When I set out in sear
intention of killing hi

I left Istanbul before f
how could I forget? –
the month of Rebiulah
891*. A few last stars
the heavens above the sleeping city when
the boy Yani brought my horse to the
front of the house. It was bitter cold and
not a soul was abroad when I passed the
Mosque of the Conqueror – may God
reward him for his innumerable victories
over the Infidels! – on my way to the
Edirne Gate. As I approached I saw
some Janissaries of the guard warming
themselves by a brazier. I recognized one
of them and greeted him by name. He
peered up at me through the darkness
and I pulled down my muffler so that he
could see my face, and showed him my
pass. 'Make way for Captain Barak!' he
called out to the others, as I sharply
reined in my horse and it reared up on its
hind legs. 'Jump to it boys, jump to it!
Will you delay an officer of the Sultan on
official business?' I raised my whip, and
as the great doors swung open the beast
leapt through the gateway and rushed
out onto the open road towards Edirne.

* 14 April 1486

Author's Note:
The *tuğra*, or monogram, which appears on the title page, when deciphered reads:
Jem, Son of Mehmed Khan, Ever Victorious.
Calligraphy by Nahla Nassar

Jem

Memoirs of an
Ottoman Secret Agent

Roderick Conway Morris

CORGI BOOKS

JEM

A CORGI BOOK   0 552 13280 2

Originally published in Great Britain by
Bantam Press, a division of Transworld Publishers Ltd.

PRINTING HISTORY
Bantam Press edition published 1988
Corgi edition published 1989

This book is set in 10/10¾ pt Symposia
by Colset Private Limited, Singapore.

Corgi Books are published by Transworld Publishers Ltd.,
61–63 Uxbridge Road, Ealing, London W5 5SA, in Australia
by Transworld Publishers (Australia) Pty. Ltd., 15–23 Helles
Avenue, Moorebank, NSW 2170, and in New Zealand by
Transworld Publishers (N.Z.) Ltd., Cnr. Moselle and
Waipareira Avenues, Henderson, Auckland.

Printed and bound in Great Britain by
Cox & Wyman Ltd., Reading, Berks.

To
Victor Ménage
and
the memory of Stavros Papastavrou
With affection and gratitude

Non dubito fore quin haec posteris
non facta sed ficta videantur.

I do not doubt but that these events
will seem to posterity not fact but fiction.

Sigismondo dei Conti,
Rome, 1495

Contents

ISLAM AND CHRISTENDOM
AT THE DEATH OF
MEHMED THE CONQUEROR
AH* 886 — AD 1481
• AH (Anno Hegira) according to the Muslim Calendar.

Prologue

It was September 1983. I was staying, as I used to almost every summer in those days, with my friends Alexis and Sophia Makrahouridis in their delightful house in Corfu. This venerable structure – which is said to have been built originally by a disgraced and exiled Venetian senator in the days when the Most Serene Republic ruled the island – overlooks a small, unfrequented bay, a couple of kilometres off the road that runs between Corfu Town and the northern village of Kassiopi. The only other building in the vicinity is the tiny chapel of St Nicholas, which sits perched on an offshore islet and is seldom visited except on the saint's feast-day. The house itself lies in an olive grove, tastefully dotted about here and there with graceful cypresses, and is surrounded by a lush, well-tended garden, watered by a cool spring that bubbles up from a mossy cleft in a rock outcrop at the back of the house. The ample terrace, flagged with pinkish limestone and, in summer, shaded by bright-green vines, affords an uninterrupted view across the turquoise waters of the gulf to the imposing mountains of southern Albania that rise almost sheer from the sea on the mainland beyond. Thus, like some dilettante eighteenth-century traveller, equally addicted to both creature comforts and wild romantic landscapes, one can savour the prospect of these barren sun-scorched slopes and peaks from a breezy pastoral enclave of almost indecent loveliness. But the season was drawing to a close, my hosts were preparing to return to their flat in Rome and I to my house in Athens. No more guests were expected.

11

Throughout the summer and occasionally during the autumn, the shores of the island are subject to a strange phenomenon, produced no doubt by conflicting currents of warm and cold air in the atmosphere and on the surface of the sea. Within less than a minute or two, a dazzlingly clear day can be plunged into a fog of the density and opacity of an old-fashioned London pea-souper. It doesn't even seem to roll in from the sea, but appears rather to emanate from the very earth itself. The whole business rarely lasts more than a few minutes before the mist disperses with such rapidity and completeness that one is left wondering whether one hasn't dreamt the whole thing.

It was out of just such a mist that quite unexpectedly Dimitri Dimitriou emerged one afternoon. We had lunched late, after spending the morning on the beach below the house, and were slumped around the table on the terrace, when the cicadas' infernal scratching changed key, the cheeping of the birds became curiously tentative and the mist enveloped us. The vaporous blanket lingered for a few minutes and then began to disperse, gradually revealing the figure of Dimitri, clothed just in an ancient pair of baggy swimming trunks and clutching a canvas bag, standing dripping with sea-water on the terrace not two yards away. After a stunned interval of silence, we all leapt to our feet to greet him. (Actually he was famous for appearing out of the blue in the most unlikely places. I was about to cross the road one winter morning by the Old Parliament building in Budapest when he rumbled by, waving benignly from behind the half steamed-up window of a passing tram; or there was the time I was taking a photograph of a temple in India when Dimitri, deep in conversation with an aged Brahmin wearing a dhoti and carrying an umbrella, loomed up from nowhere, filling the viewfinder; not to mention the occasion when Alexis trekked up Mount Ararat one summer with a local guide, only to be confronted, on coming round a bend in the path, with Dimitri sitting on a boulder, quite alone and eating a pomegranate.)

'How on earth did you know we were here?' said Alexis.

'Ah, but Count Lithrinios saw you all in the Esplanade a few days ago watching the cricket . . .'

'But what are *you* doing here?'

'Well, of course, I wasn't intending to come here at all. But a great-aunt of mine – Evgenia Doukas, have you met her? – died last week and I had to come to help sort things out.'

'I didn't know you had relatives in Corfu,' I said.

'Good heavens, yes. I must at least have told you about my uncle, Odysseus Dimitriou, the obstetrician, who assisted in 1921 at the birth of Prince Philip – as you know, he was born here in Corfu, on a dining-room table, actually . . .'

Dimitri was one of those rare people you can know for years, spend countless hours talking to, and yet who is capable of continually surprising you by casually unveiling some hitherto unsuspected facet of his knowledge or experience. He was descended from an illustrious Constantinopolitan family. Some of them remain in Istanbul to this day, whilst other branches can be found in various parts of Greece, Bucharest, Odessa, Alexandria, Mombasa, Tugssaq (Greenland), Buenos Aires and Yokohama. Most of his ancestors had been merchants and seafarers; some, high officials in the Ottoman administration during the great days of the Empire; others, scholars; others still, adventurers, pirates and rogues. He liked to claim that he was related to Stamati Crassiolo ('on my mother's side'). This notable figure succeeded one night in sawing through the bars of the Treasury of San Marco in Venice and carrying away a number of priceless gems and artworks. He had committed the perfect crime. It remained totally undetected until he boasted about his exploit to a crony in a tavern. They hanged him between the pillars on the side of the Doge's Palace facing the Piazzetta – the place reserved exclusively for the most notorious criminals.

Dimitri himself was born in Smyrna but was brought to Greece by his parents during the twenties. He was a polymath, a linguist, a classical scholar of distinction, an

13

expert on literature and the genealogical ramifications of the royal and noble houses of Europe. He had taught in Paris at the Sorbonne's Institut des Langues Orientales Vivantes, at Heidelberg and at the Marcus Peachy School for Graduate Studies, Wisconsin. He had retired, for the moment, to Athens.

Dimitri was persuaded to stay to dinner and the talk went on long into the night. As the others drifted off to bed, Dimitri and I stayed chatting a little longer. He screwed a fat Turkish cigarette into his amber holder, lit it, blew out a fragrant cloud of smoke and said, 'A few days ago, I came across something quite remarkable at Aunt Evgenia's place when I was sorting through her papers. A manuscript. Fifteenth century. It seems to be a collection of memoirs, written by . . . well, a secret agent. . . . Why don't you come into town, take a look, see what you think . . .?'

Aunt Evgenia's house, in which she was born and had lived for over eighty years, turned out to be a large ochre-coloured two-storey mansion, typical of the kind constructed throughout the last century by the Corfiot aristocracy, and now showing signs of neglect and decay – the faded stucco falling off the walls in places and the bleached green paint peeling on the firmly bolted shutters. Originally it must have stood amidst fields, vineyards and orchards, but now it had been engulfed by the town, and rattling buses and lorries, their air-brakes hissing, now thundered past its high walls and great wrought-iron gates. Next door there was a petrol station, and bangs, thuds and what sounded like somebody slicing an oil-drum in half with a chainsaw emerged from a furniture workshop opposite. Hideous examples of the fruits of the labours of those within littered the side of the road, the sickly smell of freshly applied varnish vying with the petrol fumes of the traffic in the fetid morning air.

Dimitri opened the gate and we made our way up a gravel path lined with dusty orange-trees. A gnarled and tanned old man, barefoot in khaki shorts and a vest, stood

14

on a patch of emerald-green grass directing a fountain of shining water from a hose into a bank of rhododendrons. He raised his wide-brimmed straw hat gravely in greeting. We said good-morning and went into the house.

An impressive white marble staircase led upstairs. Off the landing, which ran like a sort of gallery above the hall, double doors opened into a large study. Dimitri threw open the shutters and the room filled with bright morning sunshine. Glass-doored cabinets stood empty, half-filled cardboard boxes of books lay scattered about, and tottering piles of disintegrating periodicals stood drunkenly propped against the walls: *The Illustrated London News, Politiki Epitheorisis, Revue Asiatique, The Quiver, Bollettino della Società Letteraria di Verona* . . .

Dimitri opened a drawer and produced an oilskin package tied up with tape. He opened it and placed on the desk a heavy, vellum-bound volume. The book consisted of about three hundred or so unnumbered pages covered in small but neatly formed Greek letters. There were numerous crossings-out and corrections, all in the same careful Greek hand. Here and there were odd words, sometimes whole passages, in the old script of Ottoman Turkish. In some places words appeared in Ottoman followed by letter-by-letter transcriptions into Greek. It was evidently a translation, but a sort of rough draft, not a final copy. At the end of the text there appeared the words *Entaftha eteleioun ta Apomnimonevmata tou Barak Reis* ('Here end the Memoirs of Captain Barak') and, at the foot of the page, the initials 'E.I.'

The dissonant jangling of an ancient doorbell sounded in the hall down below.

'Ah,' said Dimitri, 'that will be Kyr' Andoni, the family lawyer,' and striding from the room, added over his shoulder: 'Make yourself at home. I'll get Anna to bring you up some coffee.'

My business is buying and selling old manuscripts and books – Near and Middle Eastern mostly, though I've had some Japanese and Chinese material pass through my

15

hands. I studied Arabic and Persian at university. I learnt to speak Greek from my Greek mother. At one time I used to go to Turkey a great deal. I even married a Turkish girl. We used to speak Turkish at home – until we stopped speaking to each other altogether. I realize now it was entirely my fault. It didn't seem like that at the time. I haven't remarried.

I flicked through the volume that lay on the desk before me. It wasn't exactly a joy to behold. The general condition was good, but there were too many corrections. It would lose a lot in value as a result – yes, even academic libraries like something to look pretty if they're going to shell out a lot of money for it. No pictures either. Shame about that. I started to read.

The next thing I knew Dimitri was calmly sitting on the opposite side of the desk. His hands were folded on his chest; he was smiling. I hadn't even heard him come into the room.

'It's nearly two o'clock. Come and have something to eat.'

I had been reading for over four hours.

After lunch we retired to the study. The shutters were half-closed now against the glare of the afternoon sun; a soft breeze blowing from the hills behind the house could be heard stirring the trees in the garden; even the noise of the traffic had subsided and sounded as though it was coming from far away. We settled ourselves down in creaking old cane chairs on either side of a little octagonal Indian table. Anna brought up cups of pungent black Turkish coffee and glasses of iced water.

We sat for a while in silence, sipping our coffee. Then I began: 'The provenance of a manuscript can, of course, be nearly as important as the manuscript itself . . .'

'Quite so,' said Dimitri.

'As you know, during the fifteenth century, even before the Fall of Constantinople to the Ottomans in 1453, thousands of Greek manuscripts were brought to the West. They say that at one point there were literally cratefuls of them sitting rotting on the docks at Venice – but to try to

16

explain how a Greek translation of a Turkish manuscript came to be in Corfu might be more difficult.'

'It would be impossible,' said Dimitri, 'if it weren't for some surprisingly good detective work carried out by Evgenia's father, Nanos Doukas. You will have noticed the initials "E.I." at the end of the text?'

'Yes?'

'They belong to a . . . well, a kind of distant cousin of mine, an Orthodox priest, Emmanouil Iakavidis.'

'Was he a Corfiot?'

'No, no. He spent almost all his life in Turkey. Then, quite suddenly, he took it into his head to come here. He was in his seventies by that time, hardly the sort of age to start gadding about, and unfortunately he walked straight into the middle of a typhus epidemic, caught the disease and died within a few weeks of arriving. That was in 1503.'

'So you assume that he brought the book with him then?'

'Yes,' said Dimitri and, draining his glass of iced water, he got up and walked over to a small teak filing-cabinet. Opening a drawer, he pulled out a series of large, yellowing index cards covered with spidery handwriting in black ink.

'Among Nanos' numerous projects,' he went on, 'none of which, unfortunately, was ever completed, was a history of the family. Quite an undertaking. Not surprisingly, he was rather interested in Emmanouil. From letters written by Emmanouil to a fellow priest in Venice and preserved in the archives at San Giorgio dei Greci – you know, the Greek church in Venice – it appears that Emmanouil was parish priest of Mega Revma, a small village on the European shore of the Bosphorus. In some of his letters, he mentions in passing a certain Captain Barak . . .'

'Aha,' I said, 'the author of the original memoirs. But what possible reason could Captain Barak have had for getting his memoirs – which deal with events surely known only to the Sultan himself and a mere handful of the most highly trusted members of the Ottoman secret service – translated into Greek? I'm amazed that he ever allowed Emmanouil even to take a look at them.'

'Ah, but he didn't. In fact, he left strict instructions that his memoirs were to be destroyed if anything should happen to him. And, in the end, they were destroyed – but not before cousin Emmanouil had made a translation of them,' said Dimitri, as though nothing could be simpler.

'And how the devil did Emmanouil lay his hands on them in the first place?' I said, finding the whole story becoming increasingly incomprehensible.

Dimitri raised a calming hand. 'That we know from one of the letters in Venice. It was written in the spring of 1499. Nanos has copied out the relevant passage on to one of these . . .'

He shuffled through the cards until he found what he was looking for. 'Listen:'

> *"The Turk Barak has gone to sea again. His house was damaged by a fire two days before he was due to leave. It seems that a servant was grilling aubergines in the yard and the sparks set fire to some quilts hanging from the windows. Barak told me that his servants are fools, that he could not delay his departure any longer and they would no doubt finish the job of burning his house to the ground while he was away. He gave me a small box, saying I was to look after it. He said: 'Promise me that if I do not return you will put it in a sack with some heavy stones and throw it in the water where the whirlpool is. Do not let anyone see you do it.' I promised and he went. The box is strongly made, with brass rings around it, and it is locked. I have no idea what is inside it."*

'It's quite simple,' said Dimitri. 'Barak never came back.'

'But', I said, 'does Emmanouil say anywhere in his letters that he did in fact open the box one day, and that it was the memoirs he found inside?'

18

'Of course not!' said Dimitri, looking quite horrified. 'That's the last thing he would have risked doing. Picture the scene. Barak leaves the box. Time passes. Weeks turn into months, the leaves turn golden and fall from the trees. The wind turns cold and the autumn rains begin. Emmanouil eagerly awaits the return of his Turkish neighbour – he is a bit frightened of him, but we know from the letters that the two men were friends and enjoyed each other's company. And anyway, the Captain should have an interesting tale or two to tell when he returns. . . . The last few stragglers of the Black Sea and Mediterranean fleets sail into port; the Imperial galleys and warships are laid up for the winter; the Sultan's crack infantry, the Janissaries, return to winter quarters to while away the long evenings till campaigning begins again in the spring. But alas, still no sign of the Captain. . . . And all the while he's consumed by curiosity – remember, my friend, that Pandora was a Greek, the fact that she was a woman is irrelevant. So, eventually, he convinces himself once and for all that Barak is dead. Drowned, killed in action, a victim of fever – it doesn't matter. He's not coming back. And yet, Barak has made him promise . . . But just to throw the box into the whirlpool, having looked after it so carefully for so long? Madness! At the dead of night, when the whole village is asleep, he quietly prises open the box. What is he expecting? Gold ducats, fabulous jewels, rubies, diamonds, pearls . . . What does he find? Just a pile of useless papers. But he starts to read – very slowly at first, the candle is guttering in the draught, the handwriting is a little difficult to decipher – and realizes that he has stumbled upon a gold mine. Why, any state in Christendom would pay a king's ransom for the information these memoirs contain . . .'

'So,' I said, 'he surreptitiously makes a translation, noting down problem passages here and there to work on at a later date; he puts the original manuscript in the box, weighs it down with rocks and hurls it into the whirlpool. He simply disappears one day and, clutching his precious bundle, sets off for the West in search of a suitable buyer . . .'

'But the Almighty has other plans for him. Having

19

successfully slipped out of Ottoman territory and across the narrow straits to Corfu, he dies before he is able to realize the immense profit on his extraordinary discovery,' said Dimitri, quietly laying Nanos' index cards on the little table between us.

'Perhaps it was God's punishment for breaking his promise to Captain Barak,' I said.

'Did he break his promise?' replied Dimitri, affecting surprise. 'After all, he did destroy the original.'

'A very Greek way of looking at things,' I said, laughing.

'Perhaps . . .'

'There's one thing I still can't understand,' I said. 'And that's why the family here – who must have found the manuscript when poor Emmanouil was struck down in the epidemic – didn't try to turn it to their own profit.'

'Ah, but in those days,' said Dimitri, 'the family was rich, much richer than they were in later years. They were well-established members of the Corfiot nobility – why risk it? The whole thing could have backfired on them. After all, their Venetian rulers do not emerge from the memoirs with flying colours, to put it mildly. No, it would have been too dangerous . . .'

'Well,' I said, 'I can think of one or two people who might be interested. It will be difficult to put a price on it before I've made a few enquiries. Naturally, as it's for you, I'll waive the commission.'

'But, my dear friend,' said Dimitri, 'I have no intention of selling the manuscript.'

'Oh, I see,' I said in confusion. 'Then, what *are* you going to do with it?'

'I'm not sure,' he said, getting to his feet. 'Anyway, we're supposed to be meeting the others at the Esplanade for drinks. If we don't go now we'll be late.'

I returned to Athens a few days later and didn't hear from Dimitri for several weeks. I tried phoning his flat but he never seemed to be there. He turned up, unexpected and unannounced as usual, during a spectacular thunderstorm one evening. The street outside my house always flooded when we had heavy rain and Dimitri looked almost as wet as when he had emerged from the waves in Corfu that September afternoon. He didn't seem to mind. To my surprise he'd brought the manuscript with him. He said he had decided to ask me to attempt a version of it in English. I protested rather feebly that I was far too busy, and in any case hardly qualified to undertake the task.

I was being far from honest. Barak's pursuit of the fugitive Prince Jem had already begun to obsess me. I had been itching to have another look at the manuscript and had been trying to think of a way to ask Dimitri if I could borrow it.

Dimitri waved my objections aside impatiently and, pausing in deference to a blinding flash of lightning and a great crack of thunder that shook the window-panes and set all the lights in the house wildly flickering, said: 'It is such a miracle the manuscript should have survived at all that, now it has been rediscovered, it is our duty to make it available to others.'

'Well, Dimitri,' I said, 'I will look at it. But I make no promises . . .'

'Good man!' he said in English and, as though afraid that I might change my mind, he retrieved his shoes, which were drying by the stove. Claiming that he was already late for a rendezvous in Kifissia, he opened the front door, erected a sturdy umbrella and hurried out into the rain.

'You'll never find a taxi in this weather,' I called after him, but he was gone.

That winter I spent all my spare moments – and a great deal more time besides, when I should have been doing other things – working on the manuscript. By May a reasonably respectable first draft was complete. I continued to work on it until September, when I returned to England. Not knowing quite when I would make it back to Athens and not wanting to leave something so valuable in an empty house, I decided to leave the original manuscript with Dimitri. I spoke to him on the phone. He was on his way to the airport, going on a trip, he didn't say where. I could leave the manuscript with his housekeeper, Frosini; she would put it in a safe place.

That autumn, while I was still in London, Dimitri suddenly died. I didn't hear about it until weeks afterwards. When I got back to Greece the following spring I found that everything he owned had been dispersed to the four winds. I made enquiries – some of the more important books and manuscripts had gone to libraries – but Emmanouil's volume had vanished.

I hesitate to offer my translation of Captain Barak's memoirs for publication. But I hope that whatever the faults and shortcomings in my work – which I know in advance will be legion – Dimitri would still somehow approve. We all miss him very much.

RCM

Book One

The City

When I set out in search of Jem I had no intention of killing him.

I left Istanbul before first light. It was – how could I forget? – the ninth day of the month of Rebiulahir, in the year 891.* A few last stars still sparkled in the heavens above the sleeping city when the boy Yani brought my horse to the front of the house. It was bitter cold and not a soul was abroad when I passed the Mosque of Mehmed the Conqueror – may God reward him for his innumerable victories over the Infidels! – on my way to the Edirne Gate. As I approached I saw some Janissaries of the guard warming themselves by a brazier. I recognized one of them and greeted him by name. He peered up at me through the darkness and I pulled down my muffler so that he could see my face, and showed him my pass. 'Make way for Captain Barak!' he called out to the others, as I sharply reined in my horse and it reared up on its hind legs. 'Jump to it, boys, jump to it! Will you delay an officer of the Sultan on official business?' I raised my whip, and as the great doors swung open the beast leapt through the gateway and rushed out onto the open road towards Edirne.

My father's name was Abdullah. He was of the opinion that he was Greek. From Thrace, from Macedonia, perhaps. But he was never entirely sure because when the Imperial officers gathering the levy of Christian boys came to his village and chose him to be taken from his parents

* 14 April 1486

25

and sent to the capital, he was very young, so he could remember little about his early life. Fortune smiled upon him: Sultan Murad – our present Emperor's grandfather, whose abode is Paradise – picked him out personally the day he arrived for duty as a page in the Palace. Thus, one of the weakest, the most insignificant of God's servants was elevated by the goodness and boundless generosity of the Sultan to be raised according to the precepts of the True Faith, and educated in all the sciences and arts, the martial skills and courtly graces necessary to make him a worthy servant of the State.

Of course, at first he spoke only Turkish after entering the Sultan's household – but one day he went with his master's entourage to Gallipoli and heard some Greek shipwrights chatting, as they took their midday meal in a shady corner on a ramp in the arsenal. Although it wasn't the first time he had heard Greek spoken, it was the first time he had heard it spoken not by ambassadors and grandees but by humble men going about their business. Suddenly he was possessed of the realization that he could half-understand what they were saying. That's when he made up his mind that he must have been Greek – not that it's the done thing for slaves of the Felicitous Sultan to speculate about their origins. And he never did – except occasionally at home after the death of my mother (and certainly never in front of the servants).

The circumstances of my father's meeting with my mother, Mara, are worth relating. He was involved in operations with Isa Bey in Serbia. On the orders of the Conqueror, they laid siege to Novo Brdo, the place the Italians call Novomonte. The 'Mother of Cities', as it used to be known in those days. Miners came from all over the world to work the fabulous seams of gold and silver that existed in seemingly infinite quantities on the plain and in the mountains around the town. It was said that even small children scrabbling in the dust had been known to come up with whole nuggets of these precious metals. But my mother's people were Serbs from a nearby town who had moved there some twenty years before.

26

The siege lasted for forty days and forty nights. My mother's father was killed during an assault while defending the ramparts. When the city fell she was separated from the rest of her family in the fighting. She never saw any of them again. The town's officials (who had stubbornly refused to surrender even though Isa Bey guaranteed that if they did, not a single person or piece of property would be touched, so long as they paid an annual tribute) were beheaded. Over three hundred boys were enrolled into the ranks of the Janissaries and seven hundred women and girls handed over to the troops as a reward.

My father was supervising the removal of some church bells from a tower, to be broken up as scrap for casting cannons, when a Janissary corporal emerged from a side-door of the church, leading an exquisite fair-haired young creature – 'An angel, an angel!' my father used to say – on the end of a rope. She must have been about fourteen then. He was amazed by the look of unperturbed aloofness on her face as she proceeded along the streets with her captor, as though out for a stroll to take the air. 'How much do you want for her?' my father said. 'I'm sorry, sir, but she's not for sale,' said the corporal. But eventually the man's avarice got the better of his lust and my father bought her from him. When, during the journey back to Istanbul, he attempted to exercise his legitimate rights as an owner, she bit him. When she gave birth to me, he married her. She remained a Christian all her life and, although she came to love my father, she was unshakeably convinced that she had married below her station. When my father was angry with her he used to say that he had unwittingly purchased the means of his own destruction that day in Serbia, and he might just as well have spent his gold on a good strong dose of poison and done away with himself on the spot, rather than let her kill him by degrees. After she died giving birth to my youngest sister, he never recovered. Even years later, I used to avoid mentioning her name, it caused him so much pain.

My father remembered that the village where he was

born was by the sea, and he must have learned to swim very early. But he didn't discover this ability until, one spring morning, one of his fellow pages at the Palace slipped into the Tunja at Edirne (where the Court used to be in those days) and my father, as much to his own astonishment as to that of the bystanders, threw himself into the rushing waters and saved the boy from drowning. Attracted by the cries of the onlookers, Sultan Murad himself rode over to the place on the riverbank in time to witness the incident. He rewarded my father for his courage there and then, and afterwards treated him with special favour.

His whole Destiny seemed to lead him to water, ships and the sea. For after the death of his benefactor Sultan Murad, he was fortunate to be retained in the service of his son Mehmed, and soon his life took a maritime turn. All the world knows that from the very first day of his rule Mehmed was determined to fulfil the words of the Prophet Muhammad which say: *'Verily they will conquer Constantinople. How excellent a commander shall be that commander. And how excellent an army shall be that army!'*

Sultan Mehmed knew the story of my father's plunge into the river Tunja and on the eve of the expedition, almost as a sort of joke apparently, summoned him and gave him the command of a squadron of ships that was to take part in the assault. My father was overcome with terror, and saying that he was far too young and inexperienced for such an honour (he was then no more than twenty-three), added that he was totally ignorant of the art of naval warfare. But the Emperor merely laughed and said, 'Come, come, Abdullah, at least if you fall in the water we will not have to waste time trying to rescue you.'

The siege went on for over a month and although our artillery was the most formidable and powerful ever brought together in one place, and our soldiers the most hungry for glorious martyrdom in defence of the Faith, still the Christians managed to hold out. Our onslaughts were repeatedly repulsed because we could only attack from two sides: the land side, where the walls were so massive as to defy a decisive breach, and from the heavily manned and well-defended side of the city facing the Marmara Sea. The third side facing on to the Golden Horn was closed to us by a great chain running across the wide entrance to the inlet, from Istanbul to Galata. My father and the other commanders had lost hundreds of men and dozens of ships trying to breach this boom – but all to no avail. When an Infidel warship and three supply ships from Chios bearing relief to the beleaguered Christians managed to burst through our blockading fleet, Sultan Mehmed – who was observing from the shore – fell into a furious rage and, riding into the sea, brandishing his sword and calling down terrible imprecations onto the heads of our sailors and marines, ordered them on pain of death to hurl themselves afresh against the enemy. But it was too late. The result of this humiliating failure was that Admiral Baltaoglu was ignominiously stripped of his rank and office, and was lucky not to lose his head into the bargain. My father and the other commanders were now becoming reconciled to the fact that they would certainly soon lose theirs.

The Council of War met to deliberate and there was even talk of abandoning the siege altogether. But that night as my father, unable to sleep, was gloomily pacing the deck of his flagship he remembered a conversation he had once had with a renegade old Greek. The man, who worked in the Palace translating diplomatic communications, had devoted himself for many years to scholarship and was very knowledgeable about the writings of his ancestors. My father spent some time working as an assistant in the same department and recalled the old man's talking once about how, to shorten the journey around the Morea, the Greeks used to drag their ships across the narrow isthmus of Corinth – from the Aegean to the gulf on the other side – by building a great wooden roadway and hauling their vessels along it. He even said that he had been to Corinth many years before and had seen for himself the original slipways that had been cut into the rock.

Why not, thought my father, take some ships out of the Bosphorus and drag them overland in the same way?

He presented himself at the Sultan's tent. The Emperor scowled at him when he saw him enter, and turned away, cursing. In a trembling voice my father put forward his suggestion. When he was about halfway through his discourse (he told my mother afterwards), a vision appeared before his eyes of the old Greek's face – with his big hairy nostrils and blotchy bald pate – contorted with mirth. Perhaps the whole story was a complete fabrication, thought up by the wicked old renegade to dupe a bright but rather credulous young apprentice from the Palace school. My father had fallen into a sort of trance and had no idea, when he tried to remember later, what he had been saying. But somehow he managed to finish. There was an eerie silence, then uproar.

'Captain Abdullah', said the Aga of Janissaries above the din, 'has finally taken leave of his senses.'

Another said, 'He's trying to make fools of us . . .'

Another, 'Let this purveyor of marvels produce a potion so that my men can drink it, sprout wings and fly over the walls into the city!'

But Mehmed just sat there in silence, his chin sunk on his chest in thought. When the commotion died away, he said, 'If it is true that the Ancients, the artful compatriots of the mighty Emperor, the world-conqueror Alexander the Great, did this thing – then so shall we.'

My father did not need to be told what would happen to him if his scheme should fail.

The Commander of the Faithful had spoken. He and his senior officers sat up most of the night planning the operation. In the morning it was begun. A path was cleared through the vineyards, trees and scrub, and a broad road of planks laid down along it all the way from a bay in the Bosphorus, over the hill of Pera and down the other side to the shores of the Golden Horn. The boards were greased with the tallow from a thousand sheep and cattle, and soon the first ship – a small one, as an experiment – was on its way. The captain stood on the deck shouting encouragement as his vessel – hauled by the crew and roared on by the watching army – majestically sailed up the hillside towards Pera and then, cresting the ridge, disappeared in the haze like a phantom vessel dissolving in a dream. In no time ship after ship, large and small, followed in its wake, and ship after ship glided down the slope on the other side to surge into the waters of the Golden Horn, crews cheering wildly, banners flying, sails unfurling and cannons booming. In a few days, more than seventy vessels were launched into the waters denied to us until then by the Infidels' iron chain.

And so the city fell and my father kept his head. And the disreputable clanging of church bells was replaced by the Muslim call to prayer, and the chanting of the Adorers of the Cross by the sweet murmur of the five-times-a-day-repeated confession of the True Faith. And so, having won a famous naval victory by land, Abdullah – may God Most High have mercy upon him! – went on to spend the rest of his days harrying the enemies of Islam across the oceans of the world. And so it was that, when he grew to be a man, his unworthy son, Barak, followed his father to sea.

I was born in Istanbul in the fifth year of Mehmed the Conqueror's reign. As a reward for his part in the conquest of the city, Sultan Mehmed had given my father the palace of some Greek noble who had fled to Europe on the eve of the siege. The palace itself was damaged during the fighting and my father had it gradually restored during his breaks from campaigning on land and leading his squadrons of ships at sea. But the real glory of the place was its gardens, which occupied a series of steep terraces on the hillside below the palace, overlooking the Golden Horn. My father was a very keen gardener – having acquired a taste for cultivation in the magnificent parklands laid out in Edirne on Tunja Island by Mehmed's father, Sultan Murad – who dwells for eternity in the cool shade of the gardens of Paradise. Not only did he grow many rare kinds of exotic flower and fragrant shrub and bush but he

31

also grew a multitude of fruit and vegetables of every variety. When, one year, he sent some of his famous peaches as a gift to the ladies and slave girls of the Sultan's harem, it was said that when they ate them they swooned and fainted, the fruit was so delicious. And afterwards, the eunuchs were not given a moment's peace until they promised to go to my father and beg him to send some more. Perhaps the story is true, because I myself can remember the Chief Black Eunuch coming to our house, chatting and taking sherbet with my father, then departing, followed by a train of servants bearing basket-loads of ripe peaches.

All my earliest memories are of those gardens. Looking back, it seems they enjoyed an eternal spring, with almond-blossom, roses, tulips, peonies and magnolias always in full bloom; the branches of the trees laden with peaches and apricots, cherries and pears; the vines heavy with green and purple bunches of grapes; the ponds bright with water-lilies; and the borders of the verdant lawns erupting with crisp vegetables and plump honey-melons. There were animals too. Fastidious cats, amiable dogs, lumbering tortoises, a tame gazelle, a monkey picked up by my father off the Barbary coast – found treading water, presumably having fallen overboard from a passing ship, although there wasn't another vessel in sight – and a peculiar talking bird with a yellow beak and bead-like black eyes, all the way from India, that we thought little of (its Turkish accent was atrocious) until one day one of my father's fiercest falcons broke loose and the demented creature took it on, defeated it in single combat and chased it, shouting curses, halfway across the city. (Quite where it had learnt some of the words it used remained a mystery.)

But nothing in this world is permanent. One day I was wandering among the bird-filled trees in search of butter-flies when I came upon my mother lying weeping on the grass, surrounded by distraught and tearful maids. For it had just been learned that my father had suddenly, and quite unexpectedly, fallen from the Sultan's grace. And, my mother informed me between sobs, it was to his pre-eminence as a gardener that he owed his downfall.

The real reason for the Emperor's taking against my father cannot be known for certain – but there can be no doubt that it dated from the day when Sultan Mehmed (himself a fanatical horticulturalist who dug, planted, watered and weeded with his own bare hands) deigned to visit my father's celebrated gardens in person. Everything was going well, apparently, until the Sultan came to some vegetable beds where my father was nurturing cucumbers. The Emperor was reputed to take more pride in his cucumbers than almost anything else in the world, and it was said that they astonished those who beheld them with their almost unworldly perfection. But when he saw my father's cucumbers nestling among their leaves, so sleek and bright and green that they looked as if they had been fashioned out of some awe-inspiring, hitherto unknown element, his face grew pale. Mumbling something inaudibly to himself, he indicated with a wave of the hand that the visit was at an end. When the Imperial party reached the gate of our house and my father bowed to kiss Mehmed's hand, the Sultan distractedly patted him on the back as though only half-aware of his presence and, murmuring quietly 'Yes, yes . . .', mounted his horse and rode away, hastily pursued by his baffled entourage. By the following morning my father had learned that Mehmed was mightily displeased with him.

At first it seemed that the dark shadow cast over him would be as fleeting as a black rain-cloud passing momentarily in front of the sun on a hot midsummer's day – but in truth it was several years before my father won back the Sultan's favour. He bore his unhappy lot with characteristic fortitude, saying to me that I should learn from this example that Fortune in this life is fickle and that God has set a measure for all things and we can never know what event He may, in His mercy, bring about. At one point his friends at court warned him that he might be sent into exile and even that his life was in danger – though God spared him this unjust Fate. After a period of ominous uncertainty, when my father expected

33

hourly to be summoned to the Sublime Porte for the last time, he was allowed once more to wield the sword of Islam in the service of his Sultan. At last he went to sea again, but was honoured with lesser commands.

During his time in the wilderness, my father decided to build a modest house on the Bosphorus at the enchantingly beautiful spot where the channel narrows at the Cape of the Current (or Mega Revma, 'the Great Current', as the Greek fisherfolk call the little village there). The building work had just been completed and a small garden laid out when a terrible plague broke out. My father was by then cruising in the Aegean in search of the Catalan pirates who were devastating our coasts and pillaging our towns and villages.

But alas, the ravages of the plague in the city that year were infinitely worse than those of any raiders or corsairs. Within a short time of its arrival in the city, hundreds – men, women, children – were dying every day. Some fled their homes never to be seen again, others locked themselves in their houses, refusing even to speak to others. Families abandoned their dying relations, rendered deaf by terror to their lamentations and pitiful appeals for help. Those that were fortunate enough to receive burial were buried at first two or three in the same grave and then indiscriminately in vast pits. And he who was burying the dead one day was himself being buried the next. By the end of the summer so many people were sick or dying that there were no longer enough people to bury the dead at all; corpses lay rotting in the streets where they had fallen, and the air became foul with the smell of death and putrefaction.

When Mehmed, who was on his way back to Istanbul after campaigning in Albania, learnt of the scale of the calamity taking place there and that the pestilence was at that very moment raging in Macedonia and Thrace – through which he was about to pass – the Ever Victorious Conqueror, suddenly overcome with fear, fled northwards and took refuge in Nikopolis. Thus, the greatest city in the world and the most powerful stronghold of the

34

Faith was abandoned by the Emperor and – so it began to seem to us who were left there – forsaken even by the Almighty.

My mother was in despair as to what to do. Hearing no word from my father, she took matters into her own hands and decided that we should flee with our servants to the house in Mega Revma in the hope of escaping the dreadful contagion. And there can be no doubt that our lives were spared by her resolve and wise action.

When the plague died down we stayed on. There I was allowed out to play with other children along the shore and in the thick woods on the steep slopes behind the village. Many of my young companions were Christian Greeks, so I learned their tongue at an early age. In the years that followed, the family spent more and more time on the Bosphorus and less and less time in the city. You could almost say that I grew up in Mega Revma, for it was here that I learnt to swim and sail a boat in the deep and dangerous waters below the whirlpool, here that I learnt to catch fish with a line and hunt animals with a bow, and here (at the age of nine) that I first fell in love, with a sulky, dark-eyed young beauty (aged ten), and it is here too that I write these memoirs that nobody will ever read.

The Inner Apartments

God alone knows what brought me to Kivami Bey's attention. But one thing is certain – it changed the course of my life for ever. For although it happened quite some time before the disappearance of Prince Jem and that fateful dawn when I rode out westwards on the Edirne road in search of him, whenever I ask myself when it was that my Destiny became inextricably entangled with the Prince's, I have to say, yes, it was then, it was on that night that my involvement in those extraordinary and terrible events first began.

It was in the autumn of the year when the last war with the Republic of Venice came to an end. I was back again in Istanbul after my galley, the *Osprey*, had been sunk in action in the Aegean, and I had been waiting several weeks, hoping to be assigned to another vessel. But with hostilities now suspended, I had to admit to myself there was little chance of a new command until the spring. The prospect of an idle and tedious winter lay before me. Well, idle at least.

And so, after wasting a great deal of time in the city in the hope of finding something useful to do, I decided to take myself off for a while to Mega Revma. I had left it rather late before I said farewell to my beloved Sofia at her house in the Fener district where I had been paying her an amorous visit, and started for home. The light was fading rapidly as I set off down the hill towards the waterfront, intending to find a caique to row me across the estuary to Galata (whence I would continue on horseback along the shore to Mega Revma).

The wind was blustery and a persistent drizzle had begun to fall. Ten days or more had gone by since St Dimitrios' Day – and judging by the immense black clouds massing on the horizon to the north-east of the city, the first storm of winter would surely break before the night was out.

I quickened my pace, striding through the twilight down the empty Friday streets between shuttered shops and deserted warehouses, pulling my cloak around me and lowering my head against the rain. Presently, I passed through the city walls and came onto the quay. Curtains of rain, driven before the wind, were drifting in from the Bosphorus and sweeping over the choppy waters of the Golden Horn. The encroaching night was remorselessly swallowing up the hills behind Pera and only a few scattered smudges of yellowish light now indicated the presence of the Frankish quarters on the lower slopes of the opposite shore. I made my way along the water's edge, passing by skiffs and fishing smacks rocking and bouncing about at their moorings, their flimsy hulls slapping against the waves.

When I neared the landing-stage at the Harbour Gate I saw there were still half a dozen people standing around waiting to cross and, narrowing my eyes, I could just make out the indistinct grey form of a boat approaching through the drizzle from the Galata side. Oars could be heard splashing in the water and muffled voices rose intermittently above the wind.

As I drew level with a row of upturned fishing boats and ghostly nets draped between poles to dry, a figure came out of the shadows into my path. I took a step back. At the same time I sensed something else moving up behind me. I glanced round and saw another man standing motionless a few yards to the back of me. I was now only a stone's throw from the passengers on the landing-stage. I could have called out to them, but something – I can't explain what – prevented me. The figure before me said:

'Captain Barak?'

'Yes.'

'Would you care to come with us, Captain? Kivami Bey would like to see you.'

'The name means nothing to me. What people are you?' I said.

The figure reached inside his heavy dark cloak and slowly drew out something small and flat about half the size of a Frank playing-card. He held it up in front of my face. I could see all too clearly the bold black pen-strokes of the Sultan's monogram, but the words below it I could not decipher in the dimness.

Seeing my difficulty, the man said flatly, 'Imperial Security.'

The card disappeared into the folds of his cloak.

'Perhaps you would care to tell me what your name is, if that is allowed?' I said.

'My name is Atik.'

'And your companion's?' I said, turning round to try to get a better look at him.

'He cannot hear you. He is deaf and mute. And anyway, his name is unimportant. Shall we go now, Captain?'

'Where to?'

'You'll see,' he said, walking past me and going off in the direction from which I had just come. I could have made a break for it, but what would have been the point? Throwing a last glance over the darkening waters of the estuary and observing with numb detachment that the grey boat was at that very moment about to draw alongside the landing-stage, I turned away and followed the receding figure of Atik. The other man stood aside politely and waited for me to pass, then silently brought up the rear.

For some time we made our way through the dank cobbled streets up the hill again, in the direction of the Grand Bazaar. I tried to delve into my memory, to think of some seditious or ill-advised words I might have spoken. Or of some evil-minded person I had encountered who might have reasons for trying to get me out of the way by falsely denouncing me to the authorities. My efforts proved fruitless. I could think of nothing. So, as I trudged disconsolately along, I was soon reduced to silently and impotently cursing my ill-luck in not going down with my ship in the company of the other brave men who were martyred for the Faith that day, thus depriving these people of the pleasure they would no doubt take in breaking my limbs and strangling me, or slitting my throat in some noisome dungeon.

We were now approaching the barred and imposing portals of one of the entrances to the Bazaar, but a few yards before we reached it we turned sharply to the right and went off in the direction of the Old Palace, where the Emperor lodged with his harem in the early days following the conquest of the city. Then we turned off once again, this time ascending a steep flight of steps between high blank stone walls. Dark plane trees overhung the narrow passageway, water dripping from their mournfully creaking branches. The ground underfoot was sticky and slippery with fallen leaves. Obscene visions of gouged flesh and welling blood began to steal forth from the dark recesses of my fevered mind.

After ascending for a while, the steps veered slightly to the right. Atik came to a halt ahead of me. When I caught up with him, I found myself standing before an arched gateway. Atik tapped softly on the heavy doors. Abruptly, a panel slid open. A dull glimmer of light shone through and, for an instant, an eye appeared on the other side of the grille covering the hole. The panel slid shut again. A key turned in the lock. Without a word being spoken, we went inside. Then, almost soundlessly, the door was shut and locked again behind us.

Emerging from an echoing, ill-lit passageway, I found myself standing before a spacious courtyard. On three sides there ran a kind of cloister and in the centre of the courtyard was a large domed building that looked like a mosque or church, before which two lofty black cypresses stood sentinel. The pavings of the yard gleamed darkly in the drizzle. Somewhere water splashed noisily from a spout into the deep trough or basin of a fountain. Not a single star penetrated the dark mantle of the sky above, and suddenly I was overcome with the eerie, almost vertiginous sensation that this place I had entered was hundreds of miles from anywhere and outside its daunting walls there was no longer an extensive and populous city but some vast uninhabited tract of desolate wilderness.

We started off beneath the wind-swept colonnades of the cloister, which was lit at intervals by small flickering lamps set in niches in the walls. Then Atik broke the silence so unexpectedly – we had not exchanged a single word since leaving the waterfront – that for a moment I could hardly grasp the meaning of the words he spoke.

By the time I had recovered from the surprise, he was saying: 'Yes, it used to be a sort of monastery for women before the Conquest. It was called Aya Irini – "Divine Peace", that's a joke! – like that church up at the New Palace that the Janissaries use as their armoury. From the outside this place doesn't look like anything much, but there's enough room in here to accommodate the Imperial harem three times over. Mind you, it seems it was pretty well empty by the time the city fell and the soldiers broke down the doors. Hardly more than a dozen ancient crones and their servants left by then, or so they say. There used to be an old Armenian porter here who knew all about it. But he died . . . oh, it must have been a couple of years back now.'

At that point we reached the end of one side of the courtyard and came up to a pair of green bronze doors that still bore the scars of axe and hammer blows. Atik knocked again and we were admitted into an antechamber by a giant villainous-looking Nubian girded with a great two-handed sword. At one end of the antechamber there was a desk (unoccupied) and some shelves piled with documents. By this time the nameless mute had vanished, though he was so jinn-like in the subtlety of his departure that I cannot say even to this day at which stage in our progress along the cloister he had caused himself to dematerialize.

Atik removed his shoes and gently pushed open a door leading off the antechamber and disappeared inside. A voice from within barked, 'Well, what are you waiting for, then? Send him in.'

Atik reappeared and said, 'Kivami Bey is ready for you now.'

I looked at him, trying to read the expression on his face. A blank sheet of paper would have been more revealing. Avoiding my eyes, he bowed and with a graceful gesture of his arm indicated that I should proceed across the threshold.

I took off my shoes and handed him my cloak. Until that moment I had assumed that, initially at least, I would be questioned and asked to give an account of myself. And, if they were not satisfied with what I had to say – and it was perfectly well known that they were seldom satisfied – they would move on to more persuasive methods of interrogation. But then all at once it struck me that perhaps they would dispense with such formalities and dispose of me immediately. It looked horribly dark on the other side of the door. I felt the muscles of my throat starting to constrict as though the bowstring was already tightening around my neck. My tongue felt thick and heavy and repulsive, a suffocating intruder in my mouth.

I stepped into the room. The door was shut behind me. I thought my knees were going to give way beneath me. At first I stared into the darkness straight ahead of me, expecting to be seized at any moment. But when nothing happened I cautiously looked to left and right. Gradually adjusting to the gloom, my eyes began to travel about the room. It was big, with a high vaulted ceiling and two fairly large square windows at one end. In one corner there was a wide hearth – surmounted by a handsome canopy covered with glazed and decorated tiles – in which a fire was burning. The floor was covered with carpets that felt to my toes as though they were made of silk.

At last my eyes rested on a low divan to the right of the fireplace. On it sat a small fat man, with one leg tucked under him and the other dangling but barely touching the floor. Beside him were propped two stout black wood canes whose polished shafts and silver handles gleamed in the firelight.

The man's beard was white and trimmed rather roughly

41

to a point; his fleshy, misshapen face pallid, pockmarked, and foxed with unsightly freckles; his nose aquiline but crooked, as though the bridge had once been badly broken; and his white hair receding and closely cropped. He wore a skull-cap but no turban. His robes looked crumpled and neglected, his sable pelisse matted and moth-eaten. He regarded me with an unblinking fishlike stare.

I bowed nervously, touching my lips and forehead in the most respectful manner. He looked impatiently on and said, 'All right, all right. Sit down, will you?'

I approached him and lowered myself onto a thoroughly worn and lumpy cushion on the floor opposite him. I shifted a little to try to find a more comfortable position.

'What's wrong?' he said irritably.

'Nothing, Kivami Bey,' I said.

Between us stood a long narrow table. On it lay a vellum file. He opened the file and by the light of a candle started to cast his eyes over the papers it contained. Without looking up, he reached out for a silver flask and poured himself a cup of dark liquid that smelt like wine. Still studying the papers, he emptied the cup and set it on the table. A blood-red trickle ran down his beard. He wiped it with his sleeve.

The long silence that ensued was broken only by the rain beating against the windowpanes, the crackling and hissing of the fire in the hearth and the occasional sigh of a log settling itself down among the embers. My heart was now beating so thunderously I was becoming convinced that my interrogator could not fail to hear it. I tried to swallow but seemed to have forgotten how.

Speaking as though to himself, Kivami Bey said, 'So, so, so . . . You're Abdullah Reis's boy. He was a courageous man and a good soldier. Intelligent too. People expected him to end up on the Imperial Council. But he seemed blighted in some way. One minute Mehmed was singing his praises and the next he'd fly into a passion at the very mention of his name. I could never for the life of me understand why. You know Mehmed was thinking of having Abdullah's head off. But that was going too far and all the

Pashas said so. He had me investigating him for months, but I couldn't find a shred of evidence against him. In the end Mehmed just seemed to forget about it.'

He poured himself another cup of wine and said, 'I'd ask you if you'd care to join me, but you don't drink wine. At least, according to what it says here, you don't.'

'That's true,' I said warily.

'So some of this information is . . . you're twenty-three years old, good brain, no physical defects. None, that is, that we know about. Your war record's excellent. Youngest commander serving in the Imperial Navy . . .'

'Hakki Reis is younger than I am, sir,' I said.

'Hakki Reis was killed on the Albanian coast two weeks ago.'

In confusion, I said, 'I didn't know . . .'

'I should think not,' said Kivami Bey. 'I only heard about it yesterday. You speak Greek, Italian, Persian. Some Arabic and Serbian. That's good. You've also done some surveying and mapping in the islands. That's good too. If your dispatches and your letters home are anything to go by, you seem to be able to string a sentence together on paper reasonably well. That makes a change. I don't know what people learn at school these days, if anything, but half the men of your age that I come across seem barely able to spell their own names.'

He continued to sift through the file in front of him and then went on: 'The only thing that worries me about you is that you seem to be a little reckless.'

'I don't quite understand, sir,' I said, now completely baffled at the turn that our conversation was taking.

'In your last engagement you lost your ship.'

'I did lose the *Osprey*,' I said, 'but the Infidels got the worst of it and in the end all of their vessels were either sunk or captured.'

'Yes, yes. I know exactly what happened. I've got a report about it here. And you needn't think that Gedik Ahmed wasn't pleased with you. He was. In fact, when I asked for you to be transferred, he refused to release you. I thought I was doing him a favour, but he didn't seem to look at it that way. I had to get Mehmed to intervene. The trouble is that your beloved Admiral seems to think that we here aren't a proper military organization – though he's happy enough to use the information we pass on to him. He's a fine commander in many ways – nobody would deny it – but in some matters he's hopelessly old-fashioned. Anyway, none of that need concern you any more. From now on you take orders from me, not from Gedik Ahmed Pasha, or the Imperial Council, or the Grand Vizir, not even from Mehmed himself. Is that clear?'

'Yes, sir,' I said, more in the dark than ever.

Kivami Bey hauled himself round and picked up a short sword lying on the divan beside him. Unsheathing it from its scabbard, he leant towards me, holding it horizontally between his hands. I pulled myself up onto my knees and took it.

'Well, go on, then,' he said.

I lowered my head and kissed the blade and handed the weapon back across the table to him. He took it and laid it aside, then pushed a small bowl of salt towards me. I took some grains between my thumb and finger and placed them on my tongue.

Kivami Bey settled back on the divan and gazed at me intently. 'And from now on you're going to have to learn to be more careful. I don't need heroes and martyrs in this section. It's no good spending weeks gathering intelligence if you don't live long enough to tell me about it. And you're going to have to start exercising some self-control in other departments too.'

'I'm sorry, sir,' I said, 'I'm not quite sure what you mean.'

'I know you're young,' he said, 'but this intrigue you've been conducting with that Greek woman Sofia – a bit dangerous for a man like yourself, with the kind of knowledge you possess about the Navy, don't you think? For all you know, she might be an agent in the pay of a foreign state.'

'There's obviously no point in denying that I'm involved

44

with her,' I said, 'but she's scarcely more than a girl and the likelihood of her being a spy . . . it's impossible.'

'You've much to learn,' said Kivami Bey, 'but you'll see.'

'Well,' I said, 'you may think me a fool, but I haven't told her anything that would be of any use to our enemies, I'm sure of it.'

'Of course you haven't,' said Kivami Bey testily. 'You'd be of no use to me if you had.'

He drained the silver flask into his cup and lifted it to his lips. Then all at once his face contorted into a ghastly grimace as he spat the wine he had just drunk into his cup. For a moment I became quite alarmed but then, coughing violently, he said, 'I keep telling that thundering idiot to make sure it's properly strained. What's he trying to do – poison me? Great God in Heaven. I'm surrounded by complete imbeciles. I might as well be running a lunatic asylum.'

I could hardly prevent myself from smiling. Kivami Bey caught my eye and gave me a baleful look, wheezing loudly as his great stomach heaved beneath his clothes.

Hoarsely, he began, 'I'm going to send you to the south of Italy. I want you to have a look around. Especially the coast. Harbours, roads, fresh-water supplies, strength of garrisons, that sort of thing. It shouldn't be too difficult if you're really as resourceful as you seem to be. We'll soon find out. Of course, you'll need some training and a new identity. Greek refugee probably. You can stay here until you leave.'

Rapping the table with his silver-handled cane, he called out: 'Atik!'

Atik reappeared, and came to stand beside me.

'Find Barak here a place to sleep and something to eat.'

Atik nodded.

As I got up, Kivami Bey said, 'I suppose you're wondering how I could be so sure that you hadn't told the Greek woman anything?'

'All right, sir,' I said, 'yes, I am.'

'She works for us. Though of course the Venetians think she works for them. And by the way, don't bother to try to contact her again. She left the city an hour ago and she'll probably be away for quite some time.'

Try as I might, I could not wholly conceal the dismay I felt on hearing this crushing piece of news. Seeing this, with a malicious glint in his eye Kivami Bey continued:

'You seem disappointed. But I suppose I shouldn't be surprised. I gather that you were – how can I put it? – somewhat indefatigable. I only hope you'll find yourself able to redirect your formidable energies into an activity of more benefit to the Empire.'

I was about to say something when I felt Atik's hand gently squeezing my shoulder. He slowly lowered his eyelids to indicate to me that I should remain silent. By the time I had got to my feet Kivami Bey had already reached for another file from the pile on the floor beside him and seemed to have utterly forgotten my presence. I watched his small fat hands clumsily fumbling with the tapes to untie it.

'That's all,' he said without looking up. 'Good night, Captain.'

What agonies I suffered that night! So utterly besotted was I with my Sofia that I do believe I would rather have been stretched out on the rack than endure the prospect of that cruel banishment from my sweet betrayer's bed. And when I imagined her, for all I knew, lying at that very moment cool and white and naked in someone else's arms, I groaned with grief and could barely contain my hot tears of jealous rage. Thus in the grip of these unbearable thoughts, I tossed and turned for half the night until, as the rain continued to pour down outside unabated and the first grey light of dawn began to creep through the barred window of my prison, I fell into an exhausted sleep.

Atik woke me a little after daybreak, bringing me some bread and milk and clean linen, saying, 'The Old Man wants to see you.'

The rain had stopped at last. A damp chilly mist lingered in the courtyard, defying the feeble beams of the weak autumn sun. I caught sight of Kivami Bey sitting

46

alone on a stone bench between the cypresses in front of the church, morosely prodding with his black sticks at the weeds growing up between two uneven paving stones.

I greeted him.

He grunted and said gruffly, 'Come with me.'

He started off round the side of the church, awkwardly lurching forward and leaning heavily on his sticks.

'May I give you an arm, sir?' I said.

'No, you may not,' he said, panting painfully as he proceeded doggedly on his way. I fell in beside him.

'You're probably thinking why the devil they've got an old cripple like me running this place.'

'Sir?'

'Well, that's probably what I would have thought at your age. I'm old and tired and ill. I should have retired long ago, but they can't find anybody to replace me. As for how my legs got like this, I'm going to tell you even if you don't want to hear about it. You might learn a lesson from it for the future.'

Behind the church we came to a small grove of trees, through which a broad path led to an archway and a second courtyard beyond. Hobbling determinedly onwards, Kivami Bey continued:

'I slipped into the city several weeks before Mehmed's attack and all through the siege I kept him informed of what was going on in here. I even managed to leave the city twice and get back in again via the sewers. When a first-class argument broke out between the Greeks and the Genoese on how best to deploy the troops to continue the defence, some parts of the walls were left virtually undefended. I thought it was an opportunity too good to miss. I threw all caution to the winds and released a carrier pigeon in broad daylight from the roof of the house where I was hiding. Well, some sharp-eyed fellow saw where it had come from. It didn't take them long to find me. First they crushed my feet in vices and then started smashing up my legs with hammers. They were going to have me publicly flayed alive in the Hippodrome the following day, but the city fell before they had the chance. I wasn't found for

47

several hours. The surgeons were going to have my legs off, but the Jew Maestro Jacopo, Mehmed's own physician, sent them packing. I was delirious for a month. When I came round I said, "Well, at least you got the message." And Mehmed said, "What message?" I suppose the Greeks had shot the damn bird down, or something. So you see, it was all useless in the end. I had sacrificed myself for nothing.'

Going under the archway into the next courtyard, I followed Kivami Bey through a wide doorway to the right guarded by two armed men.

Once inside, we passed through a series of rooms where a small army of clerks sat cross-legged at their desks, working away industriously in complete silence. Some surreptitiously glanced up, but made no attempt to greet their master. As we went from room to room Kivami Bey gave curt explanations, such as: 'Ciphers: coding of instructions to be sent out, decoding of agents' reports as they come in . . . Mapping section . . . Shipping movements . . . Frontier observations . . .' As we passed before an open doorway I saw within a large chamber in which half a dozen clerks laboured in a massive locked cage that nearly filled the room from floor to ceiling. Also within the cage I could see a line of heavy chests. My guide announced, 'Our Treasury.'

Finally, turning to the left and entering the wing that ran at right angles along the next side of the courtyard, facing the archway and the rear of the church, we entered a series of smaller rooms where men sat around low tables or reclined on divans in groups of two or three.

'These gentlemen', said Kivami Bey, 'work on creating new ciphers for our use and breaking the ones used by the enemy.' Some of them gravely acknowledged him as he limped past them and he in his turn unsmilingly raised a stick now and then in reply.

We emerged once again into the courtyard, which, now that the sun was beginning to break through the mist, was bathed in watery light. He pointed to the third side of the yard at a long grey two-storey building.

48

'Over there is domestic security. Surveillance of suspects, informers' reports, foreign residents and visitors, that sort of thing. But that needn't concern you now.' Then, indicating a dark passageway barred by a strong set of iron gates, 'That's where we accommodate our guests while we're questioning them. Beyond that are the stables, storerooms and kitchens.'

Then, looking down at the cobblestones at his feet and sharply tapping the ground with one of his sticks, he said, 'Below here are the vaults where the files and records are kept. Every file has to be signed in and out if it's needed. Nobody but me is allowed in there alone, the rest have to go down in pairs.'

We crossed the courtyard again in silence and went back through the archway. Kivami Bey came to a halt and turned to face me.

'I've no doubt we look to you like just a bunch of pen-pushers. Well, that's exactly what we are. That's the nature of the work. The opposition's getting better every day and the only way of making sure we keep ahead is by running a superior organization. I've got men in just about every city, major town, court and port in the world. If the King of England, the Prince of Muscovy, the Shah of Persia or the Pope of Rome gets a boil on his arse, sooner or later I get to hear about it.'

'How much', I said, 'do the Infidels know about this place?'

'A bit. But they seldom co-operate with each other and of course we feed them with a great deal of false information – some of which they swallow. Naturally you can't run an operation of this size without a certain amount leaking out through the cracks. The Venetians even sent a man in here to have a look round a few years ago. He got over the walls completely undetected, found a loose grille in an airshaft leading to the vaults and spent the night rummaging through the archives. *And* very nearly got out again, by God! A very brave man indeed . . .'

Kivami Bey fell silent for a few moments, musing to himself and chewing his moustache with gloomy ferocity.

Then he raised one of his silver-handled canes and jabbed it in the direction of a soft green patch of grass shaded by a clump of trees.

'He's buried over there.'

It was midwinter before I found myself wading ashore at nightfall in a blizzard and setting foot on a rocky headland in the Kingdom of Naples. Kivami Bey's instructions were to bring up to date our knowledge of military activity and the strength of the fortresses in this region of Christendom that lies at the mouth of the Adriatic, not fifty miles across the straits from the Empire's western front. I passed the hours of darkness huddled in a freezing cave for, although the countryside appeared devoid of human habitation, I could not take the risk of drawing attention to myself by lighting a fire. When morning came I set out along the coast towards Otranto, a strong-walled city that lay some dozen or so miles away to the north.

During the following weeks I made my way from place to place in the direction of a port called Brindisi. Whenever possible I avoided speaking to people and they usually left me alone. But inevitably there were some occasions when I had to give some kind of explanation of who I was and the purpose of my wanderings. And when this happened the story I told was this:

I was an orphan, a Greek from the town of Yannina, in Epirus. My parents were both long dead, but through my labours I had managed to support myself and my young sister in a poor but honest and Christian existence. I had a little education and worked for some time for a merchant. But then I came to the attention of the local Pasha, who offered me employment in his household. Ever mindful of the necessity to earn enough to provide my sister with her dowry, I accepted.

At first the Pasha was kind to me and rewarded me quite well. But then – accursed day! – the Pasha happened to be returning one evening from the hunt (such details are important) and by chance passed by our humble cottage on the outskirts of the town. He demanded water. My

50

sister, trembling, brought him some. Alas! her beauty, modesty and virginal demeanour instantly aroused his jaded and loathsome ardour. Soon afterwards a messenger arrived to summon me to his mansion. To begin with, he tried flattery, cajolements and promises of preferment in his efforts to persuade me to let him have her. Then he offered me gold (hearing which, my Infidel interrogators would invariably slyly interject, 'How much gold?'), which of course I haughtily rejected ('Of course,' the Infidels would echo without conviction). Then, seeing I was obdurate, the Pasha resorted to threats of imprisonment, torture, even death.

At last one night the unclean dog came round with a band of men to seize her by force and carry her away to be a slave and concubine in his harem. But forewarned just in time by the barking of our neighbours' dogs, my sister and I managed to get away and escape into the mountains. After numerous adventures we finally made it to the coast. We squandered our meagre savings on a boat – it was barely seaworthy, but what else could we do? – and awaited a fair wind to set sail for Corfu, where we proposed to throw ourselves on the mercy of the Venetian governor of the island. But just when we thought we were safe, news reached us that the enraged Pasha had learnt of our whereabouts and was hard on our heels. Preferring death by drowning to dishonour, we put to sea in a gale.

After many days of being carried hither and thither by the wind and current, we had been cast up upon the shores of Apulia. Our boat was smashed to pieces by the waves and as we lay there on the strand, more dead than alive, one of those marauding bands of ruffians that infest the countryside in that wild part of the world came upon us, stripped us of our remaining possessions, beat me senseless when I tried to resist and, leaving me for dead, carried my poor dear terrified sister away with them.

And ever since that day, my story concluded, I had been wandering the land, from town to town, village to village, castle to castle, in search of my sister, hoping against hope that she was still alive. 'Have any of you good people seen or heard anything of her?'

The first time I was obliged to relate this preposterous catalogue of woe – to the Governor of the castle of Otranto, who had seen fit to have me arrested within an hour of my setting foot in the city – I thought my mission was about to come to a speedy end on the gallows. But when I stuck to my story in spite of the slaps and kicks and punches designed to persuade me to confess that I was nothing more than an impudent vagabond who hoped to extract money from the gullible with this shameful pack of lies, the Governor seemed impressed by my sincerity and contented himself with having me hurled, bruised and bleeding, out of the fortress.

But God is with those who persevere. And, as it happened, the beating I had received was thereafter to prove invaluable as confirmation of the truth of my story (which I told and retold in the following weeks so often that, eventually, I was beginning to believe it myself).

I remained in the Kingdom until the early spring. And then, after spending the best part of two weeks lurking in my cave, only narrowly escaping detection by a real band of brigands and cut-throats (I concealed myself on a dark ledge above the cave's entrance), a vessel arrived to take me off.

On landing at Avlona, I found orders awaiting me from Kivami Bey to dispatch detailed reports in cipher of what I had seen, and remain in the port until further notice. And as summer wore on, galleys and sailing vessels of every description began to arrive, night and day, in the harbour. Then one morning Grand Admiral Ahmed Pasha's flagship, her long red banners floating on the breeze and her great golden lantern flashing in the sunlight at her stern, dropped anchor in the blue waters of the gulf.

Eventually, a war fleet of one hundred vessels put to sea and, crossing the straits, sailed into the Bay of Otranto. The Infidels were taken completely by surprise. Our *Gazis*, bold warriors for the Faith, poured ashore like hungry lions uncaged, roaring, 'God is Most Great!' and 'To Rome! To Rome!' The crash and peal of our cannons filled the ears of the stupefied enemy like the annihilating

52

blasts of the Resurrection Trumpet. The walls of the city began to sway and crumble as though shaken by a mighty earthquake, and the smoke and dust of battle rose up to the heavens, making a dark night of noon.

But the doomed Infidels fought well and for several days put up desperate resistance until, thanks to Divine Help and our knowledge of the weak points in the fortifications (so Providentially increased by the Governor's order to have me arrested and brought within the fortress), our adversaries were driven back and the *Gazis* swarmed through the gaping rents in the walls.

Within an hour our victory was complete. And while our sappers and engineers set about rebuilding and strengthening the ramparts to secure a foothold on Italian soil, our troops went forth, ravaging and laying waste the countryside for miles around, making of the Misbelievers food for their swords and targets for their arrows.

Now the road to Rome lay open, and Sultan Mehmed and the main body of the army were expected daily. Every available vessel returned to Avlona without delay, in readiness to ship reinforcements of the invincible Imperial host across the straits. Even a sizeable flotilla of Venetian galleys and transports appeared off the Albanian coast to assist in the operation – for not only had they hopes thereby of gaining a large sum in gold but they also saw in us the means of curbing the power of the King of Naples and humbling the pride of the Pope of Rome.

After some time, reports began to reach us that this same Pope had declared an unholy crusade throughout all Christendom and was arming a fleet against us. But, as our spies and agents in Europe soon confirmed, even the prospect of the conquest of Italy seemed insufficient to divert most of the Christian states from their incessant rivalries and squabbling. The weeks passed and not a solitary Infidel banner appeared on the empty plain to landwards, nor a single sail on the clear sea-horizon; and we remained as tranquil and unmolested as if we were reclining on our own couches, taking sherbet in our gardens back in Istanbul. And yet still the Emperor did not come . . .

Then strange, scarcely credible news began to arrive from the Sublime Porte. A fleet of one hundred and sixty ships had been dispatched in the early spring to the Isle of Rhodes by Sultan Mehmed, in order to uproot, once and for all, from the midst of his dominions, those meddlesome Infidels and Enemies of the Faith – may God resist them! – the Knights of Rhodes. But the foul cuckoos had clung like grim death to their unclean island-nest and – on the very day our *Gazis* stormed ashore, carrying all before them at Otranto – the final assault on the Knights' castle was badly bungled and repulsed with such ferocity, and with so many men on our side killed and wounded, that the siege had been abandoned altogether.

Such a reversal was unheard of in all the thirty years of the Conqueror's reign and there were even some who ventured to suggest that they saw in it the hand of God warning that a man might achieve only so much in a lifetime. But all the while Sultan Mehmed – who had never until then failed personally to lead the Imperial Army, sword in hand, into battle against our enemies – remained in his Palace in the city, apparently as indifferent to shameful defeat in Rhodes as to glorious victory in Italy.

And as the summer faded we in Otranto waited, our eyes still fixed on the shimmering image of Rome, little knowing that before twelve months were out the Empire would be torn apart by internal strife and our brave visions of conquest would soon amount to no more than a confused heap of impossible dreams.

Sovereignty

Kivami Bey sat in his inner sanctum perched on a windowsill, gazing out across the rooftops of the city and over the wide channel of the breezy foam-flecked Bosphorus to Uskudar and the cloud-topped hills of Asia beyond. As I entered the room he said, 'You've made good time.'

'Thank you, sir,' I said.

'Bring me something to drink, will you?'

I filled a cup from the silver flask on his table and carried it over to him.

He took it with a grunt and, indicating the window ledge beside the one on which he had installed himself, said, 'Sit down.'

His expressionless grey eyes came to rest on my face.

'Well,' he said at last, 'a second winter in Italy doesn't seem to have done you much harm. I thought you were supposed to have been roughed up or something.'

'That was quite some time ago, sir.'

'Yes, I suppose it was. What was the state of affairs over there when you left?'

I shrugged. 'Very much the same. The Infidels have been making some feeble attempts to harass some of our forward positions since the weather improved, but it's a half-hearted business. Whenever we send a detachment out of the city most of them take to their heels. The king's son Alfonso came and rode up and down outside the walls until one of our marksmen shot his horse from under him and he removed himself to a safe distance. I gather from some prisoners we took on a raid that he may even have gone back to Naples.'

'And what's happening at sea?'

55

'As I suppose you'll know by now, some Infidel ships have been standing some distance away offshore during the past few weeks – but they're obviously in no mood to engage us, and our vessels have been coming and going quite freely. It's all rather curious really.'

'What about the men?'

'Naturally, they're pretty bored,' I said. 'But when Gedik Ahmed Pasha returns with the fresh troops he's been mustering in Albania and Greece they'll liven up soon enough. And there are no difficulties with supplies or horses.'

I fell silent.

'There's something you want to say. Go ahead, say it,' said Kivami Bey.

A little fearfully at first, I began: 'What nobody can understand, sir, is why the Emperor has delayed so long. Of course, I know what happened in Rhodes but, in my opinion, it would be easy enough to blockade the island and prevent the Knights from doing any mischief behind our backs while we advanced in the peninsula. We caught the Italians on the hop last year, but now they've had plenty of time to prepare and the Pope's patched up his differences with his neighbours – they're bound to be able to put up a stiffer fight this summer.'

'Yes, yes . . . I suppose so,' said Kivami Bey with a dismissive wave of his pudgy hand. 'So when is Gedik Ahmed expected back in Otranto?'

'I gather he was about to sail when I passed through Avlona.'

An angry scowl came over Kivami Bey's pale pock-marked face.

'I trust', he said with menacing slowness and precision, 'that you did not disobey my express orders not to inform the Admiral of your departure?'

'God forbid!' I said indignantly. 'Hayreddin Mustafa Pasha – he's the one who's been appointed Governor of the garrison at Otranto – thinks that I have gone on another reconnaissance trip behind enemy lines, and by now he will have reported the fact to Gedik Ahmed Pasha.

I crossed the straits to Avlona in the hold of a freight ship. The only person who knew that I was aboard was the captain, who is a friend of mine and won't breathe a word to anyone.'

'And when you landed?'

'I waited till dark before leaving the ship disguised as a civilian. I saw nobody that I know or that knows me. And I got the horse from the man whose name you, sir, had given me. It was he who told me that Gedik Ahmed Pasha was about to sail.'

Kivami Bey nodded slowly, thoughtfully, apparently satisfied – though it would take a first-class fool to believe that he could ever be really sure what was going on behind that ugly, misshapen brow.

After a while he said in his most dangerous off-hand manner, 'You have something else to say, Captain? I have the feeling that there's something bothering you.'

'I heard rumours on the road that Sultan Mehmed has left the city with the army and that part of the fleet has sailed.'

'That's perfectly true,' said Kivami Bey blandly. 'Mehmed left several days ago.'

'And yet the army is marching eastwards, into Asia?'

'Indeed . . .'

'But I don't understand . . .,' I said.

'My advice to you, Barak, is not even to try. Who does not know, in East or West, that the Sultan will never be satisfied until Rome is his?'

'Yes,' I said. 'Even the prophetic books of the sages of old speak of the coming of a Turkish Emperor who will go into the Infidel lands of the West and win possession of the Red Apple – which all the learned doctors agree means Rome. Why, then, now that Rome lies before him for the taking, does the Emperor turn his back upon it and march instead into the East?'

'Ah!' said Kivami Bey in mocking tones. 'Sages, augurs, sooth-sayers, oracles . . . the Red Apple! Listen and I will tell you something about *that*.

'One day, even before you were born, Mehmed, myself

57

and some others fell to talking about these very prophecies, and whether, in our time, they could ever be fulfilled when Rome was so far away, so deep in the heart of Infidel territory. Well, Mehmed said that certainly they would, and even then he knew how to achieve it. And to show us how, he took an apple and placed it in the middle of a great carpet, and challenged us all to take it without once treading upon the carpet. And when we said it could not be done, he said: "Nonsense!" And he took the edge of the carpet and very slowly he began, like this, to roll it up, until—'

Kivami Bey ceased speaking, and with a sudden swipe of his short arm he seized the imaginary apple from the sill in front of him and held it up to me in triumph.

'And how wise and far-sighted His Majesty was in this matter!' I responded vehemently. 'Rome is now within his reach, but the opportunity will not last for ever.'

'Perhaps,' said Kivami Bey. 'But Mehmed is too experienced in conquest, too knowledgeable in the ways of winning and holding on to power not to know that, if he is permanently to expand the borders of the Empire to so great an extent, he must first make certain its foundations are secure. He *will* go to Italy, but not before another account has been settled that has become somewhat overdue . . .'

'An account with the Infidel Knights of Rhodes, Kivami Bey?' I said.

Ignoring this, without even so much as a blink, Kivami Bey said, 'Mehmed has read your reports and the details of the other sorties you made inland during the autumn and winter. He was very interested in what you had to say and wants to question you further himself. In fact, that is the reason you have been recalled.'

'I see, sir,' I said. 'Then I am to wait here until His Majesty is pleased to return to the city?'

'Good God, no,' he said. 'He absolutely demanded to see you as soon as possible. And, fortunately for you, the expedition has got off to a rather slow start. The army's now camped on the Gebze road. If you start now you'll be able to get there tonight.'

'But what can I tell his Majesty that you or Gedik Ahmed

58

Pasha would not be able to tell him so much better?' I said, suddenly filled with apprehension at the thought of being cross-questioned by so lofty and awe-inspiring a person as the very Emperor himself.

'My dear Barak,' said Kivami Bey, giving me a strained look, 'I can only assume that he wishes to speak to somebody with personal experience of the terrain in the Italian hinterland. Which is something that neither I nor, as far as I am aware, your precious Admiral has to offer. Or it may be for some other reason . . .,' he added with an ironical curl of his lip. 'Perhaps he has it in mind to appoint *you* Admiral of the Fleet. He's done stranger things than that in his time.'

Lying on the windowsill was a small folded piece of paper. Picking it up with his clumsy and, I now noticed, slightly trembling hand, he passed it to me, saying, 'He left this pass for you – it will give you immediate access to him in the camp. And he wants everything done as discreetly as possible; that means you're not to reveal to anybody – not even to members of his Staff – where you have just come from and the reason Mehmed wishes to see you. He's signed the pass himself, so don't let them keep you waiting around when you get there. There are also some other documents that you might as well take with you. Atik has them.'

Kivami Bey turned away and resumed his contemplation of the shifting formations of billowing white clouds passing high in the sky over the low Asian hills.

As I left the room he said, 'Remember. Nothing of this to anybody but the Sultan himself.'

'I would sooner', I said, 'part with my head than with this secret.'

'If you part with this secret your head will not be long to follow,' he said quietly, 'of that you may be sure.'

And, thus instructed, I made my obeisance to Kivami Bey's resolutely averted back, and went in search of Atik.

At dusk I came upon the Imperial host encamped in the foothills overlooking the Marmara Sea on that rolling plain of grassland called the Emperor's Meadow. As I drew near, the sumptuous tents of Sultan Mehmed and his entourage

59

of generals, councillors, courtiers and favourites came into view – rising up on a green eminence in superior grandeur over the vast sea of humbler tents pitched by the rest of the army – the gold-tipped pinnacles of their dazzling white cotton pavilions catching the last iridescent rays of the sinking sun. The sweet smell of horses, woodsmoke and cooking food, and the confused sound of neighing beasts, barking dogs and human voices filled the cool stillness of the evening air.

Leaving the paved way, I rode on soft turf through the broad avenues of tents, past bands of irregulars, detachments of cavalry and companies of Janissaries lounging and chatting with their comrades around their fires and cooking pots, until eventually I came to an advance picket of guards who demanded to know my identity and my reason for wishing to approach the Imperial Presence. I showed them my pass bearing the Sultan's monogram and went on up the slope towards the royal encampment.

When I reached the brow of the hill I dismounted. As my animal was led away by grooms of the Sultan's Household I proceeded with an escort to the portals of the Emperor's tent. I was detained outside while my pass was borne within by a sergeant. The flaps of the tent fell closed behind him, but not without leaving a narrow gap through which I could keep surreptitious watch on the curtained entrance to the inner room of the tent beyond the antechamber. For some time I waited for some courtier to go through this door in order to present my pass to the Emperor, but the heavy folds of the curtains remained still, forbidding, undisturbed.

After a few minutes I was ushered into the outer chamber of the tent, where I was presented to a regal gentleman who received me with an air of suave and polite indifference. His robe was of the finest white silk, his cloak of heavy brocade lined with some costly fur, and about his waist he wore a wide gold sash in which was tucked a dagger with a jewelled hilt and scabbard. After the usual formalities I found myself alone with this resplendent gentleman, who said:

'His Highness is resting at present.'

'Then I will wait,' I said.

'That will not be necessary,' he said. 'His Highness is suffering from a slight indisposition and he has deigned to instruct me to deal with any urgent business that might arise.'

'I'm afraid my orders are to speak to no one but the Emperor.'

'Do you know who I am?' he said with supercilious disdain.

'Of course, my lord,' I said. 'You are Mahmud Pasha, the Sultan's Grand Vizir.'

'Well, then?'

'I'm sorry, my lord. But my orders were quite specific and unless they are countermanded in writing with the Sultan's signature I have no choice but to follow them.'

'You are an officer in the Imperial Navy?'

'Yes.'

'Then, in the absence of the Grand Admiral you are obliged to obey my orders as Commander-in-Chief of the Army,' said Mahmud Pasha calmly.

I said nothing.

But Mahmud Pasha seemed curiously indifferent to what I thought he would take to be this gross example of insubordination on my part.

With a sigh he said, 'Very well. You may go now and return in the morning. Perhaps His Majesty will find time to deal with this mysterious matter then.'

'His Majesty *has* been informed of my arrival?' I said casually.

'Naturally, this document was shown to His Majesty,' said Mahmud Pasha, leaning forward slightly to return my pass, 'but, as I have told you, he does not deign to give you an audience tonight. Tomorrow, perhaps.'

'The matter is important,' I said. 'Tomorrow may be too late.'

'Come back tomorrow, Captain, and we shall see.'

And with that Mahmud Pasha, affecting to stifle a yawn, indicated that our interview was at an end.

When I emerged from the tent into the open air the last blood-red streaks of light were draining out of the western

61

sky and darkness was descending on the surrounding hills. I led my horse slowly down the slope again into the main body of the camp and wandered around, apparently aimlessly, until the blackness was complete and I was sure that I had not been followed. The moon that rose that night was nothing more than the faintest silver crescent and – fortunately, in view of the desperate enterprise I had in mind – cast down no more light on the earth than the most feeble constellation of distant stars.

A little distance from a camp-fire and a small collection of tents, I came upon a boy, all by himself, brushing down one of half a dozen horses by a stream.

'How would you like to earn yourself a few aspers, my friend?'

'For what?' he said, continuing to brush down the animal's coat with even strokes.

'Feed and water my horse and give it a rest from the saddle while I go to visit someone,' I said.

'Is that all?' he said suspiciously.

'And keep an eye on my bags. That's all.'

He shrugged and came over and took my horse by the bridle. Then he hesitated, glancing down bashfully at his feet. I reached into my sash for my purse and counted out three pieces of silver into his grubby hand. In the twinkling of an eye they had vanished into his shirt.

As I walked away I glanced over my shoulder. The boy was already patting the side of my beast's neck and reaching down to unfasten the saddle.

Getting past the guards at the bottom of the slope was surprisingly, even scandalously, easy. I went slowly on my stomach and kept to the shadows. The grass was soft and wet, and very satisfactorily deadened the sound of my painstaking progress. At one point I practically crawled between a sentry's legs without his having the slightest inkling of my existence. Working my way around the side of the hillock, I managed to locate a shallow gully, which had been cut into the incline by the downward passage of rainwater. Following its course, I made my way upwards.

By a stroke of exceptional good luck the gully I had chosen reached the top of the hill only yards from the rear of the Sultan's tent. I wriggled forward and was about to make a dash to cover the last few feet when suddenly two figures loomed up above me out of the darkness. I lay completely still – and one of them came so close that he nearly trod on my hand as he passed. I pulled myself up a little to observe their receding forms and could discern from the silhouettes of their turbans against the night sky that they were members of the Sultan's bodyguard, patrolling the environs of his tent with that lethally soft and stealthy tread they perfect lest their footfalls disturb the repose of their resting master. Then, just in time, I sensed the equally silent approach of another pair coming hard on the heels of their fellow guards, and flattened myself against the ground again.

I lay concealed behind some tufts of grass for some time, observing the guards as they made their regular circum-ambulations of the tent. The interval between each pair was so small – perhaps the count of ten or twelve – that I began to despair. But then I noticed that as they rounded a corner at the very back of the tent they seemed to take a slight detour away from the canvas walls. Awaiting an opportunity, I raised myself up and, peering through the darkness, could just make out that at that point there was a slight depression in the ground, filled with shadow like a small pond brimming with dark water. Also, it seemed that the wall of the tent was sagging slightly on the other side of the depression as though the ground was too uneven there to pitch it properly. So much the better if there was some slack in the canvas . . .

As soon as the coast was clear I slithered forward and into the depression. I held my breath as the next pair of sentries passed but – Praise be to God! – I seemed to be invisible. Gradually I worked loose the pegs holding down the skirt of the tent – pausing at the approach of each patrol – until they could be silently removed. When there was sufficient loose canvas to form a funnel through which I could squeeze my body, I crawled up from my hiding-place and into the narrow gap between the heavy canvas of the outer walls and the fine silken layer of the rich inner linings, through which I could now see the glow of the lamps illuminating the Sultan's private chamber.

For a long time I lay there, trying to slow down my breathing and listening out for any sounds within. The heady scent of aloes-wood assailed my nostrils, mixed with a sweeter, more sickly smell, like incense. I was in terror that the Emperor would – despite his indisposition – be enjoying the artful ministrations of one of the ravishing and nimble-fingered girls of the harem, or (more likely, if the rumours were to be believed) be caressing and fondling some pliant and beardless boy in preparation for the act of delicious, if forbidden, penetration. But there was silence. Absolute silence.

Cautiously I pulled the folds of the silken hangings from beneath the carpets of the other side and, lifting them gingerly, crawled into the spacious room.

At first it seemed to be empty. But then I saw the form of a man lying on his side on a low padded couch beneath a quilted cover. His back was towards me so I could not see his face. But then my eyes fell upon a small table beside him and on it lay the Emperor's turban and sword.

Remaining on my knees, I whispered, 'Forgive me, Your Highness, your slave Barak comes to you with news from Italy.'

I waited with bated breath, but he did not stir.

More loudly, I said, 'Your Highness . . .'

I rose to my feet and, keeping one eye on the flaps covering the door to the next chamber of the tent, I edged nearer him. Laying my hand gently on the Sultan's shoulder, I said again, 'Your Highness . . .'

No response.

His head was turned slightly to one side and, leaning forward, I found myself looking into his face. His skin was chalky white, his eyes deeply sunken in bluish sockets, his lips a strange purplish colour and drawn back in a lop-sided grin. His fine aquiline nose seemed pinched and bloodless, almost translucent. Then I noticed with a start that his eyelids were open a little and behind them black irises glistened darkly. But the eyes opened no further.

I reached for his hand, which lay awkwardly across his broad chest. It was cold and stiff, the fingers bent inwards like a claw. Catching sight of a small silver dish, with a trembling hand I held it before his lips. Not a hint of vapour clouded the polished mirror of its surface.

So there I stood, alone, gazing upon him: this King of Kings, Great Monarch, Mighty Ruler, Invincible Commander of the Faithful, Victor of Constantinople, Subjugator of the Empires of Byzantium and Trebizond, Humbler of puissant despots and princes, Subduer of ancient cities, proud states and warlike nations, Conqueror of the Kingdoms of Karaman, Albania, Serbia, Bosnia, Wallachia, the Morea, the Islands of the Archipelago, Scourge of the Infidels, the Shadow of God on Earth, Lord of the Age . . . his feet stretched out, his arm flung across his chest, his eyes unseeing, his turbulent mind and ambitious heart stilled for ever, his powerful body a ghastly lifeless corpse . . .

Surfacing as if from a feverish dream and finding that I had been all the while awake, my self-control almost deserted me. I was even about to call for help. But then the full realization of my position took violent hold of my racing brain. Unless I succeeded in removing myself from this place of death forthwith, and without being seen by a living soul, I, who had found the Emperor dead and cold, would without question be taken for his assassin. And if that should happen, the best I could hope for would be to die on the spot, hewn to pieces by the enraged members of his bodyguard – for it was evident even to my inexpert eyes that the Sultan had not died a natural death.

I started to make for the place where I had lifted the inner lining of the tent in order to crawl underneath, determined to be away and out into the night before some solicitous chamberlain discovered the inanimate mortal remains of his master, but then I heard muffled voices in the next chamber of the tent. I spun round and seized Mehmed's own sword from his table, and moved silently over to the curtained door. Raising the sword, I waited – for I had the utterly mad thought that if I could cut down the first person that came in I might just be able, in the ensuing surprise and disorder, to hack my way out of the canvas walls and escape into the blessed darkness.

But nobody came through the door. Warily I sank onto my haunches and, still gripping the sword, opened one of the curtains a fraction. Four men were sitting huddled together in a circle. One I could see in profile – the Grand Vizir, Mahmud Pasha. The others, as was evident from their uniforms, were senior officers of the Imperial Army, but I could not see their faces very clearly. They spoke so quietly that I had to strain my ears to follow the conversation passing between them.

One officer was saying, 'But what fiend could have been responsible for poisoning His Majesty?'

'It is impossible to say,' said Mahmud Pasha. 'There are suspects, but nothing can be done at the moment without letting the whole army know about it. And now that he *is* dead – Lord have mercy upon him! – only one thing is essential and that's to keep Mehmed's demise secret until his successor has reached Istanbul and has been proclaimed Emperor. Otherwise there will be chaos.'

'But how can this be done?' said one of the other officers. 'It is already two days since the Sultan fell ill. If many more days pass and His Majesty still does not appear before the troops, they will start asking questions.'

'Later tonight,' said Mahmud Pasha, 'the Emperor's body will be placed in a closed carriage and driven back to the Palace in Istanbul with an ordinary guard. Not more than a dozen men will be in the escort – all of them completely trustworthy. Most of the camp will be asleep and it should not be possible for anybody who happens to see it leave to know whether it is carrying Mehmed, some other official, or even one of the ladies of the Household. Tomorrow I'll make it known that Mehmed has returned to Istanbul for a few days to take baths for the treatment of his gout. He's been suffering quite badly from it lately – so, God willing, the story will be believed.'

'What of the other members of the Imperial Council?' said the officer who had spoken first.

'They know nothing of this matter yet,' said the Grand Vizir.

There was a murmur of surprise.

'You'll see the reason why very shortly,' said Mahmud Pasha, raising his hand to quieten them. 'The Imperial Council will not be informed of Mehmed's death until the day after tomorrow – which is when I propose to call a meeting. And the meeting will take place not here in the camp but in the Palace.'

'But they will be enraged when they discover that you have concealed the death from them for so long,' said the first officer.

'No,' said Mahmud Pasha. 'They will be informed that Mehmed expired only the night before the meeting – in other words, *after* returning for treatment to Istanbul.'

'But what possible purpose is there in this elaborate deception?' said the first officer in tones of growing perplexity.

'As you know,' said Mahmud Pasha, 'Prince Bayezid is ruling as Governor in Amasya, and Prince Jem in Konya. Bayezid is the elder of the two, and so is heir apparent.'

'Yes, yes . . .,' the officers growled impatiently.

'But the fact is', said Mahmud Pasha, 'that it is Jem, not Bayezid, who will be proclaimed the next Sultan of the Sublime and Ever Victorious House of Osman.'

There was a silence as profound as if all three officers had been struck dead where they sat. My heart seemed to miss a beat. Could my poor soul have known then what lay in store for me? But no, only to the Lord God is known what shall happen on the morrow.

At last the first officer said, 'But Bayezid is twelve years older than Prince Jem.'

'And yet Prince Jem is more fitted to succeed, more worthy of his illustrious birth, stronger both in arms and intellect,' said Mahmud Pasha. 'That is the reason Sultan

Mehmed entrusted it to me – the First Officer of the State – to make certain, for the sake of the Royal House, the Empire and the Religion of Islam, that Jem, not Bayezid, ascends the throne at his death. And I swore to him on my father's soul and the Holy Koran that I would see that this thing was done – and so it shall be, by Almighty God!'

There was a long silence as Mahmud Pasha, his face flushed red and his forehead shining with perspiration in the lamplight, looked defiantly from one officer to another.

The one who had not spoken before began cautiously, 'There is not a subject or slave in the whole Empire who has not heard of Prince Jem's valour in arms, his nobility, his grace, his learning, his ambitious pride. Why, they say his men worship the very ground he walks on, and even the people of Karaman, so recently brought within the borders of our Empire, love their Governor as though he were a prince of their own blood! There is not another like him of the same age in East or West, and indeed he gives every sign of being born to rule and overcome our enemies and win glory for our Nation and our Faith. Perhaps he would be greater even than his father, for they say he has all his father's virtues and he lacks only – God forgive me! – his father's cruelty. Those that have seen him hold court in Karaman say that this boy of twenty-two can sway by eloquence and persuasion where others twice his age must resort to bribes, promises of pensions or threats of evil consequences. And in the field of battle they say he is a lion.'

'And yet this is a dangerous game, my lord,' said one of the other officers ominously. 'The expectation is that Bayezid, not Jem, will succeed his father. Nor is Bayezid wholly without friends, even if they are not so numerous as Prince Jem's or even, as we now learn, so eminent as the Grand Vizir himself.'

Mahmud Pasha sat impassive and unmoved, not deigning to reply to these stern words of warning. Meanwhile, the other members of this council of the night appeared to be plunged in deep and sombre consideration of what their brother officer had said.

Then the first officer broke the spell of silence, saying:

'Tell me, is Prince Jem aware of his father's wishes?'

'He is,' said Mahmud Pasha.

'Then,' said the first officer, 'even if Bayezid were called to Istanbul and put upon the throne, Jem would still attempt to fight his brother for it?'

'Inevitably,' said Mahmud Pasha, opening his hands wide in an uncharacteristic gesture of helplessness. 'Prince Jem will be satisfied with nothing less than the Sultanate. And nobody knew this better than his father!'

'So,' said the third officer, 'if Jem can be brought to Istanbul and declared his father's successor before Bayezid even learns of their father's death, there is – if it please God – some chance that war between the brothers may be averted?'

'Faced with an accomplished fact, Bayezid will accept what the Heavens have seen fit to decree. When he learns that Jem is already in Istanbul and girded with his father's sword, he will not dare to oppose him – on this I will lay my head and neck,' said Mahmud Pasha.

'That is all very well, my lord,' said the first officer in an almost mocking voice, 'but Prince Jem is now in Konya, not in Istanbul.'

'And that is why', said Mahmud Pasha briskly, 'you three must start for Karaman tonight. From here you can reach Konya in five or six days. When you have told Jem the news, you can return with him. I have prepared letters advising the Prince what he should do. It would be best if he travels incognito with the smallest possible escort. If it becomes known that he has left his province Bayezid's suspicions will be aroused.'

'But how will you handle the Imperial Council in the mean time?' said the third officer. 'It will be at least eight days before we can get back to the city with Jem.'

'When I reveal the Emperor's death to the Imperial Council I will, of course, say nothing of Mehmed's wish that his adored Jem should succeed him. As a matter of course the Council will agree that the death should be kept absolutely secret until the very moment the new Sultan is proclaimed. The members of the Council will then expect messengers to be dispatched immediately to Amasya to call Bayezid to Istanbul. This will be done. But the journey to Amasya cannot be covered in less than eight or nine days – it may even take longer if the weather is not good – which means that by the time the news of Mehmed's death reaches Bayezid, Jem will have already arrived in Istanbul and – God willing – been declared Sultan. And after that, gentlemen, Bayezid will come to realize that the tide of events has flowed so far beyond his control that he is powerless to resist. He will then have no choice but to bend to the inevitable and concede defeat.'

And with these words the Grand Vizir rose to his feet amidst murmurs of 'God willing' from the officers, while I, letting the curtain drop and laying down the Emperor's sword, hastened to make good my escape from that fetid mausoleum into the cool refuge of the spring night.

I roused Kivami Bey from his slumbers at the time of the dawn prayer. The fire in his room had burned out and I sat before him huddled in my travel-worn cloak, shivering with hunger and fatigue. He received the tidings of the Emperor's death in complete silence. As usual his features betrayed nothing. When I described the conversation I had overheard in the outer chamber, I believe I saw one of his eyebrows on the verge of being raised a little – but I had ridden a great many miles and been up all night. I probably imagined it. When I finally dried up he said, 'Anything else?'

'I don't think so, sir,' I said.

'Well,' he said, 'now you can guess what Mehmed was doing leading the Imperial Army into Asia and not to Italy.'

I looked at him blankly.

'Come on, man,' he said irritably, rattling one of his

70

silver-handled canes against the table in front of his divan. 'Put two and two together.'

My mind seemed to have ceased to function. Then I heard myself saying, 'Bayezid.'

'Very good, very good,' said Kivami Bey, nodding slowly in mock admiration. And then with ponderous irony, 'You have hidden depths.'

'Then it is true', I said, 'that Sultan Mehmed had decided that Prince Jem, not Bayezid, should be his successor?'

'What did you think when you heard the Grand Vizir say that was what the Emperor had decreed? That it was just another dastardly Palace intrigue? Mahmud Pasha fixing things so that the Prince that suited *him* best should come to the throne?'

'I thought it possible,' I said defensively.

'Well, I suppose you were right to think so. But, as it happens, for once that old fox Mahmud Pasha was speaking the truth. Mehmed had decided that Jem should succeed.'

'How many people knew of this?'

'A handful. But Mehmed knew that it couldn't be kept like that for ever, and sooner or later he'd have to make up his mind what to do about Bayezid. That's why he couldn't risk leaving the city to go campaigning last summer – in case Bayezid got to hear of it while he was away.'

'And did he?'

'I think he may have begun to suspect. But, according to my information, he didn't know that Mehmed was marching on Amasya. And now that Mehmed's dead, perhaps he never will. After all, it was not Mehmed's habit to confide his plans, even to his generals. And the army was so large that Bayezid must have thought it was on its way to Rhodes or the eastern borders. Of course, that was a deliberate ruse on Mehmed's part, and I suspect it worked.'

'If Sultan Mehmed was so determined to remove Bayezid from Prince Jem's path to the Sultanate, I'm surprised he didn't simply have him called to Istanbul on some pretext and imprisoned or—'

'Assassinated?'

'I suppose so, yes,' I said uncertainly.

71

'It had become too late to recall him to Istanbul,' said Kivami Bey. 'Jem had become too obvious a favourite. If Mehmed had tried to call him to the Porte, Bayezid would have smelt a rat and refused to come. Assassination? All very well if the attempt was a success first time, but if anything went wrong it would merely have alerted him to the fact that his life was now in danger. Either way, Bayezid stood a good chance of being forewarned that something was up and of being able to take measures to defend himself – and, given that he has friends in the Army, even attempt a coup against his father. No, Mehmed's plan was best: secrecy, complete surprise – or it would have been, if death had not surprised *him*.'

Kivami Bey let out a savage laugh, then sank back on the divan and began to stroke his beard in moody meditation, murmuring almost inaudibly to himself:

'So, the old cripple outlives his master. Who would have thought it? So much for expecting to find me in Hell waiting patiently to greet you, you old dog.'

And then, shooting me a penetrating glance: 'Poisoned? Are you sure?'

'I can't be, Kivami Bey. I'm not a physician. But it looked like that and obviously Mahmud Pasha thinks so.'

'He should know,' said Kivami Bey darkly. 'And it stands to reason. I never thought Mehmed would give up the ghost from old age – not his way of doing things at all.'

'Forgive me,' I said, 'but if Prince Bayezid *had* begun to suspect that his younger brother was being prepared to usurp his place on the throne when their father died . . .'

'You mean, could Bayezid have had Mehmed poisoned? I don't think so. If he'd realized that his father's sword was poised above his head, he might have tried it to save himself. But I'm still convinced that he didn't know how imminent the danger was.'

'Perhaps the Infidels are behind it, sir,' I said.

'To get at the Emperor himself? Most of the Infidel states wouldn't even know how to set about it, let alone pull it off. Not that that's prevented them from trying from time to time in the past. Except the Venetians, of course. They've been trying to poison Mehmed ever since the Fall of Constantinople, but at the moment they haven't got an agent left alive in the city or court who has not been turned to work for us – or at least as far as I know they haven't.'

'Then, who?'

'Mehmed had as many enemies as you'd expect. There have been more plots against his life than you can imagine, but conspiracies involving several people are easier to deal with. A man with a grudge working patiently on his own, revealing nothing to anybody – that's another matter. There'll have to be some kind of investigation, but not until the problem of the succession has been solved one way or the other.'

'What are we to do till Prince Jem comes?' I said.

At this, Kivami Bey really did raise an eyebrow.

'Nothing,' he said.

'Nothing?'

'What else do you suggest we do?' said Kivami Bey in tones of exasperation. 'Mehmed is dead and ensuring the succession is a matter for the Grand Vizir and the Imperial Council. This section reports directly to the Sultan. That was the system in Murad Khan's day and Mehmed saw no reason to change it. So, as far as we're concerned, it's quite simple: until the new Emperor has been proclaimed by the Imperial Council and recognized by the religious authorities and the Army, we don't have anyone we *can* report to.'

'But if Prince Jem is to be Sultan, would it not be more prudent to declare our allegiance now?' I said.

'If Jem wins the race to Istanbul and gets himself proclaimed over his older brother's head – then so be it. That's the way it's done. But in the mean time, I'm going to make damn sure that Imperial Security doesn't get itself mixed up in the machinations of Mahmud Pasha and his crew.'

And with that Kivami Bey ordered me to go and get some rest and report to him later.

Atik was not at his desk in the antechamber so I went

73

out into the bright morning sunshine and wandered across the courtyard to his room. Squatting outside his door in the shade of the cloister was one of the nameless Convent mutes, who gave me to understand in the sign language peculiar to them that my friend had gone into the second courtyard to collect some documents. I indicated to him that I would wait inside. I don't think a broken-backed old couch ever looked more inviting. I don't even remember lying down on it before I fell into a deep and dreamless sleep.

Battle Array

I don't suppose it will ever be known for certain how the Janissaries got to hear of the Emperor's death. I suspect that even the omniscient Kivami Bey never really got to the bottom of it. Not that I ever asked him. After all, it's not as if he would have told me – if he was as much in the dark as everybody else seemed to be about it.

Some say the Janissary astrologers saw signs in the heavens – I saw none. Others, that the evil tidings became known in the Imperial harem and the loud lamentations of the ladies and girls within were overheard by a Janissary guard without (a durable chestnut this, suitable for all court occasions). Others still, that when the body was hurried at dawn through the Palace gardens to a secret entrance to the Sultan's apartments, a Janissary cadet caught sight of a deathly wax-coloured hand projecting from the covers of the litter (I can see it now – bouncing up and down in a grotesque parody of a regal wave to a non-existent multitude), recognized Mehmed's signet ring and surmised that its wearer had departed for another world; and that, within the hour, the boy, along with the rest of the corps, was under orders from Mahmud Pasha, who was anxious to get the cadets out of the way, to go and help repair a bridge on the Asian side; from there he was able to slip away and inform his commanding officer, the Aga of the Janissaries . . .

But no matter how exactly the news leaked out and how it reached the ears of the Janissaries, reach them it did and by the afternoon of the second day after Mehmed's death the flower of his troops were in open revolt and hotfooting it back to the capital, defiantly determined to see their beloved master, whether he be dead or alive.

So it happened that hardly had the Imperial Council met, been informed of the Sultan's sad demise and, at the suggestion of the Grand Vizir, dispatched the Royal Chamberlain Keklik Mustafa to call Prince Bayezid to Istanbul to ascend the throne of his illustrious forebears and take up the reins of power, than companies of mutinous Janissaries began to appear with their banners on the shore of the Bosphorus opposite the Palace. A message to this effect was passed to Mahmud Pasha but, as he had the day before taken the precaution of severing all communication between capital and camp by ordering every vessel of whatever description, great and small, to leave the Asian side and tie up at the harbour below the city walls or anchor in midstream in the Golden Horn, the Grand Vizir saw no reason to interrupt the calm deliberations of the Council on the Emperor's funeral arrangements.

Meanwhile, convinced by the Grand Vizir's elaborate measures to exclude them from the city that the news of Mehmed's death was no idle rumour and fearing even that Mahmud Pasha was himself attempting to seize the throne (or so they claimed afterwards), the Janissaries began to roam up and down the Asian shore, howling with fury and anguish, in search of some means to cross. But all to no avail – for by the time the Janissaries reached the waterfront at Uskudar even the boat that had deposited Keklik Mustafa and his escort on the Asian side on their way to Prince Bayezid in Amasya had set sail on its return journey to the city.

And so the mutinous troops might have vainly searched the far shore of the Bosphorus for hours, even days on end, without finding a single boat, had not a small fleet of fishing smacks appeared on the horizon on their way back from their fishing grounds in the Marmara Sea, their oars dipping rhythmically in the haze like the wings of a flock of gulls flying low over the water.

All eyes were now upon these boats, and when at last they bobbed gaily into the little bay on the eastern coast that was their haven they didn't even have a chance to reach shore and land their catch. Mobs of Janissaries, wading into the water to meet them, surrounded them on every side. Fish, nets, baskets, lines, tackle and any fishermen who dared even to ask what was happening, were unceremoniously tossed overboard. Several boats, precipitously filled to the gunwales by a struggling mass of heavily armed soldiers, sank to the bottom. Others capsized. But finally the remainder – rowed by terrified fishermen – put to sea again.

And even these were so grossly overloaded that if there had been the faintest puff of wind or heave of swell they would all, without a shadow of doubt, have been instantly swamped and every last man aboard drowned long before they had made it halfway across the channel. But the hand of Fate seemed hell-bent on denying the Grand Vizir even this small respite from the Furies in human form that were now bearing down on him with such inhuman speed and singleness of purpose, and appeared almost actively to still the wind and smooth the surface of the waters.

Thus shielded miraculously from the elements, in due course the first of the overburdened craft began to approach the mouth of the Golden Horn – where they slid into the line of vision of Kivami Bey, who was at that very moment at his window, surveying the estuary with his unblinking gaze, a dishevelled, truculent old eagle in his eyrie.

With all the other field agents available already deployed at points around the city, I was rudely roused from my slumbers (I was still trying to catch up on sleep) and summoned for duty.

'Something nautical's going on down there,' said Kivami Bey, pointing with one of his sticks. 'Go and find out what it is and get back here as quickly as you can.'

As he finished speaking a breathless messenger arrived, saying, 'Master, there are some soldiers coming over from the Asian side in small boats.'

'I can see that, I'm not blind,' snapped Kivami Bey. 'What kind of soldiers are they?'

'I don't know, sir,' said the messenger. 'They were too far away to tell when I left to come up here.'

The Old Man snorted derisively. He turned to me. 'Well, go on, then. And if there's fighting, don't get mixed up in it. That's an order. I've got a feeling something very nasty is about to happen.'

I rode down to the harbour and came onto the waterfront just as Mahmud Pasha, descending from the Palace with a large mounted entourage, debouched from the Fish Market Gate and thundered onto the quay. The first of the fishing smacks were now drawing alongside some of the larger vessels anchored in midstream and Janissaries were swarming aboard with blood-curdling cries and flashing swords.

Seeing that it was the Janissaries' intention to commandeer the vessels and return with them to collect their comrades, Mahmud Pasha – grey-bearded, erect, haughty and majestic in his Grand Vizirial robes – rode over to the water's edge calling on the captains and crews to remain where they were and to convey this order to the ships anchored too far away to be within earshot of the shore. But the Janissaries' unsheathed scimitars soon decided any of the mariners who might have found themselves in two minds as to what to do and, in no time, anchors were being weighed, rowers taking up their positions on the benches and crewmen busying themselves about the rigging.

Oars were unshipped and blades splashed into the water, lateen yards hoisted aloft and cascades of loose canvas released. And then Fate intervened once again and showed her hand: a light breeze from the west, which had held off only long enough to allow the fishing smacks to get safely across from the other side, now began to freshen a little and to fill out the sails that were blossoming like spring flowers all over the Golden Horn. Nudged forward by this unexpected current of air, vessels were soon in motion and visibly gathering speed. Before long, half the fleet seemed to be getting under way.

Such naked defiance was more than the Grand Vizir could bear and, falling into a terrible passion, he stood up in his stirrups and began to wave his curved sword above his head, swearing by the Almighty, Muhammad and the souls of all the Prophets that he would personally decapitate every man in every vessel that did not turn back forthwith – but his words were carried away by the wind as one vessel after another glided past him out of the estuary and, pitching and tossing on the swelling waves of the channel, relentlessly forged on in the direction of the Asian shore.

And even when it became clear to everybody present that only some thunderbolt out of the clear blue sky, some cataclysmic freak occurrence, some intervention by the Divinity could prevent the ships' returning with the troops, Mahmud Pasha continued to ride up and down on the quay as though hypnotized by the unfolding drama of his own downfall, scarlet with impotent rage, blaspheming loudly and cutting with his sword at any poor devil who found himself in the path of the Vizir's charger.

By now a considerable crowd of civilians had gathered to watch the excitement and as most of these were on foot I began to grow afraid that, if Mahmud Pasha passed too close by, he might recognize my face. So, to render myself less conspicuous, I dismounted and took my animal by the bridle. Pushing forward, I reached the front just as two of the other Pashas had caught up with the Grand Vizir and started to plead with him to return to the Palace with them.

Wild-eyed, he shouted, 'Go to Hell, damn you!' Then, pulling his horse round, he rode off, muttering to himself, 'I'll make those bastards pay for this, by Great God in Heaven, I will. They'll wish they had never been born!'

The Aga of the Janissaries was the first to set foot ashore from the vessels now recrossing, laden with their wrathful and embittered human cargoes. Seeing the mustachioed, strong-limbed old veteran of a score of the Emperor's campaigns leaping onto the quay, Mahmud Pasha rode over to him, saying, 'General, this is a disgrace. Take your men back to the camp immediately. This insubordination is intolerable. Order your men on no account to disembark. The Emperor will be furious when he gets to hear of this.'

The Aga said nothing but grimly strode up to the Grand Vizir, seized the folds of his sumptuous robes and, still without uttering a syllable, pulled him off his horse. Then the Aga calmly drew his sword, apparently with the intention of cutting off Mahmud Pasha's head. A great gasp went up from the crowd. But before he had the chance to raise his weapon on high to deal the fatal blow, the Grand Vizir's bodyguard rushed the Aga, who, after a violent and confused struggle, toppled over and crashed to the ground, bellowing like a wounded elephant.

At the sight of their revered commander thus assaulted a mighty shout of outrage was raised by the watching Janissaries and they began to pour ashore. And it was only in the nick of time that Mahmud Pasha's minions managed to drag him clear and help him back on his horse to ride turbanless, his rich robes covered in mud, and pursued by a baying mob of soldiers into the city through the Fish Market Gate, ignominiously clinging for dear life to his horse's mane.

Civilians fled in panic in all directions. The Janissaries streamed into the city and up the hill towards the Royal Palace. I followed on. When they arrived, finding no one to oppose them, they rushed from courtyard to courtyard and then surged in a tide from room to room, breaking down doors wherever they found them locked and calling out the Emperor's name, until eventually, in an empty, out-of-the-way storeroom with bare walls and a grey flag-stoned floor, they found Mehmed's cold, forlorn and unattended corpse lying stretched out on a table.

Wailing pitifully, they paused only to cover their heads with dust from the Palace courtyards and flowerbeds before setting out in a mob to seek out the Grand Vizir, who had last been seen fleeing in the direction of his palace. And there they found him, trying to conceal himself amidst piles of bedding in a cupboard. He was pulled out by his feet, and eager swords set about clumsily hacking off his head. Fountains of blood spattered the walls, the floor,

80

the ceiling. White linen from the cupboard, strewn across the floor in the struggle, was soaked by the hot jets of crimson. Severed at last, the head was driven onto the point of a lance and the body, rigidly convulsed in the twisted agony of death, left lying in a pool of its own gore.

The riotous throng outside the palace was becoming greater by the minute as more and more Janissaries disembarked at the harbour and hurried up the hill to join their comrades. Abandoning Mahmud Pasha's palace, they took to the streets again, touting their ghastly trophy and, at the instigation of their Aga and their officers, began chanting, 'Bayezid! Bayezid! Long life to Bayezid!' until, growing tired of marching in tumultuous procession, they began to long for further action.

Seeing that control was slipping from their grasp, their officers attempted to order them back to the city barracks. But the men paid them no heed. For now that they had had a taste of murder and destruction they would not be calmed until their ungovernable appetite for more blood had been satiated and the fiery humour burning in their veins had been allowed to run its full course and spend its energy. They began to break ranks, officers were knocked to the ground. What followed was inevitable.

The first street-vendor's stall was overturned, the first passer-by set upon and beaten up, the first door kicked in, the first shutters wrenched from their hinges, the first shop invaded, looted and destroyed. And for some little time they contented themselves with such aimless and wanton acts of violence.

But then their bestial energies turned to more practical targets and they set about plundering the houses of the rich, the Christians, the Jews. Soon, like a ravening pack of wolves, they were ranging far and wide about the city, terrorizing Infidels and True Believers alike wherever they found them and stripping them of everything they possessed.

I made it back to the sanctuary of the Convent only minutes before a sizeable band of Janissaries laid siege to the outer gate. God be praised, their efforts to batter down the

81

oak doors failed – but not before Kivami Bey had issued the order that if the gates showed signs of giving way they were to be flung open to let the rebellious troops rush into the first courtyard. For it was his plan that, if necessary, they should be enticed inside and the gates slammed shut behind them. In this way they could be isolated and shot down by our archers who lined the cloisters and rooftops in readiness to destroy any intruders. But, fortunately, it became clear that not a man amongst them seemed to have the faintest notion of what deadly secrets and vast hordes of gold and silver lay behind the walls and, finding that the gates were strong enough to withstand their initial assaults and that their threats fell on deaf ears, they soon lost heart – brave fellows! – and went off in search of easier pickings.

Meanwhile, the dreadful anarchy was spreading across the water to the Infidel districts of Galata and Pera. By the late afternoon Venetian, Florentine and Genoese mansions and warehouses were being sacked and set ablaze. And it was not long before every tavern and wine-shop on both sides of the estuary had had its doors broken open and was the scene of vile misrule and drunken orgy. As night fell a kind of ominous calm, broken now and then by brutish subhuman shouts and the sounds of distant swinish carousal, descended on the city. The smell of burning hung in the air and black columns of smoke could be seen billowing skywards from fires still not put out in the Frankish quarters across the darkening waters of the Golden Horn.

At about the time of the night prayer Kivami Bey demanded my presence once again. As I crossed the shadowy courtyard a solitary muezzin in a nearby mosque began to call out from his minaret over the rooftops of the city the sweet summons of the Muslim Faith:

'God is Most Great . . . Come to prayer . . . Come to security . . . God is Most Great . . . There is no god but God . . . Prayer is better than sleep . . . O Lord . . . My sins when I think upon them I see to be

many, but the mercy of my Lord is more abundant
than my sins . . . I am not solicitous on account of
good that I have done, but for the mercy of God I am
most solicitous . . . Extolled be the Everlasting . . .
He hath no companion in His great dominion . . .
His perfection I extol: exalted be His name . . .'

I lingered for a moment or two to listen and then went inside. No sooner had I been gruffly bidden to sit and 'stop hovering around like some blessed executioner' than there were raised voices and sounds of a struggle in the ante-chamber outside and seconds later in marched a robust farouche individual whose face and garb were stained and filthy, boots caked in mud and headgear in disarray, but who none the less managed still to look every inch an officer of the Imperial Army.

'What in God's name is going on in this madhouse?' he demanded in a booming voice. 'It's a shambles out there. I was beginning to think the Infidels had made a surprise attack. What's happened to the Pashas – have they all been murdered or something? There are soldiers lying around all over the place – roaring drunk every blasted one of them, like animals. And there isn't a bloody officer in sight. I've never seen such a disgusting spectacle in my life. Has everybody here gone stark staring mad?'

Then, suddenly seeming to remember himself, he looked around and bowed most respectfully to Kivami Bey. He gave me a quick nod. Overcome with embarrass-ment, he started to mumble, 'I'm sorry, sir. I'm just abso-lutely astonished, that's all.'

'All right, all right,' said Kivami Bey with a frown. 'Now that you've managed to compose yourself, perhaps you'd care to tell me what brings you here so suddenly – though, God knows, we've got enough to keep us occupied at the moment.'

Shaking his head, the visitor said, 'So I see, so I see.'

'I wasn't expecting you until the autumn,' said Kivami Bey. 'Where have you just come from now?'

'From Bursa, sir.'

83

He seemed about to go on but then shot me a sideways glance and gave Kivami Bey a questioning look. I started to rise.

Kivami Bey said, 'Sit down. You'll go when I tell you.' And to the officer, 'Well, get on with it.'

'I suppose it's true then, sir?' he said. 'About the Emperor, I mean.'

'What's true?'

'That he's dead.'

'Yes, it's true. Do you think the city would be in this state if Mehmed were still alive?'

The officer bowed his head and seemed almost visibly to grow a little paler.

'Well, I don't suppose you've ridden all the way from Bursa just to ask me that,' said Kivami Bey.

'No, sir,' said the officer, drawing himself up. 'It's about Prince Jem, sir. Last night I was dining with some officers of the garrison at Bursa who told me that the Governor-General of Anatolia, Sinan Pasha, had suddenly ordered the closing of all the roads and passes to the east – without giving any reason to anybody. And shortly afterwards three men riding eastwards were arrested for trying to get through in spite of the orders. Well, sir, they were hauled off and brought before Sinan Pasha himself – but refused to say what they were doing. He had them searched but couldn't find a thing. Then for good measure he had one of the blighters hanged. The others still wouldn't talk. Eventually he had them searched again and found some letters to Prince Jem telling him to come to Istanbul. Sinan Pasha's daughter is married to Prince Bayezid, as you know, so he didn't like that one little bit. And, as far as I could gather, he sent messengers to Bayezid to tell him all about it straight away.'

'Was any of the letters signed?' said Kivami Bey.

'Apparently not.'

'Did you learn anything else about this business?'

'Not much, I'm afraid, Kivami Bey. I had to be careful not to ask too many questions. They would have got suspicious and I might have been detained myself. I pretended

I'd drunk too much and said I was going off to my billet – and instead I set off immediately to come here. And it wasn't that easy to get through, even coming west. Sinan Pasha has patrols posted all over the place and the countryside is swarming with his troops.'

'You did the right thing,' said Kivami Bey. 'I'll talk to you again later. But for the moment leave us.'

The officer got to his feet and withdrew. When the door had closed and we were alone the Old Man said, 'It looks as though your officers have been intercepted.'

'So it seems,' I said, 'but if Sinan Pasha closed the roads and passes *before* the officers were arrested, somebody must have tipped him off that Sultan Mehmed was dead.'

'Probably the Aga of the Janissaries. Sinan Pasha and he are thick as thieves. The Aga must have got wind of the fact that something was wrong, but not that Mehmed was actually dead. If he had known that, he wouldn't have waited till today to bring his men into the city. Anyway, if Sinan Pasha was in any doubt before, those letters to Jem should have made it pretty clear to him what had happened.'

'So,' I said, 'Prince Bayezid will receive the news before Jem, after all.'

'Yes,' said Kivami Bey, and I almost thought I heard a tone of regret in his voice.

'And now that Mahmud Pasha's dead as well,' I said, 'by the time Jem gets to hear of it I don't suppose there will be very much he can do about it, whatever grand plans Sultan Mehmed – God sanctify his soul! – might have had for him.'

'Don't count on it,' said Kivami Bey sharply. 'Jem's got other supporters in high places. I know. It's my business to. But they're hardly going to show their hand now, with the Janissaries on the rampage, out for blood. And as for Mahmud Pasha – yes, the old fox finally overreached himself, and paid the price for it too. But he was no fool when it came to judgements of character, and what you heard him say about Jem is true. When he does get to hear of his father's death, he'll still be prepared to fight Bayezid for the throne, however much the odds seem stacked against him. After all, he came very close to being declared Sultan once before.'

'How can that be?' I said.

'Why,' said Kivami Bey, 'don't you know the story?'

'No,' I said, 'what story?'

'I suppose you would have been too young to remember. It happened when the Conqueror marched against that scorpion Uzun Hasan and his Horde. Bayezid was there as well. Jem couldn't have been more than thirteen, fourteen years old – about your age then, in fact – so he was left behind in Istanbul. For forty days there was no news at all, not a word. Then those Persian dogs started to spread rumours saying that there had been a battle at the border, Mehmed's army had been defeated and Mehmed, Gedik Ahmed, Bayezid – every one of them – had been killed. So the Imperial Council called Jem in and told him to prepare himself to take his rightful place on the throne, but that night a courier arrived from the East with the truth: Mehmed had wiped Uzun Hasan's men off the face of the earth at Otluk Beli and was on his way home in triumph.'

'I see, almost a kind of omen,' I said.

'Indeed,' said Kivami Bey grimly. 'But this time Mehmed really is dead and Jem knows his father didn't want Bayezid to succeed. So he'll fight all right. And he'll go on fighting until either he or Bayezid is destroyed. All we miserable slaves and subjects can hope for is that they don't end up bringing the entire Empire down with them.'

At daybreak, while marauding bands of Janissaries still wandered the empty streets and the intimidated populace remained closeted in their houses, the Imperial Council met in secret session in the Royal Palace. The oldest among them, one Ishak Pasha, a wily old survivor of countless intrigues, backstairs conspiracies and Palace coups, was pressed by the other members of the Council – who, following the events of the previous day, had become curiously self-effacing and devoid of ambition – to take the murdered Mahmud Pasha's place. This Ishak Pasha at last

86

agreed to do, but prudently disclaimed the title of Grand Vizir, which he maintained was only within the Sultan's power to grant, and insisted that, in view of the gravity of the crisis, he be invested with absolute authority to do what he thought best – a demand that the Pashas, usually so jealous of their rank and privileges, conceded with almost indecent alacrity. These matters settled, the venerable old gentleman lost no time in calling for the Aga of the Janissaries to find out what was being done to reimpose discipline on the mutinous troops.

The news that the Aga had to offer was of a kind that Ishak Pasha and the Council would have given almost anything not to hear. For he told them bluntly that as a result of the foolish actions of the Grand Vizir and his attempts to conceal from them the death of their beloved master, the Janissaries had lost all faith in the Pashas – even he himself, their general, despaired of how on earth he was to bring them again to order. And the circumstances were made worse, he said, by the fact that, before the outset of the last campaign, it was understood that the Emperor – God grant him Paradise for his resting-place and abode! – had had it in mind to increase the salaries of his Janissaries in recognition of their selfless devotion to his person and had, it seemed, only been prevented from doing so by the necessity to attend to more urgent affairs on the eve of the Imperial expedition into Anatolia.

The Aga paused for a moment, expecting no doubt that objections would be raised to this assertion of Sultan Mehmed's intentions which, by some mysterious oversight, had never been conveyed to his own Council. But what would have been the point?

So the Aga continued with growing confidence, saying that naturally, now that the Sultan – God sanctify his soul! – was dead, the men would be fearful that the Emperor's intentions might not be honoured, and this uncertainty could only help the unruly and dissatisfied elements in the ranks to stir up more trouble and encourage worse disobedience. In fact, he felt it his painful duty to inform the Council that things were already so bad that it was now difficult to see how the Pashas could reassert their authority without the promise of an immediate rise in the men's pay.

A despondent silence fell on the chamber as the Council pondered the deplorable implications of the Aga's words. After a pregnant pause, Ishak Pasha spoke: the city was still at the mercy of the mutinous troops; it would be at least two weeks before Prince Bayezid reached Istanbul; there was even the possibility – God defend us from it! – that Prince Jem might dispute the succession . . . in short, if the revolt was not nipped in the bud, chaos and anarchy could spread throughout the Empire, leaving it exposed to mortal danger from its enemies.

Therefore, said Ishak Pasha with a sigh, however distasteful it was to succumb to blackmail – his cold grey eyes rested for a moment on the Aga of the Janissaries – circumstances conspired to make this unavoidable. Accordingly, he proposed to announce an increase in the men's pay without delay. A brief and icy exchange occurred between Ishak and the Aga as to what might be sufficient to satisfy the troops. A figure was finally agreed upon: an increase of five aspers a day for officers, two for other ranks. In addition, as a token of the State's gratitude for their continued fidelity, a sum of a thousand silver pieces for each man in the cavalry, three hundred for every foot soldier. Deathly pale, the Minister of Finance nodded his assent.

Thus, by the time the midday call to prayer rang out from the minaret of the great mosque of Aya Sofia, the whole business was concluded. As the afternoon wore on, the news spread, Ishak Pasha's desperate remedy began to take effect and the men drifted back to their barracks to sleep off the prodigious quantities of wine – the use of which they were normally forbidden on pain of the severest punishment – with which they had befuddled their unruly brains. So covetousness overcame riot and drunkenness, and it came to pass that some semblance of order returned to the city (but at what price!).

Sixteen days after the death of the Emperor, reports

began to arrive from the interior of the approach of a party of horsemen several thousand strong riding swiftly in a column towards Istanbul. In no time the whole city was buzzing with speculation, and rumours even began to circulate (put about by the younger brother's partisans) that it was Prince Jem, not Bayezid, who was approaching.

The next day the shores of the Golden Horn were thronged with a great multitude as the bazaars were shut, all business ceased and the entire population turned out. And as for the Bosphorus, it was so thick with vessels of every shape and size that it appeared as though a mighty forest of pines had sprung up overnight on the face of its blue waters.

Meanwhile, the Imperial barge rode at anchor in the harbour at Uskudar, waiting to convey the new Sultan to the Royal Residence. At last, as the crowds were growing restive, following hours of patient vigil, an immense cloud of dust began to rise on the eastern horizon, indicating that the rumoured column was fast drawing near. A profound silence fell, disturbed only by the blustering breeze, the flapping of flags and banners, the sucking and slopping of the water below the quay and the hiss of white foam breaking on the waves.

Then, as the column came all at once, a mass of mounted men and animals, onto the waterfront of Uskudar, the indistinct sound of isolated shouts was heard wafting across the channel. Before long, a low confused murmur of voices began to rumble like a surge gathering in the deep as the word was passed from vessel to vessel, man to man, until the cry became audible to us watchers on the European shore, and the multitude gave tongue with one universal voice, roaring out, '*Bayezid! Bayezid! Bayezid!*'

Soon the Imperial barge could be seen drawing away from Uskudar and, rowed strongly and swiftly along the azure avenue that opened up between the forest of masts, its golden prow came nearer and nearer with every moment until it glided past the Palace Point and into the estuary of the Golden Horn. Amidst an ear-splitting tumult of cheering, the barge came alongside the quay. A gilded gangplank was lowered. The Prince with his retinue of officers and courtiers descended and stepped ashore, and for the first time I set eyes on Bayezid.

He was dressed in the simple woollen robes and black turban of mourning. He was gaunt, dark and strangely lifeless. Although only in his thirty-third year, he struck me as much older, for his skin was sallow, like yellowing vellum, and his beard already quite grey. He seemed sickly and ill at ease, and looked about him nervously as the mob pressed forward on all sides, joyfully calling aloud his name.

Behind Bayezid walked a small group of outlandish fellows, also clothed in black, whom I could almost have taken for Infidel monks or priests had I not known them to be those dervishes of the world-renouncing Halveti sect who had of late enjoyed the patronage of the Prince, and whose insidious influence on his eldest son the Conqueror was reputed so much to detest and deplore. And who, according to Atik, had so successfully played on the religious fervour Bayezid had exhibited from his younger days, and so poisoned his mind with their evil counsels, that the Prince had recently been overheard saying in Amasya that, whatever qualities his father had as a military commander and ruler, these were eclipsed by his sensual and unholy way of living, and if the truth be known his father believed in neither the Prophet, God, Heaven nor Hell, and in his heart had no religion whatsoever.

Hardly had Bayezid put a foot on dry land when, to the dismay and amazement of the crowd, the old man leading the pack of Halvetis (who was walking barely half a step behind the royal person) dared to lay a hand publicly on the Prince's shoulder just as he approached his horse and, when the Prince inclined his head, whispered something in his ear. Bayezid listened for a moment and nodded. Then a silver footstool was placed beside the heir apparent's glossy black steed, the Imperial Herald called out the acclaim 'God give long life to our Lord Bayezid!' and the Prince mounted. Followed by the Master Sword-Bearer in his robes of gold and scarlet, who carried on his shoulder the Imperial scimitar, Bayezid set off through the teeming multitude along the path forged for him by the Royal Halberdiers.

An astonishing spectacle awaited the Prince at the Palace. For in front of its awe-inspiring portals were arrayed twelve thousand Janissaries fully armed and drawn up in battle order. The royal entourage came to a halt. Bayezid showed no fear and surveyed them, frowning. There was an ominous pause. Then, bowing low before the Prince, the Aga of the Janissaries came forward on foot. Bayezid's bodyguard closed in around him. In a clear voice and in a most respectful manner, the Aga sought to present a petition on behalf of his men. With a dignified but troubled air, Bayezid indicated that he deigned to know its contents. The bodyguard jumpily fingered the hilts of their swords as the Aga calmly withdrew a large folded piece of parchment from his robes. The captain of the bodyguard stepped forward and took it from him.

Passed from hand to hand over the heads of the bodyguard, the petition finally reached one of Bayezid's mounted officers, who, at a sign from his master, unfolded it and began to read in a low voice to appraise the Prince of the contents. The men humbly begged forgiveness for killing the Grand Vizir and for the pillage of the city, boldly incorporating in their suit those words from the Holy Koran where the Lord – may He be exalted! – says, *'Paradise is for those who bridle their anger and for those who forgive men'*, and not hesitating to include the sublime words that follow, *'For God loveth the beneficent'*, the Janissaries craved there and then confirmation of the increases in their salaries and the gifts of silver promised them by the Imperial Council.

The officer finished reading. The Prince's features remained impassive, betraying nothing. For a little while he scanned the row upon row of men-at-arms who stood between him and the throne of his illustrious ancestors. Some began to stir uneasily, others to look down at their feet to avoid his penetrating gaze. The Aga stood alone, his head bowed in supplication. Then, with a proud

91

perfunctory wave of his hand and the slightest inclination of his head, the Prince indicated that the Janissaries' petition was granted.

The solid phalanx opened. The men who, before the revolt, had been and – if it please God – may yet prove to be the pride of the Empire abjectly prostrated themselves in the dust and Bayezid rode slowly through their ranks and passed under the Imperial Gate into the Palace.

At the time of the evening prayer on the day after Bayezid's entry into the city, I was crossing the first courtyard of the Convent when Atik beckoned to me to join him in the cloister where he stood lurking behind a pillar. He said:

'Have you heard the news?'

'What news?' I said.

'Aha, so you haven't—'

'Come on, my friend,' I said, grabbing his wrist in my powerful paw and turning it gently.

Affecting agony, he gasped out, 'Prince Jem's mustering an army in Konya to fight Sultan Bayezid.'

'Dear me, you're not very good at resisting torture,' I said, releasing his hand. 'But seriously, my friend, should you be telling me this?'

'Why not?' said Atik. 'The whole world will know it in a day or two. Jem's been sending out messengers far and wide, calling his supporters to arms.'

'So he finally got to hear that his father was dead.'

'Several days ago, apparently,' said Atik, 'from his friends here in the city.'

'Is he intending to march on Istanbul?'

'No. They say he's planning to take Bursa first.'

'H'm,' I said. 'Have you seen the Old Man today? He didn't seem to be in his room earlier.'

'Of course he wasn't,' said Atik scornfully. 'He's been kicking his heels at the Palace since early this morning. I was with him. And before they let him see the Sultan in private, those Halveti dervishes Bayezid brought with him from Amasya had him *searched*. Imagine! He was absolutely furious. He's gone to take some medicine to calm himself down.' Atik made a furtive quaffing gesture and then added: 'I'd keep out of his way today if I were you.'

I noticed out of the corner of my eye that one of the mutes was padding along the cloister towards us. I assumed he had come to fetch Atik. I said hurriedly, 'Tell me, what is our new Emperor like?'

'I don't know, it's difficult to say,' murmured Atik, avoiding my eyes.

The mute was upon us. I patted Atik on the shoulder and, deciding to take his advice and wait until the following morning before trying to see Kivami Bey, turned to go. But the messenger caught me lightly by the sleeve and indicated that it was me, not my companion, he was seeking.

'I'll come over with you,' said Atik. 'I've got some papers to sort through.'

When we reached the antechamber Atik sat down cross-legged behind his desk. He spread his hands and looked heavenward in a gesture of prayer, then with a bow invited me to proceed into the inner sanctum. I knocked, and hearing a menacing growl from the other side of the door, I went in.

Kivami Bey, startlingly attired in the rich robes of a Pasha, was perched on his divan in his customary manner, with one leg tucked under his small fat body and the other hanging loosely over the side. He was pouring himself a generous glass of wine from his silver flask and glowering like a thoroughly bad-tempered sort of jinn who had been turned into human form against his will by some evil-minded magician. The table and divan were piled high with bundles of fresh reports and dispatches. He gave me a tremendous scowl when I greeted him. As I sank to the floor he emptied his glass, spilling half of it down his front in his haste to drink it, and fell to cursing while he refilled it.

'What are you staring at?' he said belligerently.

Then, looking down at the unaccustomed splendour of his attire, he said with a dismissive wave, 'Yes, I am a Pasha. And that's been my rank since the day Mehmed in his wisdom made me Head of Imperial Security, close on twenty years ago. But we're an old family and the title Bey was good enough for my forefathers and it's good enough for me. Does that answer any impertinent enquiries that might be preoccupying your mind?'

'Yes, sir,' I said.

'Good. Well, now that we have a Sultan at last,' he said, 'let's get down to business, shall we? I've got a little job for you. This time in Anatolia.'

'Bursa?' I said.

'Damn you people!' he said, exploding. 'You know the rules. But you all seem determined to break them. Is it surprising that I'm driven to drink when I'm surrounded by such idiots?'

I stared intently at the floor, trying to look contrite but secretly revelling in the fact that I had scored a direct hit. Picking up a hefty pile of documents, he slid them across the table in my direction.

'Take these away and study them. I want to make sure you're properly briefed before you go off to – all right, don't look so pleased with yourself – to Bursa. There are other agents who know the place and the area well. You don't. I know that. But I'm sending you because your face isn't known there, so if the city does fall to Jem there shouldn't be anybody who will be able to expose you. I've got people there permanently of course, but things are very unstable in the interior at the moment and, to be on the safe side, I've decided that you're to act alone and not even to try to make contact with them. We are fortunate that our Sultan does not underestimate his brother's powers of persuasion and abilities to win people over to his cause – which is more than can be said of some of his self-appointed advisers. Some of them seem to think, now that Bayezid has managed to get to Istanbul before his brother, that's the end of the matter. Huh! Anyway, I'll speak to you again tomorrow.'

I got up to leave. I had almost reached the door when Kivami Bey said:

'Tell that pest Atik to come in and see me.'

I said, 'I should say, sir, the breach in the rules was my fault, not his.'

'Nonsense,' said Kivami Bey. 'But don't worry, I'm not going to give him the thrashing he richly deserves. He knew that I'd decided already to send you on this mission. If that hadn't been the case, by God, I'd have had him beaten to within an inch of his life, and he'd have been getting off lightly at that. You can't run an organization like this if half the people in it are like leaky sieves. And I'll tell you another thing: if you lot spent half as much time performing your duties as you do standing around gossiping like a bunch of washerwomen, we might actually get some work done occasionally. Now, get out!'

Ah, Green Bursa . . . who that has not seen it for himself could believe such a place exists anywhere in this imperfect world? For in Bursa, nature and man's art conspire to make of it something near to an earthly paradise. Or so it seemed to me then.

The city stands on the sheltered and wooded slopes of the Great Mountain (which the Greek Infidels of the region still call Olympus), looking down over a vast cultivated plain – covered with fields and groves, orchards and meadows – that lies spread out below like a brightly coloured map, as far as the port of Mudanya and the sandy shores of the Marmara Sea. And to wander in the shaded streets of this town abounding in noble domes, slender minarets and stately edifices is more like walking in the midst of a beautiful garden studded with exquisite pavilions than through a thriving and populous city. For everywhere you look there is water flowing, cold and clear and drinkable; trees and plants, flowers and fruit delight the senses with their verdant loveliness; and all around the air is filled with the glad song of birds and the humming of bees.

Small wonder that Sultan Osman Khan, founder of the Royal House, hearing, as he lay dying, that Bursa had fallen to his *Gazis,* desired that his mortal remains be buried in this terrestrial Eden, and small wonder too that his worthy son Orhan not only honoured his father's wish but also made of the city the first capital of the Ottoman Dynasty. And small wonder that Prince Jem, their proud descendant, should resolve that no place would be a more fitting citadel in which to raise his standard than this, the God-guarded cradle of the world-conquering Ottoman State. For in those early days of his struggle for the throne, the Prince's touch was so sure, his every step so firm that he seemed guided on the shining path to glory by the kind and unerring hand of Fortune herself. But Fortune is a fickle mistress and, as the Prince's vicissitudes were soon all too clearly to show, nothing is certain on this earth save the inconstancy of the lives of all created things.

By the time I managed to reach the city – after landing by night at Mudanya and crossing the plain on horse-back – news had arrived in Bursa that Jem's army was approaching. Governor-General Sinan Pasha's forces were by then retreating precipitately north-eastwards towards the capital in the face of the Prince's advance, seemingly abandoning altogether the defence of the cities of western Anatolia. Yet the people of Bursa seemed tranquil and unconcerned, and life was going on as usual, as though nothing untoward was happening. When I arrived there, the gates stood wide open, as they would have done on any normal day. I lodged at a caravanserai near the Grand Mosque and the Covered Bazaar, giving myself out as a merchant's agent from Edirne in search of samples of the fine materials manufactured in the town from the silk-worms that feed on the abundant mulberry trees of the region.

The next morning, though, the gates were at last shut, as the first men of the Prince's army – a mounted vanguard of skirmishers led by Gedik Nasuh – made their appearance and encamped in a quiet and orderly fashion in a small valley near the famous mosque built by the First Sultan Bayezid, he whom we call 'the Thunderbolt'. Within hours, another force was sighted crossing the plain from the direction of the sea. And before long it had established itself on the other side of the town, in that place where hot sulphurous springs well up in muddy pools among the rocks. This, it was soon learned, was a detachment of two thousand Janissaries, sent out from Istanbul under the command of Ayas Pasha by Sultan Bayezid in the hope of preventing Bursa falling into his brother's hands.

The city now found itself in the position of a much sought-after but jealously guarded young girl, wooed by two persistent and warlike suitors, neither of whom will take no for an answer, as now one, now the other camp dispatched envoys, begging to be admitted within the walls. But the Governor refused to yield to their entreaties or, as time went on, their politely worded threats, seemingly determined to preserve his richly dowered charge in veiled seclusion a while longer. The townspeople in the meantime, who had heard lurid (and regrettably quite true) accounts of the excesses of the Janissaries in Istanbul after Mehmed's death, made vehement representations to the authorities that the Sultan's troops should on no account be admitted. The Governor, however, was understandably loath to risk his neck by defying Istanbul and rendering up the city to Jem's advance party. Thus, there was stalemate. But a resolution was not long in coming.

At dawn Gedik Nasuh led a ferocious surprise attack on the Janissaries, destroying their camp, throwing them into panic and sending them running like so many startled hares across the plain. Hardly a man escaped being killed or captured. Ayas Pasha, their commander, was taken alive. The townspeople seemed to lose their heads completely in the face of this display of military prowess: the populace erupted in jubilation, the gates were thrown open and amidst noisy and universal acclaim Gedik Nasuh and his wild Anatolian horsemen – looking somewhat bemused by the intemperate enthusiasm of their reception – clattered into the city. From that day forth the place seemed to fall into the grip of a kind of communal hysteria, the like of which I have never seen before or since. Suddenly Jem's name was on everybody's lips and the people, Muslim and Infidel, male and female, rich and poor – who knew nothing of the Prince save his glittering reputation – began to talk with almost mystical expectation of his arrival, as though a long-awaited prophet was about to come into their midst. Nor was their saviour long in coming.

97

On the third night, under cover of darkness, Jem slipped into Bursa, and the city that his forebears had besieged for twelve years, before the Greeks were defeated and the golden crescent was planted in its high citadel, fell like a ripe apple into his princely palm.

By morning the main body of his army – regular Ottoman and Karamani cavalry and foot soldiers, fierce mounted Turcomans, Varsaks and Tatars – arrived on the plain and began to pitch their tents and bivouac under the trees in orchards and olive groves. By noon Jem had made a proclamation declaring himself sole legitimate heir to the throne, in accordance with his father's wishes, and Eighth Sultan of the Sublime Ottoman State.

On the Friday it was announced that Jem would attend public worship at midday in the Grand Mosque. The square and courtyard before the Mosque were crowded long before the appointed hour. I made my way through the multitude and with the utmost difficulty managed to squeeze past the main doors of the building. Picking my way through the densely packed rows of worshippers, I found a space on the carpets from which I could get a clear view of the raised platform reserved for the royal suite. But the platform was empty and there was no sign of the Prince.

However, as the imam was moving towards the pulpit to deliver the Friday sermon, Jem and his entourage arrived quietly through a side door, took their place on the royal dais and began silently kneeling and prostrating themselves in performance of the preparatory prayers. When they had completed their devotions the imam, who had by then reached the top of the tall pulpit stairway and sat down, rose to his feet and began his oration. I didn't hear much of what he had to say. I was too busy observing the Prince. And in this I was not alone, for a finer and more striking-looking fellow would be hard to imagine.

He was dressed in a dark pelisse trimmed with sable, dove-grey robes with silver buttons, a red silk sash and a voluminous turban as clean and white as snow. He had the distinguished aquiline nose, the lively blue-grey eyes, the arched eyebrows, the small but shapely mouth and sensual red lips of his father. Yet his features were altogether more refined – was not his mother, Chichek Hatun, a Serbian princess of surpassing beauty? His skin was exceptionally smooth and white, but with a glow in the cheeks bespeaking health and vigour. His beard, which he wore clipped short, was sleek and thick and shone with a deep lustrous sheen when it caught the light. His hands looked strong, with long well-formed fingers. He was of a good robust stature, with broad shoulders, and when he moved, even beneath his loose attire it was evident how lithe and powerful were his limbs. Indeed, seeing him in the flesh, at close quarters, it was no surprise that he had gained a reputation as a wrestler and barefisted fighter without equal in the land, and not difficult to believe the stories that he had by now added so many iron rings to his mace that few could even lift it, let alone wield it in martial exercises. Yet for all his obvious strength and manly attributes, his movements were graceful, his manner pleasant, and his demeanour modest, restrained and in no way overbearing.

The sermon came to an end. In a loud voice the imam called on the people to make their supplications to God, and amid cries of 'Amen! Amen!' sat down. Then the congregation silently offered up their private petitions to the True Helper, and the imam also prayed in silence. After some time, rising to his feet, he spoke again:

> 'Praise be to God, abundant praise, as He hath commanded. I testify that there is no deity but God alone. He hath no companion. I affirm His supremacy, condemning him who denieth and disbelieveth; and I testify that our lord and prophet Muhammad is His servant and His apostle, the lord of mankind, the intercessor . . . God bless him and his family as long as the eye seeth and the ear heareth . . .'

A silence now fell upon the congregation, so heavy that it seemed to press down upon me like a tangible weight. For, as everybody present knew, it is the prerogative of the

Sultan alone, who owes allegiance to no master but God Himself, to have his name invoked in the Friday prayers that follow directly on the sermon. And now the single consuming question gripped the mind of every living soul in that great gathering: whether Jem had issued instructions to the imam to replace the name of Sultan Bayezid with his own, thus publicly arrogating to himself this supreme privilege before the Most High, the Lord of Heaven and Earth, the Eternal Issuer of Decrees, while yet the throne was in dispute and his bid for power in its infancy.

The imam intoned the sacred text evenly and unhurriedly. And although the prayers were in Arabic and few of the congregation could understand them exactly, the sense of universal expectation was rising to a fever-pitch as the anticipated passage drew nearer, moment by moment. Anxious faces gazed up at the pulpit. Here and there the silent lips of learned greybeards moved in unconscious unison with the imam's words.

All at once there was a whirr of wings above our heads as a small bird, which must somehow have flown into the mosque earlier and was now trapped, took to the air from the ledge where it had remained concealed. Some of the Faithful peered upwards. The bird circled two or three times under the dome, swooped and dipped. Involuntarily looking up for a moment, then quickly looking down again at his book, the imam raised his voice slightly and went on. Dropping lower and lower in a series of spirals the bird made for the burst of sunlight streaming through the open main doors, fluttered over our heads and flew out into the bright airy freedom of the day. I glanced at Jem. He sat calmly looking up at the imam, his body immobile, his face revealing nothing to my searching eyes.

The imam stopped for a split second to draw breath. The pause opened up like a gaping chasm, a dizzying abyss. I closed my eyes. The voice rang out again:

'O God, pardon the believing men and the believing women, the Muslim men and the Muslim women,

100

*those who are living and the dead; for Thou art a
Hearer near, an Answerer of Prayers, O Lord of the
beings of the whole world. O God, aid Islam and
strengthen its pillars and make infidelity to tremble
and destroy its might, by the preservation of Thy
servant, and the son of Thy servant, he who is sub-
missive to Thy might and majesty and glory, he
whom God hath aided, our master the Sultan, son of
the Sultan, the Sultan Jem Khan: may God assist him
and prolong his reign. O God, assist him and assist
his armies, O Thou Lord of the Religion and of the
world present, and the world to come . . .'*

I watched Jem's face intently as his name was spoken
and even then he remained completely tranquil, his expression utterly unchanged. Not even a flicker disturbed the
steady gaze of those bright blue-grey eyes.

But the people could contain themselves no longer. A
low growl of approval ran through the ranks of the
worshippers. The imam stopped reading, looked up and
frowned. Even then the murmur of approbation continued
for some seconds. When at last it died away the imam read
the final words: *'Praise be to God, the Lord of the beings of
the whole world!'*

The special Friday prayers now at an end, the imam
descended from the pulpit so that the customary noonday
devotions could commence – though some took the
opportunity to slip outside to convey the news of what had
taken place to those waiting in the courtyard and the
square. At the close, the congregation remained standing
in respectful silence as Jem and his entourage retired by the
side door through which they had come. Thunderous
cheers greeted the Prince as he stepped outside and the
people lifted up their voices in tumultuous acclaim.

I left the mosque and, mingling easily with the jostling
crowd of country folk returning to their homes outside the
city walls, passed through Bursa's gates without incident
as I set out once more for Istanbul.

*　　*　　*

101

I had never seen the Convent such a hive of activity as it was that day I returned from Bursa. And as a result it was two or three hours before I had the chance to make my report – because the Convent had its own way of doing just about everything, and making a report there was not simply a matter of giving a written or verbal account of what you'd done, things you'd seen and heard, names and descriptions of people you'd encountered, and so on. That kind of thing might have been all right for the amateurs who ran military and naval intelligence operations – but for Ottoman Imperial Security? Perish the thought!

The Old Man must have spent years perfecting that fiendish system of his (standard by the time I was recruited), whereby each agent returning to base from 'enemy territory' was given a full-blown interrogation by an Investigator, with a couple of scribes present to take down word for word every last detail of what was said.

And in this murky world where, as I gradually came to appreciate, it was so often necessary to hide the truth behind a deceptive veil of calculated lies, it should, I suppose, have been obvious that this method had an additional unconfessed purpose. I didn't realize this at first, but when I did, it frightened me half to death.

For although the interrogations were ostensibly carried out merely to make certain that every last drop of potentially useful information was squeezed out of each mission, these rigorous, sometimes seemingly interminable sessions of cross-examination were also a subtle means of investigating agents whose trustworthiness had come into doubt, without letting them know they were even suspected; of distinguishing the 'clean' from the 'unclean', and rooting out those who had 'fallen by the wayside', so that they could be assigned to new roles or eliminated.

For it is a lamentable fact that there will always be some individuals in this corrupt world who can be bribed, seduced or coerced into working for the deadliest enemies of their Nation and Religion, and others still who will fall prey to the temptation to try to play a double game for their own ends. And whereas such people once unmasked can prove invaluable in misleading the enemy (it is surprisingly difficult to fake the real thing), as long as they go undetected they represent a mortal danger not just to their fellow agents but also to the entire fabric of the State.

Sometimes the Old Man attended these formal interrogations, sometimes not. And since every room used for the sessions was furnished with a double wooden lattice set in the wall shared with a small adjoining room from which the proceedings could be invisibly observed and overheard, you could never really be sure if he was there or not. On this occasion, though, I'm pretty sure he was – as I had hardly finished giving my deposition before the call came to attend Kivami Bey in another interrogation room not then in use by the Investigators.

He was sitting on a divan, my report lying beside him, the ink from the scribe's agile pen barely dry on the last page. In his hand was one of the coins I had brought back from Bursa with me: a silver asper bearing on one face Jem's monogram, in which the Conqueror's name and title were artfully entwined with his own, and the whole device adorned in the traditional manner with the noble epithets of the Royal House of Osman. Kivami Bey peered at it intently, tilting it from left to right, and read aloud:

' "*Sultan Jem Khan, Son of Mehmed the Conqueror, Ever Victorious.*" H'm!' He turned it over. 'What's this? "*Imad-ed-din.* Pillar of the Faith." And what about this, then? "*Kolona tis Pisteos.*" The same words in Greek, by God! Following in his father's footsteps even in wooing the Greeks. Cunning fellow . . . Our dear Christian subjects will take him for a second Messiah after this. A good move – some of them are immensely rich and would pay a great deal to have another Sultan as tolerant of their religion as Mehmed was.'

'Of that there can be no doubt,' I said. 'And yet our people seem to hold the Prince in high regard for his piety and observance of the obligations of the True Faith.'

'Well, by all accounts,' said Kivami Bey, giving me a searching glance, 'he's a better Muslim than his father. But a good deal more tolerant of the Christians and Jews than his brother.'

He picked the tiny coin out of his fat palm with his finger and thumb and said: 'Are there many of these about in Bursa?'

'Quite a number, yes . . .'

'Ha!' said Kivami Bey. 'Sultan Bayezid would sooner be seen dead than start plastering Infidel letters all over the Imperial coinage, that's for sure. And he'll certainly have something to say about it when he gets to hear that not only is our friend issuing coins from his own Treasury but also having prayers read in the mosque in his own name, as though his elder brother didn't exist.'

He picked up the report and affected to look through it, then went on:

'You say that Jem's people are putting it about that he has no desire for war and there won't be one if Bayezid can be persuaded to see reason and negotiate a peaceful settlement to their rival claims.'

'That's right,' I said. 'And they were also saying that Jem had already sent his great-aunt Seljuk Hatun and some mullahs to Bayezid to discuss the matter. But I can't confirm that definitely one way or the other. Maybe it was just a way of trying to allay the people's fears of what might happen to them if there is a war.'

'There'll be a war all right,' growled Kivami Bey. 'But the story about the delegation is quite true. Seljuk Hatun even tried to appeal to Sultan Bayezid's finer feelings of brotherly love! That didn't get her very far.'

'What did the Emperor say?'

'For a long time, nothing. But eventually he lost patience and said to her, "*La arhama baina'l muluk.*" '

' "There are no ties of kinship between princes," ' I said. Kivami Bey looked momentarily stunned that I really did know some Arabic after all. He seemed about to say something, but thought better of it and scowled at me instead.

'And then?' I said.

'He tried to send her and her mullahs away. But she refused to budge until Bayezid had heard out the proposals she'd brought from Jem. In the end he gave in and agreed to

104

listen. Not that he had much choice. He could hardly have an elderly royal relative manhandled out of his presence in front of the entire Imperial Council.'

'And what did she propose?' I said. 'If it is permitted to ask.'

Kivami Bey shrugged and said: 'It's no great secret and anyway you're involved in this case now, so there's no reason why you shouldn't be told. Jem proposed that he and Bayezid split the Empire between them – with Jem keeping the Asian provinces and Bayezid the Imperial possessions in Europe . . . And an agreement that which-ever of them outlives the other should inherit the lot.'

'My God!' I said. 'And what did Bayezid have to say to that?'

'He said that the Empire is a bride whose favours cannot be shared. Rather elegant, don't you think? Not original, of course. But to the point, by Heaven! And admirably restrained, given the utter insanity of the suggestion.'

'But tell me, sir,' I said, 'do you believe that the Prince made the suggestion seriously, or is he perhaps just trying to play for time. Surely he can't really have believed that Bayezid would agree to it?'

'I rather think Jem believed he might,' said Kivami Bey, shaking his head. 'As far as Jem's concerned, his father had promised him the throne, so now he feels cheated of it. Of course, the promise was an empty one as long as Bayezid was still alive – because not even Mehmed was going to be able to rule from beyond the grave! But empty or not, to Jem it's all the same. He's in a state of mind now that will drive him to any lengths to carve out some kind of king-dom for himself, even if it means splitting his father's Empire down the middle. At first, that is.'

'At first?' I said.

'Certainly. If he could get half now it would be a matter of time before he got everything. Bayezid's twelve years older than he is, and Jem knows his brother's health has not been particularly good of late. Whereas Jem – well, you've seen for yourself. And he must have calculated that he might not have to wait even that long. As I've said

105

before, he has got a lot of supporters who think him a more worthy heir to Mehmed than Bayezid, and their numbers have been growing ever since he's shown that he's prepared to fight his brother for the succession. It seems even the loyalty of the Janissaries – confound them! – can't be relied upon since Mehmed died.'

'Aah,' I said wearily. 'This whole business will bring joy to nobody but our enemies . . . Perhaps it is not fitting for a mere slave like myself to speak of such things, but would it not be possible, Kivami Bey, for Sultan Bayezid to make some kind of concession to his brother?'

'Not only would it be possible,' said Kivami Bey, 'he already has made such an offer. He sent word back to Jem with their aunt that if Jem agrees to retire to Jerusalem he'll overlook the present foolish insurrection and make over to him the entire revenues of the province of Karaman – though not, of course, the governorship – for his own personal use so that he may live in the Holy City in honourable and peaceful exile. It's a generous offer and not a wholly inappropriate one: after all, Jem's a scholar, a poet of distinction and a man of taste. He would have his wife and children with him, and there can be no doubt that most, if not all, of his officers and companions from the court at Konya would happily join their beloved Prince in exile. So there would be no reason why he shouldn't find ways of occupying his time agreeably and profitably.'

'And what', I said, 'has Jem himself had to say about all this?'

'There has been no reply as yet. But you've seen the Prince in action – what do *you* think will be his response?' said Kivami Bey.

'He won't accept,' I said.

'Precisely.'

Kivami Bey stretched out his arm towards me and signed to me to help him up. Once on his feet, he shook off my supporting hand impatiently and made for the door, hobbling along with the aid of his silver-handled black canes. He turned slightly and with a jerk of his head indicated that I was to follow him outside. I went out after him into the morning sunshine. He said nothing more until we had passed under the arch into the first courtyard and rounded the church. He lowered himself painfully onto the stone bench beside the cypresses. With a wave of his fat blotchy hand, he showed me that I was to sit down beside him.

For a while he sat wheezing, his great stomach heaving, as he regained his breath. Then, with a terrible scowl, he reached inside his robe and pulled out a crumpled and folded square of paper bearing Sultan Bayezid's monogram and seal. He handed it to me.

I took it, saying, 'What is it, sir?'

'Bayezid has already crossed to Uskudar and is mustering the army that was supposed to destroy *him* to march on Jem. But there have been some desertions to the Prince, and His Highness now says he needs every available man. God knows, I did everything I could to keep him from requisitioning my men for cannon fodder – but when it came to able-bodied officers like you, it was hopeless. Some of your colleagues have already gone.'

I opened the paper. My orders were to report to the Arsenal on the Golden Horn as soon as I returned to the city, to take command of a company of eight hundred marines (at present in the charge of a lieutenant) waiting to cross to the Asian side, and join the main body of the Army, encamped at the Emperor's Meadow.

'And another thing,' said Kivami Bey, gloomily prodding a clump of dried-up grass in the crack between two paving stones. 'Gedik Ahmed Pasha's been recalled from Otranto to act as Commander-in-Chief of the Sultan's forces. He's on his way here now.'

'I thought . . . ,' I began.

'I know, and so obviously do you, that there's no love lost between Bayezid and Gedik Ahmed,' said Kivami Bey. 'And I've no doubt the Admiral's told you at some time or another how it all came about – discretion in such matters was never his strong point. Bayezid didn't want him recalled and I've no doubt Gedik Ahmed didn't want to come – especially as, with the fresh troops he was about to ship over from Albania, he was damn near certain of taking Rome this summer. But with Jem carrying all before him in Anatolia, in the end the Imperial Council went down on its knees and begged the Sultan to call Gedik Ahmed back. And they were quite right to do so. Because, to be honest, Bayezid still might not win *with* Gedik Ahmed, but the way things look at the moment he certainly can't win without him.'

I do not believe that since the times of the Great Alexander or the far-off days of the Siege of Troy there was ever a soldier more audacious, headstrong and fearless than Gedik Ahmed Pasha. He was, like my father, a slave of Infidel birth, taken from his parents in the annual levy of Christian children from the European provinces – in his case, from a poor mountain village in Serbia, or so he used to say. He began his career serving as an ordinary infantryman in the lowest ranks of the Janissaries, but in a short time his boldness, intelligence and perseverance raised him above his peers, until he became, when yet a young man, a commander in the Imperial Army. And soon after that, he found himself elevated to the rank of Vizir and he took his place on the Imperial Council. But his promotion owed not a jot to servility or a willingness to flatter his superiors' vanity by telling them what they wanted to hear. For just as he was contemptuous of every danger in battle, likewise at court he stood in awe of no one – not even Sultan Mehmed himself. Indeed, this refusal to defer to any man, however great and powerful, came close to bringing about Gedik Ahmed's downfall on numerous occasions. But time and again he managed to outwit his enemies and emerge unscathed from the shameful plots laid against him by lesser men whose jealousy and anger had been aroused by his rapid rise to power and the forthrightness of his words and actions. And even Mehmed seemed prepared to go on indulging him, no matter how outrageously irreverent and outspoken he became.

Finally, though, he went too far, openly coming into conflict with the Sultan on how best to curb a rebellion in

Albania. Exasperated by his favourite Vizir's calm and obstinate refusal to adjust his opinions to the royal view, Mehmed had him thrown into a dark dungeon in the fortress at Rumeli Hisar. There he languished for a year, only to be abruptly forgiven, released and appointed Grand Admiral of the Imperial Navy (an honour he accepted with the cheerful and unrepentant self-assurance of one at last receiving just recompense for his merits, nothing more or less). And that was the manner of his whole life – and in the end, alas, of his death.

For if Gedik Ahmed Pasha's relations with Sultan Mehmed were habitually stormy, they were none the less sustained even through their most tempestuous passages by the tacit respect and admiration with which these two formidable men regarded one another. Sadly, this could not be said of the Grand Admiral's relations with Bayezid. For Gedik Ahmed and the Prince had such a falling-out – when the young Bayezid was still Governor of Amasya – that few of those who knew of it believed that they could ever be reconciled again.

It happened during that dark era when Uzun Hasan was threatening the eastern borders of the Empire. Learning of the White Horde's intention to overwhelm the Asian provinces of the Empire by a surprise attack, Mehmed had hurriedly gathered his forces at Uskudar, and he and Gedik Ahmed had led them as far as Amasya before the winter snows closed in, blocking the passes. There the army encamped on the Plain of Geese.

The winter that year was exceptionally cold and took an appallingly heavy toll of the Sultan's troops. To make things worse, spring the following year was late in coming and as a result the hoped-for reinforcements were yet further delayed. But as the weather improved, reports began to arrive from the border confirming the alarming news that Uzun Hasan and his hordes were already on the march westwards. Without waiting for the reinforcements, Sultan Mehmed struck camp immediately and set off – now in conditions of burning heat that beat down relentlessly on mountain and plain day after day – in a series of forced marches eastwards. With him, Mehmed also took Bayezid, who was then twenty-five or -six years old, so that the Prince could gain experience of war and join in the defence of the menaced realm.

The two armies confronted each other on the banks of the Euphrates. Our forces were decimated by thirst, starvation and exhaustion, whereas Uzun Hasan's were well fed, watered, fresh from an advance made in easy stages and already in command of the heights of Otluk Beli on the river's furthest bank. Our position looked well-nigh hopeless even to the most optimistic eye. But withdrawal was by now out of the question and there was nothing for it but to stand and fight, and trust to the favour of God.

On the eve of the battle Uzun Hasan sent a messenger to Sultan Mehmed. The man brought with him a great sack of millet and, without a word, had it set down before the Emperor's tent.

'What's this?' said the Sultan.

'My master', said the messenger, 'sends you greetings and says that Your Majesty would need as many men as there are grains here to prevent him from overthrowing you and your army.'

At first the Sultan made no reply, but narrowed his eyes and looked around. Then a camel nearby, loaded with provisions, seemed to catch his eye. He strode over to it and began to pull down from its back its load of wicker baskets filled with live chickens and, upsetting them one after the other, set free several dozen of the birds. Then he drew his sword and slashed it across the bag, releasing a golden torrent of millet onto the ground.

The hungry creatures needed no prompting. They rushed forward in a body like things possessed and, with flying feathers, blazing eyes and greedy squawks of delight, they fell upon the grain. Meanwhile, Mehmed stood back, hands on hips, observing the spectacle with an air of majestic disdain. In no time every last morsel had been gobbled up and the earth lay as stark and bare as it had been a few moments before.

As the dust settled, the Emperor turned back to the messenger and said, 'Go tell your master that, as quickly as these birds have devoured this sack of grain, my Janissaries will deal with those men of his, who may be good at herding sheep and goats but will prove of no use to him in the face of Ottoman troops.'

The messenger stroked his chin, gave a sour smile and returned from whence he had come – for in truth, despite all Mehmed's brave words, there was not a man who did not secretly believe in his heart that the Ottomans were doomed to annihilation on the morrow, unless some miracle occurred.

At first light our forces crossed the Euphrates and the lines of battle were drawn up. Davud Pasha, the Asian troops and the irregulars were on the left; the Emperor and Gedik Ahmed, the bulk of the Janissaries, the cavalry and the Sultan's bodyguard at the centre; and on the right, Prince Bayezid, the troops from the European provinces and several thousand Janissaries more.

Just before the fighting commenced, Gedik Ahmed happened to ride along the section under Bayezid's command and was overcome with horror at the uneven and shoddy nature of their deployment. Immediately, he set about hastily reorganizing the lines, calling some men forward, sending others to the rear, and arranging them with his usual skill and cunning to take best advantage of the terrain. As this was going on, Bayezid himself rode up and asked what the devil was going on.

Gedik Ahmed turned to him and said, 'I am merely doing those things that you should have already done yourself, Your Highness.'

'Why,' said Bayezid, cut to the quick at being thus humiliated before his men, 'what impudence is this?'

'Impudence it may be,' said Gedik Ahmed, 'but you need have no fear that I will interfere in the future. For I can assure you that if you and I should survive this day I will never do the same for you again.'

Gedik Ahmed Pasha turned to go, but then pulling his horse round for a moment, he said, 'And let me tell you this, Your Highness: should you ever come to the throne, I swear by my father's soul that I will not gird my scimitar in *your* service.'

With that, he rode away to continue the reordering of the right wing, the task barely being completed before the enemy, with a great and terrible cry, swarmed down from the heights in their first attack.

For eight hours the battle raged. Against all expectation, not only did the entire line hold like a solid wall against the onslaught but the attacks were beaten off with such violence that over and over again the enemy were sent reeling back in confusion, leaving their dead and dying strewn on the ground. At last news spread that Uzun Hasan's son had been slain on the left wing. The severed head was swiftly conveyed to Mehmed by one of his captains and thrown into the dust at his feet. The Emperor ordered it to be spiked on a lance and held aloft. Seeing this, the enemy suddenly seemed to lose heart, and God – may He be exalted! – turned the tide in favour of the Ottomans. Uzun Hasan himself soon left the battlefield, his army's retreat dissolved into chaos and the Janissaries stormed forward, butchering Hasan's men in their thousands as they tried in vain to escape.

But despite the happy outcome of this most perilous of ventures, after the battle Bayezid and Gedik Ahmed Pasha could neither of them humble their pride and extend the olive branch of peace. And from that day forth, neither the Prince nor the warrior addressed a single word to the other.

Now, nearly a decade later, those of us who knew of the quarrel and of Gedik Ahmed's vow waited in trepidation at the Emperor's Meadow, one moment believing that only the presence of the famous general could rally the Imperial troops, the next that his arrival would only reopen old wounds and that another public disagreement would prove a fatal blow to the Army's already disastrous state of morale.

At length, with the Army about to march on Jem – who was now reported to be ready to quit Bursa and move against Yenishehir, on his way to Istanbul – and still no

112

sign of Gedik Ahmed Pasha, I concluded that he was deliberately hanging back and thereby offering his implicit support to Jem's cause. In this I did him a grave injustice. I should have known that, headstrong and obstinate though he was, if called upon, Gedik Ahmed would do his duty to the State. What is more, he had always been a man absolute to his word, and he had promised the Sultan and the Imperial Council that he would come. And come he did. Though even now, in spite of everything that has happened since, I cannot – God forgive me! – prevent myself from wishing that he had stayed away.

He arrived with his entourage at dusk the very day before the Imperial Army's departure for Yenishehir. I happened to be nearby when, by chance, the Emperor's suite (which was returning from a tour of inspection of the troops) ran into Gedik Ahmed Pasha and his Staff just as they were entering the camp, after riding the last stage of the long journey from Otranto.

As soon as Gedik Ahmed saw that it was Bayezid himself leading the party he had come face to face with, he called on his men to halt, smartly reined in his beast and hastily dismounted. Meanwhile, all around, men rose to their feet, abandoned their camp-fires, leaving their evening repasts half-eaten, or dropped whatever else they were doing and hurried over to get a closer look at this grand personage who had suddenly and unexpectedly appeared at the Meadow in the twilight. The Sultan, realizing who the new arrivals were, had also given the signal to halt and was watching intently as Gedik Ahmed approached on foot, striding across the grass towards him with a forceful and determined air. Silently the crowd of onlookers pressed forward as their numbers were swelled moment by moment by new arrivals.

Soon Gedik Ahmed Pasha reached the Emperor's horse and with grave dignity he bent and kissed the royal stirrup. Reverently taking in his hand the hem of Bayezid's cloak, he brought it to his lips and kissed this too. Then he stepped back and stood with his head humbly bowed before his new master, awaiting His Majesty's command.

The Sultan, who had looked for a moment anxious, almost reproachful, seemed visibly to soften at this display of public homage from the renowned soldier, and an expression of mildness began to creep into his melancholy black eyes. He now greeted the Grand Admiral quietly and affably and bade him repair to the quarters already set aside for him that he might wash, change his clothes and take a little rest before attending on his Sultan formally at the royal tent.

At this Gedik Ahmed Pasha bowed again very deeply and respectfully and began to withdraw, walking backwards at a measured pace towards his horse, lest by turning round he should suggest any disrespect to the Sultan's person. And the Sultan watched him as he went, his face displaying for all to see his relief and satisfaction.

But then the Emperor's features slowly began to harden, the look of a haunted man began to darken his eyes again and a bitter smile came to his lips. By this time Gedik Ahmed was about to reach his own horse once more. I was utterly baffled by this sudden change in the Emperor's countenance, for I could see no reason for it. I looked over yet again at the Grand Admiral. He was standing now by his beast, taking hold of a stirrup so as to climb once more into the saddle. As he swept back his heavy black cloak to free his foot to mount, I saw that, unaccountably, there was no sword at his side. Then my heart sank as I raised my eyes and saw that this was no unintended omission. In fulfilment of his fateful vow at Otluk Beli, Gedik Ahmed Pasha's scimitar was hanging from the silver pommel of his saddle, where he had left it whilst he bent his proud knee in submission to Bayezid.

But the Sultan himself spoke not another word and by the time I glanced back at him he had turned to depart for his tent. And, as I later gathered from one who was present at that evening's Council of War, when Gedik Ahmed Pasha attended on Bayezid in the royal quarters, the Sultan seemed determined not to rise to this latest challenge, and so successfully did he dissemble his anger that he managed

114

to appear supremely indifferent to the Grand Admiral's effrontery. When I learned this I was amazed and – though, Heaven forfend, I wished no harm to Gedik Ahmed – I took it for a display of weakness on the Sultan's part that he did not seem to dare upbraid his slave for this ostentatious act of wilfulness. But then I utterly underestimated the Sultan. So, I believe, did nearly everyone else – none more so than the Grand Admiral himself. For, in truth, Bayezid had not the least intention of letting the matter pass and, in due course, he was to exact a terrible price for Gedik Ahmed's obduracy.

But for the moment the Sultan was content to bide his time until more pressing and weighty affairs had been taken care of, before avenging himself on a mere slave. The next morning the Imperial host struck camp and began the march eastwards in the hope of blocking Prince Jem's threatened advance on the capital.

At the end of the week, after encountering only Gedik Nasuh and his mounted irregulars – Sinan Pasha's Asian cavalry dealt with these along the way in some small and insignificant engagements – we ascended the heights above Yenishehir to find that the Prince's army had arrived there before us and, having crossed the river that meanders through the broad rolling plain to the south of the city itself, had already encamped outside the walls of the town. That night we remained on the wild and desolate slopes from which, as darkness fell, we could observe the twinkling camp-fires of the enemy, scattered like bright jewels across the velvety blackness of the grasslands below. And, alas, many was the man who lay down that night on mountain and plain to sleep the last fitful sleep he would ever know on this earth!

Both armies were stirring well before daybreak. As the first yellow glow appeared in the eastern sky, the muezzins in both camps called upon us wretched sinners to prostrate ourselves in the worship of the Creator of Heaven and Earth, the All-seeing, the All-wise. Our solemn devotions completed, the signal was sounded to advance and we began to descend in columns onto the lightening plain.

A daunting spectacle awaited us there. The Prince's army looked superb. It was drawn up in an immense encircling crescent – the regular Ottoman and Karamani troops in the centre, the fierce mounted Varsaks, Turcomans and Tatars on the wings – rank upon rank of foot-soldiers and horsemen standing silent and absolutely motionless in strict battle order before us, their green and gold banners stirring in the dawn breeze. They waited, calm and unwavering, as we streamed down the hillsides onto the flat ground and took up our preordained positions, regiment after regiment, detachment after detachment, company after company, squadron after squadron, according to Gedik Ahmed Pasha's battle plan.

I led my marines onto a low ridge at the centre, behind our front line, where I had been instructed to remain in reserve in case the central phalanx of the Sultan's Janissaries should by any chance be breached. From there, on a slight rise almost opposite, I caught sight of the Prince surrounded by his staff and mounted on a magnificent grey charger, his brilliant white turban catching the first rays of the sun as it rose above the mountains to the east, flooding the plain with golden light.

When both armies were in position, a great hush fell. The wind whispered through the grass. Harness, bits and saddles creaked and jingled, hoofs stamped and pawed at the ground, here and there animals whinnied and snorted, but not a single human voice was heard.

All at once, at the wave of a banner from the hillock where the Sultan and Gedik Ahmed Pasha sat on horseback surveying the awe-inspiring scene, our kettle-drums began to beat, cymbals to clash and trumpets to blow forth their warlike music. Then the entire army filled its lungs and cried out with one voice *'God is most Great! Bayezid! Bayezid!'*

The drums, pipes and brass of the enemy wasted no time in taking up the challenge, and thundered out their defiant reply as the Prince's host raised its voice with the impassioned shout: *'God is our support! Jem Khan! Jem Khan!'*

116

With that, both sides surged forward simultaneously and rushed at one another, causing the ground to shake beneath their feet; and, beating their lances and swords against their shields, they set up a fearful, ear-splitting din. With a frightful and mighty crash the armies came violently together. In an instant the whole length of the line was reduced to a murderous mêlée.

Never in all my experience of war had I seen such carnage as I saw in those first few minutes. Everywhere there were men charging and being charged, striking and being struck, wounding and being wounded, maiming and being maimed, slaying and being slain. The air was thick with an unspeakable noise – of shouting, blaspheming, threatening, swearing, groaning, cursing. Battle order was almost immediately abandoned as men broke ranks and fought at will in a struggling mass, hand to hand – stabbing, hacking, slashing and raining frenzied blows on each other's head, furiously vying with one another to commit more and more horrible acts of cruelty and mutilation. And as men fell, butchered by the hundred, comrades and adversaries, the dying and the dead were all brutally trampled underfoot by those hurling themselves, wave upon wave, into the fray from behind, hell-bent on dealing out destruction.

Absolute chaos reigned. On all sides men fought more like savage beasts than human beings, yielding themselves wholly up to blind wrath and mercilessly cutting one another to pieces. For now they were completely drunk on battle and seemed to set their own lives at naught, not caring if they were slaughtered if only they could slaughter others before they were themselves struck down. Before long it became all but impossible to distinguish friend from foe as, in the relentless mayhem, men's weapons, clothes, limbs and faces were drenched in one another's blood.

So it went on for the best part of an hour, the line swaying and buckling as now one side, now the other appeared to be about to gain the upper hand, but with neither able to win a decisive advantage. But, in time, Jem's front line was seen to be gradually creeping forward, while the

Janissaries were driven back by the irresistible pressure of the Prince's seasoned Ottoman and Karamani regulars. At one point some of Jem's cavalry broke through and appeared without warning to the right of our redoubt, but my brave archers ran forward, discharging arrows as they went, and shot down half a dozen men and horses in a hail of darts, forcing them to retreat.

Some little time later, a messenger arrived with an order instructing me to lead my men along the right wing, behind the battle area, in the direction of the river. We set off and, as we got clear of the dust clouds raised at the centre where the fighting was at its bloodiest and most intense, I saw that a detachment of Janissaries was already ahead of us, making for a bend in the river, apparently intending to ford it and thereby get behind the enemy's lines. Coming closer, I saw that they were led by the Sultan himself. But, to my surprise, the Janissaries seemed to be hanging back, as though uncertain whether to go on. It was not long, however, before I saw the reason for their delay: a mass of several thousand men and horses from Jem's rearguard – fresh troops as yet uncommitted to the field – were advancing at a brisk pace along the riverbank towards them. But as we hurried over to reinforce the vastly outnumbered Janissaries, an astonishing thing occurred.

We were scarcely a bowshot from Bayezid and his men when the troops from Jem's rearguard began to slow down. The officer leading them rode forward and gave a broad wave of his arm above his head. To this the Sultan replied in like fashion and, before I knew it, Jem's men were lowering their banners one by one. At first I could not for the life of me grasp what was going on, but then I realized with incredulity that they seemed to be signalling their willingness to surrender without a fight.

What had been, a moment before, a more or less well-disciplined section of Jem's army now broke down into disorder with startling rapidity and the troops milled about in confusion. Some hung back, shouting angrily at their comrades not to surrender in this shameful way, but

118

most seemed utterly bewildered. Soon more and more of them, following the example and exhortations of their officers, began to throw down their arms and come forward, holding their weaponless hands before them to show that they were empty. In the mean time, one of the Sultan's bodyguard rode over to us with the order to assist in taking the surrender of these men, disarm them and drive them as quickly as possible onto the high ground behind our lines lest they should think of changing their minds. But by the time they reached us, hardly a man among them was carrying a sword or lance or shield, and most of them were running so fast we were forced to open our ranks to let them through as they blundered blindly towards the safety of the hills behind.

From that moment the breeze of victory began to unfurl the Sultan's standard. And, although I did not know it then, it was entirely to his foresight and cunning that the Imperial Army owed this alteration in its declining fortunes on that fateful day. For, despairing of success by ordinary means, Bayezid had managed by secret negotiation to suborn one Yakub Bey – a commander only recently appointed by the Prince – with the promise of one hundred thousand silver aspers and a governorship in Anatolia, if he would come over during the battle and bring with him the troops entrusted to him by Jem.

Yet, at first, this treacherous deed seemed to have come too late to affect the outcome of the desperate conflict. By the time it took place the Janissaries at the centre were falling back, unable to withstand a moment longer the horrific punishment being meted out to them by the crack Ottoman troops now pressing forward under the personal command of the Prince himself, whose fearless presence seemed to inspire them to new, previously undreamed-of heights of boldness and fanaticism.

But that alone shall be successful which accords with God's decree . . .

Sinan Pasha's Asian cavalry broke through on the left wing. The Prince's Varsaks and Turcomans in that section feigned flight in their customary manner, with the intention of drawing off their attackers, abruptly wheeling round and, with the help of the rearguard, encircling them. But when they retired to regroup they found the reserves in turmoil after the defection of Yakub Bey and his men. The more cowardly among them were already taking to their heels in the direction of the river, and seeing now the tribal irregulars apparently flying for their lives before Sinan Pasha's cavalry, panic took sudden hold of the rest. Within the twinkling of an eye, almost the entire rearguard was dashing, terrified, towards the river in pursuit of those who had already taken themselves off in the wild hope of making it back to Bursa.

News of this latest disaster soon reached the front line and before long, deprived of the protection of the rearguard, Jem's men found themselves being harried from behind by Sinan Pasha's horsemen. Now forced to turn round and fight to defend their backs, the line began to collapse. Jem's Staff begged him to flee while there was still time. He refused even to listen to them and rode off along the line, waving his blood-stained sword, calling on his soldiers to stand firm.

But eventually he saw to his dismay that his attempts to rally his men were hopeless. And so, as the sun reached its zenith in the cloudless blue summer sky, shedding bitter tears, the Prince turned his back on the spacious plain of Yenishehir and with a tiny band of his trusted companions rode eastwards into the mountains of the interior.

Exile

Summer was long gone before I was discharged from the
Imperial Army and free to return to my duties at the Convent. At Yenishehir I had been drafted by Gedik Ahmed
Pasha into the small force sent by the Sultan in pursuit of Jem
as soon as it was confirmed that the Prince had fled the field.
But Jem proved more elusive than we could have imagined in
our wildest dreams. For days on end we followed in his
wake, sometimes even coming within sight of the dust raised
by his furiously galloping beasts, but somehow he managed
always to keep one or two steps ahead of us. Within less than
a week he was back in Konya and we thought we would soon
have him in our grasp. But he tarried there no longer than
was needed to gather up his mother, Chichek Hatun, and his
young bride and children (a son and daughter, then scarcely
more than babes-in-arms), and set out with them to cross the
Taurus Mountains in the hope of reaching Syria, which lies
within those rich and fertile domains belonging to Kayitbay,
Sultan of Egypt.

By the time we were approaching the border – beyond
which we knew we could not go – no more than a single
hour separated us from the Prince and his party, and we were
gaining moment by moment. But Fortune, which had so
cruelly deserted Jem at Yenishehir, now guided him swiftly
along the winding mountain pathways, through the maze of
ravines, gorges and defiles, and finally brought him and his
people safely through the Cilician Gates to the Syrian city of
Tarsus where, as we learned in due course, he was received
by the Governor with open arms and granted immediate
sanctuary.

121

And so, cursing ourselves for our failure, we abandoned the chase and turned again for Konya, where Gedik Ahmed Pasha had been ordered to meet up with the Sultan (who had been following in our footsteps at a slower and more cautious pace with his bodyguard and the Janissaries). But when we arrived in that city we found that, on hearing of our lack of success in capturing the Prince, Bayezid had already departed for Istanbul.

Nor did these events mark the end of the bloody insurrection. Jem's supporters fought on in the mountains of Karaman for many months to come, at one point showing their strength by laying siege to Konya itself, until Gedik Ahmed Pasha – who had gone back to the capital on the Sultan's orders, only to be commanded to return once again to fight the rebels – arrived with a fresh force of cavalry, Janissaries and marines to drive them off and relieve the sorely beleaguered garrison.

Soon afterwards, as a consequence of the Old Man's repeated appeals to the Sultan that his men should be allowed to resume their former posts, word came from the Porte recalling me to Istanbul. Thus, for the second time I took my leave of the Grand Admiral, who grimly assured me that, should they ask me, I could tell our masters from him that, the way things looked then, he would soon be reduced to extirpating the entire population with the sword to suppress revolt and re-establish peace in the eastern provinces of the Empire. But for me, God be praised, the war appeared to be at an end.

I had barely time to cross the threshold of the Convent before Kivami Bey summoned me to attend on him.

Night was drawing in and the lamps had been lit. The air outside was damp and cold and a fire burned in the hearth, filling the room with warmth and the pleasant smell of woodsmoke. Kivami Bey sat huddled in his old pelisse on his divan, just as he had done on the first night I set eyes on him. His ugly, freckled and pockmarked face was yellow in the lamplight. There were dark, purplish shadows under his eyes and he looked older and more worn out than ever. As I entered, he put down his wine cup and wiped his fat glistening lips with his sleeve. The austere and abstemious regime the new Sultan was rumoured to be attempting to impose on Palace and Council Chamber was clearly yet to find favour in this shadowy department of the Sublime Ottoman State.

'Ah, about time too,' said Kivami Bey. 'Sit down, I want to ask you something.'

I bowed and sank to the carpet on the other side of the long low table that was piled high as usual with miscellaneous papers, files and reports.

Kivami Bey said, 'There's a notion in certain quarters here in the capital that Gedik Ahmed Pasha dragged his feet after Yenishehir and deliberately let Jem get away. What do you say to that, Barak?'

'That's absurd,' I said indignantly. 'What evil-minded person could possibly believe that the Grand Admiral didn't do everything in his power to prevent the Prince from escaping?'

Kivami Bey gave a short mirthless laugh. Then, fixing me with his fish eyes, he said, 'You certainly have a way with words sometimes, my poor dear fellow. The "evil-minded person" is none other than your Sultan . . .'

'Forgive me,' I murmured, dropping my eyes, my cheeks burning with shame.

But Kivami Bey merely waved his arm in an impatient, dismissive gesture and said, 'Bah! Who cares who said it? So, there's really nothing whatsoever in it?'

'No, sir,' I said firmly.

'Then how in Heaven's name did Jem manage to get away?'

'It seemed to me,' I said, 'that Gedik Ahmed Pasha did everything he could in the circumstances. But we were small in number and in hostile country most of the time. Everywhere we passed through seemed to be crawling with Jem's supporters – even after the news of the defeat became known. Why, as you know, operations against them are still going on now! We were expecting to be ambushed at every turn – and several times we were. And of course once the Prince got to the Syrian border and over into Kayitbay's territory, there wasn't anything more we could do, without risking a war with the Egyptians, that is . . .'

'H'm,' said Kivami Bey. 'That's exactly what I keep telling Bayezid. Not that he seems to believe a single word I say on this particular subject. But then Gedik Ahmed Pasha has only himself to blame after that damn fool performance at the Emperor's Meadow.'

'You heard about it, then?'

'Heard about it?' said Kivami Bey, arching an eyebrow and glaring at me ferociously. 'I should say I did. And from about nineteen separate sources too. One of these days Gedik Ahmed is going to come a cropper, mark my words. Still, that's hardly the worst problem we've got to contend with in view of the fact that, for whatever reasons, Jem did succeed in getting clean away.'

'Is it known where the Prince is now?' I said.

'It's known all right,' said Kivami Bey. 'He's in Cairo. He got a reception worthy of a Roman Caesar. The whole darned city turned out to see him, and Kayitbay even left the citadel to greet him personally – that in itself is almost unheard of – and embraced him like a long-lost son. After that, the celebrations went on for days apparently.'

'Where is he staying?'

'The Sultan's given him one of the finest palaces in Cairo as his residence for as long as he wishes to remain there. He's installed his mother and his household in it and they're all living like kings. To think that Kayitbay was quaking in his boots only this spring when Mehmed was mustering the Army, because he thought that Mehmed was about to annex Syria. Well, he must feel safe enough from any designs Bayezid might have had in that direction, now that he's got his troublesome brother in Egypt as his guest.'

'But how long will the Prince be content to stay there?' I said.

'That's just it,' said Kivami Bey, waving a bundle of reports. 'My people there tell me that he'd hardly set foot in

Cairo before he was asking Kayitbay to lend him money and troops to help him win back what he's pleased to call his "rightful inheritance".'

'I see,' I said. 'And yet, would the Egyptian Sultan really give them to Jem? If he did, it would amount to a declaration of war.'

'If Mehmed – God forgive him! – were alive, Kayitbay wouldn't even consider it. But against Bayezid, he might chance his arm. At present it seems he's telling Jem to be patient and wait until the time is ripe – or so my people there have been led to believe. But if I know that wily old devil at all, Kayitbay's not going to let an opportunity like this slip through his fingers. The moment he thinks Jem is strong enough to come back with a chance of beating Bayezid a second time round, he'll give him what he wants, and more, I shouldn't doubt. He'd be a fool to do anything else. There's been all kinds of rubbish talked lately about the invincible Imperial Army at Yenishehir – but you don't imagine that I believe a word of it. Jem's a fine commander and absolutely determined, like his father. What's more, he's shown that the men he commands will go to hell and back for his sake. He came damn close to beating Bayezid and, given a second chance, who's to say he won't pull it off? And if he does it with Kayitbay's help, Jem will owe him a debt of gratitude that the Egyptian knows will have to be repaid with interest.'

'An agreement not to expand our borders in Syria at Egypt's expense?'

'Something like that,' said Kivami Bey with disgust. He lapsed into a brooding silence, morosely pulling at the untidy white hairs of his clumsily trimmed beard.

'So what does the Sultan propose to do now?' I said.

'Bayezid believes that his brother can still be persuaded to retire to Jerusalem, as he's already asked him to,' said Kivami Bey. 'Or, at worst, to remain in Cairo and undertake not to try to raise another revolt.'

I said: 'Pray God that for all our sakes he will do as the Sultan asks. But if you'll allow the worthless opinion of an insignificant slave like myself, after what I've seen of the

Prince, I should say that it would be a miracle if he does.'

'And there isn't a Pasha on the Imperial Council', said Kivami Bey, 'who does not secretly think the same, whatever they may say openly.'

'And yet, Kivami Bey,' I said, 'does it not bring shame upon our nation that a prince so full of qualities, who could be of such service to the Empire and the Faith, cannot be found some kind of position that would befit his talents and his birth?'

Kivami Bey slowly shook his head.

'My dear Barak,' he said at last, 'I see that even you have fallen a little under Jem's mysterious spell.'

'Then tell me, Kivami Bey, what is to be done?' I said.

'For the good of all, even perhaps of the Prince himself – since he has made it clear that he will never abandon the struggle until he gets what he wants – Jem ought to be sacrificed as cleanly and speedily as possible.'

I confess I felt a profound sense of shock when I heard these words and found myself stammering out, 'But he is now far away. Besides, he will certainly be on his guard against any attempts we might make on his life.'

'Come, come, Barak,' said Kivami Bey with irritation. 'What kind of talk is this? It might not be easy, but it could be done. I have men in Cairo even now who have the skill and experience to carry out the task. But the obstacle is not a practical one. The problem is the Sultan himself. He refuses even to discuss such a solution.'

'I am surprised,' I said. 'You would have thought that His Highness had more to gain than anyone by getting rid of Jem. And, besides, was it not the case that, when Murad died and Mehmed came to the throne, he consulted the Doctors of Holy Law and they conceded that a Sultan may lawfully have his brothers killed if it be for the sake of peace and security in the land?'

'So they did,' said Kivami Bey. 'And Mehmed had his baby brother strangled forthwith, although there were some who asked what threat could there possibly be in such a tiny child, and called Mehmed a monster and cruel young tyrant. But there were factions then, as there

126

are now, and Mehmed was right to do what he did. And look, my friend, at the result: thirty years of undisputed dominion, during which time our Empire – may God defend it! – has become the most powerful and extensive on this earth!'

'Even so,' I said, 'it is evident that Bayezid is of a much milder nature than his father. Perhaps that is why he still hesitates to commit such an irrevocable deed. Has he consulted the reverend Doctors anew on what actions it would be proper for him to take?'

'He hardly needs to,' said Kivami Bey, leaning forward with a grunt and, after shuffling through a file of papers, removing a sheet. 'Four or five years ago – though of course it never became generally known – Mehmed suffered from an illness so grave that it was feared he might not recover. It was a time of terrible danger to the Empire. That year it looked for the first time as though the Infidels were about to set aside their differences and gather a massive and wicked crusade against the Muslims. So, at Mehmed's behest, a legal opinion on the matter of royal fratricide was sought once again. And when he received it the Emperor instructed that these words be added to his will: "*And to whomsoever of my sons the Sultanate shall pass, it is fitting that for the good of the world he shall kill his brothers. Most of the Doctors of the Sacred Law allow this – so let my successor act upon it.*" '

'I see,' I said. 'What is it, then, Kivami Bey, that holds His Highness back?'

'That', said the Old Man, sinking back on his divan with a sigh, 'is not an easy question to answer. To be quite frank with you, much of the time it's virtually impossible to work out what's going on in that dark mind of his. But one thing is certain: Bayezid could not abide what he saw as his father's irreligion and . . . well, it has to be admitted that Mehmed – God forgive him! – could have led a purer life. And perhaps he should not have surrounded himself so much with Greek and Italian Infidels and Persian heretics – even if they were men of culture and science. But when Bayezid says his father won an Empire but in the example of his impious life he reviled Islam, by Heaven, he goes too far! Nevertheless, if it be just or not, that is how Bayezid thinks, and now that Mehmed is dead and it has pleased the Divine Will to make Bayezid the Conqueror's heir, our new Sultan is determined that *his* rule will not be as his father's was.'

'You mean', I said, 'that His Highness refuses to sacrifice his brother for the good of the State simply because his father urged that it should be done?'

'Certainly for the moment he is not prepared to do it,' said Kivami Bey, 'but not merely because he wishes to defy his father. You must remember that Bayezid is by nature superstitious – look how he surrounds himself with astrologers and soothsayers, not to mention those accursed Halveti dervishes he brought with him from Amasya! So it is easy to see why he should fear that his reign will be blighted in some way from the outset if he begins his rule by shedding his brother's blood – though, God knows, Jem's given him cause enough to feel justified in doing so. But there's something else more important still. Bayezid knows perfectly well that Jem was his father's favourite. And now that he's seen Mehmed's will, he knows that his father had secretly condemned him to death. And yet God has been merciful to him and not only spared his life but also brought him to the summit of worldly glory. Who's to say it's mere superstition that stays his hand from putting Jem's name on a death warrant intended for himself?'

Throughout that grim and uncertain winter it was Kivami Bey's oft-expressed belief that things could only get worse. Encouraged by the sudden death of Sultan Mehmed, the mere mention of whose name had long caused mortal terror among the Infidels, and by the news of the civil war between the Conqueror's sons, the Worshippers of the Cross had begun to besiege Otranto boldly and in force. Hayreddin Mustafa Pasha, whom the Grand Admiral had left in command of the garrison when he himself returned to Istanbul in answer to the Sultan's call, now appealed to

128

Bayezid to send more supplies and troops. But the Sultan either could not or would not do so. He ordered Hayreddin Mustafa to yield up the city to the enemy and withdraw with his men to Avlona. So, our brave work was undone and our precious foothold in Italy lost – may God aid us to regain it for Islam!

Whole weeks passed without a full meeting of the Imperial Council. Instead, the Sultan, who seemed to suspect virtually every one of his ministers and officials of being secret partisans of Jem, took to inviting the Pashas in ones and twos to attend on him in his private apartments, in the presence of a couple of mute Nubian bodyguards and, as often as not, an elderly black-robed Halveti dervish, who presided silently, like some death's-head, over the icily formal proceedings. It was as much as Kivami Bey could do, when he went to the Palace, to persuade Bayezid to dismiss such superfluous attendants so that their meeting could take place, as they always had done in the past, 'with no third but God'. But even then, when Kivami Bey sought guidance on some matter, Bayezid would not infrequently say, 'Do as you think best.' Or, 'We cannot concern ourselves with such questions at present.'

Spring brought news that Jem had quietly left Cairo during the winter to go on the pilgrimage to Mecca and Medina. This plunged the Sultan into new depths of dejection and despondency – not least because he himself had for many years wished to journey to Arabia for this purpose, but had been prevented by Mehmed's stern orders that he was on no account to leave his post at Amasya – a command ominously reaffirmed at the time when, on the eve of his death, the Emperor was mustering the Army to destroy Bayezid and make way for Jem.

And it was from this time that the errant Prince became known at the Convent as 'the Hajji' (that is, 'the Pilgrim'). Atik said that the name originated in some cynical remarks made to Kivami Bey by the Sultan himself regarding the religious purity of his brother's motives in undertaking the expedition – for Bayezid was not slow to appreciate that Jem's action would lend a halo of sanctity to his struggle to usurp the throne. But whoever was the first to call him thus, 'the Hajji' soon became a kind of code-word amongst us and quickly acquired official status by appearing in written reports and documents. And, without the smallest shadow of doubt, whether the Prince undertook the journey for the purpose of spiritual salvation or temporal gain, the experience appeared to instil in him a renewed vigour and an even greater sense of conviction that he had been cheated of the Sultanate merely by ill-luck and unfavourable circumstances, as was presently revealed by an extraordinary incident, which Kivami Bey witnessed at the Palace and related to me not long afterwards.

It was a bright morning early that summer and the Old Man was alone in the presence of the Sultan when their discussion was interrupted by the Royal Chamberlain, who entered the room in a great state of agitation, bearing a letter, which he said had just arrived from Egypt. It had been brought by a Tatar courier who claimed he had sailed from Alexandria to a port near Tarsus in one of Kayitbay's galleys and ridden post-haste from there to Istanbul. The man, said the Chamberlain, would say nothing more, other than that if the Felicitous Emperor deigned to reply he would bear the letter back to Cairo.

Bayezid took the letter, instructed the Chamberlain to withdraw and, when the door had quietly been closed, broke the seal and very slowly opened it. Having carefully unfolded it, with a furrowed brow he cast his eyes over its contents. At first his face registered no reaction, but then a strange grimace began to spread across his features. It took Kivami Bey quite some seconds to realize that the Sultan was actually smiling.

The Old Man was already considerably astonished at the effect that this mysterious missive seemed to be having on Bayezid, but was even more thunderstruck when, without a word, the Sultan leant forward and handed it to him. To begin with, Kivami Bey hardly dared to look at it, but then, encouraged by a gracious gesture from Bayezid, he lowered his eyes. The paper was headed with the swirling and intricate device of the Prince's monogram and, glancing down, Kivami Bey saw that the message below was written in Jem's own elegant and stylish hand. There were just four lines that read:

> Whilst thou on a bed of roses dost lie in all delight,
> Downcast, forlorn, forsaken, I languish in blackest night
>
> — why, why is this?
> And though a pious Pilgrim to the Holy Shrines am I,
> Yet thou to me, O cruel one, still justice dost deny
> — why, why is this?

Kivami Bey looked up to find that Bayezid was now sitting with his head bowed, stroking his beard and obviously deep in thought. After some time the Sultan smiled again and rose to his feet. He went over to a small desk where the scribes normally sat. Bending down, he took some sheets of paper, pens and an inkstand and handed them to the Old Man.

The Sultan then sank down once again at his divan and, reclining against a bolster, began to drum his fingers, staring at the ceiling with a look of intense concentration. The minutes went by. Several times he seemed to be about to speak, even opening his mouth a little once or twice, but at the last moment stopped to think again. He closed his eyes. After a while his face became quite animated. First he frowned. Then a look of quiet amusement played on his lips. He became grave. He began rhythmically to tap his knee again. Finally, the Sultan spoke, in even and measured tones, and the Old Man's pen started laboriously to scrape and scratch its way across the paper. When the last strokes were complete, the last black point dotted over the concluding word, the Sultan opened his eyes and sat up.

Bayezid now looked at Kivami Bey expectantly, his dark eyebrows slightly raised. The Old Man cleared his throat and read aloud:

> E'en before God framed this world, Emperor was I decreed,

131

But yielding not to Destiny, thou still wilt pay no heed

— why, why is this?

And though a pious pilgrim to the Holy Shrines thou art,

Yet still on an earthly Sultanship hast thou set thy heart

— why, why is this?

Within that very hour these words were transcribed under the Imperial monogram by the Sultan himself, in his own hand, and entrusted to the Tatar messenger so that he might convey them swiftly to his master. Thus, in brotherly fashion Bayezid rebuffed Jem's eloquent but unreasonable reproaches and urged him to accept the condition assigned to him by Destiny.

But, alas, as events were soon to show, it would take more than a Sultan's verses to deter the Prince from venturing to alter his lot once more by force of arms and again submerging the unhappy Empire in the innocent blood of his fellow Muslims.

There is a story that, when Sultan Mehmed was once leading forth the Imperial Army, one of his young commanders had the boldness to ask him what were his plans, and the Conqueror replied, 'If a hair of my beard knew them, I would pluck it out and burn it.' The Prince now showed that he was his father's son in this respect, as he had already proved to be in so many others.

Jem's movements in Egypt were as closely watched as they could be by our agents – and the Prince knew this only too well. But not long after returning from Mecca and Medina, he had it discreetly put about that he was suffering from a slight illness, brought on by the exhaustion of his desert journey, and had taken to his bed to rest. After some weeks an agent reported that he seemed to have recovered – he had been seen one dark night leaving his palace with an escort on his way to the citadel (presumably for some secret conference with the Egyptian Sultan); and then again, some days later, riding on the plain between the Nile and the Great Pyramids (though his face could not be seen very clearly as, naturally, his fair features had been partly masked against the burning African sun).

Thus, it was without any warning that, after making his way northwards completely undetected, while his veiled double ran rings round our agents, Jem led his stealthily gathered forces over the Taurus by the obscure mountain-tracks and high passes known only to his trusty Turcoman guides, and suddenly reappeared at the head of a new army on the plains of Karaman. In no time he had surrounded Konya and was vigorously laying siege to that city, which he had governed with such dazzling success until just twelve months before.

Within days, the eastern provinces, fanned by the raising anew of the Prince's proud and warlike banners, were ablaze with the flames of revolt once more. But Gedik Ahmed Pasha's merciless rooting out and deportation of Jem's followers in Konya itself now paid off: the garrison there not only refused to surrender but put up the most tremendous resistance to the besiegers.

The delay caused by this failure to take the city immediately gave Bayezid the vital few days he needed to dispatch a mounted vanguard of Asian cavalry to ride eastwards while he mustered the main body of the Imperial Army at Bursa. But as things turned out, Jem had at his side, even then, a far more lethal, if unwitting, agent of Fate than any vanguard, in the form of one Mahmud Bey, a former Aga of the Janissaries from the days of the Conqueror, who had secretly made his way from Ankara (where he was then Governor) to pledge his support for the Prince's cause. For Mahmud Bey began to fear that his wife and family, whom he had left behind, might now fall into the Sultan's hands. With tears in his eyes the venerable old commander begged the Prince to allow him to take a force northwards to secure Ankara against Bayezid's vanguard or at least to rescue his own people, who were in danger of being captured.

There can be little doubt what the Conqueror's response

would have been to such a request. But, equally, few that ever knew the Prince would have been surprised by the nature of *his* reaction. Without hesitation he assigned the Aga several squadrons of his finest horsemen and sent him on his way with his blessing, urging him to return as soon as possible to the safety of the army.

When Mahmud Bey had departed, some of Jem's allies came to his tent to upbraid him for taking such a risk while Konya still remained unsubjected. But the Prince, using the words of the Prophet, merely said, 'When the generous man stumbles, God takes him by the hand.' And that, as far as he was concerned, was the end of the matter.

Yet it was not the will of God that Mahmud Bey's mission should be crowned with success. When the Aga came near Ankara he learned that Bayezid's vanguard had got there before him and, on the orders of the Sultan, had arrested all his people and dragged them off to the capital. In a fury the Aga launched an assault on the town — but his enemies had been forewarned of his approach and were well prepared and fortified against the attack. Mahmud Bey's vastly outnumbered forces were utterly routed — one of the first to die being the Aga himself, whose severed head was duly dispatched to the Sultan.

Meanwhile, learning that Bayezid was marching on Ankara but hearing nothing as yet of Mahmud Bey's violent demise, Jem temporarily raised the siege of Konya and set off by forced marches in the hope of reaching and occupying the city in advance of his brother, and of there rallying the troops to confront the Imperial Army head-on for a second time. But as the Prince and his men drew near their destination, a ghastly spectacle began to unfold before them. For now they saw the grim testimony of the Aga's defeat with their own eyes. The countryside was littered for miles around with the bodies of Mahmud Bey's slaughtered men and horses. Many had evidently been struck down fighting, but clearly many hundreds had been captured alive. The fly-blown rotting corpses of these unfortunates lined the route of Jem's silent progress, some having been bound hand and foot before being decapi-

134

tated, some impaled on stakes or disembowelled, and others mutilated and hanged from the boughs of trees, where they dangled like the suppurating black fruit on the thorn trees of Hell . . .

That evening the Prince's army encamped in a desolate rock-strewn valley not far from Ankara. Frightened half out of their wits that day by the grisly vision of the remains of their fallen comrades, and now by the packs of wolves and wild dogs that filled the empty darkness with their howling as they ranged the surrounding hills in search of human carrion, men began to melt away into the night. By dawn the scouts sent ahead to assess the strength of the Sultan's army were returning, saying that the approaching Imperial host looked more like a mighty rolling ocean than a body of mere mortals. And when asked to say how many troops they judged were marching beneath the Sultan's flags and banners, even the most sober and experienced among them – men known not to be given to foolish talk and exaggeration – averred that there must be more than one hundred and fifty thousand.

By nightfall Jem had ordered the total destruction of the camp and commanded his remaining loyal followers to take to the hills to save themselves to fight for his just cause another day. And he comforted his weeping and loudly lamenting men with the promise that, as God was his witness, he would thenceforth not leave his native soil unless driven from it by the direst necessity, but would take to the mountain fastnesses of the Taurus and there await the hour when, smiling upon him at last, Glory summoned him to receive the Imperial inheritance solemnly pledged to him by his father, the Conqueror, the eventual attaining of which he knew in his heart to be written in the stars.

Perhaps, in view of everything that happened afterwards, it is no wonder that Jem would one day come to look back on those days spent on the wooded slopes and high summer-pastures of the Taurus as a brief sojourn in a kind of demi-paradise.

His palace was then a grove of ancient, spice-scented

135

cedars; his portico, the spreading shade of their dark green branches; his fountains, the bubbling springs and tumbling mountain streams; his lawns, the flower-spangled upland meadows; and his royal canopy, the clear blue vault of the open firmament of Heaven. And there he lived like one of his nomad forefathers of old on the wide Asian steppe – his sheep and horses supplying his every want and need, his table furnished with meat by the herd or by the chase, his foaming cup filled with the sweet wine of fermented mare's milk – the lord and master of everything he surveyed. Nor did he lack for cultured and civilized society, for with him he still had his faithful ministers, officers and retainers from the court at Konya: his Chancellor, Sadi (nicknamed 'Jem's Sadi', so inseparable was he from the Prince); his treasurer, Haydar; his chamberlains Sinan Bey and Ghalib Bey; his scribes Nasuh Chelebi and Frenk Suleyman; and a dozen or more other companions of his childhood and youth.

But the idyll of the Prince's existence in this breezy domain was doomed to fade even before summer had turned to autumn. For with every hour that passed the Sultan was closing in as his men overran the foothills, scoured the valleys and clambered up even the highest and most dizzying peaks, tirelessly searching every forest, wood, copse, thicket and glade, every gully, hollow, ravine, crevasse and cave for some sign of the fugitive and his men.

At length, the Prince learned through the Turcoman shepherds with whom he shared his remote upland kingdom that Bayezid wished to open negotiation with him. After parleying for some days through these same Turcoman intermediaries, Jem sent Sinan Bey to a secret rendezvous to speak with the Sultan's ambassadors. Once again, via Sinan, he demanded that his brother cede to him at least some of the Asian provinces, and once again he was told that Bayezid refused to entertain the request, repeating that the Empire was a fair mistress who could have but one master, and calling upon Jem to put an end to the spilling of the blood of the Faithful by retiring with honour to the Holy City of Jerusalem, where he would yearly receive all the rich revenues of Karaman.

The shepherds in due course candidly informed the Prince that his brother had put upon his head a price of one hundred thousand gold ducats to the man who could lead him to Jem, with the solemn assurance that the Prince would come to no harm but merely be restrained for his own good until he could be brought to see the folly of his enterprise. Meanwhile, the fires of the soldiers combing the mountains were visible in the darkness, slowly creeping nearer and nearer night by night. Every pass out of the Taurus, north and east and west, was now closed by Bayezid's forces and the road to Syria and the entire length of the eastern border sealed by Gedik Ahmed Pasha's troops.

The net closed on Jem's lofty silvan refuge. His camp lay empty and deserted, the ashes in the fire in his regal hall beneath the cedars grey and cold. Sheep and horses quietly clipped the grass and birds picked through the remains of a last feast. But for the wind and the gentle creaking of the branches, there was not a sound and the snow-covered peaks above silently kept their counsel.

Then the strangest news reached the ears of the Emperor. A mounted search party had heard rumours that a group of thirty or so men had been sighted unhurriedly making their way on horseback down the steep southern slopes of the massif in the direction of the sea. The search party went off after them. Coming to a high eminence, they looked down upon the golden Cilician coast and the small port of Korykos and saw that a single vessel was tied up down below. But as they descended the winding track to the rocky shore the ship, which raised no colours and hoisted no flag either Infidel or Muslim, cast off and slowly started to slide out of the harbour. Then, before their very eyes, it spread its dazzling white canvas, its banks of oars began to beat regularly upon the waves and the vessel carrying the Prince and his companions set off westwards over the calm blue summer sea, whither no man knew.

137

Congealed Blood

It was three weeks after St Dimitrios' Day when Gedik
Ahmed Pasha, who had only recently returned to the capital from the south-eastern provinces, was summoned at
dawn to attend on the Sultan at the Palace. The Imperial
Council had at last begun to meet again more or less regularly, but there was no meeting that day.

The autumn was well advanced, most of the trees nearly
bare, the leaves scattered over the damp ground piled up
here and there in little mounds by the wind. The hour was
early, but the sun had risen and its moist light was just
managing to penetrate the haze that hung high in the sky
above the city.

The Palace guards stood briskly aside, saluted and
called out respectful greetings to the Grand Admiral as he
rode through the Imperial Gate, followed by a single
young groom. The first court was hushed and virtually
deserted: a couple of pages – one with a bandaged leg – sat
whispering on the steps of the Palace Infirmary; half a
dozen Janissaries lounged about, idling away their time
under the majestic plane-trees it is their privilege to gather
beneath; and a little further off, some porters crossed the
broad central expanse of the court, stooping under their
mountainous burdens of freshly chopped logs, on their
way from the woodyard to the Imperial kitchens. The
fragrant smell of new-baked bread and sweetmeats still
lingered in the motionless air.

The Grand Admiral and the boy neared the Middle
Gate, ascending the sloping cobbled path at barely more
than a walking pace, their horses treading so lightly and

softly that even they seemed awestruck to be approaching the Royal Presence. The massive iron doors already stood wide open before them. The dark vaulted passageway that leads into the Court of the Imperial Council between the Gate's tall twin towers and narrow mullioned windows appeared from a distance to be empty and unattended. Since beyond this gate no man save the Emperor himself may proceed on horseback, the groom now drew alongside his master and, skilfully sliding from the saddle, held his own reins in one hand and took his master's bridle in the other. When they came to a halt Gedik Ahmed dismounted with a grunt and set about straightening his turban and cloak in preparation for his audience with the Sultan. At that moment some rather tardy grooms of the Royal Household came running from the stables at the corner of the court and took both beasts in order to lead them aside until the riders required them again.

But as Gedik Ahmed Pasha and the boy walked the last few yards of the cobbled way and came to the threshold of the Middle Gate, they saw in the gloom of the sunless passage three figures standing in their path. Gedik Ahmed strode towards them, his footfalls echoing hollowly against the gateway's curving stone walls and ceiling. When he reached the men, realizing that they showed no signs of stepping aside, he stopped in front of the most imposing and heavily built of the three, a man with thick moustaches, attired in a black turban and robes.

Gedik Ahmed said in an affable manner, 'What is this, gentlemen? The Felicitous Sultan has called me to his side on some urgent business – I received the summons not an hour ago. Perhaps you have not been informed?'

'Certainly we have been informed,' said the man in black. 'And, my Lord Admiral, it is for you that we are waiting.'

'Why should His Majesty send *you* of all people to meet me at his gate?' said Gedik Ahmed indignantly.

'But surely you understand what this means?' said the man.

'What is there to understand?' said Gedik Ahmed. 'What

139

enormity, what crime am I supposed to have committed that I should find myself talking to such as you?'

The man drew a document bearing the Imperial seal from his robes and handed it to the Grand Admiral without a word. Gedik Ahmed took it and unfolded it, and in the dimness cast his eyes over the contents. After some time he handed it back to the man and said, 'These charges are preposterous. Let me pass and speak to the Emperor that I might defend myself against them.'

As he spoke the Admiral sensed that the boy, who was standing a pace or two behind him, was tugging gently but insistently at his sleeve. He turned round and the boy indicated with a very slight, surreptitious jerk of his head that something was going on behind them. Taking the boy by the arm, he walked with him back to the threshold of the gateway. Gedik Ahmed shaded his eyes against the glare of the hazy morning light. The pages, stable lads and the handful of Janissaries beneath the plane tree had all disappeared. At the far end of the sloping cobbled path the Imperial Gate had been shut fast. Before it there now stood a sizeable detachment of Royal Halberdiers and Archers. Gedik Ahmed released the boy's arm and made his way back towards the men.

'Then I am condemned by the Sultan himself?' he said in a clear and unwavering voice.

'Yes, my Lord Admiral,' said the Chief Executioner, avoiding his penetrating glance by lowering his eyes.

Gedik Ahmed's young groom moved forward silently and clutched his master's cloak. Tears began to swell up in the boy's eyes. He slipped to the ground, sobbing and clinging to the Admiral's sleeve. Tenderly, Gedik Ahmed raised him to his feet. He put his arm around the boy's shoulders, stroked his cheek and began to wipe the tears away with his rough fingers, saying:

'Come, come, my dear boy. There is no reason to be afraid. No harm will come to you.'

The boy buried his head against the broad chest of the Grand Admiral, who looked up at the men, his eyes full of uncertainty and mistrust. The Chief Executioner, seeming

140

to read his thoughts, spread his hands in a wide gesture of horror and said:

'My Lord, what kind of men do you take us for? Why, if the boy wishes to, he may go now and nobody will stand in his way. His Majesty has no quarrel with him, or any other of your people. You have just seen the warrant yourself: there is no other name on it but your own.'

Gedik Ahmed now sighed deeply and very gently started to prise the boy's fingers from his sleeve. Pushing him away from his side, he slowly took off his rich fur pelisse and handed it over to his young servant. Then calmly he unbuckled his belt for the last time and passed this to him as well. He said to the boy:

'Now, stand aside a little, there's a good fellow. And show these gentlemen how brave you are, or I shall be ashamed of you.'

Still weeping inconsolably, the boy obeyed and, taking some steps backwards, stood against the wall of the dark passageway, covering his face in his master's cloak. Gedik Ahmed Pasha turned to address his executioners.

'I did not think', he said with a bitter laugh, 'to end my life like this . . . but what of it? No man can know the hour and place appointed for his death – Sultan or slave.'

He reached inside his sash, brought out his purse and handed it to the Chief Executioner. The Executioner took it with a bow and passed it to one of his assistants.

Then Gedik Ahmed Pasha said, 'Allow the boy, if you will, to keep my cloak and sword that he might remember me.'

'They are his,' said the Executioner.

'Then there is nothing more to be said, save to tell me where you wish to do your work.'

The Executioner drew his curved sword and held it out at an angle to his side, saying, 'Where you stand now would be as good as any place, if it would please you, my Lord Admiral.'

'What difference does it make to me?' said Gedik Ahmed with a shrug. Then with dignity, and apparently complete tranquillity, he gathered up the folds of his robe and knelt

141

on the stone floor of the passageway. The assistants stepped forward noiselessly and drew back his robe and shirt to expose his neck. The Executioner signalled to them to stand back, took his place beside Gedik Ahmed, with his feet apart, and murmured almost inaudibly, 'In the name of God: God is most Great . . .'

Then, raising his sword high above his shoulders, with a swift effortless swing of his powerful arms he brought the blade down with such force that it sheared through the Admiral's neckbone, severed his sinews and arteries and cleaved his head from his body with a single blow, sending it somersaulting across the threshold into the sunlight. At the same time his body fell heavily forward, a welter of hot blood gushing from the gaping hole in his shoulders onto the cold grey flagstones of the passageway.

In this way the Sultan finally settled his account with his recalcitrant slave Gedik Ahmed Pasha, and set at liberty the brave soul of the Victor of Otluk Beli, Kaffa and Otranto that it might go in search of God's mercy and enjoy for all eternity a martyr's reward in Paradise.

Kivami Bey remembered later that when he arrived at the Porte, about two hours before the time of the midday prayer, it certainly struck him as strange that, although the pavings had only recently been sluiced down and the ground was still wet by the fountain where the Chief Executioner invariably washes his sword and hands after fulfilling his latest commission, no vizir's or official's head adorned the spikes above the Middle Gate. And when, having passed through the Gate into the Inner Palace beyond, he made his awkward and painful way across the Court of the Imperial Council to the room where he customarily conferred with the Sultan, and found waiting for him there not Bayezid but Davud Pasha – who had only weeks before been made a vizir – the Old Man began to suspect that something very strange indeed was going on.

But it must have taxed his inscrutability to the limits to receive unblinkingly – as, according to Davud Pasha in later years, he did – the announcement that this newly appointed vizir delivered almost before Kivami Bey had time to seat himself in his usual position on the divan.

For he heard that not only was he to be relieved forthwith of his position as Head of Imperial Security but there was at that very moment a small naval vessel lying under sail in the Golden Horn waiting to convey him to the Thracian port of Tekirdag. Not far distant from there, on a secluded part of the coast, the Sultan had, in a display of boundless generosity, set aside a small estate (substantial house, fine gardens, views over the Marmara Sea) as a place of retirement where Kivami Bey might end his days in the peaceful repose that he no doubt craved after such a tireless and active life of service to the Royal House . . .

At this point Kivami Bey finally objected in an uncharacteristically mild fashion that perhaps, owing to some oversight by his advisers, the Sultan was unaware that he already possessed ample estates in the region of Bursa, to which he would willingly now retire if His Majesty would deign to allow him to do so.

Davud Pasha shook his head sadly, saying that, whereas His Majesty was naturally perfectly aware of the ancestral lands belonging to Kivami Bey's illustrious family, in view of the recent troubles in the Asian provinces the Sultan had deemed an estate in Europe as a more suitable place for his future residence. It was, after all, said Davud Pasha, merely a necessary precaution for the continued protection of one who for nearly three decades had been privy to the most closely guarded secrets of state, as Kivami Bey himself would surely be the first to understand . . .

He understood. Kivami Bey said no more but only raised his fat hands in a gesture of submission and let them fall back limply on his knees. And although he now strongly suspected that this talk of exile might well be a mere ruse to remove him with the minimum of fuss from the city to some more discreet place of execution, suddenly he felt so weary of the world that he now hardly cared what was to happen to him. He hauled himself to his feet and started out laboriously on his sticks towards the door. Davud Pasha hurriedly rose to his feet and solicitously offered his arm. With a shrug, the Old Man accepted it.

Not, of course, that I knew of these momentous events until a very long time after they took place. I suppose if I had done I would not have been so surprised when they came to arrest me.

Unfortunately, I wasn't at the Convent when Atik returned there almost speechless with grief to announce that Kivami Bey had been toppled and was to be replaced by a favourite of the Sultan, one Mustafa Bey. I was then at the house at Mega Revma on a few days' leave before being dispatched on a new assignment (the details of which I shall never know), and I was as blissfully unaware of the Old Man's being haled away as I was that my former Admiral's severed head and corpse were now food for fishes at the bottom of the Bosphorus.

And, as things turned out, this was a great pity. Because the next thing that happened was that Davud Pasha and the State Investigators turned up at the Convent, hot on Atik's heels, with a list of agents – all people they suspected might have been involved in the Jem case, one way or another – whom they wished should give evidence to a secret inquiry, instituted that very day, into the whys and wherefores of the Prince's miraculous escapes. Seeing my name on the list, Atik then did something very touching and extremely foolish. He tried to get word to me to make myself scarce until he found out exactly what was going on and sorted out what he took to be some kind of misunderstanding. If only it had been as simple as that.

As a member of Gedik Ahmed's Staff at the time of Jem's flight to Egypt after Yenishehir, I was already under suspicion of conspiring with the Grand Admiral to allow the Prince to get away. But as the intended recipient of an anonymous coded message sent to Mega Revma by somebody within Imperial Security instructing me for my own safety to disappear, I was obviously a very dangerous customer indeed. Of course, if the signal had not been intercepted by the Investigators things might have been rather different, but the fact is that it was. And once it had been, it was not as if I could tell them that it was Atik who had dispatched the warning. And – God be praised! – despite exhaustive enquiries they never found the culprit for themselves.

The first few weeks were very bad. I don't much like thinking about them even now. Their methods were rather crude – not the kind I ever saw employed at the Convent. After a while I was afraid that if I ever did get out – which, admittedly, was highly unlikely – I would not really be of much use to anyone. By then I could only get about on my hands and knees. It felt very permanent at the time. But, mercifully, I was still a young man – I doubt if an older man would have made such a remarkable recovery. Even so, it took the best part of a year before I could walk anything like properly again.

At some point, quite why I don't know to this day, they began to get it into their heads that I was telling the truth. But by then I was hardly in a state to be released. However, I can't complain – they didn't take the easy option, though I would have almost been thankful if they had put me out of my misery.

In fact, I discovered afterwards that it was the Sultan himself who insisted that as soon as I was in a fit condition physically I should not only be set free but even given a small pension in keeping with my former position as a captain in the Imperial Navy. But, to be honest, even though I was told that I could resume my former rank, it was difficult to believe that I would ever really be trusted again.

And yet, after a year, armed with my papers of honourable discharge ('retired owing to injuries received in action') and with the help of some old naval colleagues, I did manage to get some work in the shipyard of the Arsenal, supervising the building and fitting out of new vessels for the Fleet. I counted myself lucky, too. The Grand Admiral was by no means the only officer who had vanished during those terrible months, never to be seen again – may God's mercy be upon them all!

And still, nearly four years after Gedik Ahmed's execution, it seemed nothing certain was known about what had happened to the Prince and his companions. Rumours

145

as to his whereabouts were rife – but I managed to gather from dark hints dropped by Atik, whom I encountered from time to time, that not even people at the Convent knew where he had gone and what daring plans he might be hatching. Indeed, nobody had ever known of such an extraordinary mystery, and the strangest thing was that, now that Jem had disappeared into thin air, to the Sultan's despair the population seemed to have become more obsessed with him than ever. And despite the fact that it was treason even to speak his name, hardly a week passed without some news of sightings of him from one or another far-flung region of the Empire.

That I myself would ever become entangled in the Prince's affairs again never occurred to me for a moment. After all, it was not as if I would ever set foot in the Convent again – an assumption that had the seal set upon it when Atik confessed to me that it was now the general belief there that the Old Man was no longer alive. Yet nothing happens that is not written in the Book of Heavenly Decrees, and it almost seems to me now that I survived those evil days following the fall of Gedik Ahmed Pasha, when so many others perished, for one reason alone – and that was so that I might once more resume my inevitable part in the drama of Jem's ill-starred existence on this inhospitable earth.

It was one of those winter days when, from dawn till dusk, the mist clings to the city like a sodden shroud, the frost lingers hard and white on the ground until well into the afternoon and, though there's not a breath of wind, your face and hands are numb with cold the instant you step outside and you can feel the damp eating at the marrow of your bones.

I had just left the Arsenal and was on my way down to the waterfront to get a boat back to the Stambul side of the Golden Horn. From some distance off I saw that a boy of maybe nine, ten years old was stopping passers-by on their way down to the landing-stage and speaking to them one after another. I thought he was begging for small coins or something, but he didn't appear to be having much luck – everybody he accosted seemed just to shrug and walk on. I reached inside my sash to see if I could find him something. Then he stopped an old mustachioed marine who bent over for a moment inclining his ear before straightening up and, with a smile, pointing in my direction. I was practically upon them by that time.

The boy planted himself in my path, folded his arms and gazed up at me expectantly. When I got to him he said, 'Please, sir, are you Captain Barak, sir?'

'I might be,' I said.

'That man,' said the boy with a jerk of his head towards the departing marine, 'said you were.'

'Then perhaps I am, if *he* says so,' I replied. 'Who wants him?'

'I can't say,' he said, 'unless I know for certain that you are this Barak.'

'All right,' I said, holding up my hands in a gesture of surrender. 'I confess that I am "this Barak". So tell me who wants him, quickly now before both of us freeze to death standing around like this.'

The boy solemnly put out his hand.

'Yani,' he said.

I took his hand and clasped it. He peered at me for a few seconds as though still sizing me up, withdrew his hand from mine, turned on his heel and set off down the lane towards the landing-stage, saying in a business-like fashion, 'Follow me . . .'

I shook my head. I was going that way in any case, so there wasn't much else I could do but go after him. We boarded one of the caiques that had just drawn up amidst the usual commotion and cries from the ferryman of 'That's enough!' and 'Come on, boys, let's go!' We cast off and, straining at their oars, and even sweating from their exertions despite the cold, the boatmen pulled us out over the grey and foggy waters of the estuary.

The boy and I sat jammed up against each other in the bottom of the boat. I was about to speak to him, but he squeezed my forearm and shot me a meaningful look with

147

his bright black eyes, warning me to remain silent.

We landed at the other side. Yani scrambled nimbly out of the caique ahead of me. He reached down, offering me his hand to help me up onto the landing-stage.

'I think I can manage,' I said, 'but thanks just the same.'

'This way,' said Yani, looking piqued and striding off.

I caught up with him in half a dozen easy steps and laid my hand gently on his shoulder.

I said, 'Just one thing, Yani. I don't live that way, I live *that* way.' I pointed along the quay in the opposite direction.

'I know,' said Yani nonchalantly. 'I went to your house just now and your man said you were still on the other side at the yards – so I crossed over to look for you there.'

'My man had no business telling you, a stranger, where I was,' I said severely.

'Bah!' said Yani scornfully. 'He had to. I showed him this.'

He fumbled inside his shirt and pulled out a small, somewhat smudged and crumpled piece of paper. I took it. It had an official seal, that day's date and the words: '*Barak, accompany the bearer of this letter to the Church of the Most Blessed Virgin in the Fener quarter.*' There was no signature. I didn't recognize the handwriting. My stomach tightened as if gripped by a fist.

The boy looked up at me quizzically. 'What's wrong?' he said.

'Nothing.'

He reached up, gently slid the letter from between the light grasp of my fingers and replaced it inside his shirt.

'Shall we go?' he said.

'Of course,' I said, my voice sounding odd and unfamiliar even to my ears. 'Why not?'

Yani and I walked along the shore of the Golden Horn for some way, turned left at a narrow gate in the sea walls and started up the hill through the dank twilit streets of Fener amidst the ramshackle jumble of wooden houses built by the Christians. I knew this quarter well. I had come here countless times before to keep those delicious clandestine trysts with my Christian mistress, Sofia. For seven years I had hoped, but she had never returned to Istanbul, and God only knew where she was now.

The uneven pot-holed cobbles underfoot were icy and slippery, and the boy, who could have done with warmer clothes in such weather, was beginning to shiver. I offered him my coat. Disdainfully he refused and hastened on ahead of me, proceeding jerkily on his thin legs, his teeth chattering.

At last the grey walls and squat dome of the church loomed up, swathed in fog at the summit of the hill. When we reached its portals Yani said, 'Wait here.'

The building stands alone on a kind of open terrace overlooking the rest of the quarter and the estuary below. There are cypresses and, to one side, a grove of tall plane trees, where the Greeks gather on Sundays and feast-days during the summer to drink their wine and pass the time. But the trees were quite leafless now and the meagre grass beneath them scattered with bluish patches of still-unmelted snow.

Occasionally old men and women shuffled past me in and out of the church door, avoiding my eyes and mumbling darkly to one another when they thought they were out of earshot. When the boy had left me he had gone off down one side of the church. With still no sign of him, I wandered after him. The mist was very dense on this exposed piece of flat ground and I could hardly see two yards in front of me. I turned to go back to the main door of the church. A figure, his head and shoulders enveloped in a cloud of his own freezing breath, rounded the corner of the building and moved rapidly towards me. When we came face to face he said, 'Ah, thank goodness, it's you, Captain. My apologies, sir. I thought for a moment you'd got fed up waiting and gone off. But you understand that we had to make sure that you weren't being followed.'

Although he spoke good Turkish I could tell by his accent that the man, like the child Yani, was Greek.

'Where's the boy?' I said.

'He's gone home, sir,' said the man. Then he added,

149

'He's my nephew. He has no parents, so I look after him.'

'Perhaps you'd care to tell me what all this is about?' I said.

'You've seen the letter, haven't you, sir?' he said. 'I can assure you it is all perfectly official.'

'That's what I was afraid of,' I said.

He eyed me with a look of puzzlement.

'Come on,' I said, 'let's get it over with.'

We walked down the steep deserted street I had come up, turned into a gloomy alleyway and followed its winding undulating course until we came to a tiny square dominated by a large wooden house with two floors, of the sort the richer Christian merchants had started to build in those days. Heavy icicles hung from the protruding eaves and a dusting of undisturbed snow on the shutters and windowsills showed that they had not been opened recently.

The man produced a key and unlocked the door. We stepped into a square hall furnished with a couch, a small copper brazier and a large carpet that almost completely covered the polished boards of the floor. On one wall a lamp flickered above some icons on a shelf. The man shot a heavy wood bolt across the door behind us and indicated a narrow staircase going up to the first floor.

'I'll wait down here, sir,' he said.

As I started to climb the stairs I saw that he took the letter the boy had shown me and began to tear it into long strips and drop them into the brazier, where they smouldered briefly before catching light and going up in smoke.

At the head of the stairs there was a long dark hall, lit by a single dim oil-lamp, with three or four doors giving off it to right and left. They all appeared to be closed. But at the end of the hall opposite me another door stood very slightly ajar and showed a crack of golden light. Treading softly, I walked towards it. I paused for a moment and listened. I heard what sounded like a man breathing heavily, almost as if he were asleep. I cautiously pushed the door with my foot.

It swung back with a mournful creak to reveal a

spacious, sparsely furnished room. At one end, by a small open fire that burned brightly in a blackened hearth beneath a deep-set chimney-piece, a solitary dwarf-like figure sat with bowed head, hunched up in a fur-trimmed pelisse on a sort of couch. At first the dazzling brilliance of the fire and the shifting shadows cast by the flames made it impossible to make out anything of the apparition's face. But then it slowly began to raise its head, disclosing a broad furrowed forehead, crooked pockmarked nose, and finally a pair of gross glistening pinkish lips. I stepped across the threshold into the light. The face was lifted sleepily towards me, the firelight momentarily catching the moist and shining eyes. Then the lips gradually curled themselves into a leering grimace, a kind of grotesque twisted smile.

'God Almighty!' I whispered hoarsely, utterly unable to restrain myself for sheer amazement. 'I thought you were supposed to be dead.'

'I'm so sorry,' said Kivami Bey with sour precision, spitting the words out one by one, 'to disappoint you, Captain.'

'Forgive me, sir,' I said, 'but, you see, Atik believed that they'd done away with you as well.'

'Atik is a feckless and incurable optimist. You should know that by now, Barak,' said Kivami Bey with a dismissive wave of his hand.

I laughed – I couldn't help myself – from nerves, surprise, relief. But the Old Man wrinkled up his brow and fixed me with a withering stare.

'Well,' he said, 'don't just stand there grinning like some nincompoop – close the door! I know you naval types don't mind the wind whistling about your ears the whole time, but I do. There's a bloody awful draught coming down that hall, so kindly shut it out before this room becomes like an ice-house again!'

I pushed the door to and leant my back against it. He beckoned to me impatiently.

'Come here,' he said.

I walked towards him, the boards squeaking with

151

unnatural loudness under my feet. When I reached him I bent down to kiss his hand, but he avoided my grasp and caught me by the elbows, saying brusquely, 'Never mind that . . .'

His arms were surprisingly strong. Gripping my sleeves with his small fat hands, he swung me round and pushed me firmly down on the couch beside him.

In front of him was a long, low, elaborately carved chest on which there stood a tall glazed jug brimming with red wine. He leant forward and filled a cup, spilling some onto the lid of the chest. He wiped the bottom of the cup with his sleeve and proffered it, raising an enquiring eyebrow.

I lifted my hand in a negative gesture.

He shrugged and emptied it himself at a single gulp. He stifled a belch and wiped his mouth with the back of his hand. He turned his grey fish-eyes upon me.

'I hear you had it pretty rough,' he said.

'Others suffered worse than I did,' I said. 'And if I may say so, sir, I'm glad to see that Atik's information about you was incorrect.'

Kivami Bey said, 'H'm! Perhaps I'll tell you about it some time. But not now. You and I have work to do. You see, the fact is that our beloved Sultan has seen fit in his infinite wisdom to have me recalled to my former position. And he's also deigned to let me have *you* back again – in spite of your unsavoury relations with the late lamented Grand Admiral.'

'The Sultan is merciful indeed,' I said, bowing my head and placing my hand on my chest over my heart. 'But why here, in this place?'

'And not in the Convent? I have my reasons, as you'll see, all in good time.'

He refilled his wine cup, drank a little and settled back on the couch. The fire sputtered and crackled in the hearth. He peered at me for some while with that unblinking, dispassionate gaze of his, almost as if he'd never set eyes on me before. I looked back at him steadily.

Finally he said, 'I have a new mission for you. Something very big.'

I said nothing.

152

'It concerns Prince Jem. As you've probably gathered, he's still at large. I'm going to give you the job of finding him before he has the chance to start another war and plunge the whole damned Empire into chaos all over again.'

For an instant it seemed to me that the atmosphere in the room grew quieter and more chilly, and all at once I felt as if somebody was very lightly, very slowly running a cold finger down my spine. I don't know if my face betrayed anything. Fortunately, by then Kivami Bey had put down his cup and was fumbling clumsily behind him. He turned back again gripping a voluminous roll of heavy paper. He reached down to the floor and produced a piece of cloth. He tossed it to me.

'Here,' he said, 'wipe the top of the chest.'

While I did this he shifted himself crabwise a little further down the couch and lifted a lamp that had been sitting by the fire and placed it on the end of the chest.

'There's another lamp over there,' he said. 'Light it, would you, and put it on your side. I want to show you something.'

The roll of paper turned out to be a large chart, which we spread out over the lid of the chest, weighing down the curling edges with empty clay cups, our knives and some hastily dusted stones I found lying to one side of the hearth. An admirable and skilful piece of work the map was too. It depicted the entire Mediterranean and Black Sea from Tangier and the Pillars of Hercules to Kaffa and the Crimea, marking all the mountain ranges, deserts and plains of the hinterland, and every city, town and port of note, and showing in detail not only the territories already won by the Muslims but also those of the numerous Infidel kingdoms and states that lay yet unconquered to the north and west. Here on the left hand before us was Italy: the Kingdom of Naples; the lands of the Pope of Rome; the Marquisates of Saluzzo, Montferrat and Mantua; the Duchies of Modena, Ferrara, Milan and Savoy; the Republics of Venice, Florence, Siena and Genoa. Here the heathen kingdoms of Castile, Aragon, France, Bohemia,

Hungary and Poland; the petty principalities of Germany and the Archduchy of Austria. And here on the right hand the lands of the True Believers, and supreme and most glorious amongst them the vast and prosperous dominions, Asian and European, of the Ottoman Empire, the Sanctuary of Islam and Abode of Security – may God preserve it till the Day of Doom!

We sat there for some little time, scanning the chart by the light of the lamps, in silence, lost each in our own thoughts. But presently Kivami Bey broke the spell:

'I don't suppose I need to tell you', he began, 'that after being absent for so long myself, piecing together Jem's movements since he left these shores has not been easy. I've been working on it day and night ever since I was recalled several weeks ago. But I can't pretend I can tell you the full story even now. Anyway, for what it's worth, this is what I've got so far:

'It seems our friend quickly came to realize that if he remained in the Taurus, Bayezid would catch up with him sooner or later, especially when he learned that he had a hundred thousand ducats on his head. So he formed a plan to make a dash for the European provinces of the Empire in the hope of raising another army there. Nor was it such a bad idea. Apparently he'd been receiving messages from various commanders and governors in Greece and Albania – most of them old campaigners from Mehmed's day – pledging their support for his cause. We know this because some of their letters were intercepted.

'So Jem obviously reckoned that if he could reach Greece quickly enough he might make a surprise attack on Istanbul before Bayezid managed to get back there – perhaps even before he realized that Jem wasn't still hiding out somewhere in the Taurus. But Greece was a long way off and to risk going overland was, of course, out of the question. So he sent some of his men down to the coast in search of a vessel of some kind.

'Meanwhile, Bayezid's troops are getting closer and Jem realizes that he hasn't got much time. The Prince comes up with another idea. He sends a messenger to Pierre

154

d'Aubusson, the Grand Master of the Knights of Rhodes. Jem knows the man – he dealt with him personally some years before while conducting negotiations with the Knights on Sultan Mehmed's behalf. That was in the days when there was talk of a truce if the Knights would agree to pay tribute to the Porte – not that it came to anything.

'Anyway, what the Prince asked for was basically this, "Provide me with a suitable ship and a safe-conduct to pass through your island on my way to Greece and if I succeed in toppling Bayezid you will not find me ungrateful in the future." '

'My God!' I said. 'Sultan Mehmed must have been turning in his grave.'

'Possibly. Possibly not,' said Kivami Bey guardedly. 'Sometimes princes and kings must resort to stratagems of one kind or another, whatever their religious scruples, and you'd be surprised what alliances even Mehmed himself proposed in his time . . . Besides, at this stage at least, Jem was promising nothing very specific in return for any help these Infidels might give him.'

'I see . . .,' I said. 'Anyway, I interrupted you. What happened?'

'Pierre d'Aubusson agreed. After all, Jem might not be offering him eternal peace, but it must have been immediately clear to him that the longer Jem and Bayezid went on fighting each other, the better it would be for the Knights – you must remember they had still barely recovered from the last attack Mehmed made on their fortress before he died. So, Jem was granted his safe-conduct and the Grand Master sent off a galley to rescue the Prince from the mainland and bring him back to Rhodes before Bayezid managed to get hold of him . . .'

'That explains where that mysterious ship came from,' I said.

'So it would seem . . . but the peculiar thing is that once Jem got safely to Rhodes, after staying there as a guest of the Grand Master and the Knights for a month or so, he seems to have changed his mind about going to Greece and set sail instead in one of the Order's ships bound for

Europe – where eventually he landed . . . here, in this place called Nice.'

Kivami Bey leant over the map and stabbed his pudgy index finger at a small coastal town on the gulf between Italy and France, to the north of the islands of Sardinia and Corsica.

'Perhaps he was beginning to doubt his chances of raising sufficient support in the western provinces,' I said.

'That's possible,' said the Old Man. 'And we can be fairly sure that he wouldn't have felt too secure in Rhodes since by that time Jem had received word that Bayezid had learned of his flight to the island. He was probably afraid that Bayezid might have assassins sent after him, or that his brother might even try to attack the place in force.'

'What happened when he got to Nice?'

'Well,' said Kivami Bey, 'you can imagine that Jem hadn't been there long before the Infidels began to wake up to just how useful an enemy prince of such importance could be to *them*. And in no time just about every king and prince in Europe was working on some kind of scheme for offering him money, arms, ships and troops to assist him to overthrow his brother.'

'In exchange for certain assurances and promises, presumably?'

'Exactly so, my dear Barak. After all, bargaining with the Knights at a distance was one thing, but striking deals now that he was actually on Infidel soil and several hundred miles from home was quite another. Even that damnable scoundrel the Pope tried to get in on the act, with talk of forming some kind of league of all the states of Europe to launch a crusade against Bayezid, putting Jem at its head!' said Kivami Bey, scowling at that place on the map where Rome was marked with such intense ferocity that I would not have been surprised had the paper suddenly burst into flames.

'Surely,' I said, 'the Prince would never have agreed to such a diabolical plan – whatever he might have to gain from it?'

'A man could justify a great deal to himself and make

156

many concessions even to his enemies when the prize at stake is the richest and most powerful Empire on earth,' said Kivami Bey gravely, looking up at me with a sideways glance. 'Why, even the most sacred scruples can be cast aside when they come between a man and his ambition! And never forget that the Prince is utterly convinced, to the very bottom of his being, that it is Bayezid who is the usurper and that he, Jem, is the one who has been ill-used and cheated of what is his by right . . .'

'But if Jem is, as you say, prepared to enlist the assistance even of these unclean wretches and sworn enemies of our Race and our Religion – why has he waited so long before making war on us?'

'Another mystery!' said the Old Man. 'We know from our agents in Buda that Jem was all set to leave Nice and go to Hungary to join forces with King Matthias to invade Bosnia, Serbia and Greece. Then something happened, what exactly isn't clear, and the Prince sent word that he'd have to put off his journey to Buda for a month or two. And a few weeks after *that*, our man in Nice informed us that one night Jem had hurriedly left the city with his companions and an escort of Knights, supposedly to escape an outbreak of plague, but not a soul seemed to have any idea where they were going.'

'How long ago was that?' I said.

'Close on three years now,' said Kivami Bey.

'But surely our European agents must know something of where the Prince has been all this time?'

'Some seem to think he's in France, preparing to sail with the French fleet for the mainland of Greece. Others that he's somewhere in Hungary, biding his time until Bayezid leaves his back exposed by embarking on some kind of expedition into Asia. Kayitbay has lost no opportunity recently to launch raids across the border from Syria – perhaps even at Jem's instigation. But wherever Jem is now, there's one thing we can be sure of: sooner or later he'll be back and most likely with some kind of Christian army behind him. And as long as this uncertainty continues, the whole damned Empire is effectively paralysed

157

by the need to remain perpetually on the defensive; and, worst of all, the Infidels are gaining precious time to sink their differences and strengthen their hand against us. So now, my dear Barak, perhaps you understand why Jem must be found at all costs before some disaster occurs!'

'I see,' I said, 'but where to begin? Is there absolutely no clue as to where he could be now?'

Kivami Bey said, 'My hunch, from what I've found in the reports and what our more reliable people in Europe have been saying pretty consistently, is that he *has* been in France – and probably for most of the time he's been missing. What he's been doing there – God knows! But it seems from the most up-to-date dispatches from the Italian ports that he's back in Nice again. If he's not, you're going to have a devil of a job finding him, for sure.'

'All right,' I said, 'let's say he is back in Nice or somewhere nearby. And let's say I manage to find him there. What will I be able to do then? He's bound to be extremely well guarded – I'll be extremely lucky, I should think, to get within a hundred yards of him . . .'

'That's not your problem,' said Kivami Bey sharply. 'All you have to do is find out where he is, as much as you can about how his accommodation is arranged, how strong his guard is, how regularly it's changed, whether there's a garrison in the area. That sort of thing. After that, your job will be done, apart, of course, from getting the information safely back to us.'

'But what then?' I said.

'Perhaps I shouldn't tell you this,' said Kivami Bey, furrowing his brow and stroking his straggling beard, 'but if I don't, you won't know what to look for when you get there. The plan is to stage a raid from the sea. With any luck, since Jem is so far from home, it'll be the last thing the Knights are expecting, so we'll be able to take them by surprise. With a reasonable force of marines we shouldn't have too much difficulty in seizing the Prince, getting him aboard one of our vessels and out into the open sea before the Infidels even catch on to what is happening. And once Jem's back in Turkey he can be kept somewhere secure for as long as it takes to reconcile him to the fact that he will never be Sultan while Bayezid is still alive.'

'And if Jem resists arrest?'

The Old Man did not reply at first, but set about replenishing his cup with wine. He raised it to his lips but did not drink. Without looking at me, he said:

'As a last resort His Highness has agreed that his brother is to be killed if at any point it looks as if the Prince might fall into the hands of the Infidels again. However, if the operation is properly organized and carried out – which it will be if *I* have anything to do with it – that eventuality, God willing, should not arise.'

He drank from his cup now, emptying it to the dregs at a single draught. He put it down, leant forward over the map again, and pointed to the area showing the mountains of northern Greece and Albania.

'The passes to Avlona should be open in a month or so. You'll need that time in any case to be properly briefed for the mission and to familiarize yourself with the procedures and some new codes. From Avlona you'll have to find your own way across the straits to Italy because I don't want to involve the Navy. I've been looking for a guide to go with you – and I think I've found one. He's a Genoese merchant who's acted as a courier for us occasionally in the past. He's in Istanbul at the moment dealing with some business affairs in Galata, but I gather he was intending to go back to Italy this spring in any case. So, for a suitable consideration, there's no reason why he shouldn't take you with him. When you get to Genoa you can make contact with Messer Gaspar Grimaldo – an excellent man who's been working for us for years. I'll tell you more about him later.'

'And in the mean time?'

'You'd better stay here. You can send for anything you need from your house – Mano and the boy will look after you.'

'What about the Arsenal?' I said.

'The Palace will inform them that the Sultan has decided he wants you as an adviser on his Staff. When they hear that, they'll probably think you've been arrested again, which will be all to the good from our point of view – they'll be less inclined to ask too many questions.'

'Thank you, sir,' I said drily.

'As for me,' said the Old Man, 'I'll be going back to the Convent shortly. But don't on any account try to contact me there. You may as well know that close on a dozen agents have already been dispatched to find the Prince since he vanished from Nice – though not by *me*, needless to say – and every single one of them seems to have been killed or captured by the Knights long before they got anywhere near him. Perhaps they were incompetent or just extraordinarily unlucky. But perhaps not. In fact it's almost as if the Knights had been forewarned every time one of our people has been sent off.'

'Somebody in the Convent?' I said uneasily.

'I'm afraid it's possible. And that's why I've set up this place. Everything you need will be brought to you here by me personally – so the only people who'll know about *this* assignment will be you, myself and Bayezid. In the meanwhile, let's hope, if there is some nasty little cuckoo in the Convent who's been singing to the Infidels on the sly, that it won't be too long before I get my hands on him.'

Kivami Bey twisted his corpulent body awkwardly round and started to grope down the side of the couch, grunting from the exertion. At last he produced one silver-handled cane and then another. By this time he was quite red-faced from the effort and breathing heavily. He signalled me to pour him another drink. I did so, emptying the jug in the process. He took a couple of sips.

Still wheezing, looking puce and with wine trickling down his chin, he said in a strangled voice, 'Go tell Mano to bring my animal round to the front.'

I got up and moved towards the door. As I opened it he said to my back: 'And when you've done that, come back and help me get down those blasted stairs.'

I turned and bowed, and said, 'Yes, sir.'

Then I went out into the dark hall, quietly closing the door behind me, and made my way down the passage.

Book Two

Those That Are Sent Forth

I had sent word to Paolo da Garibaldo, the Genoese who was to act as my guide through the lands of the Unbelievers in my quest for Prince Jem, to join me at the time of the dawn prayer where the road from Galata meets the Edirne road beyond the Golden Horn.

When I reached this spot he was nowhere to be seen – but then, shielding my eyes against the early light, I caught sight of a mounted man approaching at a brisk trot from the east. Presently the Infidel was by my side, and after greeting one another, we turned our backs on the pale wintry sun and set off together westwards.

On the third day we came to Edirne and as we passed through that fine city I witnessed the great works recently begun there by Bayezid. For the Emperor – whose heart is as wide as the ocean – had ordered the building of a magnificent foundation for the care of the sick and the infirm. I saw many large buildings already taking shape that were to house a new hospital and asylum for the insane; beautiful lawns and gardens for those recovering from illness; a medical college for the training of physicians; a hostel for those studying at the college; a bakery for the staff and inmates; a kitchen that would provide meals for the poor of the city; cisterns for clean water; capacious storerooms for every kind of food; and innumerable other edifices and courtyards, all surmounted by a mosque and slender minarets as mighty and as high as any built by the Sultan's most illustrious forefathers – may God reward him in the next life for his pious works in the present one!

*　　*　　*

After travelling for twelve days more through Rumelia and Albania, Paolo and I were within less than a day's journey of Avlona. In the evening we came upon a burned and ruined church by the roadside and decided to spend the night there. Part of the roof was still standing, so we could shelter ourselves and even our horses from the downpour which had not let up since that morning. It was an eerie place, abandoned now to spiders, bats and owls.

I managed to find a few twigs of dry wood to light a fire. As the flames illuminated the walls around us we could see that these were covered with crumbling paintings. Some depicted the figures of the True Prophets, but others the Unsaints worshipped by the Christians in their folly. One wall was entirely devoted to scenes of naked men and women condemned for their sins to Eternal Damnation. Some were being tossed on pitchforks into raging furnaces; some crushed between giant millstones; some hurled, fettered hand and foot, to the bottom of pits full of venomous snakes and scorpions; some were being forced to drink from boiling fountains and others driven into an ocean of blazing pitch to be devoured by great scaly fish with monstrous gaping jaws. The light cast on the wall by our flickering fire seemed to make the devils dance about and the whole spectacle was made yet more ghastly by the glass-like sheen spread over the picture by the rainwater streaming down the wall from a hole in the roof above. God guide us along the Path of Righteousness, lest we be found wanting on the Final Day!

I averted my eyes and busied myself with cutting up some meat we had kept from the day before and skewering the pieces to cook them over the fire. As we ate we fell into discussion.

'Certainly,' said Paolo, 'if we find a vessel bound for Otranto or Brindisi, the crossing will be short – but it would be very unsafe for you after you land. In those parts every foreigner is now a Turkish spy.'

'But,' I said, 'should we be separated for whatever

164

reason, at least I am familiar with the countryside.'

'Perhaps so, Excellency,' said Paolo, 'but I passed through those regions myself on my way to Istanbul last autumn. The population is still half-mad with fear of another invasion. They talk of nothing else: "When the Turks were here they did this, when the Turks were here they did that." Why, if the roof of a man's house is in danger of falling in on his head, he hardly thinks it worth repairing: "What for, since those" – forgive me, Excellency – "filthy barbarians the Turks will be back tomorrow to kill us all and set the house ablaze?" Those southern scoundrels even think that we, the northerners, had something to do with the invasion. If you run into trouble there won't be much I can do to help you, believe me, Excellency.'

In the end his arguments began to convince me and I came round to thinking that it would be more prudent to land, if possible, further north. My sleep was disturbed by horrible visions of hellfire and I was finally awakened by the howling of wolves in the mountains above the church. Try as I might, I could not get to sleep again on account of the Genoese's abominable snoring (which had driven me to such distraction night after night that I had once or twice seriously considered cutting his throat, or strangling him, or smothering him with a blanket, just in order to get a proper night's sleep).

In the morning, before setting out on the last stage of our ride to Avlona, I revived the fire and, taking off my outer garments, burned them along with my turban. I put on the kind of black robes and fur-trimmed hat worn by Greek merchants – for this was the disguise I had decided to adopt, at least for the first stage of my journey into Europe. Although I could speak Italian well enough, my experiences in the south some years before had shown that, if challenged and questioned closely, it would be easier to pass as a Greek than as a native. At the same time I packed some small squares of gold brocade in different designs, together with some needles and thread, in a small leather bag.

165

'What are those?' asked Paolo.

'Samples,' I said.

By midday we were within sight of the minarets and roof-tops of Avlona. The sky was low and grey. A north-west wind was blowing in gusts off the Adriatic. The narrow streets and little squares of the port were glistening with water after a recent squall. The entire population seemed to have shuttered themselves in their houses to escape the icy rain. The waterfront was all but deserted. Only three dozen or so vessels were tied up or at anchor in the harbour. A sizeable swell was running in before the wind and murky green waves banged up against the quay, shaking the ground and sending up sheets of freezing spray.

We put up in a tavern on the quay. I hoped I wouldn't be recognized by any acquaintances from the past. Especially as, just before I had set out, Kivami Bey had warned me – one of our men in Venice had got word to him – that there was an informer working in the Governor of Avlona's secretariat, who apparently was providing the Most Serene Republic with regular bulletins about our shipping movements all along the coast.

Soon afterwards, Kivami Bey sent out an Investigator posing as a Treasury man on an audit of the Customs House accounts. The culprit was found within less than a week – usual story: debts, family troubles – but kept on so that we could continue supplying intelligence cooked up by the Convent.

However, the Venetians must have got wind of it. A few weeks later some fisherman brought the poor wretch's body up in their nets. An expert job, too – a single blow to the heart with a stiletto, so neat that at first it was thought that he had died by drowning.

I left Paolo sitting by the warm hearth at the tavern, drink-ing hot spiced wine with the Infidel proprietor, and set off in search of the Harbour Master. A few weak beams of sunlight were at last beginning to shine through the gaps in the ragged grey clouds that rolled overhead. I found the

166

Master's office at the end of the quay. I listened at the door for a moment but the noise of the waves and the wind made it difficult to hear if there was anybody inside. I gently pushed the heavy oak door and silently it swung open. The office's bluish-green windows suffused the whole room with an unearthly luminous glow and I felt that I was wading into some sea-cave half-flooded with water by the rising tide. As my eyes adjusted to the dimness of the light I could gradually make out the toilers in this enchanted cavern. In front of me some clerks were sitting cross-legged at their desks, making entries into ledgers; while a couple of others were standing making notes in front of lists chalked on to grey slate boards fixed in highly polished wooden frames to the wall at the far end of the room. The boards showed the names of ships – *Ay Varvara, Porpoise, Thunderbolt, Ay Nikolaos, Sirocco, Mary, Swan* – their ports of origin, arrival and departure dates, details of cargoes and harbour dues paid.

At the centre of the room, like a seal-king surveying his watery domain from the vantage-point of a solitary reef, a smooth-skinned man with a luxuriant moustache reclined in a fur-lined cloak against a bolster on a raised platform draped with quilts. Below him sat a boy – a servant or apprentice scribe perhaps – on a little cushion.

Hearing the door open and feeling the wind from outside swirling into the room, the man slowly turned his head and gazed at me with lugubrious, charcoal-black eyes. At the same time, the busy tapping of pens against inkpots and the scratching of nibs against paper came to an abrupt halt as the clerks looked up from their ledgers.

I was about to speak when the man raised his hand to signal that I should wait and, turning to the clerks, said softly:

'Please, gentlemen, do not let us distract you from your work.'

As the scribbling and shuffling of papers recommenced with renewed vigour, the man turned back to me and indicated by the faintest incline of his head and an

167

almost imperceptibly raised eyebrow that I should proceed.

Feeling rather ridiculous, and clutching my Infidel's hat in front of my chest, I said, 'May I be so bold as to assume, sir, that you are the Harbour Master?'

'You may,' he said.

'I am a cloth merchant,' I said, putting on a Greek accent, 'hoping – God willing – to make my way to Italy on business, with the help of a Genoese guide who has ridden with me from Istanbul.'

'You have a travel permit, of course,' he said.

'I do,' I said, giving it to the boy, who unfolded it and handed it to his master. After glancing at it without comment, he returned it to me again by way of the boy.

'There are several vessels', he said, 'waiting for a favourable wind but none, as far as we are aware, intends to cross the straits. There is very little direct traffic at the best of times, let alone so early in the year.'

'In that case,' I said, 'perhaps there might be a vessel going northwards in the direction of Venice?'

Turning towards the clerks manning the shipping lists at the end of the room, he said, 'Tell me, are Captain Shehu and his *Dolphin* ready to leave yet?'

'Indeed they are, Ahmet Bey,' said one of the clerks.

'Good,' said the Harbour Master and turning to me once again: 'Well, my friend, you may be in luck after all. Shehu will usually take passengers – though make sure he doesn't overcharge you – and he's no more likely to drown you than any of the other ruffians running the merchantmen in this part of the world. Go and speak to him today – if the wind turns he'll be off straight away. Take my boy with you. He'll help you find somebody to row you out to the *Dolphin*.'

The boy jumped to his feet and made for the door. I hastily took my leave of the Harbour Master (who kindly wished me a fair wind and a safe journey, in case we did not meet again before I departed Avlona), and then hurried after the boy out into the rain, which was falling now more heavily than ever, as the blustering wind rattled the doors and shutters of the houses along the waterfront and darkness began to envelop the town.

At first light the Genoese and I embarked in Captain Shehu's caique. The wind had veered round during the night and, fully laden though the *Dolphin* was, blown along by the southerly gale she glided swiftly through the waves. Even when, leaving behind the protection of the gulf, she hit a heavier sea – still she forged ahead, ploughing a great furrow through the rolling ocean swell. But the mighty billows proved too much for Paolo and soon the unfortunate fellow was sick over the side.

I was sitting aft by the rudder with Captain Shehu, who said, 'What is wrong with the Frankish Infidel, surely he has been on a boat before now?'

'I don't think that's the problem,' I said. 'He drank a great deal of wine yesterday and now he's paying the price.'

Shehu laughed and said, 'Now I know the reason. That Yorgi's wine is pig's piss – why else would he waste good money throwing spices into it?'

And the Genoese gasped for air; then, groaning 'Misericordia!' and calling for intercession from the Mother of Jesus, began to be sick all over again.

An even and unfailing wind blew night and day for the whole voyage, and after ten days at sea we made landfall in Italy at Ancona. This place is a small independent principality that lies within the territories of the Pope of Rome, and since a great amount of traffic passes through the city the Anconans seem to take little interest in those who embark and disembark at their port. Thus my fears that I might be questioned or have to give some account of myself to the authorities proved groundless.

In next to no time we had obtained horses and provisions so that we could continue our journey. The day was hot, and after riding northwards for a couple of hours, we stopped to rest and take some food under the shade of some spreading pine trees. On a sandy hillock overlooking a deserted beach that stretched away in either direction as

169

far as the eye could see, we sat eating some fresh cheese and bread we had bought in Ancona, and for a little while watched the waves breaking on the shore without saying anything. Then I spoke:

'I am surprised that you have asked me so little about the purpose of my mission.'

'Sometimes, Excellency,' he said, 'it is better not to know too much.'

'That is certainly true,' I said, 'yet I have a feeling that you know more than you pretend to.'

'Your masters asked me if I could take you into Europe. I said I could. As you know, I have rendered some small services to them before . . .'

'And why, do you think, should my masters wish to send me to Europe?'

He gave a hollow laugh and said, 'Forgive me, Excellency, but do you Turks take all us Christians for fools? Why, the Sultan wishes to find his brother Jem. The one who has – how shall I put it? – disappeared. That is obvious. If it were another kind of business your Emperor would not send a man such as yourself.'

'Good,' I said, getting up. 'Now we can stop playing games. First we must go to Nice.'

'But why Nice?' he said, also getting to his feet. 'They say the Knights of Rhodes took him away from there and into France three years ago or more.'

'Perhaps they are lying,' I said, 'perhaps they are hiding him somewhere nearby. After leaving Rhodes, it was at Nice he first landed. That at least is certain. Everything else is mere conjecture. With so few facts at my disposal, what else can I do but begin my search there?'

'Perhaps so, Excellency,' said Paolo, 'but still, a long time has passed since he was last seen there. And although your masters do not believe it, it may even be that the Prince is no longer alive.'

'That', I said, untying my horse and mounting it, 'is exactly what I intend to find out.'

'Very well, then, Excellency. I shall take you first to Nice,' he said, throwing his bag over his saddle. 'I only hope that you will not be disappointed if we find nothing there.'

'Put your mind at rest,' I said. 'Whatever we find there, I will not blame you for it.'

'May your Excellency not live to regret your words!'

I kicked the sides of my horse and, turning away from the shore, trotted out of the pine wood and back on the road to Rimini.

When a man is at sea he understands instinctively that his Destiny is not in his own hands but is decided by the winds and tides and stars; yet when he comes ashore, his perception becomes clouded, he forgets what he has learned and he falls prey to the illusion that he is the master of his Fate. If I had but known what awaited me . . . yet this is foolish talk! Only God knows what the future holds in store.

At first following the coast road – which runs dead straight, mile after mile, parallel with the seashore – at Rimini we turned inland and crossed the saltpans of Cesena, which are vaster even than those at the mouth of the Merich in Thrace and blind the eyes with their snowy brilliance. From here, riding through flatlands, we passed through Forli and Imola and on to Bologna. This bell-tormented city is a veritable forest of soaring towers, which, when viewed from a distance across the rolling plain, look like the masts of a mighty battlefleet becalmed on a grass-green sea. From here we passed on to Modena and Reggio, leaving the lands of the Pope and entering the territories of the Duke of Milan, on to Piacenza, Sarmato, Castel San Giovanni and Stradella. At Voghera we turned southwards to Tortona and thence to Serra Valle, where the Duke's domains border with those of the Republic of Genoa. And then, mercilessly whipping on our stumbling horses, we ascended a great mountain wall, and coming through a high pass, we at last looked down upon the sweeping Bay of Genoa and the deep-blue Ligurian Sea.

The day was fast declining as we descended the rocky road towards Genoa and, bypassing the city itself, came

171

down to the seashore a little to the west at Voltri. Here we spent the night. At dawn the following day we boarded a ship bound for Noli, another town on the coast of the Republic, which Paolo told me was his birthplace.

The waterfront tavern where we lodged at Voltri was a pit of a place and, what with Paolo's trumpeting snores, fleas hopping around all over the bed and rats scuttling around amongst the roof beams over our heads, I slept very poorly. So as soon as the vessel had put to sea, I found a space on deck at the bow of the ship, folded my cloak for a pillow and lay down to get some rest.

The next thing I knew, Paolo was shaking my shoulder and saying, 'Wake up, my friend, we're about to dock at Noli.'

I struggled into consciousness and saw that we were approaching a little port on a narrow plain at the foot of some mountains. I drank some water brought to me by Paolo. Still feeling very groggy, I filled a bucket with sea water and splashed it over my face and neck to try to clear my head. My limbs were so stiff that I could hardly move them. Looking westwards at the sinking orb of the sun, I said, 'How far is it from here to Nice?'

'The road is not too good,' said Paolo, 'but just the same, one and a half, two days at most. But now that you are here, first you must come to my house and rest.'

'I will rest easier when I've made it to Nice. There are still some hours of daylight left, we could make a start at least.'

'But look how tired you are!' he said. 'We will make much better time if we are feeling fresh.'

My bones ached, my clothes were filthy and although I had slept for several hours I still felt very drowsy. I barely had the strength to argue.

'Very well,' I said. 'But we must start again early tomorrow.'

'Just as you wish,' he said, 'just as you wish . . .'

Paolo's house was near the top of a steep hill in a run-down, half-derelict part of the town. Many of the houses were roofless and empty with gaping doorways and windows, a refuge for bats and birds. Some had wide cracks in their walls and the whole district had the appearance of a place the people had fled to escape the devastation of an earthquake or a plague.

I cannot forgive myself for what happened next. When we reached the house that Paolo said was his, I was surprised that the door seemed to be unlocked. But I didn't think quickly enough. When I crossed the threshold, the door slammed shut behind me and three Infidels fell upon me. I had no time to reach for my dagger and in any case they were armed with axes and swords. Before binding my hands behind my back with cord, Paolo wrenched my gold ring from my finger. As one of his accomplices held a knife to my throat, the Genoese tore open my shirt, and finding my leather money-belt, cut it free with his knife. He laughed like a lunatic as he emptied onto a wooden table at the centre of the room the ninety gold ducats given to me in Istanbul to meet the expenses of the mission. Picking up handfuls of the coins, he thrust them under my nose shouting, 'Take a last look, Turkish cur, at your precious Sultan's gold!'

I struggled violently, throwing the man with the knife at my throat across the room. Barging aside the other men pinioning my arms and shoulders, I rushed at Paolo, trying to butt him in the face with my head. But he eluded my lunge and the others got hold of me again and forced me up against the wall. Paolo started slapping me repeatedly about the face, cutting a deep gash above my right eye with the heavy ring he was wearing.

'God damn and blast you, you devil,' I said, 'release me or you'll pay for this.'

'Release you?' he said. 'Don't you know, you stupid barbarian, that the brother of the Lord of this place, Fra Fabrizio, is one of the Commanders of the Knights of Rhodes? He'll reward me well enough for your capture, heathen dog!'

'Capture? You stinking pile of ordure,' I said. 'By God, I swear you will not live to enjoy the spoils of your treachery, you cockroach.'

'Take him outside,' said Paolo to the others.

I was hustled across the room through a kitchen into a small courtyard at the back of the house. It had high walls, but I noticed that in one place the stones had collapsed leaving a jagged hole through which I could see a path leading into a dense wood. I made a run for it, but was brought down by one of the Infidels, who tripped me with his foot. Half-blinded with blood and struggling to free my hands, I rolled over and over on the ground, trying to escape the blows and kicks that rained down upon my head and body. I tried to get nearer the hole in the wall, but was driven back by Paolo, who picked up a fallen branch and hit me with it over and over again until it snapped in two. My ears were buzzing from the blows and a noise like a jangling bell began to fill my head.

Suddenly, there was a terrible high-pitched shrieking and a banging of wood and a clashing of metal. Blinking the blood from my eyes, I saw an army of screaming women in black robes pouring through the breach in the wall. Some were brandishing spades and various garden implements, some kitchen utensils, and others sticks and brooms. They wasted no time in falling on the accursed Infidel and his confederates, one of whom was almost immediately knocked to the ground under a hail of blows.

'Wait! Wait! Stop it, you demented hags,' shouted Paolo as he was driven back towards the house. 'This man is a Saracen, a spy from Turkey . . .'

'Do not listen to him!' I roared from the ground as two of the good sisters struggled to untie my hands. 'I am a Greek merchant and these men are trying to rob and kill me.'

'I tell you,' screeched Paolo, 'he's an enemy, an impostor, a spy!'

'Bear false witness as well, would you?' said one of the women, who appeared to be the leader. 'Impious fiend!' she said, catching Paolo a terrible blow on the side of the head that sent him staggering backwards against the wall of the house.

'You're mad, mad, mad . . .,' he groaned, slipping on to his knees, clutching his head.

174

The Infidel's accomplices were now nowhere to be seen. Helping me to my feet, the nuns speedily carried me away up the path through the trees to the safety of their convent, slamming shut the massive doors when all the sisters were once again inside. They took me into a big white room with long tables and benches. They brought me warm water and clean towels, and sitting me down on a high-backed chair at one end of the room, they gently began to wash my wounds. I felt dizzy and sick, and must have passed out for a while. I came round to find – God forgive me! – that they were forcing fiery liquid into my mouth from a flask.

'It's aqua vitae,' they said. 'Drink it, it will do you good.'

Coughing, I pushed the flask away. As I did so, I shifted slightly in the chair. My clothes were so badly torn that in places they hardly covered my naked flesh. Some of the younger sisters started giggling. At first I couldn't understand what they were laughing at, but when I looked down I discovered to my horror that my genitals were half exposed to view. I tried to cover myself with my hands, but this only made the girls laugh even more than ever. The Mother of the House reprimanded them sternly and finally ordered some of them from the room.

After they had finished dressing my wounds and rubbing soothing balms on my bruises, they brought me some clothes and turned their backs while I put them on.

'They are not new but they are clean,' said the Mother Superior (as I learned she was called, when the other sisters addressed her). 'We beg them from the great houses in order to give them to the poor.'

'I am very grateful', I said, 'for everything you have done for me.'

'Think nothing of it,' she said. 'Are we not all Christians? And has not Our Merciful Saviour taught us that we should love others as ourselves?'

'Indeed,' I said, 'but you also put yourselves in great danger for my sake and showed great courage.'

'Those that put their whole Faith in Our Lord need have nothing to fear,' said the Mother Superior, and murmur-

175

ing 'Amen', the other sisters made the sign of the cross. 'We are only thankful that He sent Sister Anna up our tallest ladder to knock down a cobweb in the dormitory. Otherwise she would not have seen what those wicked men were doing to you.'

'When I heard the bell ringing,' I said, 'I thought it was in my head.'

She smiled and said, 'You must rest now. Sister Francesca has gone to look for Father Fresia, our priest. I'm sure you will be able to stay with him until you've properly recovered. You are lucky to have no broken bones.'

Darkness had fallen. I knew that it was only a matter of time before Paolo alerted the Knights and they came in search of me. I didn't even know how long I had been unconscious.

'I have a friend,' I said, 'another Greek. I must try to find him at the harbour. He will be wondering where I have got to.'

'But', said the Mother Superior, 'you are too badly hurt to go anywhere.'

'I must,' I said, getting up and limping to the door and out into the courtyard in front of their church.

As I left, one of the young nuns brought me my leather bag, saying that she had found it lying on the road outside Paolo's house.

'Is this all you had?' she asked.

'Yes,' I said, taking it. 'It is all I had.' And thanking them all a thousand times over, I took my leave of them.

Later on, I discovered that they had secretly put into my bag some silver coins wrapped in a piece of paper on which they had written the words 'Go with Christ Our Lord'. May God bestow His Bounty on these most excellent of women!

Wincing with pain, I hobbled down towards the port. I was thankful for my new clothes, which, being Italian in style, would help me to pass unnoticed as I moved through the streets. But I knew that, however well disguised, I would not live long if I was not away from Noli within a few hours. My mind was in turmoil: one minute I wanted to scour the town in search of Paolo da Garibaldo to repay him with interest, and the next I thought only of doing my duty and trying to escape from Noli at all costs so that I might get word to Istanbul of his betrayal. For if I should not live to do so, he would be at liberty to return to the city and, offering some plausible tale for my disappearance, lead another of our agents to his death. Stupid barbarian!

My thinking still befuddled by the beating I had received, and still torn between opposing desires for revenge and escape, I came into a square that opened on to the waterfront.

The quay was lined with freighters, merchantmen and coasters. If I could slip aboard one of them unseen, I had a reasonable chance of stowing away and remaining concealed until the ship reached another port. But there were still far too many people about for my liking. I pulled down my cap and, trying not to limp too obviously, started towards the harbour. I kept to the shadows and picked my way along a colonnade of arches that ran under a large building alongside the quay.

Reaching the corner of the building, I was about to step out into the open when I caught sight of a group of men carrying lanterns and advancing along the dock in my direction. As they drew nearer I could see that some of them had their swords drawn and others were carrying sticks and clubs. They called for the captain of the vessel tied up nearest me and some of them went aboard, leaving the others standing guard on the quay. I turned round and hurried back the way I had come. About halfway along I came to an opening and, hearing voices behind me, dived into it. It turned out to be a narrow passageway, very dark and stinking of rotten fish and vegetables, and worse. As I stumbled along it, I heard loud shouts and singing coming from ahead. I rounded a corner and saw a dim lamp hanging over a doorway and realized it must be a tavern. Just as I was about to pass under the lamp, I saw a hooded figure coming towards me. I pressed myself against the wall. At the very instant the figure passed before the tavern, the door was flung open and the shrouded spectre was momentarily illuminated by a bright shaft of light from inside. Raucous drunken voices echoed against the walls of the passageway and a man staggered out. Then arms reached out and grabbed him from behind and pulled him back inside again. The door was slammed shut. But in that moment I saw the spectre's face.

Startled by the burst of light and sound, the man stopped in his tracks and stepped back, blinking. He remained still for a little, then proceeded on his way again, wheezing and shuffling forward in small tottering steps. As he passed close to me, I reached out and seized his arm. I thought he was about to cry out, so I pressed my open palm hard against his mouth. His eyes stared at me in terror and he tried feebly to pull himself away.

'Messer Marco, Messer Marco . . .,' I said in a hoarse whisper.

Dragging him with me, my hand still clamped over his mouth, I edged along the wall so that I was standing under the lamp outside the tavern. A faint beam fell on me, bathing my face in its weak yellow light. At first the old man seemed more frightened than ever; then suddenly his eyes opened even wider in wonder and began to fill with tears.

I took my hand from his mouth and he said, 'No, no, it can't be . . . my dear boy, my dear boy . . .'

The full horror of the degradation of this proud merchant prince, who had once had mansions and warehouses in Genoa, Galata and Kaffa, and could count among his friends not only commanders, pashas and vizirs but Sultan Mehmed himself, became evident when we reached the hovel he now inhabited.

It was on a beach by the harbour wall and consisted of a small ramshackle shelter of the kind built by poor fishermen the world over. It formed part of a row of similar shacks from which you could hear – over the sound of the breaking waves – children crying and men and women

178

murmuring in low voices. I looked down the beach towards the sea and could just make out in the starlight the ghostly shapes of fishing boats that had been dragged out of the water onto the sand.

Gasping for air after the exertion of his walk, Marco Spinola held open the ragged sacking door of his hut and motioned me to go inside. A small smoking lamp cast an uncertain and flickering light on the hut's rough wooden walls. I could see that apart from a low bed and a battered wooden box it was quite bare. Spinola followed me in and lowered himself painfully to the ground and with a sigh leant back against the box. When he pulled back his hood I could not prevent myself from giving a start. The once handsome face was haggard, ancient. The eyes were sunken in their sockets, the skin a dull grey. Where once there had been thick black hair, only a few sparse wisps of white remained. The edges of his mouth were flecked with spittle and most of his teeth were gone. One eye seemed covered with a milky film and stared sightlessly into space. Turning towards me, he gave a sad furtive smile, as if to say, 'Yes, I'm afraid this is all that's left.'

Then he said: 'And your father?'

'He's dead – God rest his soul,' I said.

He nodded sadly.

At last I managed to say in a whisper, 'Why?'

He stretched a bony hand towards me and I grasped it in both of mine. It was icy, the hand of a corpse.

'But where are Donna Maria and the children?' I said.

'Dead,' he said, 'all dead.'

'I can't understand it,' I said. 'My father heard that you got back safely to Italy, after the Fall of Kaffa.'

'We did, we did,' he said, 'but there was an epidemic . . . took them all away.'

'What of your wealth?'

'All lost, all lost,' he gasped. 'Mixed up in some bad business. Bankrupt. Creditors.' He burst into a fit of coughing and jerked his hand away to cover his mouth. When the fit abated, he pulled a cloth from his sleeve and wiped his face with it. I could see it was smeared with blood.

179

When he had recovered sufficiently I said, 'I must get away from this place. There are men looking for me. If they find me they will kill me. If I can only get to Genoa, a merchant there called Frenk Iskender and his partners will help me. But what am I saying? You must know these men too. They came to Istanbul to sell cloth. My father used to do business with them and they've known me since I was a small child.'

'I will see to it in the morning,' said Spinola. 'No one will come looking for you here. These people are my friends. In the morning.'

His head lolled forwards. Worn out by his exertions and the surprise of seeing me, he had fallen asleep.

I lifted him on to the bed, covered him with a coarse blanket and, finding another one, wrapped myself in it and lay down on the floor beside him. A few moments later I too was asleep.

I sat up suddenly. The bed next to me was empty. Sunlight was streaming through the cracks between the boards of the hut and I heard low voices outside. There was a rusty knife lying on the box. I picked it up, freed myself from the folds of my blanket and crouched by the doorway. The sacking parted. I was about to strike but saw that it was only poor old Spinola.

'Come quickly,' he said.

I got up and, grabbing my leather bag, went outside. A young man with tousled black hair and a tanned face stood before me.

'This is Giorgio,' said Spinola. 'He will row you out into the bay in his boat. A coaster is leaving port in an hour or two, bound for Genoa. The captain is my friend. He will take you on board at sea.' He was panting now from the effort of saying so much, so fast. But his face was alive with excitement. For a moment I could see the man I had known shining through his ravaged features. I embraced him tenderly and knelt to kiss his hand.

'No, no,' he said, 'go now, go quickly.' I got up. 'God bless you, my boy, God bless you,' he called out after me

180

as I turned and half-hopped, half-ran down the beach after Giorgio.

His boat was already half in the water. Giving it a final shove, we leapt aboard together as it bounced about among the breaking waves. Clambering to the middle of the boat, the fisherman unshipped the oars and, each taking one, we pulled her rapidly away from the shore.

Less than an hour later willing hands were reached down to hoist me aboard the coaster and we were on our way, leaving Giorgio standing in his little boat, smiling and waving as it rocked wildly from side to side in our wake. At sunset on the third day I found myself standing on the quay at Genoa – alone, all but destitute, in clothes that were not my own and exactly forty-five days out from Istanbul.

Alms

The money given me by the good sisters paid for a night's lodging in a moderately decent tavern on the waterfront. I told the keeper to wake me early and as the first rays of the rising sun were scattering their gold light across the waters of the bay I set off in the hope of finding Alessandro Giustiniani, whom we in the East call Frenk Iskender, that is 'Alexander the Frank'.

Looking out to sea, I could just discern the white sails of a small flotilla of ships disappearing over the shimmering dawn horizon, and it occurred to me that this ever restless man of business, this illustrious director of the Banco di San Giorgio – the most venerable, most powerful, most prestigious Genoese trading corporation of them all – might have set sail already to inspect his precious mastic groves on the isle of Chios, or be bound for Alexandretta to take on board bales of raw cotton, or Alexandria to load spices, or he might yet be (Heaven forbid!) on his way to Istanbul itself with a cargo of woollen cloth – for in those days were not even the uniforms of the Janissaries, most zealous *Gazis* of the all-conquering House of Osman, cut from the cloth brought from Italy by Frenk Iskender's ships at the express command of the Sublime Porte? Offering up prayers that gout, or a fever, a broken bone, or some such other non-fatal complaint had kept him at home this season, I turned my back on the sea and hurried inland as fast as my still-bruised and damaged leg would allow me.

The buildings of Genoa are exceptionally tall – many of them are five, six, seven, even eight storeys high – and densely packed together; the crowded streets behind the harbour narrow, dark and dank as subterranean passages. My cut face and shambling gait drew suspicious glances, and as I was reluctant to attract attention to myself any further by enquiring about the way, it was only after many false turns that I found myself emerging at last into the Piazza dei Banchi where, I had been assured by the tavern keeper, the city's merchant bankers and traders congregated each morning as soon as the sun was up to consult with one another before dispersing to their various counting-houses, offices and banks to pursue in earnest their own particular affairs.

Never, not even in Kaffa, had I seen such an immense gathering of men of commerce. Black-robed, with sharp noses and sallow faces, they filled the square like a seething mass of plump, glossy, overfed crows as they flocked together in the eerie blue light of the dawn. I pushed my way with difficulty into their midst, my head reeling from the bedlam of sound produced by their deafening chatter, and searched high and low, in vain, for the familiar features of Frenk Iskender.

I was on the verge of giving up in despair when I felt a sharp tap on the shoulder and a voice said over the uproar, 'Are you looking for somebody in particular?'

'Yes,' I said, turning round in the crush and seeing before me a supercilious, smooth-chinned youth with a large ledger tucked under his arm, 'but I fear that he may not be here today. His name is Alessandro. He has estates in the Grand Turk's domains in Chios. His family name is Giustiniani.'

'Why, that is him over there,' said the boy, standing on tiptoe to match my height, and pointing out, some way off, two men walking slowly with bowed heads under the arches of an imposing building at the top of the square.

I made my way through the jostling crowd towards them. I was practically beside them when they turned sedately round to retrace their steps. One of them looked up and I found myself staring into the face of Frenk Iskender. For a moment I was seized with fear that he

183

would cry out in surprise to be confronted so unexpectedly by the son of his old friend. But I need not have worried. Not a flicker of recognition registered in his eyes.

'Messer Alessandro,' I said.

'Ye-es?' he said with haughty disdain, looking me up and down with an expression of distaste.

'Sir, I wonder if you could spare me a few moments of your time?'

'I'm afraid I am rather busy at the moment, as you can see. Perhaps a little later,' he said, making as if to move off.

'It is rather urgent. It concerns a mutual friend,' I said, reaching out and taking hold of his sleeve.

A look of alarm came over his face. Struggling to free his arm from my unyielding grip, he said, 'And who might that be?'

'I would rather we spoke of him in private.'

Frenk Iskender sighed deeply and, turning to his friend, said, 'I really can't imagine for the life of me what this fellow wants. But would you excuse me just for a moment?'

When his friend had politely bowed and stood aside he turned to me impatiently.

'Now, what is all this, my man? What's all this nonsense about a mutual friend? To be perfectly blunt with you, I should be very surprised if we had any friends in common.'

'I am Barak,' I murmured quietly. 'Abdullah Reis's son.'

'My God,' he said, looking at me thunderstruck. 'But what in Heaven's name are you doing here? And all dressed up like this? If you're caught in disguise you'll be arrested.'

'I know,' I said.

Glancing around us apprehensively, Iskender said under his breath, 'We can't talk here, you'd better come with me.'

And taking me by the arm, he pushed me ahead of him through the throng. We did not speak again until we had left the square and were standing in a deserted backstreet.

'Are you alone?' he said, glancing anxiously up and

184

down the street as though expecting a detachment of Janissaries to appear from round the corner.

'Quite alone,' I said. 'I'm here on official business and I need your help.'

'But what can I do?' he said, a look of panic filling his grey eyes.

'For a start, I need somewhere safe to hide. I've run into trouble and before long some gentlemen will probably come looking for me.'

'My house is just near here, but there are far too many people at home. They'll start asking awkward questions. I have a summer place' – he waved his arm vaguely in the direction of the citadel – 'which we don't usually go to until July. I'd better take you there myself. Can you manage it with that leg? It's quite a climb, you know.'

The house stood half-concealed from view amid trees and hanging gardens on a lofty eminence high above the city. Frenk Iskender had sent a boy to run on ahead and warn the servants that we were coming. When we arrived – after a painful and laborious ascent – I was immediately shown upstairs to a spacious room furnished with a wide bed, a chest, a table and a couple of chairs. Outside in the quiet gardens I could hear the pleasant gurgle of fountains and the spry twitterings of birds. I threw open the shutters to admit the morning light and stood for some minutes admiring the stupendous view over the harbour and the deep-blue sweep of the Gulf of Genoa, until a servant appeared bearing a bowl of hot water and some soap and placed them on the chest. When she had left I studied my face in a mirror hanging on the wall. I was still far from a pretty sight – perhaps one day I might have the chance to renew my acquaintance with the Infidel Paolo da Garibaldo and repay the compliment.

I had just about finished cleaning myself up when there was a knock at the door. It was Frenk Iskender, carrying in his arms a bundle of clothes.

'Take these,' he said, laying them on the bed. 'Where on earth did you get those other ones?'

'God provides,' I said.

'And your face? An accident?'

'No,' I said bitterly, touching the swollen cut above my eye and seeing from my fingers that it had started to bleed again. 'I was on my way to Nice when the scoundrel given to me as a guide turned on me and with the help of some of his friends stole my money and damn near killed me. What's more, he said that the lord of the castle there had a brother who is a Commander of the Knights of Rhodes, and that he was going to hand me over to him – but perhaps that was just supposed to scare me.'

'Where did all this happen?'

'In Noli.'

Iskender frowned. 'In that case, I'm afraid he was telling the truth. The Marquis of Finale's brother Fabrizio is a Knight. If he'd got hold of you I shudder to think what he might have done to you.'

At this point two servants arrived bringing baskets of fruit, a dish of cold meats, bread and red wine, and laid them on the table in front of the window. Frenk Iskender courteously invited me to join him, poured two glasses of wine and handed one of them to me. I hesitated. Then, seeing that one of the servants was surreptitiously observing me out of the corner of her eye, I emptied the glass at a single gulp.

'So what do you intend to do now?' said Iskender when the women had withdrawn. 'Perhaps you would like to tell me a little more about this "official business" you mentioned in the piazza? I am, as you know, at the Sultan's service in all matters.'

'Forgive me, Messer Alessandro, but I am not at liberty to go into details.'

Iskender held up his hands. 'Just as you wish, my dear boy, just as you wish. Please forgive me for having asked. I am, after all, a man of the world! And I am aware that there are some things better left undiscussed, even with those we trust.'

'I am glad that you understand. But there is something you can do for me. I need to make contact with someone.'

'But of course.'

'Do you know a man called Gaspar Grimaldo?'

'Who doesn't? In fact, he was there in the piazza this morning. I'm surprised that you didn't see him too.'

'How could I? I have never set eyes on him before. I was merely given his name as someone who might be able to assist me.'

'I can't think how. Unlike ourselves at the Banco, all his interests lie here in the West. And as far as I'm aware, he has no dealings with your masters at the Porte. But if you say so . . . Do you intend to go and see him?'

'No, it would be safer to tell him to come here.'

'Just as you wish,' said Iskender with a shrug. 'Though perhaps you have a point. You are looking a bit conspicuous at the moment. But who shall I say wants to see him?'

'Oh, just tell him a friend of his friends in Istanbul.'

'Very well. But I ought to warn you if Messer Gaspar is not given a name of some sort, he may refuse to come. He's a prominent citizen here, you know.'

I smiled and said, 'He'll come.'

That afternoon I was sitting on a secluded vine-shaded terrace, enjoying the soft spring breeze and observing with interest the animated comings and goings of sailing vessels and galleys in the lively port below me, when I heard footsteps on the steep flight of stone stairs that led up to the house. A few seconds later a distinguished aristocratic-looking man of about forty appeared on the terrace and marched towards me with his hand extended to shake mine, saying, 'Ah, there you are . . . Gaspar, Gaspar Grimaldo.'

'Barak,' I said.

He removed his hat, sat down on the cool marble bench beside me and started mopping his damp brow with a large handkerchief.

'Your people have been taking their time, haven't they?' he said. 'It's over a year since Stalianos came to talk to me about this business – about our friend the Hajji, I mean. That *is* why you are here, isn't it?'

'Yes. I've come about Jem, all right.'

187

When he made no reply, I turned to him and found that he was peering at my face with a look of intense curiosity.

'What's the matter?' I said.

'Get mixed up in a brawl or something?'

'In a manner of speaking.' I told him about Paolo and his enterprising scheme of selling me off to Fra Fabrizio.

Gaspar tut-tutted sympathetically and said, 'Looks painful. Who d'you say this ruffian was?'

'Paolo da Garibaldo.'

'Never heard of him. Your people should be more careful. The world's full of rogues and scoundrels these days. Can't be too careful. Anyway, did you get my last reports?'

'We did. But we've heard from other sources that Jem has returned to Nice. Kivami Bey's worried that he might finally be on his way to join the King of Hungary.'

Gaspar shook his head. 'Don't know who could have told you that. If our friend had returned to Nice I would have heard about it soon enough – you know, he even stayed in a house I have there when he first came from Rhodes.'

'I know.'

'It was a pity that something was not done then. It would have been so easy.'

'The Sultan wants Jem back in Turkey alive. Stalianos told you that, didn't he?'

'Yes. He told me. But I still can't understand why. Jem's risen against him twice already. He believes he's the rightful heir to the throne. And he'll do it again. If I were Bayezid I'd want him dead.'

'It is not for us to judge these things. Besides, the Emperor's nature is a forgiving one and he does not wish to stain his hands with a brother's blood. He believes that Jem can be persuaded to see the error of his ways.'

Gaspar gave a sceptical shrug.

'So you are sure that Jem is not in Nice?'

'I am certain of it,' said Gaspar. 'My people there would have told me right away if there'd been even a rumour. No. Since going over the Alps with the Knights, I am sure he has not returned.'

'But is he still in Savoy? Or has he gone into France?'

'He was in Savoy for a little while. As you know, I am often at the Duke of Savoy's court, so I can keep an eye on things. But he crossed into France some time ago.'

'So where is he now?'

'Ah! That is something many people would like to know. There are all kinds of stories circulating – half of them put out by the Knights themselves. It's become quite impossible to tell which ones to believe.'

'Is he with the French king?'

'Apparently not. And the extraordinary thing is that not even Charles himself knows in what part of his kingdom Jem is staying.'

'And the King allows the Knights to behave like this in his own kingdom?'

Gaspar gave a hollow laugh and, shaking his head, said, 'The Knights are a law unto themselves. They go where they like, when they like. Even a king has to think twice before incurring their wrath. After all, Sultan Mehmed himself couldn't dislodge them from Rhodes – even from his very doorstep! Charles has much less power to curb them.'

'If Mehmed Khan had lived but another year they would have learned what it was to defy him, but their time will come soon enough.'

'Perhaps so. But I doubt if you or I will live to see it.'

'Do not be so sure. They feel strong against us now because they have Jem with them – and they know we won't attack Rhodes as long as that's the case. But one day they'll pay the price for daring to interfere in our affairs.'

'Well,' said Gaspar, his eyes bright with a mocking smile, 'if you ever do bring them to heel, as you say, there'll even be some Franks who will thank you for it.'

I looked out to sea for some time and then said, 'I will have to go into France and find out for myself what Jem is doing.'

'It will not be easy.'

'Then you will have to come with me.'

'That would be most inadvisable. I am too well known

189

there. And the Knights who are guarding Jem would recognize me instantly.'

'Then I will go alone.'

'How can you? How will you find your way? Do you speak French?'

'No.'

'Then you wouldn't survive a week. The last man your people sent didn't even manage to get into France from Savoy.'

'Ismail?' I said.

'If that was his name. The Knights got hold of him in Turin.'

'Is he dead?'

'As far as I know, yes.'

This was sombre news indeed. For it had been hoped that after the death of our other agents it might just be possible that Ismail was still in the field but unable to get messages back to Istanbul.

'We have one or two other local contacts in Nice,' I said. 'If I go there they may be able to help me get into France.'

'To go on to Nice after what happened to you in Noli would be suicide. Now that Fra Fabrizio knows about you, they'll be on the lookout all along the coast. If you insist on trying to go on, you'll have to go inland. At least they won't be expecting you to enter that way.'

'But how?'

'First to Turin. Then to Susa, and from Susa over the pass at Mont Cenis. But you'll need papers. Your unfortunate colleague, what was his name?'

'Ismail.'

'Ah, yes. Ismail. He didn't have papers of any kind. Very foolish of him. He was almost bound to get caught sooner or later. Though he'd have fared a lot better if the Duke's men had got him and not the Knights.'

'Did the Duke know that he'd been captured?'

'Not until some time afterwards. And he was very angry about it. In fact, the Duke had him freed, but the Knights kidnapped him again and by the time he got to hear of it your man had been spirited away to some hiding-place.

190

They may even have killed him by then. Who knows?'

'So the Duke is no friend of the Knights either?'

'Far from it. When he came to power four years ago, some of them said he was too young to rule and wanted a regent to be appointed. He cannot forgive them for that. And there's another thing: I learned a little while ago that while Jem was still in Savoy the Duke had some secret meetings with him and offered him asylum in the Duchy. But the Knights wouldn't have it and took the Prince away with them into France.'

'And where is the Duke now?'

'In Turin.'

'You say I will need papers if I am to get through this pass in the mountains – can you get them for me from the Duke?'

'I can try.'

'And a guide?'

'There are many Frenchmen at the Duke's court. He himself was raised in France. Perhaps one may be prepared to go with you.'

'A man I can trust.'

'I'll see to everything,' said Gaspar.

Over a month passed and I had almost given Gaspar up for dead when at last he reappeared at the Villa Giustiniani. After so many days of waiting without receiving word, I was in a filthy mood and made no attempt to hide it.

Seeing this, Gaspar said, 'Why are you depressed? I have spoken to the Duke. Come along, I'll take you to him.'

Gaspar had obtained a travel permit from the Duke, signed and sealed in the Duke's own hand. So we crossed the border into Savoy without any difficulties and rode post-haste together to Turin. This place lies at the foot of the Alps, on a plain, surrounded on three sides by steep wooded hills. The town is by a river called the Po and to the west there is a strong and well-walled fortress and it was here that we found the eighteen-year-old despot.

The sky was overcast and the Duke was strolling with some of his courtiers on the lawns of a private garden within the castle walls before going in to take his midday meal. Leaving me at the garden gate, Gaspar approached the Duke and spoke to him briefly, pointing in my direction. Dismissing his courtiers with a regal gesture, the Duke looked at me, then beckoned with a crook of his bejewelled finger.

I bowed to kiss his ring and, indicating that I should rise, he said:

'Messer Gaspar tells me that you wish to go to France to find Prince Jem.'

'Yes, my lord,' I said.

'Why do you wish to see the Prince?'

'The Sultan has commanded me to confirm that nothing untoward has happened to his brother.'

'If this is all that your Sultan wishes to find out, why doesn't he send an ambassador to visit the Prince?'

'He has tried to do so. But the Knights of Rhodes, who are guarding the Prince, refuse to receive an embassy and will not say where it is he is now staying.'

'The journey you propose is very hazardous. If you are caught in France you will probably be executed.'

'Yes, my lord,' I said, 'but I am not afraid to die.'

For a while the Duke said nothing and stood stroking his small beard, gazing at me thoughtfully. At length he addressed me again:

'The Sultan is said to have many slaves. What is your position? Are you a slave of the Sultan?'

'I am.'

'What is your parentage?'

'I am Turkish-born.'

'One who is Turkish-born cannot be a slave of the Sultan,' he said, his eyes sparkling with triumphant malice.

'It is as your Excellency says,' I replied pleasantly, 'but I am born of a slave, I eat the Sultan's bread, so I rank as his slave.'

'H'm,' said the Duke. 'These explanations are far from satisfactory. You will have to do better than this. Show me some proof that you are who you say you are.'

'I am sorry, Excellency, but I am not carrying official

credentials. It would have been dangerous for me to do so in some of the places I have had to pass through.'

'Then how is one to know that you are the Sultan's slave if you are not carrying the Sultan's certificate?'

'But surely', I said, tiring of this absurd catechism, 'Messer Gaspar can vouch for me?'

'How? He knows no more about you than I do!'

I could hardly restrain myself from smiling. At a loss to continue the conversation in any other way, I said, 'Then, how *am* I to satisfy your Excellency?'

'Bring me a certificate from your Sultan,' said the Duke.

I had a sudden urge to say, 'You are joking, of course', but adopting my most sickeningly urbane manner, I replied instead, 'The Felicitous Sultan is now far away. But I shall go and fetch from the Lords of Genoa a certificate saying that I am a slave of the Sultan.'

A few drops of rain began to fall, but the Duke seemed not to notice them. He appeared uncertain what to do. With an absent-minded gesture he indicated that I should withdraw. But Gaspar he ordered to remain. I stood by the gate for some time, observing their animated conversation and trying without success to read what they were saying by the movement of their lips. It was raining quite heavily now. At last the Duke finished talking to Gaspar, and acknowledging my deep bow with a wave of the hand as he swept past me, he stalked out of the garden and rejoined his waiting courtiers, who were standing politely in the downpour just beyond the gate.

Gaspar and I took refuge under a dripping cherry tree.

'What in God's name is going on?' I said.

'The Duke thinks you might be an impostor sent by the Knights.'

'Couldn't you convince him that he's wrong?'

'By telling him I'm a Turkish agent too? As things stand now, the only reason he's agreed to see you is because I've managed to persuade him that there would be no harm in his having such a powerful friend as your Emperor. If I start to press him he might smell a rat.'

'And all that business about slaves?'

193

'Jem told him when they met that no Turk, however humble, could be another man's slave – not even the Sultan's. So he thinks he's tripped you up now and there's something wrong with your story.'

'Wonderful! What next?'

'You'll have to go back to Genoa and get something from Alessandro. I'll stay here and work on the Duke while you're away.'

I returned within the week, with an elaborate document drawn up by Frenk Iskender, assuring the Duke in suitably grandiose language that I was indeed who I claimed to be – and signed at my insistence by half a dozen other illustrious directors of the Banco di San Giorgio.

I found Gaspar at the citadel. He told me that the Duke had gone out riding on the plain, so we set off together and, skirting the town, rode eastwards for about a mile across the golden stubble of harvested fields until we came to the banks of the Po. After searching for a while, we came upon the Duke's party watering their horses where the grassy bank sloped gently down to the fast-flowing stream. The Duke was still mounted and, recognizing Gaspar, he left his companions and walked his horse over to meet us.

I took Frenk Iskender's document out of my saddlebag and handed it to him. He unfolded it and examined the seal.

After perusing the text for several minutes, he said, 'Well, now that we know you are a slave of the Sultan, we will give you a man to go with you – but you'll have to provide for his expenses.'

'What will his expenses be?' I said.

The Duke replied, 'A hundred and fifty florins should be enough.'

'Gold or silver?'

'Gold.'

I turned to Gaspar. 'How many ducats is that?'

'Florins and ducats, there is little to choose between them,' he said with a shrug.

'This is a considerable sum,' I said.

'What do you expect?' said the Duke. 'The man is risking

his life. Besides, he is a free man, not a slave like you. Do you expect him to put his life in a danger for nothing?'

'I cannot meet so great an expense,' I said. 'I shall have to go to Genoa to get more money from my friends there.'

'Then do so. But be sure to return before too long – otherwise you may find I have left Turin for some other place.'

'I shall – God willing – be back before the end of the week,' I said.

'Then you may still find me here,' said the Duke. And with that, he pulled round his horse and rode back across the soft green grass to rejoin his companions at the water's edge.

It was a hot cloudless afternoon during the first days of August when I wearily descended from the rocky pass and once again looked down from the mountains of Liguria upon the red-tiled rooftops and silent towers of Genoa. The calm blue sea lay before me as smooth and flawless as a mirror and not a breath of wind stirred the trees as I trotted the last few miles along the deserted road through parched fields and dusty olive groves.

After beating for several minutes at the gates of the Villa Giustiniani, I was admitted by a sleepy servant, only to be told that Frenk Iskender had left early in the morning and since then had not returned. So I continued on foot down the hill into the suffocating heart of the sweltering city. I found him still at his desk at the Banco di San Giorgio, quite alone, in a first-floor room overlooking the piazza. The atmosphere in the room was sluggish from the heat, and small black flies darted and spiralled in and out of the shafts of bright sunlight slanting through the gaps in the half-closed shutters. At the far end in a high-backed chair sat Frenk Iskender.

Without looking up from the piles of paper strewn across the desk in front of him, he said in a lifeless mechanical voice, 'Yes? What is it?'

When I did not reply, carefully laying down his pen, he raised his head – only to lower it again and rest it on his right hand, closing his eyes and moving his lips as though in silent prayer. His face was flushed and glistening with sweat. A large drop fell from his furrowed brow, smudging a set of figures lying before him on the desk. Another followed. A purple puddle slowly began to form and spread outwards across the stiff paper.

'Forgive me,' he said at last, fighting to control his voice, 'but you should not have come here, you should have waited at the house.'

'I will not stay long,' I said.

He gazed at me with bloodshot expressionless eyes.

I gently lowered myself into the chair opposite and said, 'I need more money.'

He stared at me for some time and then said quietly, 'I have already given you forty ducats.'

'I need more.'

'If I'd had more, I would have given it to you before.'

'I need at least a hundred more.'

'I cannot raise an amount like that overnight.'

'You amaze me. To a wealthy man like yourself I would have thought a hundred ducats a trifling sum,' I said calmly.

'A trifling sum, is it? Have you gone stark mad?' he said, gripping the edge of the desk and thrusting himself halfway across it towards me, his eyes burning with feverish intensity.

'And do you take me for a fool?' I shouted back at him, roughly grabbing a bundle of bills of exchange and waving them in his face. 'What are these, then? Do you think that I don't know?'

He staggered backwards as though I had physically pushed him. Then, shaking his head and picking up a piece of paper here and a piece of paper there, looking at them and then laying them down with a sigh, one after the other, he said imploringly, 'But can't you see? This money is all on paper and my creditors are scattered halfway across the world! In Milan, in Venice, in Geneva, in Germany, in France, in England—'

'What?' I said. 'Is there nobody here in Genoa who is in your debt in some way or another?'

'Dozens of other merchants owe me money here. But large loans these days are nearly all long term. I can't start calling in debts just because you want some cash. Don't you understand? Our entire business is built on credit. If you want gold, go to the Sultan and ask him for it – why, half the gold in the Republic was sent to Istanbul this spring to pay the tribute due for our estates in Chios!'

'And what of the other directors? Are they all in the same position?'

'All of them.'

'And the Banco itself?'

'We *are* the Banco, my friend. And the coffers of the Banco can handle day-to-day expenses, nothing more. These last few years we've been on the verge of ruin.'

'Is this generally known?'

'Of course not,' he said, turning away and staring at the wall.

'Then there must be some other way,' I said in exasperation, getting up and starting angrily to pace the room.

Following me anxiously with his eyes, Frenk Iskender said, 'There is.'

I stopped and waited.

'Some of our ships will shortly be returning from Antwerp. When they arrive I can give you what you want.'

'How soon will they be here?'

'A month, a couple of months. Maybe a little sooner. You're a seaman yourself, I don't need to tell you how difficult it is to be sure about these things.'

'I'm afraid that's far too late.'

With a loud groan Iskender slumped back in his chair and stared with glassy eyes at the ceiling. After a long pause he began to speak in a slow toneless voice, like a man speaking involuntarily from the depths of a trance.

'Go back to the house, Captain Barak. I will talk to some of the other directors and see what can be done. Perhaps some silver at least can be obtained for you. I will do what I can.'

'All right,' I said.

'And another thing.'

197

'Yes?'

'Some strangers have been in the city since you last were here, saying they are looking for a foreign merchant who has cheated them in some way. They're offering a big reward in the taverns and the wine shops to anyone who can direct them to him. They have been giving a description of the man, and that man is you, Barak. Somebody is bound to have told them by now that you've been here in Genoa. You were seen by a lot of people in the square that first morning.'

'When was this?'

'Two, three days ago.'

'Thank you for telling me this. I was beginning to think that they'd given up. I'll go back and wait at the house, as you say.'

I went over to the window and, concealing myself in shadow behind a shutter, looked out over the empty expanse of the sunlit piazza. I couldn't see a soul. But of course that didn't mean a thing. The square was surrounded on every side by a warren of narrow lanes and alleys through which I would have to pass. And why bother to cut a man down in an open public place when you can dispose of him so much more discreetly in some squalid sunless backstreet?

'There is another way out of the building,' said Iskender. 'You'd better come with me.'

Leading me past other empty offices, he took me to the end of the corridor and down a steep winding staircase. When we reached the bottom he unbolted a small door. Blinding white light flooded into the stairwell. Iskender stepped outside and almost immediately slid back in again, indicating with a jerk of his chin that I should go. I just stared into his eyes. He stared back unwaveringly. Then a troubled questioning look gradually came over his face. He seemed genuinely puzzled. I couldn't be sure – you never can be – but somehow it just wasn't the look of a man about to toss a fellow creature to a pack of hungry wolves. I would soon find out.

I squeezed his shoulder and stepped out through the

door. Shading my eyes from the glare and pressing my back against the door to prevent it being shut, I glanced in both directions. It was a narrow cobbled alleyway. One end led into the piazza, the other sloped down towards the harbour. I straightened up. The door closed behind me. Then I heard the bolt being softly slid into position.

I set off jauntily as though on the way to the harbour. Then, having walked a little way and, convinced I wasn't being followed, I hid in a shadowy doorway, waited, then doubled back and hastened up the hill to the Villa Giustiniani.

It was well past midnight before Frenk Iskender arrived back at the house. Coming to my room, without a word he emptied the contents of a leather pouch onto the bed. I counted the coins. They amounted to only fifty ducats.

'Ninety ducats in all is not enough,' I said.

'It is all I could raise tonight,' said Iskender.

'Could you get the same again tomorrow?'

'To be honest, I would be lucky to raise another ten. In the autumn things will be different. Wait till then and you can have whatever you want. But I'm afraid you'll have to leave Genoa. For a while at least. I have a small farm in the hills, you could go there.'

'Why, what's happened?'

'Some of the other directors. They've been approached by a man who says he has come from Rome. Claims to be a merchant, but apparently doesn't look like one at all. Lean-faced fellow with a beard. He's been giving out the same story about a Greek merchant who owes him money. And it so happens that one of our people remembers seeing him several times in Chios when ships from Rhodes have been in port.'

'A Knight?'

'My friend is almost certain of it.'

'Will any of your people talk?'

'No, I don't think so. And as long as you stay here in the house there's not much he can do. On the other hand . . .'

'What?'

'If he goes to the Captain of the Guard and tells him that

199

I'm harbouring a Turkish agent, I'll be hanged and so will you.'

'With this amount of money,' I said, 'there is little point in going back to Savoy.'

'There is an alternative.'

'And what is that?'

Iskender looked at me steadily. He seemed about to speak, but then dropped his eyes. He got up and walked over to the window and looked out into the darkness. The fountain outside my room could be heard splashing and bubbling in the still night air. A faint breeze rustled through the vines on the terrace down below and somewhere in the trees a nightingale started to sing and as abruptly ceased.

Taking a deep breath, he said, 'One of my vessels is leaving port at dawn tomorrow bound for Chios. From there you could return to Istanbul and obtain the funds you need.'

The flow of a man's Fate is ever twisting, ever turning, ever changing course; sometimes tumbling amid tumultuous rocks, sometimes gliding noiselessly through forest glades; here rushing through barren fastnesses, there winding and looping through fat meadows. Without sufficient means to continue my quest, I could not take a single step further along the road that would lead me to Jem. Meanwhile, my enemies the Knights were inexorably closing in. Heavy with grief, I resolved to turn again for home and at first light I boarded the *San Lorenzo* and sailed for Chios.

We were barely out of sight of the city when the wind failed. For some time we drifted idly under the high summer sun on the flat surface of the sea. Then, seeing that the current was gradually carrying us in the direction of the shore and there was not wind enough to stir a feather, the master ordered the sails to be hauled down and the anchor dropped. The following day a feeble breeze began to blow off the land and we managed to move ahead – but only at a snail's pace. And so it went on like this until, on the

200

morning of the sixth day, we at last crawled into a little port called Rapallo, which lies at the foot of steep mountains and cliffs where the Republic borders with the seaboard of the Duchy of Modena. In close on a week's sailing we had covered the distance a man could ride hard in half a day. But nothing in this world happens without a purpose – as I was to find out soon enough.

The harbour was packed with vessels waiting for the wind to pick up, and preferring to while away the time in the safe haven of the port rather than risk being surprised, becalmed on the open sea, by the maritime cut-throats who infest this wild and craggy coast, we tied up alongside a fast lightweight galley of war, brightly painted and with an elaborate gilded prow. At her stern, lazily floating in the dying wind, there hung the mitred and cross-keyed yellow banner of the Roman Pope. I didn't pay much attention to her. There was no reason why I should. Or so I thought. I went ashore.

I wandered along the quay in a dilatory fashion, looking over the various vessels. What little wind there had been now expired and water, ships, waterfront, houses, earth and sky pulsated in the tremulous haze of mounting heat. Although it was at least three hours till noon, I could already feel the sun beating down on my shoulders. Sweat trickled down my face and back. If the weather went on like this we would be stuck in port for days.

I took refuge in the cool of a dark and dingy tavern. Feeling hungry, I ordered some soup. I seemed to be the only customer. I sat down at a long table and waited.

A few minutes later a party of men – sailors unmistakably from their manner and their dress – came in and, jovially calling for wine, and lots of it, settled themselves down at the other end of the table. They drank and chatted for quite some time – about the lack of wind, the heat, the whereabouts of other ships – and I was barely bothering to eavesdrop when one of them, a shrunken tanned old salt with a wheezing laugh, lowered his voice and said:

'Did you see Biassa's galley come in last night?'

'Yes, we've seen her,' mumbled one or two of the others.

'Had a word with the mate this morning. Says she's on the way back to Ostia, from Genoa.' He let his voice trail away, leaving his companions to digest this tantalizing morsel until, sure enough, the others said:

'From Genoa, you say, bos'n?'

'From Genoa,' he said, nodding sagely.

Another pause. I looked out of the window over the brilliant sunlit harbour to where the *San Lorenzo*'s masts were just visible behind the masts and spars of other vessels.

Then the old man said, 'It's all because of that barbarian that's come here from the East.'

'The Grand Turk's brother?'

'Ay, that's the one.'

'And is the Turk aboard, chief?' said one of the sailors.

'No, but the brother of the Grand Master and the Treasurer of the Knights of Rhodes were until two days ago – and the mate says that they were on their way to France to get that heathen prince and bring him back to Rome. That's why the Holy Father sent Captain Biassa to take these gentlemen to Genoa.'

There were murmurs of astonishment and one of the men said, 'What? Is the Holy Father to bring the barbarian to Italy and have him in the Holy City?'

'That's what the mate says.'

'They'd be better sending him back to his own country to fight his brother there,' said another, shaking his head. 'That might give us poor Christians some respite from their wicked plans to conquer every land in Christendom. Look what those monsters did in Otranto . . .'

'Ah!' said the old man excitedly, 'but that's just it. That's why the Holy Father wants the Prince in Rome. He's going to launch a Holy War. And mark my words now, with the Sultan's own brother by his side – he can't fail.'

'Is this Turk become a Christian, then?' said one of the seamen.

'Not yet. But when he goes to Rome, who knows what might happen? Perhaps he'll see the light and abandon his vile beliefs . . . but whatever happens, those filthy Turks will be in for a damn good hiding. They'll soon find out what's coming to them,' chuckled the old man with delight as the others crossed themselves and murmured, 'Amen, chief, amen.'

'Well,' said the old bos'n, still cackling as he swung his legs over the bench and stood up, 'we'd better be getting back.'

The tavern keeper appeared spectrally from the gloomy malodorous depths of the back room as they drained their wine-cups and prepared to leave. He hovered expectantly.

'Put it on the slate!' said the bos'n as he shuffled through the door and into the dazzling mid-morning sunshine.

'Yes, *sir*,' said the tavern keeper sourly, gathering up the cups and jugs and wiping the table with a greasy tattered rag.

I gazed at the receding figures of the party of sailors as they ambled along the dock, knowing that to return to Istanbul was now out of the question, and seized again by a renewed determination to track down the Prince whatever obstacles lay in my way.

I narrowed my eyes and looked out to sea. To my surprise the horizon, which had vanished into the misty haze just after dawn, was visible again – as sharp and distinct as a pencil line – dividing the bleached blue of the sky from the deeper azure of the ocean. Then something caught my eye, and I glanced round the harbour. Some of the flags and pennants on the masts of the ships that I could see from where I was sitting were beginning to rise and fall and fitfully to flutter. I got up and, tossing a coin on the table, walked outside.

A wind, growing fresher by the minute, had started to blow from the south. The decks of vessels – silent and deserted when I passed by them on my way to the tavern – were suddenly the scene of bustling activity as men ran hither and thither, swarmed up ladders, clambered about the rigging and called loudly to their more slothful colleagues to look alive. Flurries and eddies of warm air were now rippling the sheltered waters of the port and

203

beyond the harbour mouth the first white flecks were breaking here and there on the crests of heaving waves.

I found myself marching swiftly, then running along the quay. A great hubbub of noise and voices echoed around the harbour as last pieces of cargo – casks and sacks and crates – were swung aboard, missing crewmen called to return to their ships or be left behind and sails were hauled aloft. I came upon a high-sterned vessel, her flapping and billowing sails already up, preparing to cast off. Her master was standing, hands on hips, on the after-deck, giving the orders for the trimming of the sails. I called up to him:

'Where are you bound for, Captain?'

He replied without turning to look down at me, 'To Genoa.'

'Willing to take a passenger?' I shouted above the rattling of the ropes and squealing of tackle as the sails were hauled round to catch the wind.

Raising his hand to suspend operations for a moment, he came over to the side and peered down on me from above. Judging no doubt by my sober and respectable-looking clothes – thoughtfully provided for the voyage by Frenk Iskender – that I could well afford to pay for my passage, he said in a friendly tone, 'It would be a pleasure, sir. But as you see, we are leaving this very minute.'

The moorings had now been cast off and the gap of shining water was widening between the vessel and the dock.

'Never mind about that,' I said, 'throw me a line or something.'

Seconds later a rope ladder rattled over the side. I jumped into space and caught hold of it, clambered up and rolled myself over the side and onto the deck.

The Captain was leaning over the rail of the after-deck laughing uproariously and saying over and over again, 'Well done, sir! Why, well done, sir!'

He beckoned me to join him and then disappeared from view. I dusted myself down and went to join him at the helm.

In no time at all we slid out of the harbour and into the

open sea. The helmsman brought the prow round and the whole ship shuddered and pitched forward as a terrific southern gale caught her full astern. For a moment we seemed to stop dead, as if we had run up against a bank, but then our canvas bellied out before the wind and we were forging ahead through the rising swell, running full speed for Genoa.

At first everything went well. Too well.

I found Frenk Iskender again in his office at the Banco di San Giorgio. Dusk was falling and lamps glowed amber on the staircase and in the corridors. He was not alone this time, but with six or seven of the other directors of the Banco who had signed my certificate for the Duke of Savoy. They seemed to be holding some kind of conference. The door was ajar. I walked in and closed it quietly behind me. The conversation stopped. Frenk Iskender rose to his feet, his face as white as if he had just seen a ghost, then sank back again in his chair as though gently but firmly pushed down again by an invisible hand. The lamps flickered slightly in the cool evening breeze that was blowing in through the open windows.

'I am sorry to disturb you, gentlemen,' I said, walking slowly along the length of the table at which they sat, 'but there has been a change of circumstances. I am no longer asking you for your help – I am now forced to insist upon it.'

Half a dozen sheepish pairs of eyes followed my measured progress, gazing at me from the shadows. I reached the end of the table, rested my palms on its dark polished surface and, leaning forward, looked from face to face. A bell started ringing in a church tower on the opposite side of the square and before long other towers and belfries across the city joined in, one by one, to add their noisy jangling to the jarring cacophony.

When not one of these esteemed worthies ventured to say a word in reply, but continued to stare at me as though hypnotized and rendered speechless by my presence, I went on, 'Do not neglect your duty to the Sultan. I am the

205

Sultan's servant. Give me the funds I need to travel on the Sultan's business.'

Frenk Iskender stammered out, 'I have told you . . .'

'I know what you have told me,' I said with a menacing growl.

He lapsed into a confused silence and stared down at the glassy, dimly reflecting table-top, nervously fiddling with his hands.

A long pause ensued, during which the dissonant clanging of the bells gradually died away; until at last there was only one solitary bell left ringing in some distant tower, sonorously tolling out its baleful message over the darkening rooftops of the town.

'Well, gentlemen?'

'In view of what you say,' said one I recognized as Messer Giorgio, finally breaking the spell of inarticulacy that seemed to hold them all in thrall, 'we will, of course, have to see what can be done. But if we are, say, to draw on the Banco's reserves, we will have to take our decision jointly, you understand.'

The others nodded gravely.

'If you would excuse us for a few minutes, Captain Barak, we could even discuss it now, in view of the fact that we . . . happen to be gathered together to deal with other matters.'

Messer Giorgio, an interrogative eyebrow raised, glanced around the table at his august associates. There were murmurs of assent.

'H'm . . .'

'Quite so . . .'

'Good a time as any, I suppose . . .'

'Very well, if you insist . . .'

I straightened up and strolled over to a window at the far edge of the room. The first stars were visible in the thunderous dark-purple sky. The distant bell tolled on: boom, boom, boom . . .

Murmurs, grunts, urgent whispers, exclamations of dissent and approval rumbled on for some time behind my back. I made no attempt to listen. Finally the buzz of

206

discreet conversation subsided altogether. Even the distant bell fell silent, leaving its last reverberations portentously suspended in the air. I turned away from the window and walked back to the head of the table.

Frenk Iskender rose to his feet again. He cleared his throat, and resting his elbow magisterially on the high carved back of his chair, he began:

'We too are the Sultan's servants, Captain Barak, as you know – and Heaven forbid that we should be accused of neglecting our duty to His Majesty in any way! Therefore, we have decided that although, as you know, your appeal comes to us at a most difficult, even perilous, time we *will* provide you with all the funds that you require. To this end—'

At this point there was a tremendous commotion on the stairs outside and almost simultaneously the doors burst open and a crowd of men rushed into the room, yelling like madmen and brandishing their swords. I saw with horror that some had emblazoned on their long black cloaks the eight-pointed cross – despicable symbol of the accursed Order of the Knights.

I threw myself over Frenk Iskender's desk and overturned it, sending an avalanche of books, seals, inkpots, papers, pens cascading across the floor. Meanwhile, Iskender and the other merchants, blaspheming and shouting curses in surprise, were jumping to their feet, upsetting their chairs as they reached for their unbuckled swords that lay on the floor beside their feet.

'There's the Infidel,' bawled one of the men as I dashed towards an open window and jumped onto the sill. I looked down. Another gang of men crowded together in the square below. Snarling villainous faces and gleaming eyes gazed up at me. Cold steel glinted, caught by the sharp beams from the lamps in the piazza. I might just as well have jumped into a snakepit.

A split second later a great collision took place behind me as the intruders surged forward into the middle of the room. Chairs skidded wildly across the floor. Metal crashed and clanged on metal. Furniture splintered. Men stumbled and fell to the ground. Threats, insults, foul imprecations filled the air. A sword – knocked from somebody's hand – came spinning over the flagstones in my direction. I lunged forward and grabbed it. Then, whipping off my cloak and wrapping it round and round my left hand in heavy folds to serve me as a shield, I let forth a furious roar and hurled myself at the men, determined to hack a path through them to the door. They momentarily recoiled before my onslaught, then crowded in on me as I parried their thrusts and blows with cloak and sword.

Then someone shouted, 'Stop! Stop!'

And Iskender, who was standing beside me at the forefront of the fray, lent his voice, crying out, 'Yes, yes, hold off, damn you, hold off!'

The two sides began to disengage and after some more cursing and clattering and ringing of blades a space opened up between us. We stood glaring at each other with burning eyes and raised swords, panting breathlessly from our exertions and the excitement of the fight.

'Our quarrel is not with you, gentlemen,' said one of the Knights, visibly shaken by the violence of the resistance offered by the merchant bankers.

'Then how dare you . . .?' began Iskender angrily, gasping for air with streams of sweat pouring down his face.

Then a voice called out from behind the Knights and their wretched myrmidons, 'Messer Alessandro, gentlemen, are you all right?'

'Ah! Luca, good, you're there.' Iskender called back, looking hurriedly to left and right to make sure that we hadn't suffered any casualties. 'Yes, we're all right. Have you closed the doors?'

'We have, sir. And we have them covered from behind, sir. Are any of you hurt?'

'Praise God, no,' said Iskender.

I raised myself up a little and could see a large crowd of the Banco's men – armed with swords, clubs and staves – filling the corridor and the head of the stairs, thereby cutting off the enemy's retreat.

208

'We have other men outside in the square,' said the Knight who had spoken first.

'They cannot help you now,' said Iskender. 'As you've heard, the doors are closed against them.'

'Come, come now,' said the Knight in a conciliatory tone, 'let us settle this matter in a civil and Christian manner. As I have said, our quarrel is not with you.'

'Tell your men to clear these ruffians out,' I said to Iskender.

'Be careful,' said the Knight menacingly, 'or we shall have you killed.'

Iskender said, 'Luca. Clear the way and let these . . . gentlemen out. The time has come for them to leave.'

'One moment, we have some matters to discuss with this . . . gentleman here,' said the Knight, jerking his weapon in my direction.

'Then put down your swords.'

The Knights lowered their blades and indicated to their scowling accomplices to do the same. After some delay, they too reluctantly obliged.

'That's better,' said Iskender. 'Now tell your men to leave and wait outside.'

At first the Knights hesitated, but after conferring with furtive glances, they sheathed their swords and ordered their men to do as Iskender said. As they left, the Banco's men converged on them from all sides, swearing and jostling them, until Luca called them to order and forced them to create some space as the intruders retreated into the corridor. The operation complete, he appeared himself on the threshold and at a gesture from Frenk Iskender closed the doors behind the Knights.

The Knight who had spoken before stepped forward. The lamp-light reflected in his steely blue eyes. A jagged, fleshy, unsightly scar disfigured one side of his face. A well-aimed blow, I fancied, from some *Gazi*'s scimitar (actually, as I learned with regret some time later, the result of a hunting accident).

'Allow me to introduce myself, gentlemen,' he said. 'I am Guy de Blanchefort, Prior of the Auvergne, nephew of our Grand Master, Pierre d'Aubusson. And this', he said indicating the second Knight, who was staring at me with a look of undisguised hostility, 'is Brother Rinaldo di San Simone, our Treasurer.'

Brother Rinaldo gave a stiff bow and then returned to squinting at me with venomous concentration. The third Knight – a much younger man – remained unintroduced.

Iskender seemed unconcerned, and dispensing with the formality of introducing either himself or any of the other distinguished directors of the Banco di San Giorgio, he merely said, 'State your business and then be gone. We here·have work enough to do without having to bear disgraceful and unwarranted intrusions such as these.'

'And we have our work to do as well, Messer Alessandro,' said the Prior. Then pointing contemptuously to me with his gauntleted hand, 'Are you aware of the identity of this man?'

'Certainly.'

'Who is he?'

'Why, he is a Greek merchant from Constantinople,' said Iskender blandly. 'Michaeli Mavromichaeli. We have known him for many years. Since childhood, in fact.'

'Ha! That's a lie, as you well know.'

'Beware, Prior, whom you call a liar.'

'Perhaps you are as naïve and foolish as you make out, Messer Alessandro. Or perhaps not . . .'

Frenk Iskender said nothing.

'This man', said the Treasurer, 'is a Turkish agent.'

'A Turkish subject, yes,' said Iskender sharply. 'He is a Greek living in the territories of the Sultan. So his master is the Sultan. But what of that?'

'No. He is a Turkish agent. He is pretending to be a Greek. The man who brought him here from Turkey has confessed everything. This man even tried to murder him to keep him quiet when they arrived in Italy.'

'Scorpion,' I murmured under my breath.

Iskender gave me a wry smile.

'I'm amazed that you find anything amusing in a wretched Infidel like this trying to take the life of a

210

poor Christian in cold blood,' said the Treasurer.

'It is your absurd accusations that amuse me, Fra Rinaldo,' said Iskender.

Then the Prior broke in again. 'This man has been sent to find Prince Jem – who has had to go into hiding under our protection to avoid the vengeful wrath of his brother Sultan Bayezid.'

I guffawed. 'They would not send the likes of me on that sort of business. What need has the Sultan to do so? On this kind of business he would send someone of so great importance that a person such as myself would not even rank among his attendants.'

'For this kind of business,' said the Prior, 'the Sultan would not be so fastidious. To murder this poor wronged brother of his, what better person to choose than a miserable specimen like yourself? For that is what you have been dispatched to do, is it not, my friend? To assassinate the Prince.'

The Prior's head was now shaking with suppressed rage and his eyes burning with hatred. A froth of spittle was gathering on his lips – it almost seemed he was about to have a fit.

The Treasurer stepped forward and took hold of my arm. The young Knight moved towards me on the other side.

'Come along then, we're taking you with us,' said the Treasurer.

I did not move. The two men then seized me and tried violently to bundle me towards the door. I resisted and all hell broke loose amongst the Lords of Genoa as they all began to shout at once:

'It's out of the question!'

'Impossible!'

'Some unexpected harm may come to you,' said Messer Giorgio, grabbing hold of me and pushing the young Knight out of the way.

Recovering his balance, the Knight drew his sword and lunged at me. I dodged the blade. Then, as the Treasurer tried in vain to restrain me, I grasped the Knight's sword

211

hand at the wrist and repeatedly smashed it against the edge of the table until, howling with pain, he let his weapon drop. I released his arm. He reached down to pick up his sword and I brought my foot down as hard as I could on his hand. Then I placed the sole of my foot against his face and, straightening my leg, sent him hurtling backwards across the stone floor.

Swords flashed on either side of me and blades clashed together again. Luca appeared smartly at the door, but Iskender waved at him to withdraw, saying, 'Gentlemen! Gentlemen!'

The Knights backed off. The young Knight got to his feet, nursing his right hand. He came cautiously towards me. He looked down at his sword lying on the flagstones. Without taking his eyes off mine, he slowly began to stoop to pick it up. I put my foot on the blade and gave him my most winning smile.

Iskender said, 'Now, understand this. This man is under our protection. If anything should happen to him, *we* are the ones who will suffer. Our capital and our income are in the Sultan's domains – are they to be lost?'

'So, merchant,' said the Prior with a sneer, 'you are prepared to give succour to this enemy of Christ, this Infidel, this assassin, for the sake of your miserable profits in the Aegean.'

'It is you who say he is an Infidel. We know better. Besides, has not your own Order signed a treaty with the Sultan? And what of the profits of the Knights in those same parts?' Iskender said with dignity.

'These shopkeepers are ignorant fools,' said the Prior bitterly. 'We cannot expect to get any sense out of these men – if men they be.'

This was met with a barrage of derisive jeers from the Lords of Genoa who, as they well knew, had more than acquitted themselves in beating off the Knights' surprise attack.

The Prior came menacingly towards me. I raised my sword until it nearly touched his throat, and gazed into his cold blue eyes.

212

He made no attempt to come nearer, but said, 'What happened to all the others your Sultan sent, will happen to you. Don't think you can escape. We'll be waiting for you. You've had some luck so far, but you'll never get out of Genoa alive now. You should have come with us when we asked you. If you had come along we might have sent you home eventually. But now that you've been so stubborn, you will have to be killed.'

I just stood there and stared steadily back at him.

He turned abruptly on his heel and while the Treasurer covered his back he stalked over to the doors and pulled them open. A mass of faces, pale yellow in the lamplight, jostled at the doorway, straining to look in. Luca, a beefy broad-shouldered fellow, blocked the Prior's exit. The Prior tried to push past, but without success.

Then Iskender called out, 'It's all right, Luca. These gentlemen may go. It turns out that the man they were looking for is not here after all.'

Luca stood aside. Without looking back, the Knights, followed by their henchmen, clattered noisily down the stairs.

'We are going to need some help when the Grand Master gets to hear of this,' said Frenk Iskender, bending to pick up a handful of the papers littering the floor.

'Put your faith in the Felicitous Sultan,' I said. 'No harm will come to those who serve him loyally.'

'Ah, well, we'll see,' said Iskender pensively. 'Anyway, the sooner we get you out of here, the better for all of us.'

The hum of chatter from the curious crowd below, which had gathered, as crowds will, attracted by the rumpus inside the Banco, was now beginning to fade away as people drifted off into the night. I went over to a window and through a chink in the shutters surveyed the scene. A sizeable group of armed men still loitered belligerently on the far side of the square.

'I'll go and see what the chances are for you to make a dash for it,' said Messer Giorgio, who then quietly left the room with a couple of the other merchants.

After they had left I said to Frenk Iskender, 'There is still the small matter—'

'Of the funds?' he said. 'Don't worry, I haven't forgotten.'

Taking me by the arm, he led me to the side of the room where, against the wall, there stood a massive black iron-bound chest. Producing a set of large keys from beneath his robes, he proceeded to insert them in a series of different keyholes in the front and top of the chest and turn them, releasing with dull thuds and sharp clicks well-oiled bolts and ingenious levers. At last, with the turn of a final key, the ritual was complete. I helped him lift the lid.

Drawing aside a panel at one end of the chest, he lifted out a heavy metal tray and removed the lid. Gold coins glowed like embers in the soft light cast down on them from a lamp burning on a shelf above the chest. He counted out a hundred and fifty ducats and gave them to me without a word. He then replaced the tray with a sigh, slid the panel smoothly back into position, closed the chest and set about locking it once again. While he was engaged in this laborious operation, I folded the ducats tightly in a length of cloth and stowed them in the sash about my waist.

Then, beckoning me to follow him, Iskender sat down at a scribe's desk, took a clean sheet of paper and, after tracing tentative phantom patterns in the air for some moments, dipped pen in ink and started to write in a firm, bold, regular hand.

'This', he said, 'is a draft for a further fifty florins. If you make it as far as Lyons, you can cash it with our agent there. His name is Messer Angelo Doria. You'll find him in the Place de Saint-Jean, where the cathedral is. Everybody knows him – ask anyone and they'll direct you to him.'

He finished writing. Then signed his name with a flourish, melted some wax onto the paper and applied his seal. He handed it to me.

'And by the way,' he said, 'I didn't get a chance to tell you. Word came for you from Gaspar Grimaldo just after you left for Chios, saying that the Duke of Savoy has left Turin for Vercelli.'

'I see,' I said. 'In that case, I'll go to him there.'

Messer Giorgio and the other merchants now returned.

Messer Giorgio said, 'The Knights' men are still watching all the ways out of the piazza. I've arranged a horse for you at the city gates – but we'll have to find a way of getting you there in one piece.'

'The back door?' I said.

'No. They've got men posted at both ends of the street.'

'Then,' said Iskender, 'it had better be the roof.'

I took my leave of the illustrious directors of the Banco di San Giorgio, thanking them for their valorous display of arms in defence of the Sultan's servant and assuring them that when – God willing – I returned to the Lofty Lintel of his Felicity-encompassed Court at Istanbul, I would not fail to tell the Emperor of it.

Frenk Iskender led the way with a flickering taper and I followed along echoing passages and up narrow flights of shadowy winding stairs. Emerging at last into a musty loft, we made our way under low roof-beams until we came to a trap door opening onto a sort of terrace. Leaving the candle inside, out of sight, we crept out into the night.

We crawled up to a low parapet. Iskender instructed me in whispers how, if I could leap over the narrow street that divided the Banco from the tall building next door, I could continue unobserved over the rooftops and make my descent to earth half a dozen streets away. From there I could go on to the gates of the city, where Giorgio's men would by then have my mount waiting and would have bribed the guard to ask no questions and let me leave the city; that is, if the Knights had not got to them first. But what else could I do?

I peered cautiously over the parapet and saw, several storeys below, figures apparently patrolling the street. For some time they lingered just below where Iskender and I lay concealed. But then they started to wander back towards the piazza. When they reached the end of the street I drew back.

Embracing Frenk Iskender, I gathered my cloak around me and crouched in readiness at the back of the terrace. Iskender took a final furtive look into the street below and waved me on. I took a running jump and, sailing over the abyss between the buildings, landed heavily on a flat roof on the other side. Rolling as I fell, I crashed up against a pile of tiles. Suddenly my face was full of feathers and wing-beats as a terrified pigeon shot up screaming into the air and whirred off in blind panic into the darkness.

My heart beating furiously, I lay there holding my breath, my head spinning, blood pounding in my singing ears. It seemed impossible that I had not been heard half-way across the city. The seconds slipped by. Not a sound from the street below. No cry of alarm. No shouts. No running feet.

I warily raised my head. After a while the outline of a man's head rose with incredible slowness from behind the parapet on the roof of the Banco. Then, against the sky, an apparently disembodied arm started urgently, eloquently, waving at me to go.

I turned and crept away across the rooftops, a solitary shrouded figure under the immense dark vault of the night sky, my way lit only by the stars.

Vercelli is a strong walled town, which stands in flat country on the fertile plain of Lombardy a day's ride from Turin. When I arrived there I did not go to the citadel – for I knew from what Gaspar had told me that the Knights had informers among the Duke of Savoy's courtiers – but put up instead at an inn in a quiet, seemingly little-frequented district of the city. I had the innkeeper bring me pen and paper to my room and wrote a note to Gaspar (in Greek, a language known by few Franks but which he knew well), asking him to come to my lodgings. This missive I dispatched to the castle with the innkeeper's son, instructing him that he was to put it in the hand of none other than Messer Gaspar himself.

I idled away the afternoon in my room. At sunset there was a knock at the door. I called out to ask who it was. A familiar voice replied. I unlocked the door and in came Gaspar.

'Barak!' he said, warmly shaking my hand. 'I was

216

beginning to wonder where on earth you'd got to.'

I told him of my adventures at the Banco di San Giorgio and my nocturnal flight from the Republic into Savoy.

He shook his head. 'You have – if you'll excuse the expression – the luck of the devil, my dear fellow. I waited several days at Turin before joining the Duke here, in the hope that you'd be back. I somehow couldn't believe that you wouldn't turn up sooner or later – and . . . well, here you are.'

'What brings the Duke to this place?'

'His Grace was warned that the Governor of Vercelli – Claudio di Racconigi, Claudio the Bastard, they call him in the Piedmont – was plotting a rebellion. And when the Duke left Turin to come and see for himself, Claudio took himself off to his castle at Sommarvia. So it's pretty clear he really was up to something and it wasn't just a scare.'

'When will the Duke see me? Does he know I'm here?'

'Ah,' said Gaspar, becoming suddenly uncharacteristically vague. 'Yes, he does. I had a word with him not an hour ago.'

'And?'

'The point is, my dear fellow, he's terribly preoccupied. His problems are far from over yet. The border with Milan is only a few miles from here and his spies at the court there have sent word that Lodovico's been planning to try to take advantage of the Bastard's treachery and seize some territory in the Piedmont that *he* claims belongs to *him*. The Duke says he can't possibly see you now. I'm afraid you'll just have to wait.'

I eyed him with suspicion. He avoided my glance and looked down at the floor.

'There's another thing,' he said at last. 'The Duke's heard a rumour that Jem may be going to Rome. That would put the cat among the pigeons at the Porte, wouldn't it? Of course, it may be a lot of nonsense. But it seems to have thrown the Duke into complete confusion. He's been putting a brave face on it but, if you want my opinion, he can't decide now which way to jump.'

217

I groaned.

'I know how you feel,' said Gaspar.

'I didn't tell you just now,' I said, 'but the fact is that I overheard some loud-mouthed fool in Rapallo saying that's why Guy de Blanchefort and the Treasurer have come to Europe. I thought the story might be a load of nonsense, as you say, or even another deliberate attempt by the Knights to put others off the trail. But when the Prior and the Treasurer turned up in person to try to kill me, I began to wonder if there wasn't something in it after all.'

'The Sultan will have a fit when he learns of this – whether it's true or not.'

'His Majesty will have a fit if I don't find out where on earth the Prince is now.'

'H'm,' said Gaspar. 'It would certainly be a help if we knew that at least.'

'Look,' I said, 'can't you speak to the Duke again?'

'I'll try. But I have to tread very carefully. If I start pushing too hard, he'll begin to suspect. And if that happens, everything will be ruined.'

With little else left to say, Gaspar soon afterwards took his leave.

During the days that followed he came to see me often, usually after dark to reduce the chances of being spotted going to and from the inn – but the news was always bad. Whenever my name was mentioned the Duke dismissed the subject and adamantly refused even to hear of giving me an audience.

I seldom left my room lest someone should recognize me and betray me to the Knights. I paced my tiny low-ceilinged prison for hours on end, like a caged animal, moaning with boredom and frustration. I began to grow anxious that the innkeeper and his family would become suspicious that I went out so little, and start gossiping to the neighbours – until I heard two skivvies washing the stairs whispering to each other and saying in awed tones that the young mistress of the house (very tempting: bold eyes, white skin, masses of raven-black hair) had said that

218

the handsome foreign gentleman (I'd told her I was from Dubrovnik) was obviously in love. I suppose I had all the symptoms.

Over a week passed . . . two weeks . . . three weeks. The days were beginning to get shorter; the nights became colder; autumnal mists lingered on the damp ground long after daybreak; one day I awoke to hear rain drumming on the tiles above my head and steadily splashing from the eaves into the cobbled courtyard of the inn. And still no word from the Duke.

Then one morning I heard footsteps on the creaking wooden stairs outside my room. The door swung open and Gaspar, ducking under the absurdly low lintel, came over and stood beside the bed where I lay unshaven, unkempt, reduced to abject despair by the prospect – now almost certain, as far as I was concerned – of returning to Turkey empty-handed, a contemptible failure after all.

Gaspar's eyes twinkled and a barely suppressed smile played on his lips. 'Patience is rewarded,' he said, giving me a hearty slap on the shoulder. 'The Duke will see you.'

On hearing that the True Helper – may He be exalted! – had finally answered my most fervent prayers, I leapt out of bed and, embracing the excellent Gaspar, murmured, 'God is most Great' from the very bottom of my heart.

I shaved and washed and put on clean clothes, and together we thundered through the city gates and rode out in the crisp light dawn air over dew-drenched grasslands. We found the Duke flying some of his falcons on the poplar-lined banks of the river Sesia. As we approached we could see two of his birds gracefully swooping and wheeling in the still pale-blue morning sky. For some time he affected to ignore us – but at last he turned away from his sport and rode over to the place where we were standing, awaiting his pleasure. He dismounted and ordered his groom to lead his horse to graze a little way off.

'Well,' said the Duke, removing his hawking glove and flexing his stiff fingers, 'you are nothing if not persistent.'

I bowed.

'I told Gaspar to bring you here because I would not like it to become generally known that I am helping you in this way. I have jealous neighbours, you understand, who, if they knew of it, might try to use it against me. And what court these days does not have its spies and informers?'

'What court indeed, Excellency?'

'This deceit, this treachery, this duplicity – it is the plague of our times,' said the Duke becoming suddenly quite agitated. Then patting my companion on the shoulder with a sigh, he went on, 'Men like Gaspar here are rare, very rare. You are extremely fortunate in finding in him an advocate for your suit. For what has he to gain from it, eh, Captain?'

'Nothing, Excellency,' I said, 'but serving his prince well and giving him good advice.'

The Duke cocked his head and gave me an amused look. 'You are quite the courtier, aren't you, Captain Barak?'

'Not really, Excellency. But it is kind of you to say so.'

'Hmmpf!' said the Duke, putting his hands on his hips and laughing. 'Now then, good Messer Gaspar tells me that you have succeeded in obtaining the money.'

'I have.'

'The Lords of Genoa cannot have parted easily with so much.'

'Those who are firm-footed in their friendship with the Felicitous Sultan do not go unrewarded,' I said.

'We'll see about that, Captain Barak,' said the Duke, adopting a bluff man-to-man manner that was almost comic in one so young. 'Now listen, I want you to go and stay in Turin, d'ye hear? I'll give you your guide all right, but you'll have to wait a while. I've someone in mind, but it may be some days before he arrives in the Piedmont. Gaspar will make arrangements for you to be lodged in Turin while you're waiting – so our man will know where to find you when he gets there.'

'Very good, Excellency,' I said.

'Well, I think that is all that needs to be said.'

The Duke turned away and called for his horse; the groom brought it over at a trot, leading the beast by the reins. Replacing his hawking glove, the Duke mounted. Looking down at me, he said, 'And do not fail to come and tell me what you have seen in France.'

'You may be assured that I shall do so,' I said.

At this, the Duke spurred on his horse and rode away to his hawks and hounds.

We returned to my lodgings in town. Locking the door of my room, I took one of the squares of gold brocade from my leather bag and put it on the table. Using a small knife, I unpicked the seam down one side of it and carefully drew out the two fine pieces of paper from the space between the face of the brocade and its stiff backing. I unfolded the sheets and smoothed them out flat on the table. One was a cipher sheet covered with narrow columns of codes and their equivalents, the other blank.

I thought for a time and then, taking up my pen, began to write, consulting the cipher sheet as I went. When I had finished I waited until I was sure that the ink was completely dry, refolded the paper, inserted it again in its place of concealment and, taking needle and thread, resewed the seam. I tore the cipher sheet into strips and burned them carefully in the small brazier thoughtfully provided by the landlady.

I then took an ordinary sheet of paper and wrote on it: *Here, as requested, is a sample of the Florentine material of which we spoke. If it meets with your approval I will supply the quantity you asked for at the price we have already agreed. You may address your reply to me via Messer Alessandro Giustiniani at the Banco di San Giorgio, Genoa. Your servant, Michaeli Mavromichaeli.* I folded the brocade into the letter and addressed it to a merchant's premises that Kivami Bey had set up as a front in the Grand Bazaar.

I tied the letter with strong cotton tape and sealed it.

Handing it to Gaspar, I said, 'This is a report on everything I have seen and done so far. I've explained the reasons why I've been delayed and about these rumours that our friend may soon be leaving France for Rome. I

221

want you to arrange a courier to take it to Istanbul as soon as possible. If I do not return within a month or so of leaving Turin, write to them yourself that I am missing.'

Gaspar nodded and turned over the letter, looking at it and making sure it was properly sealed.

'I've told the Duke', he said, 'that you can stay at a house I've rented in Turin. My people there are reliable and you'll be much more comfortable and safe than in a tavern. They're expecting you already – I sent word to them a few days ago, when it began to look as if the Duke was coming round, saying that you might be coming. I've also told them to give you a horse if you need one. I will try to come and see you there if you haven't left within a week, but I may not be able to.'

As he spoke I began to gather together my few things. And within the hour I was galloping westwards through gold and russet autumn fields along the broad straight road to Turin.

I made the acquaintance of Monsieur Talabot's nose several seconds before I met the man himself. It was a prodigiously long and straight and pink and pointed nose, and it seemed to peep round the edge of the door (behind which I stood concealed) to see if the coast was clear before leading its master over the threshold and into the room.

Stopping in the middle of the somewhat murky upstairs apartment of Gaspar's rented residence in Turin, my visitor began to peer about in the semi-darkness. I stepped out of the shadows. A loose floorboard creaked beneath my foot and he spun round to face me.

'And you are?' I said.

'Talabot,' he said, drawing himself up defiantly and fixing me with the penetrating stare of his small bright eyes. His clean-shaven face was pale and gaunt, his mouth small and delicate – and suddenly I noticed his hands: lily-white, refined, almost like a girl's (but for the amazing length of his finely tapering fingers).

'I was not expecting you until tomorrow,' I said.

'Ah! So *you* are this Turkish gentleman, this Captain

Varak,' he said, his face relaxing into a charming smile.

'Barak.'

'Barak,' he corrected himself, graciously extending his hand. I grasped it. His skin was smooth and cool as marble.

I took him to the window and poured him a glass of wine and handed it to him.

'I came here with the Marshal from Vercelli,' he said. 'He will be here shortly himself. He's gone up to the citadel to collect some things for you.'

'Who is he?'

'But don't you know him? He is very close to Monsieur le Duc. He is Marshal of the Piedmont. His name is Antelmo di Miolans. A very important man in the Duchy.'

'You have told him the purpose of my mission?'

'But of course.'

There was a sound of voices from downstairs and the man I took to be the Marshal appeared at the door, followed by two servants carrying bundles. He told them to leave these on the table, then instructed them to wait downstairs.

We introduced ourselves.

The Marshal said in a friendly manner, 'Monsieur Talabot here will act as your guide. I've brought some French clothes for you. If you went dressed as you are now you would attract unnecessary questions. We have some idea where Prince Jem is staying – we think he's somewhere in the Auvergne – but we won't know for sure until you've had a chance to see him. Then you'll be able to tell us if it's really him or not. Monsieur Talabot knows the country well and I can assure you, Captain Barak, that with him you'll be in excellent hands.'

I examined the bundles of clothes. Plain shirts, a dark-blue quilted tunic, stockings, a tough pair of leather shoes. A coarse heavy woollen cloak. Also riding boots, sheepskin gloves and a stiff round hat.

'Do you have the money?' said the Marshal.

I fetched it from my bag and gave it to him. He emptied the pouches onto the table and counted it. He gave me

223

back fifty ducats, saying, 'You'll need these for your expenses.' Then he put some coins in a purse for Talabot and handed them to him. I couldn't see how many. I didn't bother to mention the bank draft. In an emergency I might need it.

Talabot said, 'We'll leave at dawn tomorrow, if that suits you, Captain.'

'The sooner, the better,' I said.

I pressed them to stay and dine with me. But they declined, and soon afterwards departed.

The Steps

On the twenty-first day of October, from the prophet Jesus 1486, Talabot and I rode out westwards together just as the sun was beginning to peep over the eastern horizon, tinting the walls and towers of the town and foothills around the plain with a watery rose-pink hue. Our long distorted shadows jerkily preceded us on the muddy road – it had rained quite persistently throughout the night – as we cantered through neat orchards and vine-yards half-submerged in a soft bluish morning mist.

We were soon at Rivoli and went on to San Giorgio – passing by a monastery called San Michele perched dizzily on a great sheer rock – and arrived at the fortress town of Susa as the blood-red sun was sinking behind the soaring snow-capped rampart of the western Alps. The curfew bell was ringing when we were admitted to the town, where we soon found an inn to sup and spend the night.

From Susa a wooded valley leads upwards towards the pass. Before we set off the following morning, as we were waiting for the stable lads to bring our horses, Talabot pointed out a curving ridge to the left of the shining ice-clad peak of Mont Cenis itself as the place where we would be able to cross over this awesome barrier that lay before us.

After riding for quarter of an hour or so from the town, we came to a clearing at the foot of the mountain, where men hire out mules and offer to act as guides.

'From here,' said Talabot, 'the paths become too steep to continue safely on horseback.'

As we entered the clearing the muleteers ran forward and crowded round us, trying to grab our bridles and tugging importunately at our stirrups. But Talabot, spurring on his horse, rode past them. Then I noticed a little way off an old muleteer with a long mane of white hair and an impressive aquiline profile, standing apart, in front of his line of mules, haughtily disdaining to take part in the general mêlée.

Raising his voice above the tumult of clamorous voices, and leaning towards me the better to make himself heard, Talabot said, 'That's Frederico. We'll go with him.'

We rode over to him. He greeted Talabot by name and politely invited us to dismount and transfer to the mules. His men brought two healthy-looking well-groomed animals from under the trees and helped us to climb into the saddles. We set off. Frederico went ahead leading our beasts, while we followed on our new mounts, with Frederico's men walking one on either side of us.

At first we rode easily through woods of birch and fir trees, crossing sparkling rills and clean bubbling brooks by small wooden bridges or stone slabs that had been thrown across them, coming every so often to pretty, gently sloping forest glades. But soon the path began to twist its way more steeply upwards and our mules struggled to get a foothold on the loose stones that lay strewn across the track.

In this fashion we laboriously zigzagged up the mountainside, our mules supported, when they slipped and stumbled, by the men who walked at our sides. At one point, on a sharp bend above a ravine, my animal lurched so violently that it almost pitched me out of the saddle and, taken by surprise, the muleteer on the outside of the path lost his footing and only by a miracle escaped being pushed clear over the side of the precipice. As I tugged him to safety by his collar, a noisy shower of stones slid over the edge and, after what seemed an eternity, could be heard rattling and cracking very faintly far, far below us.

At length we passed through a narrow defile – the clatter of our mules' hoofs echoing against its sheer rocky walls – and climbing above the tree-line, we continued on our way (no longer able to see Mont Cenis) across a wide escarpment. A long way below lay a massive pile of broken boulders that had clearly fallen recently (judging by the still fresh remains of fir trees lying smashed and flattened along their path) from the overhanging cliffs above us.

We rounded a bend in the track and Mont Cenis came into view again, much nearer now, looming above us, looking larger and more sinister than ever. Swirling clouds were beginning to gather on her desolate slopes, but her rugged summit was still visible, jutting skywards against the startlingly clear cold blue of the heavens.

We continued ever upwards. The atmosphere became palpably chillier by the minute. Our breath began to freeze. Then, completely without warning, my mule's pace seemed to quicken and we emerged at last onto a high ridge to find ourselves looking over a formidable flat wilderness of ice and snow, encircled on every side with jagged cloud-piercing peaks.

Skirting the still borders of a broad frozen lake lying directly under the great mass of Mont Cenis, we came to a small stone chapel on the shore. A steady penetrating wind blew off the forbidding mountain and the opaque surface of the lake.

We halted. I huddled for warmth in the folds of my rough cloak, which now seemed scant defence against the biting cold. The door of the chapel creaked and rattled as though feebly tugged at by the weak hand of some wretched prisoner locked within. We dismounted and I found my feet sinking into a carpet of soft snow. Frederico opened the chapel door. Crossing ourselves in the Frankish fashion, we crowded inside, out of the wind. The smell of old wax and stale incense lingered in the acrid atmosphere of the dark vault and our voices resounded hollowly in the damp dead air. Only the faintest beams of light managed to filter through the small arched windows just below the roof. Long wooden racks – whose purpose I could not imagine – lined the chapel's walls.

'La Chapelle des Transis,' said Talabot, rubbing

227

his gloved hands and clapping them together.

Not understanding the name, I said, '. . . des Transis?'

'The Frozen. The Chapel of the Frozen. The bodies of travellers – God forgive them – who die in snowstorms or falls are brought here – if they're found, that is – until they can be taken down to the foot of the mountain to be buried. Up here the ground is too rocky and too hard from the frost to make proper graves, and shallow ones are no good because the wolves come and dig them up and eat the corpses.'

I wandered round, gradually seeing better as my eyes, which were smarting painfully after the brightness of the snow, adjusted themselves to the dim light. The racks all seemed empty.

'No customers at the moment?' I said.

'It's early in the season yet,' said Talabot with a shrug, cupping his long red nose in his hands and energetically stamping his feet in an attempt to warm himself.

Frederico went over to the door and pulled it open. An icy blast swirled into the chapel. He looked up at the sky. Sniffing the air, he said, 'We'd better be on our way.'

The peak of Mont Cenis had now almost disappeared altogether, shrouded under a thick mantle of cloud. The darkening sky pressed down on the bleak wind-swept plateau. A few stray snowflakes began to fall.

We remounted and continued along the shore of the silent lake, our mules treading gingerly through the drifting snow that blanketed the treacherous uneven track. I shivered and pulled my scarf up around my face against the cutting wind. Hard frosty droplets began to encrust my eyelashes and re-formed as fast as I could wipe them off with the back of my sheepskin glove. Here and there ahead of us, flurries of fine snow rose up on the undulating waste of whiteness and, like phantom figures, briefly hovered in the air – only to melt away into the ground at our approach. It was not difficult, in the uncertain light, to imagine these spectral manifestations the abject spirits of the countless unfortunate wayfarers who must have perished on this pitiless mountain and were now condemned to incessant friendless wanderings until the Final Day. May God spare us so lonely and abominable a Fate!

After riding for some time, we left the shores of the frozen lake behind us and set off across a snowfield, following a series of tall poles that had been driven into the ground at regular intervals to indicate the path. In a final struggle our animals, urged on with shouts and slaps from our muleteers, slithered and clambered up a steep rise. We had now reached the high plateau's furthest edge. Here we dismounted, and leaving us with our horses, the muleteers hastened away, back in the direction of Susa, in an anxious race to beat the gathering storm presaged all too clearly by the ominous snow-laden sky.

Taking our horses by the reins, we led them for a short distance before two guides in heavy fur coats and boots came lumbering awkwardly towards us and took them from us. We walked on until we came to a flat platform of ice-covered rock, below which there lay spread out before us a magnificent, misty, thickly wooded valley beginning to darken in the fading light. Far off on the valley floor a constellation of tiny lights twinkled invitingly and plumes of grey smoke rose serenely heavenwards from invisible dwellings hidden among the trees.

'That's Lanslebourg down there,' said Talabot. 'It's too steep to ride with the path covered in snow – these men will lead our horses down. We can either go down on foot with them or go on one of these things.' He indicated a pile of dark-green branches and gestured to a third man – who had mysteriously materialized from nowhere and now stood in respectful silence, a little apart from the others – to lift the branches off. This he proceeded to do and a few moments later he had thrown them all aside to reveal a long, thin, extremely rickety-looking sledge, its front curved up slightly in the manner of the prow of a boat.

'Which way is quicker?' I said, feeling frozen to the marrow and secretly longing to be indoors and by a fire.

Talabot laughed and said, 'Oh, the sledge, certainly . . . much quicker.'

'All right, then,' I said.

Talabot told the guides what we had decided. As the horses were going to take longer to make the descent, we unloaded some of the baggage. The sledgeman lashed it with ropes to the back of the vehicle and invited us to climb aboard. Talabot got into the middle of the sledge and I, on his instructions, clambered in between him and the baggage.

The sledgeman retired to the rear of the sledge and started, wheezing and grunting from the effort, to roll it gently backwards and forwards. And then, the ice cracking loudly in protest under our weight, we began to slide heavily forward. Glancing to one side, I was taken aback to see that the guides leading our horses had already set off on the narrow trail down the mountain. It seemed scarcely wide enough for the sledge to get past them.

But turning to look to the front again, I saw that we were slowly but surely still gliding onwards, across the slippery shelf of rock, making directly for the brink of the precipice ahead. There was a jerk as we cleared a hard compacted ridge of frozen snow. We were gathering speed. I turned round. The sledgeman was now running, panting, behind the sledge, his teeth bared in a wolfish grin and a weird light glinting in his fanatical unseeing eyes. Suddenly, the horrible truth dawned upon me – he was about to push us off the cliff . . .

I whipped round to shout a warning to my companion. He sat impassively with his back to me as though struck dead. Something wasn't right about him . . . in a flash I realized he'd removed his hat! My heart leapt into my mouth. I lurched forward to seize hold of Talabot's shoulder. My hand was about to grasp it when the sledge-man called out triumphantly, '*Tenez bien, messieurs!*'

The edge of the abyss came rushing towards us. I shrank backwards, gripping the sides of the sledge, and let out a strangled scream as – with a loud crack of splintering ice, followed by a nauseating light smooth swish of runners – we shot over the edge and sailed out into the emptiness of space.

A split second of complete silence. The wind whistled

230

past my ears. A tremendous crash. Then the sides of the sledge were being wrenched brutally from my fingers. I lost my grip; and all at once I was sprawling like a broken puppet, my legs flailing helplessly in the insubstantial air.

Struggling wildly, I grabbed the sledge's hand-rails again and pulled myself half up. By now the whole machine was hurtling down a near-vertical slope of what seemed like highly polished glass. Faster and faster we went, slewing now to the right, now to the left, as banks of snow rose up from the ground on either side.

Momentarily, my vision cleared. Talabot was still sitting stiffly with his back to me, mechanically leaning slightly this way and then that as our uncoiling path began to twist and turn before us. Seized with the sudden notion of trying to hurl myself overboard before our flimsy vessel broke up into a thousand pieces under us, I pulled myself round onto my side and started to drag myself backwards with my arms.

And then, with disbelieving eyes, I found myself staring up at the squat form of the sledgeman – whom I thought we had left behind on being launched into the lethal void – still there, perched on the back of the vehicle like a diabolical hobgoblin.

'*Au milieu! Au milieu!*' he shouted in panic over the howling of the passing wind, as the sledge sheared sideways, and amid a hideous deafening scraping noise and a shower of blinding frosty needles I was thrown back into the middle of the sledge.

On and on we rushed, bumping, jolting, leaping, lurching from side to side. I tried to pull myself up again. We rounded a steep bend, our crazy, violently vibrating conveyance drifting sideways and climbing a concave wall of ice. Then, just as it seemed we would inevitably overturn, with a shudder the sledge righted itself again and raced headlong forward, towards a black mass of trees. But as suddenly as they loomed up, they abruptly dipped and vanished behind a colossal embankment of snow.

'*Mon Dieu,*' whispered a disembodied voice (Talabot? the sledgeman?).

The runners hit something hard. I was thrown backwards. Looking up, I saw for a moment against the sky our helmsman, his eyes wide with amazement, half-standing in the back of the sledge.

Then everything dissolved into a silent revolving blur. We rose into the air – but there was no air – we were ploughing through an asphyxiating, collapsing wall of whiteness. The entire universe began to perform a series of leisurely somersaults: once, twice, three times, then, rocking slightly, resumed its upright position.

With a tremendous jolt we came to earth. Sound flooded once again through the muffled portals of my ears. The thunderous rumble of the runners subsided gradually into a sibilant hiss as we lost speed. Then, with a final frosty crunch of snow, a dying rattle, we gently, eerily came to rest in a wide hushed clearing in the woods, to find ourselves being gravely looked down upon in the twilight by a circle of tall, imperturbable, mildly quizzical fir trees.

In this manner we descended the mountain into the land that is called Savoy.

When we awoke on the following day the cloud had lifted, and ranged before us stood chain upon chain of snow-covered mountains – beyond which lay the realm of the King of France – their white slopes gleaming in the pure light of the morning sun, their summits so high that one could fancy, were one able to ascend them, one could thereby attain access to the celestial Court of the Spheres. But my quest, alas, lay here on earth, not in the resplendent heavens.

With the small settlement of wooden houses that made up Lanslebourg still lying in a dark wedge of shadow cast over them by the peak of Mont Cenis, we set out westwards down the steep wooded valley of the river Arc. The air was clear and still and frosty, the ground covered with a soft layer of new snow that had fallen soundlessly in the night, as we slept oblivious by a glowing fire.

For some time we rode close to the banks of the river, but then the valley grew narrower and more precipitous and

the path ascended the side of a gorge, and we found ourselves following the river still, but now looking down on its
cold green foaming waters from high above. And so we
went on for a couple of hours, at some points coming upon
deep ravines traversed by makeshift bridges of pine trunks
lashed together and rendered horribly slippery by the fresh
fall of snow, until eventually the way became so narrow
and hazardous that we were forced to dismount and lead
our beasts, for fear of tumbling down the sheer cliffs into
the chasm.

Great evil-looking icicles now hung in clusters from
overhanging rocks like sharpened adamantine rods and in
places, where springs trickled from the rock face onto the
path, mirror-smooth sheets of hardened ice covered the
track and we had to go forward on our hands and knees,
breaking the ice with axes before we could risk leading our
animals across. But at last the path widened out and with
relief we remounted. As the sun slid behind the western
peaks and darkness began to fall upon the valley we came
within sight of a place called Saint-Jean-de-Maurienne,
where we resolved to spend the night.

The next day we continued on our way down the pine-
clad valley of the Arc – riding all day at the foot of a
massive snow-covered mountain – until that river passed
by the town of Aiguebelle and debouched into the roaring
torrent of another river called the Isère. On the opposite
side of the valley, high up on a spur of treeless rock, there
stood a strong solitary castle.

Talabot said, 'That's the Marshal's castle, Miolans. We
can stay there for tonight.'

Though the Marshal was not present – being still in the
Piedmont, where we had left him – his family (the mistress
of the castle, her young children and her brother) received
us kindly. I was beginning to grasp a few words of French,
but still could not understand much of what was said. But
that night it mattered little for we retired to bed early and
although our generous hosts urged us to remain some days
we departed the following morning for Chambéry, the
capital of Savoy.

233

As we descended along the valley of the Isère the abundant fir and pine trees that fill the lower slopes of the higher mountains of Savoy began to give way to wild olive, hazel, chestnut and walnut trees, and even vines (skilfully planted on the most inaccessible-looking hillsides). As we passed through hamlets and small villages and encountered groups of peasants on the road, I noticed that quite a number of the people were afflicted with goitres and grotesque swellings about the throat. I asked Talabot the cause of this. He said that they attribute it to drinking the cold waters from the melting snows. This seemed unlikely – for do not the people of Bursa and the Taurus and countless other places drink the icy waters of the mountains daily, even at the height of summer, without apparently suffering the least ill effects?

'Perhaps,' I said, 'it comes from eating too much pig-meat?' (For I had seen a startling number of these black hairy unclean creatures, grubbing about and wallowing in their own filth by the roadside and in backyards, since we had descended the mountain.)

Talabot seemed to find this quite hilarious and when he had sufficiently recovered from his mirth said, 'I had forgotten that you Turks share this ridiculous prejudice of the Jews. My dear fellow, there are Frenchmen who gorge themselves on pig-meat, as you call it, the whole year through, even – God forgive them – during Lent. And I can tell you, they get themselves big fat bellies, but never necks like these!'

'Tell me,' I said, 'is there nothing that you Infidels do not eat?'

'For other Infidels I cannot speak,' he said, 'but we Frenchmen will eat anything. Whatever is in the market-place, and more besides.'

And so, chatting and arguing in a cheerful manner to pass the time, we rode on until we came to another fortress called Montmélian, which is built on a great barren rock and commands the hills and valleys for miles around. Seldom have I seen such an impregnable-seeming castle and would have been glad to get closer to inspect its structure

234

properly, but we decided to press on to reach Chambéry by nightfall. Accordingly, we turned away from the banks of the turbulent Isère and set our course north-westwards.

However, as we passed on the road directly below the castle, we were suddenly intercepted by a rascally group of men, some dressed in a ragged kind of livery, who swarmed around us and had the impudence to catch hold of my bridle. I drew my sword and, swearing, drove them off the road pell-mell into a water-logged ditch, where they cowered, whining and pleading for mercy.

'It's all right,' Talabot called out from behind me, 'they're Montmélian's officers.'

'Officers,' I said. 'These curs?'

There was an outburst of sneers and half-audible oaths from the ditch, until I raised my sword again and this collection of fearless bravoes scrambled in terror out of the ditch and scattered in all directions, falling over each other and sprawling headlong in the mud in their haste to get away.

'You really are the most impetuous fellow,' said Talabot, laughing and leaning out of his saddle to restrain me by grasping my arm. 'They wait here to collect the toll.'

'What toll?'

By this time the band had regrouped some way off among the furrows of a ploughed field and were contenting themselves with shouting insults and making obscene gestures in our direction.

'Montmélian has an ancient right to collect a toll on the road to Chambéry. Everybody has to pay it.'

'Oh, I see,' I said, sheathing my sword.

Talabot called the men over, but they seemed reluctant to come forward. So I rode a little way ahead and waited for him while he paid them. And having submitted ourselves to this insolent levy, we proceeded on our way, travelling on one of the most wretched and badly maintained stretches of road I ever saw in all my time in Europe.

*   *   *

235

This place Chambéry lies in a wide flat valley surrounded on all sides by a ring of mountains. The whole city is encircled by strong walls and a deep moat filled with water. Within the walls there stands a citadel, which is the ancient seat of government of the Duchy of Savoy. Yet the town has an air of sad neglect – and indeed, as Talabot confirmed, the Dukes spend little time there nowadays, being more preoccupied with their domains in the rich Piedmont, which their jealous and greedy Italian neighbours would dearly love to deprive them of by seizing them for themselves.

In the church there, they have the shroud in which – they say – was wrapped the Lord Jesus after the crucifixion and which bears an outline of his body and the features of his face till this day. I did not see it, but Talabot assured me that the Christians regard this relic with intense veneration and come on pilgrimages from far and wide to pray to it and seek intercession through it. For, being ignorant of the Glorious Koran, they do not know that God in His Mercy took Jesus into Heaven and that it was one of his followers that was crucified in his stead – may He open the eyes of these Misbelievers and bestow upon them the clear light of the True Religion!

As there was nothing to keep us in that city, at sunrise we left Chambéry and rode southwards through bird-filled forested foothills towards the mountains on the other side of which lay France.

At length the road emerged from the woods into high green pastures and, leaving the tortuous rutted track, we galloped over grassy meadows towards a vertical grey wall of solid rock. As we advanced I began to slacken my pace, realizing that we were riding into a deep amphitheatre of unscalable towering cliffs. Yet Talabot rode on as briskly as before until, reaching the foot of the cliff, he turned his horse and waited for me to catch him up. I approached him now slowly, cautiously, beginning to wonder if I was being enticed into some kind of ambush. Talabot seemed to grow perplexed and called out impatiently, 'Come on, man, is your damned beast lame or something?'

236

Then, as I drew near him, the dull thud of my horse's hoofs on the damp grass reverberating ever more loudly against the blank grey face of the rock, he seemed to lose patience altogether and with vigorous blows of his whip charged full speed at the cliff, and suddenly disappeared.

Thunderstruck, I kicked my own horse on and started in hot pursuit. But when I reached the bottom of the cliff there was still no sign of Talabot. He had utterly vanished without trace, as though swallowed up by the mountain. I called out to him but, save for the dying echo of my own voice, there was no reply.

I rode forward several yards, recklessly aiming straight for the rock face until my horse shied away, whinnying piteously and rearing to avoid colliding with it and dashing both our brains out. Then, as the beast twisted round, pawing the empty air with its forelegs, for a split second I got a clear view along the base of the deeply creviced bluff – and all at once I saw it, a great dark cleft in the rock, half-concealed by clinging ivy and a dense dark-green mass of hanging creepers.

I rode through the gap and found myself descending a deep winding gorge between breathtakingly sheer walls of smooth unhewn limestone. Looking up, I could see far above a strip of clear blue sky and, hearing my horse's hoofs ringing out against hard ground underfoot, I glanced down to discover that the floor of the gorge was paved from side to side with a magnificent roadway of pure white marble. Still marvelling at this extraordinary thoroughfare, I came upon my companion.

'Aha, there you are at last.'

'Who built this road?' I said in wonderment.

'Who knows?' he said, shrugging his shoulders. 'It's been here as long as anybody can remember.'

As we went down the gorge the road became gradually steeper and then, rounding a corner, it ran straight ahead and plunged into the mouth of a gigantic cavern. When we got nearer to its silent forbidding entrance Talabot spoke again.

'At one time, they say, you could ride right through there

237

and come out on the other side of the mountain. But the roof's fallen in and blocked the way.' Then, pointing to a rough path leading away to the left of the mouth of the cavern and ascending a slope covered with loose stones to what looked like another natural fissure in the rock, he went on, 'There's another way through up there.'

He dismounted and I followed his example. Leading our horses by the bridle, we climbed up the incline and, squeezing through a gap between two large moss-encrusted boulders, we came out at the top of a long flight of very steep, irregular, pot-holed steps cut crudely into the rock. We began to descend them, guiding our horses as best we could and trying to prevent them from sliding and falling on the slippery surface, which had been worn lethally smooth by the hoofs of countless animals that had passed this way since the road through the cave had been buried for ever in rubble.

After going more or less straight down between the towering walls of the gorge, the stairway veered to one side, and coming suddenly and unexpectedly to the end of it, we found ourselves standing on a ledge with a drop of a hundred feet or so below, looking over a great sunlit valley, divided into a patchwork of green, brown, dark-red and yellow fields, studded here and there with little copses and clumps of trees. A silver river snaked through a wood just below our feet and following its tranquil meandering course, my eye lit upon the jumbled rooftops of a town nestling below a round grassy hillock on which I could descry the walls and towers of a small neat castle.

'That's Les Echelles. It means "The Steps",' said Talabot, indicating with an expansive wave the stone stairway on which we stood (and which, I now saw, continued precipitously down the cliff face to the left of where we had halted, until it ended at the valley floor). 'It's the last town in Savoy. The other side of the river is France.'

'Whose is that castle?' I said.

'It belongs to the Duke. But do you see that fortified stone house with the tall keep and the walls, in the middle of the town between the river and the castle?'

'Yes . . .'

'It's a Commandery of your friends the Knights. The Prince stayed there for some time before he crossed over into France. Its position is not so good, but it's stronger and better-defended than the castle.'

'So what do we do now?'

'We cross the river. There's a bridge in town – but we're not going to use it. The Commandery's practically right next door to it and the Knights have been watching the traffic over it night and day since Jem went on into France. Last time I crossed it they stopped and searched me. What's more, after your little contretemps with Guy de Blanchefort in Genoa, their men will certainly have a description of you and they'll be looking out for you.'

'How do we get across, then?'

Grasping my shoulder, Talabot pointed to a small spinney by the river, about a mile upstream from the town. Shading my eyes, I could see that just below it the water was catching the sunlight and flashing white, as though it became shallower at that point and was running over stones.

'There's a ford there. It's guarded, but smugglers use it sometimes and for the right price arrangements can be made. We can stay out of sight in the trees down there until it gets dark . . .'

As we prepared to descend the remaining steps that led into the leafy woods and thickets down by the river, I lingered a little while longer and looked out over the valley again to the hills of France, which rolled away gently westwards until they became indistinguishable from the quivering undulating waves of light on the bright noon horizon.

Then, hearing distant voices and hoofs echoing in the gorge behind me, I turned and hastened down the stairway after Talabot.

Night Journey

Once in France we had not ridden many hours before the hills began to give way to flatter country and for the best part of two days we rode across a spacious cultivated plain where peasants toiled in orchard, field and vineyard. Turning northwards along the banks of a swift-flowing river called the Rhône, on the third day in the early afternoon we came to Lyons. A vast and populous city, one of the greatest in all Europe, it is walled, with seven gates, and stands above the confluence of two rivers – the fast-running Rhône and a slower, dirtier stream known as the Saône – and lies at the foot of a range of hills, facing a broad fertile plain that stretches eastwards as far as the eye can see. Handsome white stone bridges span the rivers linking the city with the plain, and the innumerable houses, churches and other edifices that adorn this fine place are also built of stone. Even many of the private dwellings are five or six storeys high and, according to my companion, all have beneath them extensive vaults, well stored with foodstuffs and all manner of other provisions.

Nor, I discovered, is the population entirely French, for Infidel merchants converge on this centre of commerce not only from all over France but from every corner of Christendom; and many of these foreign traders reside in the city – as the Florentines and Genoese do at Galata – for years on end without returning to their native lands.

We lodged at a tavern called the Three Kings, where the innkeeper was a friend of Talabot's and belonged by birth, like my guide, to the Auvergne. The man was absent and not expected till the evening. We were given adjoining rooms overlooking a small courtyard.

'I don't know about you,' said Talabot, 'but I'm dog-tired and could do with some sleep. In any case we won't be able to talk to Monsieur Georges until tonight, so we may as well get some rest.' He yawned.

'I think I'll do the same,' I said. 'Come and wake me when you want to go downstairs.'

I went along the corridor to my room and shut the door loudly behind me to make sure he heard it. I waited. After a little while I got up and went over to the wall separating our two rooms. I pressed my ear against it and, sure enough, I could hear him snoring softly. I stepped out into the corridor again and, shutting the door behind me as quietly as I could, crept off down the hall and towards the stairs.

I had hardly walked half a dozen steps along the crowded bustling streets when I came upon two prosperous-looking merchants standing on a corner conversing loudly in Italian as though not another soul in the whole of France could possibly speak a word of that language or understand what they were saying. I approached them, smiling, and said, 'Excuse me, gentlemen, but could you direct me to the shop of Messer Angelo Doria? It's near the cathedral, I believe.'

They stopped in mid-flow and turned to me, sizing me up with cunning searching eyes. One of them said, 'Are you Italian, sir?'

'Ragusan, from Dubrovnik.'

'Buying or selling?'

'Just testing the water.'

He gave a harsh barking laugh and said to the other man, 'Haven't I told you before? Trying to get a straight answer out of a Ragusan . . . impossible, absolutely impossible.' Then, turning to me again, 'Where are you staying, my friend?'

I pointed up the street. 'The White Horse.'

'Are you indeed? Perhaps I'll drop by to see you. Will you be there tonight at supper time? I might be able to

241

help you, seeing that you're obviously new here.'

'I'll be there,' I said. 'Now . . .'

'You're nearly there. Keep going straight until you get to the square. His shop's right there on your left – you can't miss it.'

A few minutes later I was standing in a spacious upstairs room in front of Angelo Doria, who sat rubicund, benign, bespectacled behind a large oak table. He took Frenk Iskender's draft, unfolded it and, after glancing at it, peered up at me over the top of his glasses and said, 'Could I trouble you to return in about an hour? This is quite a large amount. I'll have to get some of it from elsewhere.'

'No trouble at all,' I said.

I left the building and, strolling off casually, took up a position by a fountain on the opposite side of the Place de Saint-Jean. I settled down to watch. Nobody went in or out except a couple of old women, half a dozen harmless-looking merchants and a ledger clerk (whom I had seen in the office), who left shortly after me and returned about half an hour later. I began to wonder if there was a back door I had missed.

The gilded hand of the square's clock crawled slowly round the dial. As it chimed five o'clock I recrossed the square and dived into the shop. I mounted the stairs with my hand on the hilt of my sword. The door was not quite closed. I peered cautiously through the crack. I was almost disappointed. Everything was just the way it had been an hour before, with the amiable old man sitting behind his large oak table. Only this time in front of him on the table, in five neat columns, ten coins in each, stood fifty bright golden florins. Less than a minute later I was back in the street with a strange feeling, almost as though I had just committed a robbery.

I returned to my room at the Three Kings. Quietly locking the door, I undressed and, after hiding the money underneath the mattress, lay down on the bed. Almost immediately I began to drift off to sleep, but awoke with a start when I heard a soft tapping at what I thought was my door. I wrapped myself in the sheet and unsheathed my sword. Then I heard Talabot's door open and a muttered exchange of greetings. His door closed again and there was silence.

I went over to the wall, shivering a little from the cold, and once more pressed my ear hard up against the wall. An urgent whispered conversation was taking place next door. Although the wall was far from thick, at first I couldn't decipher a single word of what was said, let alone understand it. But I soon realized what their conversation was about when I heard repeated now over and over again 'les Chevaliers', 'le Prince' and 'Jeem' (as Talabot's mysterious visitor pronounced his name). Suddenly the conversation ceased and Talabot's door abruptly swung open and footsteps receded down the corridor.

I hurried back to bed and lay down again. A few seconds later there was a knock at the door. I got up and let Talabot in. He seemed excited and could hardly prevent himself from breaking into a broad grin.

'I've just been talking to Georges,' he said. 'He arrived back early and came to my room when he heard that we were here.'

'Has he any news?'

'He certainly has and it looks like we're in luck.'

'What did he say?'

'This summer he was speaking to a wine trader from Bordeaux who comes to Lyons every year before the harvest to take orders from the taverns. When he was on his way here this year, he stopped at midday in a field to eat and have a rest. After a while a party of men travelling with a heavily armed escort of the Knights of St John appeared on the road and stopped nearby to water their animals at a stream. But they didn't see the merchant because he was lying in a dip in the grass, in the shade of a tree, and his horse had wandered off into some thickets to graze . . .'

'And?'

'Well, he watched them for a while before they set off again. He said the men looked foreign and he heard them speaking in a language he'd never heard before – even though, Georges says, he's been around a bit, even as far as Muscovy . . . And the thing is, he said that one of these foreigners was a powerful, very striking-looking fellow with a short black beard and . . . well, a sort of regal look about him . . .'

'Where was this?'

'Not far from a castle called Boislamy. It's on its own in the middle of a forest, miles from anywhere. Years and years ago I was travelling with my father; we mistook the road and wandering about, lost in the forest, we caught sight of it from a distance. If that's where the Prince has been hiding it's not surprising that nobody's been able to find out where he's been all this time.'

'But from what you say this was quite some while ago. And even if it was Jem this man saw, we've still no idea where he was heading and where he is now.'

'That's just where you're wrong. Georges went to see an old pal from his village earlier today who arrived back in Lyons only a few days ago. And this man swears that Jem's now staying in a priory not far from their village.'

'It could be just another story being put about by the Knights.'

'Not this time. It would be too close to the truth. Look, when the wine trader saw the Prince—'

'*Thought* he saw the Prince.'

'From the description, I'd say it was the Prince. After all, he wasn't expecting to see him and what had he to gain by making up the story? Anyway, the point is that when he saw him he was going south; in other words he was going in the right direction to be on his way to the priory near Georges' village.'

'All right,' I said, holding up my hands in a gesture of submission. 'But what possible reason could Jem have had for going to this priory in the first place?'

'No reason whatever,' said Talabot, 'except that the priory in question just happens to be Guy de Blanchefort's Priory, the headquarters of the Order for the whole of the Auvergne . . .'

*   *   *

It was still dark when we clattered over the cobbles through the empty streets of Lyons and, turning our backs on the city and the plain, set off westwards into the hills.

Towards the evening of the second day, as the sun was sinking below a dismal grey rain-obscured horizon, we came to the bank of a wide river, a little to the north of Ambert. Beyond its cloudy swirling waters there stretched a seemingly limitless expanse of barren terrain of a bleakness and hostility that would have made the stoutest and most resolute heart quail just to look upon it, let alone face the prospect of traversing it, and which, with all the fervour of some latter-day Moses on the threshold of the Promised Land, Talabot declared to be the ancient, the glorious, the incomparable land of his ancestors – the Auvergne.

Soon afterwards we arrived in Ambert, where we found lodgings for the night, and at dawn we crossed the river. For the rest of the day we rode through relentless drizzle, across wild wind-scoured heathlands, without encountering a single living soul, occasionally passing by isolated tumbledown ruins and deserted hamlets where roofless houses stood empty and open to the glowering sky, and black-visaged crows circled angrily above our heads, their raucous cawings rending the blustering air.

And so we wearily pressed on through this wilderness of gorse and heather until, on the fourth day out of Lyons, we descended into a marshy densely wooded plain and, making our way along a winding road half-buried by great damp drifts of fallen autumn leaves, we approached the lower slopes of a stark treeless range of hills.

At a clearing where the road forked, Talabot reined in his animal and, pointing to a track that led away to the north, said, 'My village is not far from here. I suggest we go there and rest our horses. Also, we may get some more news of the Prince.'

As twilight began to gather around us, we came to a fast-flowing river and followed its banks upstream. After a while we rode into a valley and came within sight of a dark group of houses and a little church lying half-concealed in a wooded hollow bathed in the dim ghostly light of a crescent moon.

'This', said my companion proudly, 'is Saint-Jean-Mozac, my village.'

A minute or two later we had reached Talabot's house – a long low stone building that stood a little apart from the other houses in the village amid grassy fields sloping gently down to the edge of the gurgling waters of the river. Warm, honey-coloured light showed through the cracks in the shutters. And as the noise of our arrival set the farmyard dogs off into a wild paroxysm of barking, the door was flung open, golden light poured out into the yard and a young woman (Talabot's sister, as I was to discover a few seconds later) came out to meet us, hurriedly wiping her hands on her apron and pushing back the long dark tresses of her tangled hair.

But any joy that poor Talabot might have experienced on returning to his native place was soon dispelled by the news that his brother was gravely ill with some kind of fever and all hope had by now been abandoned of his recovering. Despite these unpropitious circumstances Talabot and his sister insisted that we should eat. There followed a substantial repast consumed in an uneasy silence and soon afterwards my grief-stricken hosts departed for their brother's house, leaving me alone. For a while I sat by the hearth, but finding myself unable to stay awake, I dragged myself off to bed.

I awoke the following morning to the sound of rain drumming on the roof and thunder rolling around in the high hills above the village. Descending the ladder from the loft where I had slept, I found my companion by the fire, unshaven, dressed as he had been the day before and staring vacantly into the flickering flames. I joined him and we sat there for some time without saying anything. After a while he got up, patted me on the shoulder, threw on his cloak and went out into the rain.

About two hours later he reappeared, dripping wet and gloomily shaking his head. He sat down beside me by the fire.

'Any news?'

'Uh?' he said absently.

'Any news?'

'What about?'

'Your brother.'

'No, still the same. He won't last long now, God forgive him. But I've been to see some other people too. About the Prince.'

'Come up with anything?'

'Absolutely nothing. It's all very curious. Georges seemed to be so certain about everything he'd heard.'

'This is a small place. Is there a town with a market anywhere near here?'

'Riom's not far. I'll go there tomorrow and see if I can pick up anything. I have friends there.'

But when he returned from his expedition on the following day, he looked even more despondent than he had done the day before.

'Surely someone must have heard something?'

'Apparently not.'

'Well,' I said after a long pause, 'I can't see what else we can do other than go and have a look for ourselves.'

An expression of profound unhappiness came over Talabot's face and he said, 'There's no point in taking unnecessary risks. We'll hear something sooner or later. Until then you're much safer here.'

On the morning of the fourth day after our arrival in Saint-Jean-Mozac, Talabot went out early as usual, to go to his brother's house in the village. I heard him quietly pulling on his boots and creeping out, but I pulled the blanket over my head and tried to go back to sleep.

He returned much sooner than I had expected and climbed the ladder into the loft.

'Barak,' he said quietly.

I turned over.

'I've just heard something.'

I rubbed my eyes and sat up in bed.

'A salt merchant my brother knows called in at his house

247

just now while I was there. He'd heard that Jacques was ill and came specially to see him.'

'Is he from Saint-Jean?'

'No, from Riom. He's on his way home from Limoges.'

'What did he say?'

'A few days ago he was passing by Guy de Blanchefort's Priory and stopped off to see if they wanted to buy some salt . . .'

'Did he see anything?'

'Not exactly. But he said everybody was behaving very strangely. For one thing, the porter wouldn't open the gates at first – even though they know him perfectly well there – and kept him waiting for ages before letting him in. As though they were hiding something, he said.'

'There could have been other reasons for that.'

'Not according to what he heard afterwards. Before he left he paid a visit to a family in the village – he's known them for years, they put him up sometimes. And even they were acting oddly. Well, eventually they told him that there are Turks in the Priory, but the Knights have warned the villagers that they'll string everybody up – man, woman and child – if anyone's caught blabbing to any strangers about it. Apparently, they're all scared stiff.'

By this time I was out of bed and struggling to get into my clothes.

Talabot seemed thoroughly taken aback by my response and said in bewilderment, 'Where are you going?'

'For goodness' sake, man,' I said, 'there's no time to lose. Come on, let's go.'

'But I can't just run off and leave my brother the way he is now.'

'You've said yourself there's nothing more you can do for him.'

'That's not the point; he may go at any time.'

'All right, I'll travel alone.'

'Don't be ridiculous.' Talabot turned away abruptly.

I started to pack my things. As I did so I caught his eye. He tried to avoid my glance, but then suddenly let out a great sigh and throwing up his arms in a gesture of despair said, 'All right, all right. Go and get the horses ready, I'll run down into the village and say goodbye to that poor brother of mine.'

At noon we reached a place called Pontgibaud. Here an old wooden bridge spanned the turbid red-brown waters of a river swollen by the recent rains. We were in high country now and a chilly fog still lingered on the damp ground, defying the weak beams of the wintry sun. Crossing the bridge, we pushed on through a mysterious land where water seemed to be flowing everywhere, in brooks and streams and rivulets, and brimming over in countless lakes and ponds, as though the Flood was in these parts only just subsiding and the land re-emerging for the first time since the days of Noah and his Ark.

Squelching and splashing along the waterlogged road, we were soon besmirched and bespattered with mud and, after fording several streams and rivers, soaked to the skin into the bargain. Talabot had brought along a lad of about twelve years old – one of his brother's children – to add a touch of innocence to the proceedings. But we hardly met another human being anywhere along the way, and those we did – desperately poor, down-trodden, introspective hillfolk – seemed to take little or no interest in us.

At Mérinchal we passed by a little castle and a village. The whole place seemed deserted and one would have thought it empty and abandoned but for the grey smoke rising into the mist from the chimneys of the château and a handful of the cottages. The light was beginning to fade and what seemed at first a passing evening shower soon became a steady and persistent downpour.

At about midnight, with the rain now tipping down in earnest and distant lightning intermittently igniting the ink-black western sky, we came to a place where the road descended steeply into a deep ravine. When we reached the bottom we found a boiling overflowing torrent traversed by an arched stone bridge. As we crossed it – riding through a haze of spray thrown up by the water rushing

249

against the piers of the bridge – a great clap of thunder exploded directly above our heads and in the simultaneous flash of lightning I saw illuminated high on a sheer cliff the walls and turrets of an imposing castle. Panicked by the thunder and the dazzling light, our horses bucked and reared, and only by fighting hard to control them did we succeed in preventing them from bolting wildly into the night. When things had calmed a little I came alongside Talabot and pointed up to the castle.

Shouting hoarsely over the elements, he said, 'That's Aubusson . . . it's lucky the weather's so damned filthy otherwise they might have had men checking travellers on the bridge.'

Straining to peer into the night, we made our way out of the gorge up a steep rise, battling against the wind and sheets of freezing rain until, gaining the brow of the hill, we came onto a barren plateau. But we had hardly recovered our breath when the track dipped again into the Stygian blackness of what for a moment I took to be a dark expanse of heaving water, but discovered an instant later to be a dense forest, violently swaying in the gale. Terrified by the groaning and creaking of the trees, our horses shied away and tried to back off. But, wielding our whips, we drove them on, closing our ears to their plaintive cries of distress and shouting encouragement to each other to steel our hearts against our own dread of entering this hellish place.

Such was the darkness of the wood that even the brilliant flashes of lightning penetrated as little more than a dull luminous glow through the canopy of boughs, and only by continuing to call out to one another over the roar of the wind through the trees did we manage to stay together at all, and not become separated. Stumbling through the tangled undergrowth and groping our way past impenetrable barriers of deformed and twisted oaks, we repeatedly wandered off the path.

But at last the blackness seemed to lighten just a fraction, and the trees to thin out a little. Still blinking and confused, we found the track again, and straightening up in our saddles, stretching our stiff aching limbs, we were startled to be able to make out the dim white features of each other's face.

We started to laugh and even our poor horses – scarcely crediting their luck at coming out alive from that awful region – pricked up their ears and gamely broke into a jerky, slightly crazy kind of trot.

Presently we emerged into a wide blustery clearing and as we rounded a bend a church and a tiny village came into view.

'Where's this?' I said.

'Saint-Hilaire,' said Talabot.

As we approached the settlement my horse began to lag behind the others and although I gently kicked it on I could feel that the beast was now all but spent; without rest, it might collapse from fatigue at any moment. Talabot and the boy had stopped and were waiting for me by a clump of bushes not far from the church.

Seeing the difficulties I was suffering, when I reached them Talabot said, 'Leave your horse and mount my lad's.'

I climbed out of my saddle. As I did so, I looked up and saw through an opening in the clouds that the morning star was rising in the dark-blue pre-dawn sky. Talabot told his nephew to wait for us here until we returned – he could get some sleep in the back of the church. Then I mounted the boy's horse while he took mine and led it slowly away.

We travelled on for some time more and then heard the sound of bells. I asked my companion, 'What is that? There is no castle here. What is that ringing?'

At that moment a figure appeared in front of us, as if from nowhere, wearing a rough woollen cape with a pointed hood, and bent under the weight of a wicker basket full of wood. Talabot said to him, 'Where is Bourganeuf?'

Waving backwards with his arm, without looking up at us, the man replied, 'Just ahead of you.' And he continued to trudge under his burden up the road in the direction from which we had come.

As we rode on, sombre grey clouds began to gather on the horizon and roll towards us, until they seemed to fill the

251

whole vast vault of the heavens with their billowing forms. Thus the dawn came and went but the sun failed to appear and an eerie darkness lay over the face of the world.

At length a post appeared on a ridge before us with a cross fixed to it, stark and black against the murky sky. I heard Talabot murmuring what sounded like a prayer and when we reached the cross, around which was draped a forlorn wreath of dried-up yellowing laurel leaves, we found ourselves looking down into an enormous valley. It seemed at first to be devoid of human habitation, but all of a sudden a ragged rent opened in the black pall overhead. A great shaft of light stabbed earthwards through the gap and for a fleeting moment burst upon a great round tower standing at the end of a spur of rock, way down below us. Then the clouds once more closed their ranks, the celestial shaft evaporated into thin air and the valley darkened once again.

The ground fell away too steeply for us to descend from where we were, so we continued along the edge of the ridge until we came to a gushing mountain stream that tumbled down the hillside in a series of foaming cataracts and waterfalls, in the direction of the crag on which the tower stood.

We dismounted.

Leading our horses, with Talabot in front and me following behind, we set off down a path that zigzagged its way to the bottom of a gully and thereafter followed the winding course of the stream flowing towards Bourganeuf.

As we got closer I could see that the fortress consisted of a defensive wall encircled by a moat and, within the walls, a keep consisting of three round towers – one much larger than the others – with conical black slate roofs, and a heavily buttressed priory church, surmounted at the eastern end of its sharply pitched roof by the tall lantern of the now silent belfry. Below the walls on the southern side was huddled a township of some kind – inhabited no doubt by the hapless vassals of the Grand Prior and his Knights. But the most striking feature of the place was the great round tower that dwarfed the other towers and even the large bulk of the church, and seemed to grow bigger and more imposing with every step we took.

Leaving the banks of the torrent as it plunged noisily to the valley floor, we began to tramp upwards again towards the rocky promontory on which the castle and the village stood. As we came near the first houses the door of a small stone hut flew open and a big broad-shouldered Infidel stepped into the middle of the track, barring our progress and eyeing us suspiciously. When we came within earshot he said, 'What people are you?'

'We are from Saint-Jean-Mozac,' said Talabot, wiping his brow with his sleeve, 'my brother's wife's family live here.' Then he asked for them by name and the man's face relaxed, and he stood aside and waved us past. As we passed him Talabot said, 'I have not had the pleasure of coming here before. Tell me, is there a tavern where we could find something to eat?'

He directed us to one and, without difficulty, we found it. There was nobody there but ourselves and indeed the whole village had a subdued fearful atmosphere. We ate some bread and cheese and drank some stale wine as we sat by the smoking fire trying to dry out our stiff sodden clothes.

Then the Priory bells began to ring out again. I looked at Talabot and raised an eyebrow. Casually my companion said to the tavern keeper, 'Is it time for Mass?'

'Yes,' he replied, then ducked through a low door and disappeared into the backyard of the tavern.

So we got up and made our way through the narrow muddy lanes until we came to the gates of the fortress, which had been thrown open in case any of the towns-people wished to attend the service. We passed through the gates and crossing a cobbled courtyard mounted the steps of the church. Pushing a heavy, hide-covered, brass-studded inner door, we came into a dark echoing vault smelling of incense and candlewax. At the far end of the church, just below the altar, a great many Knights sat in wooden stalls, each one reading from a book held in his hand. I pulled up my scarf and stood in the shadows in a secluded corner. My companion slipped out again, closing the door gently behind him, the leather making a dull bump on the wooden frame as it swung shut.

The Knights sat engrossed in their devotions and there was no sound but for a low murmuring as they read from their books. Nobody else came in or went out. One or two of the Knights looked up and glanced round. I moved closer into the shadows, my mouth dry and bitter from the taste of the wine.

After a while the door behind me creaked open once more. I felt a light tap on my shoulder. I turned slowly. Without speaking, Talabot indicated with a jerk of his chin that I should follow him outside.

We made our way along the side of the church as a thin eunuchoid falsetto within began to sing and the Knights chanted the responses in booming voices. Rounding the end of the building, I saw the Great Tower for the first time at close quarters. A massive structure, seven storeys high, its windows barred with thick iron rods, it stood slightly apart from the other buildings of the priory, linked to them only by a long bridge-like covered gallery, some thirty feet above the ground – in case of attack it would be possible to seal off this one tower completely, making it a well-nigh impregnable independent fortress, with a clear field of fire on every side. The arrangement struck me as extremely curious, but I was soon to learn the reason for it.

When we had stealthily edged along the wall of the church to a point from which we could get an unimpeded view of the tower and its surrounds, we slipped behind a buttress; an empty cart standing before it acted as a screen.

On a lawn sloping down to the moat that almost entirely encompassed the tower, I saw six men wearing turbans. They seemed to be taking the air and were gazing out over the steep green meadows on the far side of the moat to the broad vista of the immense valley beyond.

One of them – a tall well-built man – was wearing a

large white turban and black velvet robe. He was chatting to another man with a full beard who looked to me like an Infidel, but somehow not a Knight.

Then the man in the turban turned a little towards me and my eyes rested on Jem's face. His fine features were drawn and pale, his bright grey-blue eyes slightly sunken, and I noticed that he had cut off his beard but let his heavy black moustaches grow long, which served to enhance the youthfulness of his visage and the whiteness of his skin.

Suddenly the conversation with the Infidel appeared to have come to an end. Jem turned away and now seemed, like the others, to be silently contemplating the wide empty valley and the grey cloud-filled horizon.

Guards lounged insolently everywhere around Jem and his companions, and skulked on the edges of the emerald patch of lawn. Half a dozen more, armed with pikes, swords and crossbows, blocked the narrow isthmus to the moated island on which the Great Tower stood. And at last it dawned upon me that, far from being their honoured guest, Jem was but a prisoner of these Infidels . . .

An indescribable misery pervaded the whole scene. And the more I looked upon it, the more I became overwhelmed with grief to see this noble prince reduced to this ignoble obscure confinement by those enemies of God and the True Religion, the damnable Knights of Rhodes. That such a valiant lion among men should have come to this! To see him standing there with such grave dignity and composure made me want to turn my face away and weep.

I fell into such a black reverie that I hardly noticed at first that one of the guards seemed to have caught sight of us and was now aggressively swaggering in our direction.

Talabot whispered, 'Time we were leaving . . .,' then took me by the arm and we wandered off, pretending to be deep in conversation.

The man called out to us to stop but, ignoring him, we strolled on as casually as we could, until we had rounded the end of the church again. We looked back and saw with relief that the guard – a nasty-looking, unshaven, potbellied individual – appeared to have abandoned the

255

chase and returned to loafing with his contemptible colleagues.

With a heavy heart I turned my back on Bourganeuf, on France, on the lands of the Unbelievers, and set out for home to deliver to my masters the news of Jem's whereabouts and of his captivity. When I rode out of that remote valley and began to retrace my steps, I thought that this would be the end of my involvement with the Prince and the melancholy Fate that had befallen him in Europe. But Destiny had other plans for me. And, as a wise poet once said, when the arrow of Destiny is shot, the Spheres themselves avail not for a shield.

Book Three

The Mantled One

And for two years my life seemed set to take a different course. I made my report. I told Kivami Bey of how I had discovered the Hajji at Bourganeuf, of his appearance and that of his companions; I told him of the mysterious tower in which they were held, the strongly fortified Priory, the inhospitable nature of the countryside, the immense distance of these wild uplands from the sea. He grimly cursed the perfidy, the cunning of the Knights.

He said nothing now of the audacious plan he had once had of abducting Jem by means of a raid. There was no need. Both of us knew that as long as the Infidels kept the Prince in this Godforsaken place, it was beyond the bounds of possibility that such an action could be carried out successfully.

What the Old Man's next move would be I could only guess at – for it soon became evident that whatever he proposed to do next, I would not be privy to it. He intimated that I would presently be transferred back to some unspecified naval duties. Yet, before I resumed my former existence, I learned with profound apprehension that I had a final task to fulfil. I was to appear before the Emperor himself.

I awaited the dreadful summons. It came towards midnight of the day after my return to Istanbul. I left the Convent and made my way to the Palace through the cold hushed streets under a starless sky. Admitted within the walls by a postern gate, I was conducted by a chamberlain bearing a lantern through silent courts and obscure corridors until we came to a small anteroom where a pair of

259

formidable black mutes swiftly searched my clothes. When they were satisfied that I was unarmed, the chamberlain threw open a set of double doors, the mutes took hold of my arms and I was led into a dimly lit chamber, in which I found myself at last in the august presence of Sultan Bayezid.

He sat cross-legged upon his divan, attired in a white turban and simple dark woollen cloak, motionless as a statue of stone, his face barely discernible in the dimness. I sank to the floor and prostrated myself. I remained like this for some time, then the mute bodyguards gently raised me up into a kneeling position on the carpet and remained on either side, grasping me firmly by the arms and sleeves. I heard the doors behind me being softly closed upon us. The high-ceilinged chamber resounded within to the gushing of water pouring from a row of spouts in one wall, into a deep trough that stretched nearly the full length of the room – a precaution, I had no doubt, against inquisitive ears without.

An interminable interval followed, in which the noise of the water seemed to increase by the minute. As my eyes adjusted to the light, my glance fell upon what looked like a copy of my report lying on the divan beside Bayezid.

After a while the Emperor spoke, 'You are quite certain, Captain, that it was our brother you saw that morning?'

'Yes, Your Majesty.'

There was a long pause, then he murmured, 'H'm.'

He began to stroke his bearded cheek with his index finger. Eventually he sighed and with a vague wave of the hand he said:

'Tell me exactly what happened, Captain. From the beginning, if you will. Naturally we have studied your deposition. But we should like to hear an account from your own lips . . .'

For a moment I was so overcome with awe that I seemed incapable of speech. But then Bayezid said quietly, 'From the time you made contact in Genoa with our slave Grimaldo.'

And encouraged by the unexpected mildness of his

demeanour, I found my voice and began to tell my story once again.

The Emperor listened, at first interposing questions now and then. But before long he responded hardly at all to what I had to say. At length, he seemed so immersed in his own thoughts that I almost wondered if he was attending to my words at all. Yet when I was through, he spoke to me in a kindly fashion, said I had done well and signalled to one of the mutes to call in the chamberlain. And when this courtier entered he ordered him to fetch Davud Pasha, his Grand Vizir – for even this high officer of the State had been excluded from our nocturnal conclave.

Presently Davud Pasha arrived, looking grey-faced and perturbed. He seemed relieved to discover that he had been summoned solely so that the Sultan could instruct him to reward me with a robe of honour and a liberal sum in gold. Nor was this the limit of this great-hearted Emperor's bounty – for within the week I was to receive Bayezid's personal commission to assume command of one of the superb new war galleys only recently completed and now waiting to be launched on the slipways of the Imperial Arsenal.

I soon learned that the Empire was then in sore need of men with experience of fighting at sea. Whilst I had been away, Kayitbay, the Sultan of Egypt – who still played host to Prince Jem's mother, wife and little children – had most treacherously invaded Ottoman territory and seized several frontier towns and fortresses in Karaman. At which, Jem's partisans in that province had again risen in support of the absent pretender, knowing that Bayezid would not risk committing the main body of the Imperial Army in the East so long as the menacing spectre of Jem's return loomed large in the West.

The conflict had raged in the border regions for more than a year – sometimes the Ottomans, sometimes the Egyptians and Jem's supporters winning the upper hand. But at last our enemies seemed to be slowly but inexorably gaining ground. And so it came about that in the spring following the year of my homecoming from the lands of the

Misbelievers, Sultan Bayezid ordered a powerful battle fleet into the Mediterranean to sail eastwards to bring relief to our beleaguered troops on the Syrian frontier.

Blown on by a fair and favourable wind, we sailed through the islands of the Archipelago and made our way along the southern coast of Anatolia. In the third week we encountered our first enemy vessels, and set about driving every one of Egypt and her allies' ships from that part of the ocean. We landed troops and cannon deep within Kayitbay's territories in Syria, bombarded his towns and castles, laid the countryside to waste, and spread terror and dismay amongst the insolent aggressors who had dared to violate the borders of the Guarded Domains.

Finally the malefactors' prospects looked as bleak and narrow as an Infidel's grave, and crushing defeat stared them in the face. But then, as the Imperial Fleet prepared to administer a last death-dealing blow, a great hurricane blew up, sinking ten galleys with all hands and inflicting terrible damage on several dozen other of our vessels. Thus were our endeavours overthrown on the very eve of victory. And as the storm gradually abated and the full extent of the destruction we had suffered became apparent, we had little choice but to bow to adverse Fortune and retire. Moreover, since the season was already far advanced we were compelled to abandon all hope of returning to the fray until the following year, and our Admiral signalled the Fleet to set sail at once for the safe havens of the Dardanelles, the Marmara and the Bosphorus – lest by delaying our departure longer we were caught in the annual heavy seas and storms of autumn.

On the journey back we passed through the straits that divide the mainland and the isle of Rhodes, where the Knights maintain their chief fortress and headquarters. Battle-weary and buffeted by the unfriendly elements though we were, I do not think there was a single man amongst us who would not willingly have launched an assault against them – such was our zealous desire to cause these miscreants some discomfort and inflict some damage upon their wretched refuge of Infidelity. But there was at that time a temporary truce in force between the Sublime Porte and the Order, which, as I came to know later, that sly fox Pierre d'Aubusson, the Grand Master of the Knights, had obtained from Sultan Bayezid by black-mailing him with threats of aiding Jem to return secretly to Turkey.

So we continued on our way, our guns thundering out salvo after salvo of blanks as we sailed past. To which ironic salutes the Infidels replied impudently in kind, the distant rumble of their cannons still echoing sporadically between sea and sky even as the Fleet drew away and the fortress sank from view below the purple evening horizon.

And as our master the Sultan — may God protect him! — is mighty and beneficent, and does not fail to reward the most insignificant services of his slaves, the Emperor took note in the dispatches of some successful engagements with the enemy in which I had played a part, and honoured me in due course with the command of a squadron of galleys, which, it had been decided, were to sail the following spring in advance of the main battlefleet to mount surprise attacks on the Syrian coast.

It was a good forty days before the Festival of St George — at which time the Imperial Fleet customarily puts to sea — when I received orders to prepare my flotilla to sail at the beginning of the following week. My flagship was then riding at anchor in midstream on the Golden Horn. That day, as it happened, we had just completed the task of taking on stores, powder and provisions. Since I had slept aboard for many days I decided to spend a night ashore, knowing that I might not have the opportunity again before we sailed. I left my vessel at sunset, expecting to be absent for no more than a few hours. But God decreed as He did decree, and I never set foot on her deck again.

The boat's crew gave a vigorous last pull on the oars, and we glided smoothly alongside the broad quay beneath the imposing bulk of the great sea walls. I got to my feet and, resting a hand on one of the oarsmen's shoulders to steady

263

myself, I waited my moment, then sprang onto the shore. I dismissed the men, instructing the bos'n to collect me the following morning at the time of the dawn prayer, and the boat briskly set off again across the harbour to row back to the flagship.

The declining sun was casting its dying golden glow upon the city's domes and minarets. It had been warm and clear all day and now the sky overhead was high and pale, the air tranquil without the faintest stir of breeze, the waters of the estuary flat calm and turning a dark glassy blue in the diminishing light.

I started out along the waterfront in the direction of the Christian district of Fener, where there was in those days a swordmaker, an old Greek, whom my father had employed for many years as an armourer, and from whom I had commissioned a new weapon to take with me on the impending expedition to Syria. The fellow was a brilliant craftsman, yet increasingly inclined to indolence, and in old age he had begun to affect a senile incapacity of mind (the genuineness of which was roundly belied by his unimpaired acumen when it came to setting a price for his labours). So I cannot say I was altogether surprised that, though several weeks had passed, he had neither brought the sword to the ship as I had told him to, nor sent any word at all as to why he had failed to do so. Thus I had resolved to confront the rogue in his workshop, reckoning (without much confidence) that my sudden appearance would strike such terror into him that he might exert himself to complete the weapon before I sailed.

I arrived at the gate that leads from the shore of the Golden Horn into that quarter. And savouring the thought of the fantastic and elaborate excuses he would inevitably offer (he was famous for them), if, as I hardly doubted, he had indeed failed to fulfil my commission, I passed under the archway and took a winding street leading to the cobbled main thoroughfare that ascends to the Church of the Most Blessed Virgin, near which, on an area of open ground, the Greek had both his workshop and his home. It was then that something so absurd occurred that even today I can scarcely believe that it happened in quite the way it did.

I was nearing the junction with the main thoroughfare when the street widened out a little, and I found myself passing through a kind of market where stalls selling clothes, ironmongery and household goods of various sorts lined the road on either side. Above them, lanterns hung suspended on poles; these had now been lit and were burning brightly in the dusk. There was not a great number of customers; most of them were women and some of the younger and prettier ones lowered their lashes, and coyly and half-heartedly covered their faces with their headscarves when I met their seductive glances with a bold and appraising eye. I must have been about five yards from the end of the street when a figure in a heavy cloak, clean-shaven but for a moustache, yet wearing a turban like a Muslim, came striding round the corner from the direction of the church and advanced towards me in a determined fashion.

At first I believed I was seeing things, that I myself had conjured up this apparition. But no. There could be no question about it. I had seen the man before. Two and a half years before, to be precise, in France, standing on that green patch of lawn before the great round tower, not six feet away from the Prince!

The man was very nearly upon me now. For a second I was overcome with the irrational fear that he might somehow recognize me. But then I took a hold of myself, and knew that even if he had caught a glimpse of me at Bourganeuf from afar, I was then beardless and dressed as an Infidel, and he could not possibly identify me now. Sure enough, when our eyes met, my features seemed not to make the slightest impression upon him. I turned away casually, pretending that something on one of the stalls had caught my attention. He swept past behind, his cloak brushing against me, and marched down the street into the twilight. I waited until his ghostly grey figure had receded almost out of view, then set off after him, back the way I had just come.

265

At first it seemed he was making for the waterfront and the harbour. But after a little while he veered south-eastwards and, leaving Fener, headed towards the Mosque of the Conqueror. The summons to the evening prayer was just beginning to be called out from the minarets in the different parts of the city, and as the Faithful emerged from their houses and hastened to join their fellows in the mosques, the narrow streets along which we passed suddenly became congested. Once or twice I thought I had lost my quarry. But then, quickening my pace, I caught sight of his cloak-enshrouded figure, still relentlessly pressing on at an urgent pace some little way ahead of me. Avoiding the spacious courtyard of the Conqueror's Mosque, which would by now be thronged with worshippers, he dodged down a side lane behind the Theological School and continued towards the Grand Bazaar. We crossed an open space in a partly ruined part of town that had not been rebuilt since the capture of the city. I grew anxious lest the man became aware that I was on his tail – but I need not have concerned myself. He ploughed on, looking neither to right nor to left.

Taking the wide roads towards Aya Sofia and the Palace Point, he reached the edge of the warren of streets around the Grand Bazaar. I tried to close up the gap between us. And it was just as well I did, because minutes later he suddenly plunged downhill towards the harbour and the Fish-market Gate. Some of the shops were still open on these streets and we met the crowds again. I lengthened my stride to catch up with him. There was a strong risk that if he happened to glance over his shoulder he would realize what was going on. But I just had to take that chance. Even so, a few seconds later I damn near lost him altogether.

It was just after the small square with the tall plane trees where Mahmud Pasha had built that fine new fountain. There was some kind of argument going on between a couple of porters at the bottom end of the square. They had put their loads down and were shaping up for a fist fight. As always, a large and appreciative crowd had materialized from nowhere and was beginning to mill and

266

jostle, waiting for the action to begin. My man pushed through, some way ahead of me. By the time I got to where he had been the porters were throwing their first punches and people were shouting encouragement and shoving and struggling to get a better view. I fought my way through, saw the cloaked figure some distance ahead, on the hill running down from the square, but then he vanished into some kind of side alley.

I ran forward and reached the spot where he had turned off. No sign of him. It looked like a dead end. Baffled, I set off blindly in pursuit. Then my eye caught a narrow vaulted passageway leading off to the left. Down I went, descending some steep uneven steps. It was pitch black, but after a few yards I came into the open. The path levelled out and led off across some open ground towards the entrance of another covered passage. A big stone wall rose up to the right of me. Some tall trees and the tiled roof of a house were visible on the other side.

I listened, holding my breath and straining to hear above the violent beating of my heart. I heard light footfalls and what sounded like a twig breaking. I felt my way forward, until I came to a small arched gate – but it was made of solid planks, the gaps between them filled with tar, and I couldn't find a single chink. A little way in front of me I perceived the dim outline of a large broken slab of stone leaning up against the wall. I sprang on to it, got a toehold in the rough stonework and hauled myself up with my arms just in time to look over and see my man enter the house, his hunched outline momentarily thrown into silhouette by the yellow lamplight streaming into the garden through the open door. Then the door shut and all was darkness once again.

We went in at first light. It was – even if I say it myself – a perfect operation. By then Kivami Bey's men had had all the lanes and alleyways in the immediate vicinity covered for several hours. Having run my quarry to ground, I had taken the precaution of making small nicks in the gate-posts, low down on either side, pulling a long thread from

267

my sleeve and stretching it between them. When I returned from the Convent with assistance it was still there, taut as a bowstring. Of course, it was possible the gate wasn't the only exit. I would soon find out.

As the dawn was beginning to lighten the eastern sky, I took a party over the garden wall. We made our way through the shadows to the rear of the house. The back door was bolted, but we managed to get it off with crowbars – frame and all – in about two minutes, with barely a sound. The last thing we needed was to have the suspect cut his throat or swallow poison to avoid being taken alive.

A stealthy search of the rooms on the ground floor revealed all of them to be empty. So I led the way up the stairs to the floor above. There were some nasty creaks that I thought might ruin everything. When I reached the stairhead I paused to listen for any signs of stirring. But all I could hear was a distant cock crowing and the first chirpings of the birds outside in the garden as they warmed up for the dawn chorus. I could now discern in the murky light that there was a small square landing with three doors leading off it. One door was slightly ajar. I crept over to it. As far as I could see, the room was empty but for a chest and a pile of old blankets or carpets in one corner.

The other doors were shut. I crossed over to the nearest and pressed my ear against it. I thought I heard the faint noise of a person breathing, but I couldn't be sure. I tried the latch; it seemed locked.

I returned to the top of the stairs and signalled silently to the men below what I meant to do. Then I went back to the door, braced myself on the uprights on either side, raised my knee, took aim and gave it a kick. The door gave way in a tremendous fusillade of splintering wood, jumping clean off its hinges and crashing onto the bare boards of the floor. I staggered backwards, found my balance and charged forward through the gaping hole.

The poor devil didn't stand a chance. Until that moment he had obviously been fast asleep. He leapt from his bed with a roar of surprise and rushed for his sword, which hung from a peg upon the wall. But he never got there. I hurled myself at him, bringing him heavily to the ground. And by the time the others thundered in behind me, I had him in a powerful stranglehold from which even his most violent and desperate struggles could not set him free.

It was not until late in the afternoon that Kivami Bey deigned to summon me to his inner sanctum. I had twice sought leave to depart, through Atik, and to my mounting annoyance had been refused, with no reasons given. The second time I was sorely tempted to go in any case, yet I hesitated to incur the Old Man's wrath and resigned myself to this wilful waste of precious hours that I should have been spending preparing to go to sea.

When I finally entered his room I expected to find him pleased at least at the successful arrest. But he looked more irritable than ever. He waved me to sit down on the divan beside him.

'Well,' he said, eyeing me with a sour expression, 'it is no thanks to you that we have discovered your distinguished prisoner's *exact* identity. I gather you didn't even *ask* him who he was before you brought him back here.'

I shrugged, saying, 'I'm sorry, sir, but I am no longer involved in this affair, and I thought it would exceed my duties to start questioning him.'

Kivami Bey gave a hollow laugh. Then he said, 'He is Sadi.'

'Jem's Chancellor?' I said.

'Correct.'

'And the Prince himself?'

'If Sadi's telling the truth, still in France,' said Kivami Bey. 'Sadi claims he himself managed to escape.'

'But why come here?' I said. 'He was taking a terrible risk showing himself in Istanbul.'

'Not necessarily. His face is well known in Karaman and Konya, but not here. Besides, he had no money left after his journey and needed to get hold of some before he could do anything else. His little excursion to Fener was to try to raise some from a Greek moneylender there. He was very unlucky to run into you of all people.'

'What will happen to him now?' I said.

'That depends. He's extremely bitter about the way the Knights have treated his master. This could prove invaluable for our purposes . . .'

Kivami Bey fell silent and sat hunched beside me for a while staring into space and tugging absentmindedly at his fat moist lower lip. His pockmarked skin appeared blotchier and more sickly, and his straggling beard more unkempt and unevenly trimmed than ever. He slowly nodded and turned the blank gaze of his cold eyes upon me once again.

Then he said, 'I intend to interrogate Sadi personally. I think you had better be present too. We'll start today. We have very little time.'

I spread my hands in a gesture of regret. 'I'm afraid, sir, that will not be possible. My squadron sails the day after tomorrow. Indeed, as you know, I have already overstayed my time ashore. I was supposed to be back on board several hours ago. Some of my crew are waiting even now at the harbour to take me back to my vessel.'

Kivami Bey closed his eyes, let out a loud sigh and rubbed his wrinkled forehead. 'My dear Barak . . .,' he began, but then he seemed to think better of it.

He reached for one of his silver-handled canes and rapped on the corner of the table in front of the divan. Atik appeared, bearing a file.

'Is that it?' said Kivami Bey, indicating the file.

'Yes, sir,' said Atik, darting an odd glance at me.

The Old Man waved his stick imperiously in my direction. 'Well, get on with it, then. Show it to the Captain!'

Atik took a piece of paper from the file and handed it to me, avoiding my eyes. I took it and slowly unfolded it.

I read with a sinking heart of my immediate discharge from my command in order to undertake 'vital and urgent duties related to the Security of the State'. The document was dated that day and bore the Sultan's monogram and seal. I held it out for Atik to take, and Kivami Bey motioned to him to leave us alone again.

I could not hide what I felt. I ground my teeth in anger at the insane way I had blundered back into this lethal business. Tears sprang to my eyes at the thought of the squadron sailing without me and my fine flagship handed to another.

'Come, come now,' said Kivami Bey dismissively. 'Do you doubt that this most grave matter is of infinitely more importance than some small expedition to Syria? Or that the rewards you can hope to gain will not be even greater?'

I remained silent.

For a time Kivami Bey returned to brooding, on what I know not. Perhaps even then he was forming that subtle stratagem he was to reveal to me later on. But who can tell what is in another man's mind?

Eventually he took my arm and said, 'With God's help, this nightmare that has paralysed the Empire these eight years may soon be at an end. When all is said and done, everything may well depend on you.'

I suppose I should have been gratified to be accorded this grand role in the Old Man's brave vision of a final resolution of the question of the Prince. But my grief at losing my ship was at that moment well-nigh inconsolable and his words seemed empty and without meaning.

'I will have to send word to the quay,' I said wearily. 'To tell the men to return to the ship without me.'

'I have already done so on your behalf,' said Kivami Bey, 'several hours ago.'

Alas, what can I say of poor doomed Sadi? He was then thirty years old – the same age as the Prince – and even with his master he vied in handsomeness and nobility of bearing. He was tall and very fair skinned, but his fine moustaches and hair were almost black; his dark eyes were clear and bright, his nose aquiline, his lips well formed and the colour of rubies. His limbs and hands were graceful, his gestures expressive and refined, his appearance pleasing in every way. It was not difficult to see why, of all Jem's

271

courtiers, Sadi was reputed to be the Prince's favourite. For in him were combined beauty without vanity, quickness of wit without malice, and an easy self-possession wholly untainted by arrogance or conceit. He did not deserve to die the way he did.

The interrogation went on for several days, as often as not continuing long into the night. It took place in a large room with high barred windows, in that sequestered part of the Convent beyond the iron gate in the second court where 'guests' were accommodated while being investigated. Two floors below, reached by a spiral stair, were the underground cells whence suspects were brought at the beginning of each session and to which they returned when they were no longer required.

Sadi was assigned one of the more salubrious cells, provided with a bed, clean linen and clothes. Kivami Bey issued orders that he was to be spared being put in irons, and that he be afforded every reasonable comfort commensurate with his rank. Our prisoner, none the less, though polite, proved uncooperative. Indeed, I could not see that anything would be extracted from him except under duress. Even then I suspected that he would not be broken easily.

Yet Kivami Bey remained apparently unperturbed, never once in my hearing suggesting that if Sadi persisted in his recalcitrance harsher methods of persuasion would be resorted to. But, then, I could not at that time, any more than Sadi, discern the Old Man's concealed purposes. It was only afterwards that I came to realize the labyrinthine deviousness of his approach.

Whole days, whole nights passed in what seemed like mere preliminary discussion. Kivami Bey touched only obliquely on the question of what Sadi had hoped to achieve by returning incognito to the capital. And though one could be sure that before his arrest Sadi had been planning to make contact with Jem's numerous clandestine supporters in the city, Kivami Bey demanded no names, asked for no details of the orders he had received from the Prince. And gradually Sadi's reserve began to crumble.

Little by little the Old Man disclosed what we had

learned of the Prince's movements – making the scant information we possessed take on the aspect of an extensive but unspoken knowledge of the facts. Sadi could barely conceal his astonishment that we seemed to know so much already. Yet still his vigilance did not altogether desert him, and he continued deftly to evade his interrogator's attempts to trap him. But when Kivami Bey began to allude to the part the Knights had played in the affair, Sadi's resentment began to get the better of his, until then, exemplary discretion. Soon the Prince's Chancellor was darkly hinting that it was they alone who had been responsible for the Prince's trials and tribulations in exile, and that but for them Jem might have been able to reach some kind of accommodation with his brother.

The Old Man pressed home his advantage, urging Sadi to assist the Empire in avenging the vile misdeeds of these miscreants. Sadi teetered on the edge of acquiescence – in agony that he might have said too much already. Kivami Bey reassured him and calmed his fears, saying he desired intelligence only of the common enemy. At last, one night shortly after the evening prayer, exhausted by days of relentless probing and convinced by Kivami Bey's declarations that he wished to talk only of the Knights, Sadi's resistance abruptly gave way and he began to recite the whole catalogue of false promises, broken vows, betrayal and deceit that Jem had suffered at the hands of the accursed Infidels of Rhodes. For, as he no doubt argued to himself, what harm could there be in speaking of past events so long as he kept his counsel about his adored Prince's plans for the future?

Sadi's story began on that ill-fated day, nearly seven years before, when the Prince and his band of faithful companions rode out of their camp beneath the cedars on the high summer pastures of the Taurus and set off southwards to the coast of Karaman. Sadi did not even attempt to deny that they had hoped, if the means could be found, to reach the Ottoman dominions to the west in order to resume the struggle against Bayezid in the European provinces.

Jem had sent ahead to Rhodes his trusted officer Frenk Suleyman to seek a vessel and a safe-conduct of the Knights so that he might pass through their island on his way to Greece. Reluctant though the Prince was to ask assistance of these Misbelievers, still he judged it more prudent to enter into an agreement with them than to hazard putting to sea and risk falling prey to one of their numerous ships that, taking advantage of the civil strife in the interior, were then marauding and raiding almost unchecked all along the coasts of Anatolia. Besides, Jem was well acquainted with the Grand Master Pierre d'Aubusson – from that happier time when he acted as his father Mehmed's ambassador to the Knights – and even if he deplored Aubusson's false religion, the Prince saw in this veteran campaigner a man of chivalry and honour.

Jem had instructed Frenk Suleyman to meet him on his return from Rhodes at the port of Korykos. Yet when the Prince and his officers arrived at this place, there was no sign or word of his emissary. But in the harbour there happened to be a small brigantine. So Jem commandeered the vessel, paying her Master and crew handsomely in gold, and went aboard at once with his followers, lest the Sultan's soldiers should come upon them suddenly.

That very afternoon the lookouts that Jem had posted in a minaret of a nearby mosque came racing back to the ship reporting the appearance, on a bluff above the little port, of a party of armed horsemen – whose approach had been given away by their helmets and weapons glinting in the bright summer sun. Whether they were friend or foe was impossible to say but in truth there could be little doubt in the Prince's mind that they were one of his brother's cavalry detachments sent forth in search of the fugitives.

At a word from Jem, his officers took up their stations and every crewman aboard from captain to cabin-boy leapt into action, some casting off the cables that moored the vessel, some hauling on the ropes to hoist the sails, and others jumping down onto the benches and seizing hold of the oars in readiness to speed the brigantine's departure from the harbour. In the twinkling of an eye, with their sails filling out in the warm breeze blowing off the land, they were under way. And by the time the horsemen, brandishing their swords, came at full gallop onto the shore, the ship had swept round in a broad arc and was ploughing steadily and inexorably westwards.

Next day they put into the bay at Anamur. Within a few hours a flotilla appeared on the horizon: a vast ship escorted by several smaller vessels. Those aboard Jem's brigantine, which was lying anchored out of bow-shot some way offshore in case of further alarms, watched anxiously as a light galley detached itself from the main force and set off in their direction. Then to their joy they saw floating at the masthead of the galley both the eight-pointed cross of the Infidel Order and the favour-bestowing crescent – and in due course they espied in the bow Frenk Suleyman himself, saluting them from afar.

Presently Frenk Suleyman came aboard, where he kissed the hand of his Prince and was enthusiastically embraced by his brother officers. Yet he seemed troubled – soon they would learn the reason why – but meanwhile an envoy of the Knights had also come aboard and etiquette demanded that he should be properly received. Brought before the Prince, the Knight greeted him most respectfully and, indicating the squadron that was now standing some distance away, he announced that these were the ships sent by the Grand Master to convey him with all honour and security to the fortress at Rhodes. Then handing to Sadi – whom he correctly surmised to be Jem's senior minister – a sealed document, he added that this was the safe-conduct requested by the Prince through his most distinguished emissary Frenk Suleyman Bey.

Graciously Jem thanked the envoy and expressed his willingness to go with the Rhodian ships, subject to his perusal of the letter from the Grand Master. With that, the Knight retired, saying he would return shortly so that, assuming everything would be found in order, the fleet's commander himself could welcome Jem and his companions personally aboard the galley, which would transfer them to the flagship.

275

As soon as the envoy had departed, Jem called the members of his princely council together and they gathered on the deck, sitting beneath the cool shade of an awning. Sadi opened the letter, and passed it to Frenk Suleyman to translate and read aloud – for it was written in Greek, and although the Prince was well versed in this language, there were among his courtiers some who were unfamiliar with such Infidel tongues.

Sadi remembered the contents of the execrated letter only too well, having read and reread it countless times subsequently. And I have before me now a copy that I took down at his dictation and found again not long ago among the notes I kept, at Kivami Bey's behest, during the interrogation. The letter runs like this:

'From Brother Aubusson, by the grace of God, humble Master of the Sacred House of the Hospital of St John of Jerusalem and Protector of the Poor in Jesus Christ, and ourselves, the Brotherhood of the same House, to all who read our words, Greetings!

'During these recent days there has come into our presence, on behalf of the Most Serene and Illustrious Prince the Lord Jem, the excellent Ambassador Suleyman; and the aforesaid Ambassador has apprised us by letters from the said Prince, and also in his own words, of the Prince's desire to come to Rhodes to confer with us about certain matters, and in these matters to seek and act upon our counsels, accepting them as rendered by friends who wish him well, requiring to this end our pledged word of a safe-conduct. We therefore, moved by the friendship we bear towards him from former times, and in the hope that the outcome of his visit will prove profitable, hereby grant and concede full, unconditional, and general safe-conduct to the Most Illustrious and Most Excellent Lord Jem and to those who come to Rhodes in his Most Noble Company, whether they be Turks, or Moors, or of any other Nation, so that in complete security and confidence, together with

276

their belongings, goods, moneys and jewels, they may enter Rhodes, remain there or depart, according to their own wishes or those of the Most Serene Lord Jem, without let or hindrance, and to this do we pledge our word. In witness whereof we hereby attach the joint leaden seal of the Brotherhood. Given at Rhodes, the 12th day of July, 1482.'

When Frenk Suleyman had completed the task of reading the missive a profound look of unhappiness clouded his face. Yet Jem seemed not to notice this and turned instead to Sadi, his Chancellor, and without speaking raised a questioning eyebrow to elicit his verdict.

Taking the letter, Sadi examined it carefully for himself. Then after deliberating for some while longer, he said with a shrug, 'I can find no fault in it.'

Meanwhile, however, Frenk Suleyman – who was sitting to the left of his master – had become increasingly agitated.

'Listen to me!' he said, unable to contain his distress a moment longer. 'The letter seems to me nothing more than a trick. I don't like the look of these Infidels at all. There is something about their behaviour that does not bode well. I think it would be a mistake to go with them like this . . .'

A murmur of surprise rose among Jem's officers and some gave Frenk Suleyman black looks and even bade him angrily to be silent. For it happened that Frenk Suleyman was French by birth – which is how he came to be called 'Suleyman the Frank'. (He had jumped ship in Antioch when a boy to escape the cruelty of his captain, and confessed Islam and changed his name to avoid being sent back to the vessel. After which he had wandered Anatolia for some time until he came to Konya, where the Prince was much taken with him and gave him employment as an interpreter at court.) Thus the others were quick to believe that his words on this occasion sprang from a convert's overzealous hatred of his former co-religionists rather than from any considered and rational objections.

But Jem stilled the dissension by raising his hand.

'I am moved by Suleyman's anxiety,' he said, 'for it shows that he loves his Prince and is concerned lest any harm befall me. But I think his fears, though they might be justified in other circumstances, in this case are misplaced. Do not forget that I have dealt with these people before and so I know what quality of men they are. I agree that not all of them can be trusted, but Aubusson would not make a promise in writing if he did not intend to honour it.'

The others eagerly agreed with the Prince and all in their different ways said that the Infidels had pledged their word and having done so would keep it. But Suleyman just looked on in despair. With tears in his eyes he turned to Jem.

'You must do as you think best. And wherever you go, you know that I will go with you. God knows, I would rather die than be separated from you.'

And with that, he bowed his head, and the Prince put his arm around his shoulders and sought to comfort him.

Towards the end of the day, about two hours before the evening prayer, Jem and his twenty-seven companions boarded the commander's vessel. And even those among them who had sailed the seas before agreed that it was an astonishing prodigy. The Knights called it the Great Treasure Ship, and it rose above the water like a mountain, its amazing size giving credence to the ancient stories told of the prophet Noah and his Ark. Its giant masts were three in number and carried an immense expanse of canvas, each sail – so Sadi said – looking from a distance like a billowing white cloud; its deck was of the magnitude of a spacious town square, and its fore- and after-castles towered over the waves like mighty and impregnable citadels.

The commander's own quarters had been set aside for their reception and entertainment. When they were all safely aboard they were ushered into a large and airy room high up in the stern, with windows on three sides. On the highly polished floor were spread many costly tapestries and carpets, and low tables, silk-covered cushions and bolsters were already laid out in preparation so that the

278

Prince and his officers could sit and take their ease in the Turkish fashion.

Presently there appeared a kind of chamberlain. The Knights called him their '*maître d'hôtel*' and said that he had been sent especially to tend to the needs of their guests during the voyage. The man craved permission to discuss with the Prince what dishes he desired to dine upon that evening. But as Jem was then in conversation with the commander and some Knights he delegated the matter to Frenk Suleyman.

About an hour later the *maître d'hôtel* arrived again with a train of servants bearing dishes and, as each dish was placed upon the table, he made the servant carrying it take some of the food and eat it in front of the Prince. At first Jem attempted to ignore this dumb-show, but when it went on and on, with no sign whatsoever of stopping, he began to manifest evidence of his discomfort and displeasure.

'I do not think', he said at last, 'that this performance is really necessary.'

'But, Your Majesty,' replied the man almost insolently, 'is it not the ancient custom amongst royalty *everywhere* that such precautions should be taken?'

'My dear man,' said the Prince, 'whatever the customs might be, do you honestly believe that if I expected to be poisoned by the Knights I should be entrusting my safety to them?' Then turning to his hosts, he went on, 'In any case, you, gentlemen, know my present circumstances well enough, and know that having no kingdom of my own I am royal only in name. So let us not pretend to that which is false, and set aside these royal practices until such time as they are merited and justified by the recovery – God willing – of that throne and Empire bequeathed to me by my father!'

Saying which, Jem beckoned to the remaining servants to place their platters and dishes before him on the table, and with a spoon he put a little from each on his own plate. Then without further ado he took bread and started to eat, commanding his officers to do likewise. Seeing the trust he placed in them, the Infidels were overcome with delight

279

and with many flattering words they praised his candour, his courtesy and princely modesty.

And to be sure, whatever disclaimers the Prince might have sought to make as to his status and royal prerogatives, the welcome that awaited him in Rhodes was fitting indeed for one of such illustrious birth and glorious antecedents.

As they neared the island the light galley was sent on ahead to warn the Grand Master of the Prince's coming, and when the Great Treasure Ship dropped anchor at the harbour's mouth they found the whole town and fortress decked out as for a festival or holy day. A ceremonial barge came forth to meet them. And as Jem and his companions descended on to its deck, from every rampart, tower and battlement drums began to thunder, trumpets to blare and cannons to boom out their greeting.

A floating jetty, supported on pontoons and more than ten yards long, had been built out from the waterfront so that Jem could come ashore on horseback, and this they had covered with cloth of silver and gold. Thus, on leaving the barge, he straight away nimbly mounted the animal they had provided for him and, followed by his suite, he rode slowly onto dry land, where other beasts stood in readiness for his officers. Here they were met also by an escort of Knights, their squires and men-at-arms. Without delay, they moved off together and at a stately pace passed through the gates into the city.

Within the town the streets were strewn with fresh greenery and aromatic flowers; the houses, churches and public buildings festooned with brilliant silks, damasks, gauzes and taffetas. On every side the multitude of rich and poor, nobles and commoners, eagerly pressed forward to see the Prince, whereupon they broke into excited cheers and cries of admiration. Men and boys climbed walls and trees, and clambered on to rooftops to get a better view; mothers and nursemaids held children aloft to catch a glimpse of him, while young girls leant from windows, terraces and parapets, calling to him to favour them with a single glance, and tossed sweet-smelling posies of flowers into his path.

In this manner Jem passed through the city – gathering

behind him as he went an ever-swelling army of the populace, who followed after him as though hypnotized by the magnificence of his appearance and the nobility of his demeanour – until he came to the principal piazza, where Pierre d'Aubusson and his Knight Commanders waited in front of the Church of Saint Sebastien to receive him.

The white-haired old warrior sat resplendent in velvet and jewel-studded brocades on a dazzlingly caparisoned charger, a massive war-horse, notorious for obeying none but his master, that snorted and foamed and champed at its bit, making those around cower and shrink back in terror at its incessant restless shifting and the pawing and stamping of its mighty hoofs upon the ground. And behind Aubusson, similarly mounted, and hardly less ostentatiously attired, were the members of the Supreme Council of the Order, and to their left and right, captivating young pages, dressed in scarlet satin tunics and mounted on sleek, high-spirited palfreys.

On seeing Aubusson, Jem solemnly raised his fingers three times to his lips in salutation, and three times the Grand Master stiffly bowed low in his saddle in response. When Jem reached him, the two men clasped each other's right hand and exchanged courteous words of greeting. Then, amid the acclamation of the crowd, they turned together and rode out of the square, side by side, followed by their retinues, in order that the Grand Master might in person conduct the Prince and his Turkish officers to the Auberge de France, which palace was set aside for their use for as long as it pleased them to remain as the guests of the Brotherhood in Rhodes.

The next morning, when Jem and his followers had rested after their long journey by land and sea from Karaman, the Grand Master and those senior dignitaries of the Order, who are known as the Knights Companions, presented themselves at the Auberge de France to pay their respects to the Prince.

Jem graciously received them in the great hall of the palace, the Ottomans taking their places on a raised dais covered with carpets and furnished with cushions, and Pierre d'Aubusson and his Knights seated themselves in front of them on a row of high-backed chairs. When all were in position, with calm dignity the Prince began to speak.

'It may be, my lords,' said Jem, 'that you are in some wonderment that I, who am the younger of great Mehmed's heirs, should be disputing the throne of the Empire with my brother Bayezid. Yet since you are men of experience and understanding, I will willingly explain to you how this most deplorable state of affairs has arisen.

'I freely admit that my brother is the elder. But far from vitiating my claim to the succession, I would argue that this difference in our ages gives precedence to my claim over his. Because, whereas when Bayezid came into the world my father – God sanctify his soul! – was a mere prince and not certain to succeed, when *my* mother gave birth to me, Mehmed was by then Emperor, following his most illustrious father Murad's death. Thus was I born into the purple, and indeed for this very reason, and from certain propitious signs in the Heavens prefiguring my Destiny, it was expected from the very hour of my nativity that I, not Bayezid, would one day inherit the Imperial mantle of the glorious House of Osman.

'None the less, if, in spite of the precedence conferred on me by my good Fortune in being born an Emperor's son, Mehmed had considered Bayezid a more worthy heir he would not have hesitated to declare him his successor. But he did not do so. For he saw that Bayezid, though holy and devout, did not have the temper of a Ruler; that he was too narrow in his prejudices, unworldly, withdrawn, reserved; that he feared and disliked battle, lacked assurance in arms, and did not inspire in his own people the admiration and love that would make his dominion secure.

'Moreover, as my father watched his sons grow to manhood, with every year that passed he became more confirmed in his resolve that I, not Bayezid, should be the one who, upon his death, would be girded with the victorious sword of Osman Gazi, the founder of our invincible Dynasty. Thus it came about that when Sultan Mehmed

282

suddenly and unexpectedly left this vale of tears – to go to that abode of eternal security which is Paradise – in the full knowledge and assurance of what my father had decreed, I prepared to assume my rightful place upon the Conqueror's throne.

'But some evil-minded agents of my elder brother seized the messengers sent by my father's loyal vizirs and put them to death. Then, against my father's most hallowed desires, they called Bayezid to Istanbul to usurp the position long promised to me. And when he arrived there, unable to gain the people's allegiance in any other way, he plundered the Royal Treasury and distributed vast sums in gold to corrupt the Janissaries and turn against me the high officials of the State. But even these desperate measures could not win the loyalty of the Pashas, the Army and the populace. So he compounded his misdeeds by steeping his illegitimate reign in violence and in blood – arresting, torturing and killing those men, be they ever so great or humble, whose only crime was their wish to see justice done and Mehmed's most solemn wishes fulfilled.

'But still I could not persuade myself to declare war on the usurper. Since not only did I take pity on my poor subjects, hoping to spare them the horror and misery of civil chaos, but I also knew that by taking up arms I might risk destroying that Empire – the greatest and most glorious since that of Rome – for which my father and his *Gazis* had so liberally shed their blood and sweated and toiled for thirty years to build. For, I need hardly remind such learned men as you, the annals of History are filled with terrible examples of vast Empires, mighty Kingdoms and noble Dynasties brought to ruin and disaster by such fratricidal strife!

'Accordingly, for the good of the Empire and our Faith, I proposed a compromise, saying to my brother that he might keep the provinces in Europe, whilst I retained those in Asia, and that we should rule jointly and in amity until such time as one or other of us reached the foreordained close of his span upon this earth, at which time the whole dominion, East and West, would revert to the survivor and his own particular line.

283

'But this was not sufficient for my brother. He would have everything. Nor would the heartless tyrant be satisfied until he had not only robbed me of Empire but also stripped me of royal rank, seized my possessions and driven me for ever from Ottoman lands to wander the world, an outcast, a despised and desperate exile.

'And so, because of his cruelty, war has ravaged our unhappy land for these past fifteen months, brother killing brother, father son, and son father, in fruitless and all-consuming slaughter. And now, such have been the reversals I have suffered that, not wishing for the present to provoke Fortune's malice further, I have been obliged to flee the country of my birth a second time, and even to take refuge with you, my lords, while I search out the means and opportunity of making my way to Greece, where countless more of my loyal supporters daily await my coming.

'Soon I will be leaving you. But be assured that I will remain mindful of the assistance you have given me, and in the fullness of time, when by God's grace I am Sultan at last, you will not find me ungrateful for having given succour to an unfortunate Prince, tormented both by malevolent Fate and the implacable enmity of that very brother who should have loved him above all others!'

With these words Jem's oration ended and amidst the general approbation and applause of the Knights, he fell silent.

Yet the accursed Infidels, while offering these outward displays of sympathy and kindness, nurtured in their hearts nothing but the most poisonous hatred for Jem and all the True Believers – and even then were secretly plotting to use the Prince as the means of overthrowing Dynasty, Empire and Faith and extirpating the entire Ottoman race.

At this point in Sadi's narrative, to my grim satisfaction there appeared an Infidel whom I knew only too well. For our prisoner related next that the same evening, following Jem's address to the Council of the Order, the Grand Master returned to the Auberge de France, bringing with

284

him his nephew Guy de Blanchefort – the very gentleman who, in Genoa four years later, exerted himself so single-mindedly to accomplish my destruction.

Pierre d'Aubusson most warmly commended his relative to Jem, saying that his nephew would do everything in his power to assist the successful outcome of his cause; and from that day forth Guy de Blanchefort became a constant visitor to the Prince. Yet the days slipped by with a great deal of talk but little sign of action.

When Jem began to insist that a vessel be found so that he and his companions might continue their voyage to Greece, Blanchefort said such things as 'There is not a suitable ship in the harbour at the moment – but we have sent for one and it will arrive presently,' and 'Let us first await the reports of our agents in the European provinces to make sure that it is still safe for you to go there.' And with a host of other excuses he lied and temporized and equivocated with such skill and boldness that Jem and his officers were utterly deceived as to his real intentions in delaying them.

During the day the Prince sought to divert himself by composing verses or adding new chapters to the work he was then writing on the life and conquests of his father, Mehmed. He also rode and did regular martial exercise with sword, mace and bow. And nearly every day he swam in the sea, choosing those places along the shore where the currents were at their strongest, the better to increase the vigour and suppleness of his limbs.

The Infidels looked on in amazement, for few of them can swim and so live in constant terror of falling in the water and drowning. They were amazed too at the Prince and his companions' insistence on thoroughly washing daily in hot water and sluicing themselves down with cold – for most of these Misbelievers do not wash from one month to the next, some even maintaining in their abject ignorance that there emanates an odour of sanctity from the accumulation of body filth.

As usual, the Prince was very strict in performing his devotions in accordance with the rules of the Religion. Nor

were his pious observances confined to the carrying out of
the five prayers at the appointed times. He soon learned,
through certain messages and pathetic notes and missives,
that there were a number of Muslim slaves in Rhodes, captured by the Knights at sea, on the coasts of Anatolia and in
the islands of the Archipelago. For these Knights, though
they pretend to be fighting only for their faith, pile up vast
personal fortunes by acts of piracy against unarmed merchant vessels, indiscriminately seizing cargoes and crews
and passengers. And sometimes they even become so
impudent as to land raiding parties on the shores of the
Guarded Domains whence they carry off their human mer-
chandise, committing horrible atrocities if they meet with
the least resistance. Therefore, following the exhortations
of the Prophet, the Prince searched out these wretched cap-
tives wherever he could find them, and well-nigh emptied
his coffers in paying their ransoms so that they could be
sent home to their families.

Yet in spite of all the activity with which he filled each
passing day Jem could not for long divert his mind from the
unhappiness of his position. And his melancholy thoughts
were made no better by the profound misgivings he now
began to have as to the wisdom of his decision to leave the
lands of the Muslims and go amongst the Unbelievers.

At night he wandered disconsolately from room to room
in the cheerless palace, until his chamberlains became so
despairing at his lack of sleep that they made up couches
for him in half a dozen different chambers in the hope that
he would find one at least in which he might feel comfortable and so lie down and rest. But as summer nights
became hotter and more oppressive he gave up trying to
sleep indoors altogether, and had them make up a simple
bed on a terrace upon the roof, where for hours on end he
would lie awake with open eyes, listening to the waves
breaking on the shore beyond the city walls and staring up
at the bright constellations of stars hanging silently in the
dark firmament of the Heavens.

Then one day Guy de Blanchefort came to the Prince,
saying that he wished to speak to him in confidence.

286

Therefore Jem, taking with him only three or four of his most intimate advisers, retired with the Infidel to a secluded room.

'I have intelligence', said Blanchefort, 'of the state of things in Greece . . .'

'Indeed?' said Jem with a frown. 'Your spies have certainly been long enough about it.'

'Circumstances have been exceptionally difficult, as I'm sure Your Highness will understand . . .'

'Very well, if you say so,' replied Jem. 'Tell me at least what they have managed to discover.'

Blanchefort lowered his eyes and, looking despondent, said, 'Firstly, I should tell you that your brother now knows that you are here.'

'That is scarcely surprising,' said the Prince with a long-suffering sigh, 'given the time that has been wasted . . .'

'I'm afraid that was unavoidable,' said Blanchefort. 'There was nothing to be gained by your going to Greece only to fall at once into the hands of your enemies.'

Jem shrugged and said, 'Perhaps so . . . but, anyway, go on.'

'Well, Your Highness, the way matters stand at present it would be madness to attempt to follow your original plan. Bayezid has been arresting anybody of importance thought to sympathize with you, not just in Istanbul and Anatolia but also in the European provinces. What's more, there are now several dozen vessels of the Imperial Fleet patrolling the whole length of the coastline of Greece. So it seems as if your brother is already expecting you to try to get there and will be waiting for you if you do.'

'I see,' said the Prince. Then after stroking his beard and thinking for a few moments, 'In that case, though the idea heartily displeases me, I must remain here until I can return to Karaman. After all, if Bayezid is convinced that I am about to land in the West – or, better still, if we can persuade him that I am there already, but in hiding – he will be obliged to send the Army into Europe to look for me, giving me a golden opportunity to rally my people once more in Anatolia.'

287

Blanchefort gravely shook his head.

'That strategy would be most excellent, Your Highness,' he said, 'if only it were safe for you to remain here long enough to put it into effect.'

'And why, Monsieur de Blanchefort,' said the Prince indignantly, 'should it not be safe for me to do so? Why, even my father – God have mercy upon him! – did not succeed in reducing this place two years ago – although if he had been able to conduct the assault personally, I have no doubt the result would have been very different!'

'That', said Blanchefort, 'is exactly the difficulty. We held out, but even now we have not completed the task of repairing the damage wrought by your artillery upon the walls during the siege. If Bayezid should try again, we could not be so sure of resisting him so successfully. Besides, a direct assault is not the only means the Sultan has of achieving his evil intentions. To our certain knowledge, your brother has already dispatched assassins from the Sublime Porte, with orders to cross from the mainland and attempt to take your life.'

An expression of disdain came over the Prince's face, but his advisers looked at one another with anxiety and alarm.

'The Council believes', said Blanchefort, 'that you and your officers should leave the island as soon as possible. If you agree to this we can get you to France or the Duchy of Savoy, where you would be safe for a while from your brother's schemes to have you murdered. And from there you could make your way to King Matthias in Hungary. This monarch has the greatest and most powerful army in Europe, and his dominions border those of the Ottomans for many hundreds of miles. You may be sure that he would spare no effort to assist you in driving out the usurper Bayezid – if you were ready to make peace with him when you had regained the throne.'

Jem smiled a little and said, 'Ah . . . I have often heard my dear father speak of Matthias Corvinus as a just ruler, a valiant soldier and a worthy adversary. And if peace along our common frontier were all that he would ask, I would not hesitate to seek his aid. But I fear that such an ambitious man as he would not settle for so little. He would demand that I concede some Ottoman territory to him as well, and that I cannot do. For what benefit would the Sultanate be to me if I dishonoured myself by buying it with my father's patrimony?'

'Have no fear,' said Blanchefort. 'Peace on your common borders and the guarantee that the Ottomans would desist, at least in your lifetime, from renewing their attacks upon Belgrade, and Corvinus would be more than satisfied – you'll see. All the world knows that the King of Hungary would rather make war upon the Germans than upon the Turks – mark my word upon it!'

In this manner the conversation went on, and at length Jem was persuaded that the advice of the Knights was sound, and that he should indeed sail for Savoy, whence he would be able to travel onwards to Hungary to consult with the great King Matthias. And when the Prince consented at last, Blanchefort was seen to smile for the first time since the two men had met. Had Jem only known that this was no smile of friendship but one of malicious triumph at the success of the Infidel's villainous deceit!

On the first day of September the Prince and his companions embarked with Guy de Blanchefort and a guard of fully armed Knights of the Brotherhood in the Great Treasure Ship, the sails were hoisted and they began their voyage to the West.

But the winds were contrary at first and they made painful progress. It took them a whole month to reach Sicily – an island belonging to Spain – where they anchored at Syracuse to take on fresh water and provisions. Thence they sailed through the straits of Messina, which divide the island from the mainland, and passed by Stromboli. This lofty mountain has a fiery crater that is thought by the people of those parts to be one of the mouths of Hell. During the day there rises from it a great billowing column of black and grey smoke several miles high, and in the hours of darkness gigantic flames can be seen leaping into the air, colouring the night sky an angry

289

crimson. By such awesome signs do mortal men gain intimations of the infinite power of the One God, the Lord of Heaven and Earth!

When they had continued further along the coast of the Kingdom of Naples, the wind died away and they were becalmed. At nightfall, since the evening was warm, they lit lanterns on the deck and served dinner to Jem and his officers in the open air. But it happened that the King of Naples and the Roman Pope, who was at that time in alliance with Venice, were then involved in hostilities. One of the Neapolitan King's immense warships – of the kind the Infidels call a 'cog' – was cruising in the region on the lookout for papal and Venetian ships. This cog spotted the lights in the dark from afar and started to make for the Great Treasure Ship, though the lack of wind made its progress very slow.

Yet when the following day finally dawned, it was seen to be drawing near, and Blanchefort issued orders to his men to take up their positions to defend the ship, whilst Jem and his companions were hurriedly concealed below decks. Realizing that the mysterious vessel, which then flew no flag or colours at her masthead, had no intention of surrendering without a fight, the cog lowered a boat and sent a delegation to parley. When they drew alongside, they were informed that the vessel belonged to the Order and were politely invited to come aboard.

The Neapolitans had already discovered, via their spies in the East, that the Prince had fled to Rhodes – so barely had they set foot upon the deck than they said:

'Is the son of the Grand Turk aboard with you now?'

'Good heavens, no!' said Blanchefort. 'We put him off in Rhodes.'

And to make everything look as natural as possible, Blanchefort even asked the Neapolitans to take some wine and something to eat before returning to the cog. During the meal they asked a hundred questions about Jem, to which Blanchefort replied with his customary effortless mendacity, thoroughly deceiving them as to Jem's whereabouts.

After this hazardous encounter the Knights no longer lit the ship's lights or showed lanterns on deck after dark. But a few days later their plans to get Jem safely to Europe were very nearly foiled. For all at once a terrible storm blew up. The sky turned black, lightning flashed, the ship was battered by enormous waves, raging winds tore the sails to shreds, and rain and hail cascaded down in mighty cataracts. For several days they were driven helplessly before the gale; everything on deck was swept into the sea; thick planks cracked and sprang apart, letting gallons of water gush into the hold. It was only by nailing dozens of leather patches over the holes in the hull and sealing them with pitch that the ship was prevented from foundering. But at last the Divine Being – may He be honoured and glorified! – took pity upon them and, quieting the wind and waves, saved them from the fury of the elements.

Limping northwards, they encountered a fleet of seventeen galleys taking shelter in the lee of an island. These also belonged to the King of Naples, but this time the Knights raised the colours of the Order and passed on unmolested with an exchange of salutes and shouted greetings.

Then the wind dropped altogether and they drifted on the open sea, out of sight of land. Hosts of exhausted birds, looking for a place to rest their wings, landed on the spars and rigging. One alighted very near to Jem, who was taking the air on the quarterdeck, and he called to it softly, putting out his hand. To his delight, immediately it came to him and tamely perched on his forefinger. Then he began to feed it crumbs and at length it allowed him to stroke its head and plumage.

But meanwhile the Frenchmen aboard were busy trapping the other birds, using poles with loops of twine attached to the ends. Some of the birds flew off in panic and fell into the sea and drowned. Those they succeeded in catching the Frenchmen grilled and ate, greedily consuming even the tiniest of the creatures, much to the astonishment of the Ottomans. Jem saved some by buying them, for silver, from the sailors; and these he kept in cages, watered and fed until the vessel came near the coast again, whereupon they were released.

Six weeks from the day of their departure from the Infidels' island fortress, the Great Treasure Ship sailed into the blue inlet of Villafranca, a small port in the domains of the Duke of Savoy. The following day Jem landed with his officers and, accompanied by an escort of Knights, went to Nice, which is only a few miles distant by road. That evening Guy de Blanchefort left them, saying he would ride on to France, to inform King Louis of Jem's arrival in Europe.

This place Nice is a small city, built at the foot of wooded hills that encircle the broad sweep of a tranquil sheltered bay. To the east of the city there is a citadel that stands upon a jagged rock rising above the sandy shore. The hillsides around are covered in vineyards, olive and lemon groves, orchards and plantations that murmur constantly to the sound of clear springs, rivulets and streams. The city is filled with numerous fine houses and mansions, like glittering palaces, all adorned with elegant balconies, noble terraces, marble fountains and balustrades, and surrounded by green lawns, shady bowers, sweet-scented rose bushes and thick hedges of myrtle and bitter laurel. And awaiting them there in the finest of them all was one Messer Gaspar Grimaldo . . .

Poor unfortunate Sadi! His strained and pallid features were momentarily illuminated by the happy reminiscence of their first meeting with this most affable and amusing Misbeliever. He would never know that Gaspar was not in Nice by chance – as the Prince and his companions, and indeed the Knights, were led to believe – but with the express purpose of keeping watch on the fugitives' every move. Nor that the charming Genoese, at a single word from the Sublime Porte, would have had the young Prince strangled in his bed without the slightest twinge of conscience or pang of remorse.

For Gaspar, ever vigilant on behalf of his masters in the God-guarded City, had learned a few days before – from a naval officer whose vessel had just then arrived back at the port of Genoa – that the Great Treasure Ship had been seen at anchor in Syracuse, and tavern rumours had it that there were Turks aboard bound for the Duchy of Savoy. Thus, Gaspar had left the Republic and hastened with all speed to Nice, to await developments and see for himself if there was anything in this fantastic-sounding tale. But this time the gossip turned out to be true. And within hours of the Great Treasure Ship's dropping anchor in the bay of Villafranca, the incomparable Gaspar had discovered the identity of the royal passenger and dispatched letters in cipher to the Convent, informing Kivami Bey that the Sultan's brother had appeared suddenly and unexpectedly in the West, in the company of the infamous Brotherhood.

A born intriguer and fearless framer of stratagems, Gaspar soon had an idea of how he might maintain even closer surveillance on the Prince. With brazen insouciance, he went to the Knights that very evening and begged the honour of accommodating their distinguished guests in his own house so long as they graced the city with their presence. And since Gaspar was a prominent citizen of the Republic of Genoa, a familiar figure at the court of the Duke of Savoy, and an eminent habitué of all the very best houses in Nice, they accepted the offer with alacrity, no doubt hoping that the Eastern Barbarians would be suitably impressed by the wealth, cultivation and civilization of their new surroundings. So the guileful Knights were utterly taken in by the worthy Gaspar – may God bring him to a good end and open his heart to the True Faith of Islam!

There followed many days of revelry and feasting at the Villa Grimaldo, where Gaspar spared no expense or effort to entertain his guests. He arranged hunting parties, riding on the seashore and excursions by boat, introducing them to all the noble and great families for scores of miles around. The Turks soon discovered that the young people of Nice were exceptionally attractive, refined in their taste and entirely unrestrained in the pursuit of pleasure. Gaspar summoned to the house the prettiest girls of the town. And morning, noon and night, they ate and drank wine and laughed and sang and danced. And when these lascivious nymphs were too tired to dance any more, they sat down in the laps of the strangers and kissed them on the lips and caressed them publicly in the most shameless and intimate fashion.

Moreover, there was among these girls one of exquisite beauty of countenance, whose abundant raven hair, lovely skin, narrow waist, and swelling breasts and haunches would have been the envy of the black-eyed girls in the Gardens of Paradise. Her swaying gait, sultry glances and inviting lips were enough to drive any man mad with uncontrollable ardour, and the Prince soon made it clear that he was not indifferent to her charms. One day he invited her to his apartments to look at certain jewels. She emerged three days later, her body seemingly aglow with a radiant flush and looking lovelier than ever, and scandalized the whole town by openly singing the Prince's praises and making the most thinly veiled allusions to his immense potency and irresistible physical prowess.

Meanwhile Jem, apparently much refreshed, called the Knights to him and said, 'The time has come to make preparations for our journey to Hungary.'

But the Commander of the Knights said, 'The territory we are residing in at present is under the protection of the King of France. He is a great king and will be able to give you assistance. Therefore, since we still have no word from the Grand Master's nephew, we had better send an embassy to seek His Majesty's permission before we leave the Duchy. If we do not, he may take it as a discourtesy and – God forbid – he may become angry with us. At all events, we can ask him at the same time to provide us with a letter stating that we are travelling under his guarantee lest anyone try to delay or molest us in any way.'

So Jem sent one of his officers, his scribe Nasuh Chelebi, with some members of the Order, to go to King Louis to convey the Prince's greetings and reach an understanding with him.

Many weeks passed, during which the Knights told all sorts of lies, saying that the envoys would be back any day.

294

During this time they also got up a conspiracy to remove Frenk Suleyman from the Prince's entourage. They did this because Suleyman could speak French, and so could keep Jem informed better than any of his other advisers of what the Knights were saying and what their intentions seemed to be. Therefore these wretched Infidels sent an alluring young boy to seduce the officer, and burst in upon them while they were lying naked together. Then they brought Frenk Suleyman before Jem.

'The penalty for this crime among us', said the Knights' Commander, 'is death. We must hand him over to the civil authorities so that he can be tried and executed.'

Jem was appalled that there should be so harsh a sentence for so trivial an offence.

'I forbid you to hand him over to anyone,' said the Prince. 'I will confine him in my treasury until Monsieur de Blanchefort returns, and then we can settle the matter with him.'

So Frenk Suleyman was kept locked in the room in the house where Jem had his money, jewels and other valuables. But knowing full well that his officer had been the victim of a deliberate trick, and suspecting that the Knights might have Suleyman murdered by some other means, Jem resolved to get him away from that place as quickly as possible. Accordingly, he obtained some Infidel clothes from the girls in town – who, in truth, would have laid down their lives for him if he had asked it of them – and helped him to escape. After this, Frenk Suleyman, whose prophetic words were to linger for ever after in his Prince's mind, was never once seen or heard of again, and to this day it remains unknown whether he still lives or has yielded up his soul to the Creator.

In the fourth month the plague broke out in Nice and the surrounding countryside; and the Knights told Jem that they would take him to another place free from the pestilence. On the fifth day of February, the Prince and his officers left the city, guarded by forty fighting Brothers of the Order. There also went with them two new members of the pretender's court-in-exile: a beautiful parrot, with pure white plumage and a haughty demeanour, a farewell gift from the heartbroken and weeping girls of the town; and a young, agile and exceptionally quick-witted ape that, since the day he purchased it from a wild-looking band of gypsies whom he encountered on the beach early one morning after a swim in the sea, had been Jem's constant and devoted retainer. After travelling for two days they came to a village where they found Nasuh Chelebi. And they learned from him that he had never reached the court of the King of France, since he had gone barely a dozen miles before the Knights disarmed him and brought him to a house where they confined him for several weeks, saying that there were bandits and robbers in the district and it would be unsafe to go any further. Jem protested vehemently to the Commander of the Knights. But by that time the Brothers responsible for this disgraceful deception had conveniently quitted the scene and were said to be already on their way back to Rhodes.

Going by Turin and Susa, the party came to the Mont Cenis Pass. They descended, as I did three and a half years later, by sledge, apparently much to the delight of the Prince (who had the advantage over me of having the procedure explained in advance). Then, after travelling for three or four days more, they came to Les Echelles, where the Knights lodged Jem and his people in the fortified house by the river that Talabot and I had observed surreptitiously from afar, before we slipped by night across the border into France.

There they spent the spring and early summer. And, hearing that the Knights were entertaining no less a person than the son of Mehmed, the great Conqueror of Constantinople, the nobility and gentry, freemen and peasantry of the whole country began to flock to see him and pay their respects. Not a single one of them arrived empty-handed, all of them bringing some kind of present or other. One humble hill-farmer, unable to offer anything else, came bearing a string of onions – which the Prince received with as much kindness and gravity as the more valuable gifts brought by lords and ladies, conversing with the man graciously and attentively through an interpreter.

Soon the Knights – may all their hopes be confounded! – reported that word had reached them from the French court that the Prince was free to go to Hungary with the King's blessing.

'This being so,' they said, 'you must send ambassadors to King Matthias at Buda, and let him know of your intention of joining him there this summer. Your men will also be able in this way to ascertain if the roads are open and free of brigands or any other obstacle.'

So Jem chose Ahmed Bey and Mustafa Bey, two of his most senior and distinguished officers. The Knights gave them Infidels' clothes to wear, arguing that they would be thus less conspicuous when travelling. But after they had gone, weeks elapsed with no news of them or the Christian guides that had accompanied them.

And all the while, whenever they were questioned as to what was happening, the Knights said, 'It is a long journey – we cannot expect them to return so soon.'

Then later they began to say, 'How strange that they have not come back by now! Perhaps they have met with some difficulties on the road? Still, it cannot be long now before we receive some word of them.'

Yet in reality, as Jem learned some while afterwards from the confession of one of the servants of the Order, who spoke to him secretly, Ahmed and Mustafa never even reached Chambéry. After ascending the steps and passing through the gorge above Les Echelles, their guides had taken them by an obscure path through the woods. There, among the trees, they had been ambushed by a score of armed Knights, who fell upon the Muslims and hacked them to death without mercy and buried their remains in shallow graves in that remote corner of the forest.

But none of this was known to Jem and his Ottomans then, and still they believed that the Infidels would honour the safe-conduct. Yet soon afterwards an unforeseen event finally led the Knights to drop all pretence that the Prince was their guest rather than a hostage they had managed to seize by their monstrous duplicity and the violation of sworn and solemn oaths made in the sight of God.

For it happened that Charles, Duke of Savoy, a boy of fourteen years of age, returned at that time, after paying a visit to his uncle King Louis, to his capital at Chambéry. And as Les Echelles is no more than half a day's ride off the high road to France, hearing of Jem's presence there, Charles stopped by on his way, to greet the Prince and spend a few days with him.

The young Charles, said Sadi, was like a bright heavenly body shedding golden light on all who came within its orbit, a bold and lovely faun in the garden of comeliness, a bewitching boy for whom it would be proper even to sacrifice one's life! Yet his brief reign had been fraught with difficulties, and the Duchy was then disturbed by discord and conflict stirred up by certain barons and nobles who strove to keep Charles's rule weak and ineffectual. But the Duke, despite his slender years and the daunting nature of the task before him, was even then making it plain that he would not rest until order and discipline had been restored in his ancestral domains. And he had taken for his heraldic device a sun rising in splendour from livid storm-clouds above a tempest-tossed sea, and the motto '*Non tamen inde minus*', thus giving warning to his enemies that his star was in the ascendant and he would certainly triumph over their rebellious insubordination.

Though Prince Jem was older than the Duke, the two of them loved and admired one another from the moment of their first meeting, each sympathizing with the other's sufferings, and being filled with youthful ardour to aid his fellow in adversity. This feeling of mutual regard was – Jem's Chancellor told us – further excited by the similarity of their circumstances. For Charles, like Jem, was his father's second son and he had only succeeded on the sudden and unexpected death of his elder brother. Indeed, to hear Sadi talk, you would have said that never in recorded history had there ever been such singleness of mind between two princes of such different Nations and Religions!

As the days passed and Jem's faithful officers kept watch against the eavesdropping hirelings of the Knights, the Prince unburdened himself to the Duke, telling him of his sorrows, the harshness of his Fate and the intolerable misery of his present predicament.

The Duke's chivalrous nature was more and more inflamed by what he heard. At last he began to inveigh against the wickedness of the Knights, and swore on his father's soul, the Gospels and his sword that – if it were the last thing he did upon this earth – he would wrest the Prince from the hands of the Brotherhood so that Jem might remain in Savoy a free man, or travel on to Hungary, according to his wish.

The next day Charles departed, taking with him Jem's pledge of perpetual friendship and alliance between the Empire and the Duchy when the Prince had won back his throne and inheritance. And as a parting gift Jem gave Charles a magnificent inlaid mace that he had bought in Damascus on his journey to Egypt and to the Holy Cities of Mecca and Medina.

True to his word, the instant the young Duke arrived back at Chambéry, he started to frame a plan to surprise the Commandery at Les Echelles with a crack force of Savoyard troops and set free Jem and his Turkish officers. For he knew that although this Commandery of the Order lay within his territory, the Knights would certainly defy any demands for the Prince's release and would go to any lengths to prevent it if forewarned.

But by some devious means – God only knows how – the Rhodians got to hear of what was afoot. And they wasted no time in taking action to foil Charles's daring stratagem. While one detachment of Brothers closed off the entrance to the gorge above the town, another led by the Commander himself rushed in upon the Prince and his companions, forced them at sword-point to mount horses, and haled them away under cover of darkness across the bridge over the river that divides the Duchy from the Kingdom of France.

*　　*　　*

From that day forth the Knights resolved that where Jem was held should remain an inviolable secret known only to the Brothers of the Order.

The evening after the Prince's enforced flight they embarked him in a boat on the Isère and took him southwards by river, and then by road, to another of their Commanderies at Le Poët. This place lies in wooded and hilly country, far from any highway, and they thought that on account of its location in the back of beyond they could conceal his presence there.

Yet some weeks later the Knights' spies at Charles's court in Savoy sent warnings that the Duke had received intelligence from his agents that the Prince was at Le Poët. His abductors were at first confident that Charles would not dare to make an armed incursion into his uncle King Louis' domains, in spite of his oath to Jem. But then God willed that the King of France should die, and suspecting that Charles might seize the opportunity of staging an attack while the kingdom was in turmoil following Louis' demise, the Knights became fearful that the Order might be deprived of its precious prisoner. For by now the Knights had come to realize that so long as they succeeded in keeping Bayezid in uncertainty as to his brother's whereabouts they could blackmail the Sultan into acceding to almost their every demand . . .

Accordingly, one moonless night a great body of armed Brothers, gathered from far and wide, descended suddenly on the Commandery, laid violent hold of Sadi and Jem's remaining Turkish officers and dragged them away. When Jem protested at this diabolical breach of his solemn agreement with the Grand Master, they merely said:

'What are we to do, Your Highness? We are only obeying orders. And, anyway, no harm will come to any of your people, that we can promise you.'

Thus the Prince's pleas for the release of his companions fell on deaf ears; and he heard soon afterwards that they had been taken down the Rhône to Aigues-Mortes, a port on the Mediterranean coast of the kingdom, whence they were transported in the Great Treasure Ship back to the fortress at Rhodes.

Now entirely alone and at the mercy of his captors, Jem's ordeal began in earnest. For the Knights seemed to believe that the only security lay in continually moving the Prince from hiding-place to hiding-place. First they took him northwards to Rochechinard, a lonely keep built upon an inaccessible crag high above the valley of the Isère. Then after a few weeks, travelling by night, they transferred him to another castle. This grim stronghold was situated on a bleak, windswept mountainside. Behind it, towered sheer limestone cliffs, the eyrie of bats and ravens and birds of prey; and below lay a deep ravine, through which a mighty torrent boiled night and day, sending up an unceasing and infernal roar.

The place belonged to the Baron de Sassenage, a patron of the Order, and it happened that he had a young daughter, an angelically fair maiden, fourteen or fifteen years old, called Philippine-Hélène. Soon she fell in love with the Prince and sent impassioned letters, by way of her old nurse, declaring her ardour to him. Jem responded, telling her of his love for her in no less reserved a fashion, and they contrived to touch and even once or twice to embrace one another. But the pitiless hand of Fate soon intervened to put an end to this forbidden romance.

The Knights learned that it had become known in the villages in the valley below the castle that the Prince was staying in the Baron's house, and they deemed it necessary to remove him to some spot even more secluded. With scarcely an hour's forewarning, they took him away through the ice and snow and biting winds of midwinter and journeyed westwards for many days by little-frequented roads and byways, shunning all human contact and stopping to rest only at the houses, castles and Commanderies belonging to the Order. At last, with the Prince and his guards more dead than alive from the extreme cold and the fatigue of travelling in such dire conditions, they came to the Grand Priory of the Auvergne at Bourganeuf.

This region was the ancient ancestral homeland of the

301

Grand Master, Pierre d'Aubusson, and so was deemed by the Knights to be the most secure place to hold their unwilling guest. Yet even when they had arrived there, they remained nervous lest an attempt be made to abduct or liberate Jem. Because by this time the Kings and Princes of all Europe, and the Pope himself, were rapidly losing patience with the Brotherhood's evasions and equivocations, and were demanding that Jem be employed against the Ottomans and given the opportunity of marching on his brother, with the blessings of the Church, at the head of a Christian army.

And presently the Grand Master's nephew, Guy de Blanchefort, received tidings that King Matthias had been heard to vow that he would bring the Prince to his court at Buda before the year was out, and that he had already retained the services of certain audacious adventurers and mercenaries to carry out his threat.

Learning this, Blanchefort had the Prince shifted without delay to Monteil-au-Vicomte, a strong fortress and birthplace of his uncle Pierre d'Aubusson. And after a few weeks he took him on to Morterolles, a lonely moated Commandery whose single portal could be sealed against attackers by rolling a massive round stone into position.

Then, during the second summer after Jem's flight from Karaman, Guy de Blanchefort decreed that the Prince should disappear, as though from the very face of the earth, to a place where no searcher, however persistent and determined, could possibly find him.

By a tortuous roundabout route, through dense pathless woodlands and trackless uninhabited heaths, Blanchefort brought Jem to the far north of the Auvergne. Here his brother Antoine de Blanchefort possessed a vast forested domain, utterly remote and lost to the world, known as Boislamy. In a thickly wooded valley at the very heart of this isolated preserve, there lay a secluded lake, and on its hushed shore there stood, almost hidden among the tall oaks, an ancient château. Its well-built towers were encompassed by solid stone walls and by a broad water-filled moat joined to the lake by a wide channel; its strongly

302

defended gate was reached by a causeway, raised on wooden piles, that could be instantly severed by the lifting of a heavy drawbridge in case of attack. And several dozen heavily armed Brothers of the Order walked the walls and courtyards of the castle at every hour, while beyond the moat men on horseback, with crossbows and accompanied by packs of savage mastiffs, patrolled the forest to ward off intruders.

There the unhappy Prince languished for two years. And, as Guy de Blanchefort boasted to his prisoner, not even Charles, the new King of France, knew that he was there.

All this Sadi learned when he and some of Jem's other faithful officers were brought back from Rhodes to share his imprisonment in the château. And Jem's sad existence began to improve in other ways: his property – his books, his jewels, his fine clothes – was gradually restored to him, sent on from the half-dozen places in France in which he had spent brief sojourns. To alleviate the dreary tedium of his confinement he started to write verses again and resumed work on the history of his father's glorious reign. He began to teach his ape how to play chess with him, assuring his astounded guards, dull fellows lacking the faintest spark of wit, that he discerned latent talent in the beast, and that with practice it might yet become an opponent to be reckoned with. Nor did he neglect the education of the beautiful white parrot given him by the girls of Nice. He schooled it in the catechism of the Faith and taught it to say, 'Verily, we come from God and to Him we shall return!' and whenever he left or entered the room, to shout in its stentorian tones, 'God give victory to Prince Jem!'

Meanwhile, the unholy Brothers, who never rest from hatching some new mischief or iniquity, were busying themselves at the Grand Priory at Bourganeuf, fortifying and strengthening the walls and bastions, and raising a massive and lofty tower surrounded by its own moat as a special prison for the hapless Prince and his companions.

At length the tower was completed – at a cost, it was said, of three and a half thousand ducats. It stood seven storeys high, each floor reached from the floor below by a winding stone staircase. The first and second storeys were given over to a guard-house, storerooms and a kitchen; the third, Jem's servants; the fourth, the Prince's own rooms; the fifth, quarters for his surviving officers; the sixth and seventh for the Knights, their men-at-arms and the other servitors of the Brotherhood charged with the task of acting as the Prince's gaolers.

In the early summer of the very same year of my own journey through Europe in search of Jem, he was taken by order of the Grand Master – God curse him! – from Boislamy and brought to Bourganeuf to be locked in the Great Tower. And thenceforth the Prince was never to be allowed out except to exercise twice a day on the small patch of lawn on which Talabot and I had espied him that autumn morning from our place of concealment in the shadow of the Priory church . . .

And in this manner, with the description of Jem and his loyal officers' incarceration in the Tower, Sadi's account of the hidden years in the Prince's ill-fortuned wanderings in the lands of the Misbelievers drew to a close.

As Sadi spoke the final words of his doleful tale the day dawned and the first beams of the rising sun began to stream through the high barred windows of the room in which we sat. Even the Old Man – normally so indefatigable – was now showing signs of strain, his grey features and yellowing teeth looking more than usually unwholesome in the unfriendly early-morning light. For a while the three of us said nothing.

Then, breaking the silence, Kivami Bey said, 'One final question, and you may go and sleep.'

'Very well,' said Sadi wearily.

'How did you manage to escape?'

Sadi's lip curled in an ironic smile.

'I did not agree to speak to you of that,' he said.

'I will not ask anything else,' said Kivami Bey.

'Very well,' said Sadi with a profound sigh. 'What difference will it make now? After some months the Infidels became less concerned with us who were merely the Prince's attendants. They were convinced that His Highness could not escape from the Tower – so what we did ceased to interest them very much. After all, even if it did get out eventually that Jem was being held at Bourganeuf, the place was now so well defended that it would take a whole army to lay siege to it. And as long as the Prince was locked in his room in the Tower, they even let us go into the village for an hour or two – if there were no strangers about. And the people there – God bless them! – invited us into their houses to eat and drink with them. They felt sorry for us, you see, and they hated their masters the Knights. So in exchange for gold they were quite prepared to help one or two of us get away. And I wasn't the first. Huseyn Bey got away before me; but just the same the Knights went on letting us pay visits outside the Priory.'

Kivami Bey raised an eyebrow and said, 'And what became of Huseyn Bey?'

'I don't know,' said Sadi with a shrug. 'But I would hardly tell you if I did.'

'All right, all right . . .,' said the Old Man, raising his hand in a placatory gesture. Then he turned to me and said, 'Call the guard, Captain. Sadi Bey can go back to his quarters now.'

After he had been taken away, Kivami Bey and I wandered blinking into the daylight and walked slowly back to the first courtyard. When we reached the marble bench beneath the cypresses in front of the disused church, the Old Man indicated with a wave of one of his silver-handled canes that we should sit down.

'Well,' said Kivami Bey, 'that's the end of that!'

'What do you mean, sir?'

'I'll explain later . . . first we have other matters to deal with.'

I felt light-headed with fatigue and would have liked nothing better than to be allowed to go and sleep, but Kivami Bey had that steely look in his cold grey eyes and I knew there was not the faintest possibility of my being dismissed.

'You'll be interested to hear', he said, 'that the day before yesterday, certain letters were found at the house where Sadi was staying – letters intended for Jem's adherents here in Istanbul and in several other cities.'

'But where?' I said, alarmed at my failure to locate them. 'I had the place thoroughly searched.'

'Do not blame yourself, Captain. You did what you could in the time available. They were by no means easy to find.'

'What did they say?'

'They prove that Jem has a plan for getting out of the Tower and has found local helpers who are confident they can smuggle him as far as the south coast. But he needs a vessel waiting for him there to take him on to Savoy, from where he can get to Hungary.'

'That, then, is what Sadi is supposed to arrange?'

'Indeed. And this is where you come in,' said Kivami Bey.

'But how?' I said.

'You're to go to France and make contact with Prince Jem to tell him everything has been arranged and the ship will be there to take him off. If his officers are still allowed to go out into the village you will be able to communicate with Jem through them. If not, I'm sure it will not be beyond your ingenuity to get word to him in the Tower by some other means. After all, from what you said some time ago, the Infidel Talabot and his relatives in Bourganeuf should be able to help you. Then, when everything's agreed, you can accompany Jem yourself to the coast to make sure he comes to no harm, and that he gets safely aboard the vessel we send for him.'

'But why should Jem agree to come with me?' I said. 'He may be expecting some sign to prove to him that I am sent by his supporters and not by his brother. He must have calculated that there was a chance Sadi might fall into our hands.'

'That is possible,' said Kivami Bey. 'However, we will provide you with letters written in Sadi's hand – we have samples of it that can be copied – saying that you are a friend sent on his behalf. Remember, your prompt action means that the Prince's partisans here are not aware of Sadi's arrest. And now that you have heard the whole story of Jem's adventures since he left Karaman from his Chancellor's own lips, you should not have any difficulty in convincing the Prince and his officers that Sadi really did take you into his confidence.' I shook my head at the sheer deviousness of Kivami Bey's handling of Sadi's interrogation.

'At last', I said, 'I can see what you were really after!'

'I'm very glad to hear it,' he said, giving me a mocking glance.

Then he said, 'And the sooner we get the Prince back home, the better. Because there's another even more unthinkable possibility than Jem's going to Hungary to join forces with King Matthias. For several weeks we've been receiving reports from our people in the West saying that the Knights may soon be transferring the Prince to Rome, and that Pope Innocent has grand plans for launching a Crusade in support of Jem's claim to the Sultanate.'

'Then the rumours I heard in Italy were true?'

'Indeed.'

'But why the delay?'

'For some time now,' said Kivami Bey sourly, 'His Majesty has been paying the Grand Master forty thousand ducats a year to ensure that the Prince makes no alliance with the Pope or any of the other Christian princes who have been offering to help Jem pursue his ambitions.'

The House of Osman paying tribute to the Infidels! I stared wide-eyed at the Old Man, quite unable to believe my ears. But feigning not to notice my amazement, he went on in a matter-of-fact manner:

'However, now that the *Pope* has offered to pay Aubusson a suitably tempting sum *and* make him Cardinal in exchange for the custody of Jem, he seems to have decided that he can afford to forgo what Bayezid has been paying him. As well he might – he's already amassed a vast fortune at our expense.'

'Is there no limit', I said, 'to the greed and cunning of these Knights? And is it not surprising that Innocent should allow the Grand Master to accept gold from the Ottomans, who so recently were threatening to drive the Pope and his whole pack of Misbelievers from Rome itself?'

'But, my dear fellow,' said Kivami Bey, 'neither the Pope nor any of the Christian princes knows that Aubusson has received a penny from us. And the Sultan, I might add, made this wretched arrangement entirely on his own initiative, without even telling the Imperial Council. Gedik Ahmed was the first to get wind of the deal, and he told the Emperor that he would have no part of it, which was about the last thing he did – God forgive him! – on this earth.'

'Then His Majesty', I said sadly, 'still lives in such mortal terror of Jem's return as to make a pact with our most implacable enemies.'

Kivami Bey raised his eyes to Heaven and threw up his small fat hands in a gesture of despair, letting them fall on the bench beside him. Then he took his sticks and struggled painfully to his feet. I also stood up.

'I'm going to rest for a couple of hours,' he said. 'I imagine you will want to do the same. I'll send for you later.'

I offered to take his arm and he accepted, leaning heavily against me as we moved laboriously across the courtyard towards his room.

'Tell me, sir,' I said as we walked. 'Why did you say, "That's the end of that" earlier on?'

'Ah,' said Kivami Bey, 'that's quite simple. When I informed His Majesty of Sadi's arrest and my intention of questioning him, Bayezid sent word that after seven days – if Sadi had not died on the rack – he would deal with him himself.'

I mentally counted the days. That morning was indeed the seventh since his arrest.

'What will happen?' I said as we reached the Old Man's door.

'God knows,' he said. And freeing his arm from mine, he went inside, adding without turning back, 'Now go and get some rest.'

*   *   *

They came for Sadi while I slept. By the time I awoke, it was over. I thought perhaps that the Sultan might take pity on him and let him live. But Bayezid was of another mind. It was even said that His Majesty believed that his exiled brother had sent his Chancellor for no other purpose than to procure the Emperor's assassination, or perhaps in some desperate fashion to attempt to carry it out himself. At all events, Bayezid had no intention of letting this – as he saw it – highly dangerous State prisoner into the precincts of the Palace, let alone the royal presence.

Therefore, when the detachment of Palace guards came to fetch the Chancellor, they did not return with him to the Sublime Porte. Instead they brought him on horseback – his handsome face muffled with a white scarf lest he should be recognized while he was conducted along the streets – down to the waterfront, by way of the Harbour Gate. There they put him aboard a small boat and rowed him out into midstream.

When they arrived at that stretch of deep water off the Palace Point – from which, it is said, Bayezid himself watched the proceedings from the window of one of the Imperial summer houses there – the oarsmen were ordered to cease rowing and bring the boat to a halt.

First the guards removed the scarf covering Sadi's face and used it to bind his hands behind his back. Then from the bottom of the boat they took a large stone, pierced in the middle with a hole, and tied it with a length of rope around the luckless Chancellor's neck. While this was happening he showed no fear and put up no resistance. Finally, at a nod from the captain of the guard, they pitched Sadi overboard head first, and with a dull splash, a sudden rush of bubbles rising to the surface and a brief hiss of foam, the restless waves rolled in from every side and closed over him for ever.

I passed the following days preparing to return to France. I even managed to convince myself that Kivami Bey's scheme might work. Yet on the very day I was supposed to leave for the West, I was suddenly and unaccountably ordered to postpone my departure.

I remained kicking my heels for a couple of weeks, awaiting further instructions. During this time I sensed a change of atmosphere at the Convent. The clerks and scribes seemed to hurry hither and thither more urgently, their officers appeared more than usually grave and pre-occupied, and even the Old Man acquired an uncharac-teristic air of distraction. At first I thought that a high official of State, some governor or vizir, or some member of the Royal Household – God protect them! – had fallen sick. Or that the Emperor himself was ailing, perhaps even seriously ill.

Then, one morning, all hell broke loose. Messages, let-ters and dispatches started to arrive by the quarter-hour, a torrent of reports to come from our agents and informers in the city's bazaars and inns, in the taverns, the banks, the counting houses and foreign embassies at Galata, and our couriers to dash to and fro between the Convent and the Sublime Porte.

By nightfall there could no longer be the smallest doubt about it. The unthinkable had happened. Jem had quit Bourganeuf and was now in Rome.

Ornaments of Gold

I travelled to Rome alone, and hazardous though my journey was, the perils I endured pale into insignificance before the fearful and bloody events that took place subsequently.

How shall I describe Rome? The whole world knows of the grandeur and magnificence of this city, whose rulers long held sway over East and West, and whose fame extended to the most distant places of the habitable earth and the remotest corners of the Seven Seas. Even now, the centuries of decadence have not succeeded in effacing altogether the signs of its erstwhile greatness. For within its mighty walls there remain countless awe-inspiring edifices, proud monuments and prodigious ruins that bear mute testimony to its former triumphs. Would that Mehmed's dreams of possessing this, the Red Apple, had not been ended so abruptly by his untimely death!

The walls of Rome form a circuit twenty-four miles around. They are pierced at intervals by as many gates, and are so solid and excellently built that they have the appearance of being completed only yesterday. The city is surrounded on every side by hills and through the middle of it there flows a winding river called the Tiber, which is navigable and a few miles downstream reaches the coast and runs out into the sea. In the midst of the river lies a narrow bank in the shape of a ship, known as the Tiber Island; here and in three other places the flow is spanned by noble high-arched bridges made of stone that link the two halves of the city.

Most of the inhabitants live on the Tiber's eastern side

in populous districts that crowd right up to the river's edge. Here are numerous churches, chapels, convents, monasteries, houses, palaces, aqueducts, fountains and gardens. In this part of town there are two principal concourses: the Piazza Navona, which resembles the Hippodrome at Istanbul, and the Campo dei Fiori, which signifies the Field of Flowers, but is now a paved square surrounded by buildings. And though this city is deemed by the Adorers of the Cross to be the most holy in all Christendom, there are here scores of wine-shops, taverns, gambling dens and houses of ill-repute that are nightly the scene of unbridled revelry, drunken debauch and all manner of lewdness and vice.

On the opposite bank, the western side of the river, stands a great basilica and a high bell-tower crowned by a huge cross. This church is called St Peter's and has an imposing portico approached by a wide flight of steps. The inside is like a large hall; the floor is covered in costly mosaic, and its vast roof very lavishly decorated and supported on colonnades of marble pillars. Below the altar is a chair on which, they say, St Peter sat. Nearby, there hangs between two pillars an old piece of rope the thickness of a ship's anchor cable, with which, it is averred, the traitor Judas hanged himself. On the right is a tall column where the veil of St Veronica is kept. The Infidels say that this veil belonged to a woman of Jerusalem who wiped the sweat from the brow of Jesus as he climbed with the cross to Calvary; and that after this act of compassion she found stamped upon the cloth a perfect likeness of his features. Steeped as they are in false belief, these Infidels know not that it was not the Lord Jesus who was crucified but another resembling him!

To the left of the basilica is an immense stone obelisk named Caesar's Needle. It is surmounted by three gilded orbs that are said to contain the ashes of that proud conqueror Julius Caesar. On the other side is a lofty gateway, reached by a ramp, that leads to the Vatican, wherein dwells the Pope. This palace is fortified, rises to seven or eight storeys at the front and contains several courtyards and innumerable rooms and apartments. To the north of the Vatican the Pope has a spacious walled park and on a hill, atop a series of gardens and terraces, a sumptuous pavilion called the Belvedere.

Below the Vatican walls there is a district called the Borgo, where some of the Cardinals and other clerics have built houses and mansions, and where many of the Christian kings and princes maintain residences for their envoys. And beyond this, rising up above the Tiber and dominating the entire city, stands a gigantic round fortress called the Castle of St Angelo. On its highest tower is a bronze statue of a winged angel brandishing a great sword.

This angel commemorates a remarkable occurrence. It is said that many years ago, while a merciless plague ravaged Rome, it was revealed to the Pope in a vision that he should go to a certain church in a far-flung part of the city. The next day he left the Vatican, crossed the Tiber and proceeded there in devout and solemn procession with his Cardinals. It happened that in this church there was a heathen idol that some of the Christians were worshipping in secret. But when the Pope approached the place, a noise like a peal of thunder rent the air, the idol burst open and fell to the ground, shattered into a thousand pieces.

When the Pope and his entourage were returning to St Peter's to give thanks, just as they crossed the river by the bridge leading to the Castle they looked up and saw above the fortress an angel of terrible aspect holding aloft a blood-drenched sword. Amazed and rooted to the spot, they watched the angel wipe the sword clean on his robes and sheath it once again in his scabbard. In this way the Almighty showed He was appeased and the plague came to an end. Thereafter the fortress was called by the Romans the Castle of St Angelo.

I reckoned during my time there that Rome was inhabited by scarcely more than seventy thousand souls. And the city had declined to such an extent that – beyond the Town on one bank of the Tiber, and the Vatican, the Borgo and the Castle on the other – there were within the ancient city walls wide tracts of open ground, meadows, fields, vineyards, orchards and woods where dogs, foxes, hares and other wild beasts had their lairs. Indeed, within living memory half a dozen enormous wolves had been slain within the walls of the Vatican Garden itself. Yet the fortunes of cities, like those of Nations, wax and wane from age to age. Should Rome at last be brought within Ottoman domains, perhaps the city will be rebuilt and thrive again as in former days. God assist us in conquering it!

Though the city is so much fallen into decay, the Romans bear themselves proudly, even arrogantly. And notwithstanding their inferiority to their ancestors of old, they affect contempt for those of other lands. Moreover, there are always so many strangers in their midst, not only from the other Italian states but from every part of Christendom, that a foreigner like myself could go freely about the town arousing scant curiosity.

Thus, enquiring now of one person, now another, I had little difficulty in locating the house of the gentleman who was to assist me in carrying out my mission. He was a Roman noble who had been in the Sultan's service for some time. On instructions from the Convent, he had cultivated the friendship of Francesco Cibo, whom the Pope styled his 'nephew', although everybody knew him to be the Pontiff's son, and whom many called Franceschetto, or 'Little Francis' because he shared the same name as his father. As well befitted his bastardy, this young Francesco was a thoroughly indiscreet and dissolute character, who had unknowingly proved an invaluable source of intelligence on day-to-day occurrences within the walls of the Vatican. And now that Jem had taken up residence in the papal palace, Kivami Bey hoped that I might be able to make further use of this connection to gain access to the Prince.

But alas, I arrived too late.

Although the morning was bright and airy, when I reached the house I found all the shutters closed, yet the door stood wide open. I went in and immediately encountered a servant, who wordlessly indicated the way I should proceed, as if my coming at that particular hour had been expected. Mildly puzzled by this strange reception, I walked down a long dark hall into a large high-ceilinged room.

There, sure enough, was my Roman noble, lying as though asleep on a bed. He was richly dressed and wore about his neck a gold chain and on his fingers heavy rings set with precious stones. His chin was freshly shaved, his hair neatly combed and his hands folded across his chest. He was dead.

I realized presently that in the shadows round the edges of the room there were a number of chairs pushed up against the walls and that some of these were occupied. I sensed that I was being watched intently and was in a considerable state of uncertainty as to what I was expected to do. But fortunately, at that moment, an old couple entered behind me, went past me to the bedside and bent down, one after the other, and kissed the corpse's brow. I followed suit, applying my lips to the cold waxen skin, and then I turned to go. In all this time I spoke to no one and no one spoke to me. As I retraced my steps along the hall, I exchanged perfunctory nods and murmured greetings with those I met – sombre men holding their hats in their hands, and women sniffing and dabbing their eyes with little handkerchiefs – coming in the other direction.

There was nothing to be gained by lingering in this inauspicious place, so I set out at once towards the Campo dei Fiori, where I had taken temporary lodgings at an inn. To the south of this square there is a densely populated quarter, close by the river bank opposite the Tiber Island, inhabited mostly by the Jews of the city. I had wandered the poor lanes and alleys between its close-packed houses the night before, in order to locate the shop of an apothecary named Josef. This shop served as a dispatch post for the letters and reports of our agents in the Papal States, its business providing an excellent cover since the apothecary corresponded with certain fellow practitioners in

315

Istanbul, Damascus, Cairo and Baghdad, and frequently received packages from the East containing elixirs, concoctions, simples and compounds, even sending out to these places preparations of his own devising. But not wishing to take any unnecessary risks, I had not entered the premises the previous evening, preferring not to make myself known to its proprietor until I had need of him to send some missive to the Convent.

The shop was ill-lit and cool and had that pungent bitter-sweet smell such places always have. Rows of bottles, phials, and glazed earthenware and china jars glistened darkly on the shelves. A set of brass scales gleamed on the polished wood counter, behind which a heavy curtain hung over a low doorway.

Scarcely had I entered when the curtain parted and a lean erect Jew with a grizzled beard, refined features and a patriarchal demeanour emerged, removing from his nose a pair of silver-rimmed spectacles.

'Maestro Moshe sends his greetings,' I said.

'That is good of him,' said Josef with a slight bow. 'How is my dear old friend?'

'He is well,' I said.

Josef called over his shoulder, 'Ishak!'

A few moments later a boy of about sixteen appeared. He took his seat on a high stool behind the counter. Josef beckoned to me and, going behind the counter, I followed him through the curtain.

We passed along a narrow stone passageway and into a low-beamed room with an open door giving onto a tiny sunless courtyard, surrounded by the towering walls of grim tenements at the back of the shop. We sat on chairs beside a table under the only window.

'I have been expecting you for some time,' said Josef. 'But I'm afraid I have bad news for you . . .'

'I know,' I said. 'I have just come from the house.'

'When did you arrive in the city?'

'Yesterday,' I said. 'What happened?'

'He was killed last night in a tavern not far from here. There had been an argument over cards. There was some

316

kind of fight. They called a surgeon but he was already dead. The surgeon is my friend, so I got to hear about it almost straight away.'

'Then he was not killed because he worked for us?' I said.

'I think not,' said Josef. 'He drank and brawled and kept bad company. Something of this sort was bound to happen sooner or later.'

'What of the others involved? Have they been arrested?'

A look of astonishment came over Josef's face.

'This is Rome!' he said. 'Those responsible were all wealthy – the Governor's men didn't even try to arrest them when they saw who the men were. In any case, there are murders and robberies every day – and in broad daylight too. Yet only one in a hundred culprits is ever brought to justice. Even when some malefactor is caught red-handed, if he has the means he is allowed to purchase his pardon, whatever the crime! Innocent and his Cardinals say: "Christ seeks not the death of a sinner but that he should repent and live!" But absolution costs money, and every day they get richer on the proceeds.'

I shook my head in wonderment that the Pope should allow such enormities in his own capital and that even murderers should go unpunished.

'Well,' I said, 'I suppose there is nothing to be done about it now. I will have to find someone else to help me.'

Josef rose and went over to what looked like an oven door, strongly armoured with iron strips fixed with square-headed nails, set into the stone wall. He produced some keys from beneath his garments, opened the door, took out a sealed letter and handed it to me.

'This arrived not long ago,' he said, 'with the order that it was to be given to you, but only if you were in need.'

I turned it over a couple of times and found both sides blank. I hesitated for a moment, then broke the seals and began to unfold it. As I did so a small square of flimsy paper fluttered out and came to rest on the table. I picked it up. Written on it were the words: *'Contessa Sofia Contarini, Villa Margherita.'*

I showed the paper to Josef. He seemed surprised.

'Who is she?' I said.

'The widow of a Venetian senator,' he said. 'She came to Rome a few months ago and took the house that is named there. It is in the same district you were in this morning – between the Piazza Navona and the river.'

As he spoke, he got up and brought over a small lamp that had been burning in an alcove on the other side of the room, together with a shallow brass bowl, and set them both down on the table.

'What brings her to Rome?'

'They say she is involved in some suit in the ecclesiastical courts. I do not know the details.'

'Has she ever delivered letters here?' I said.

'Never.'

I held the piece of paper in the flame of the lamp and watched it blacken, curl and catch alight. When it had been consumed I did the same with the envelope and dropped it burning into the bowl.

'I'll send the boy with you,' said Josef as we went back down the dingy corridor to the shop, 'to show you the way.'

Nothing could have prepared me for what occurred next.

The Contessa's residence was in a tranquil leafy district of the Town, on the banks of the river opposite St Peter's and the Vatican. The house was set on a slight rise a little back from the water's edge, and the Tiber's silver flow could be glimpsed sparkling at intervals in the gaps between the clumps of trees, church towers and tiled rooftops that stood in front of the Villa.

Beyond the front gate was a paved courtyard, in the centre of which was a finely wrought fountain, its round basin brimming with cool limpid water. As there seemed to be nobody about I went on through the gate and strolled towards the house. The windows were open on the first floor and I heard women's voices echoing in the rooms within, but still no one called out to me and I assumed my approach was so far unobserved.

318

Then I noticed a small arched doorway in the wall of the yard to the right of the house. I went up to it and tried the wooden door. It swung open with a creak and I stepped through to find myself in a secluded and hushed garden.

Taking a narrow sun-dappled path beneath tall pine trees, I walked round the side of the Villa. Presently, through an opening in a thick, neatly trimmed hedge, I spied a weather-worn balustrade below which was a long pergola supported on a double row of slender marble columns and shaded by a luxuriant canopy of vines festooned with pendulous clusters of ripe purple grapes.

I moved forward, treading as lightly as I could on the gravel, until I was nearly level with the short flight of stone steps leading up from the garden into the pergola. When I reached the steps, I could see on the terrace in the green shade of the vines a marble table on a pedestal, half-concealed by the dense foliage of what appeared to be a curving recess set back from the terrace itself. On the table lay a book, a pen, an inkwell and a tall crystal glass filled with pale vermilion wine.

Mounting the steps, I walked cautiously on and, coming closer moment by moment to the secluded bower, I now caught sight of a delicate wrist and a graceful white hand, its palm upturned, resting languidly on the table top. Going stealthily forward, I lowered my eyes and observed on the ground a discarded pair of red shoes and just behind them a crumpled dark-blue skirt and mass of white petticoats that had been hitched up in the midday heat to reveal a pair of smooth shapely legs and two small, elegantly arched bare feet.

Hardly allowing myself to breathe, I approached the bower. Then, almost upon it, I gave a cough and stepped out from behind a vine-draped pillar – the final obstacle that screened me from the rest of the verdant arbour's dainty and enticing occupant.

Turning her startled black eyes upon me, the nymph gave a cry of surprise, her lovely cheeks colouring as she hastened to pull down her skirt and petticoats to hide her naked legs. In doing so, she leant forward at the waist, the

319

derangement of her unfastened bodice and loose white calico blouse affording me a heart-stopping vision of two swelling and exquisitely formed breasts. For several seconds I devoured with my gaze their dark honey-coloured aureoles and delicious nipples as my sorely flustered gazelle attempted to cover her ample exposed bosom with her hands.

I looked up again at the prettily flushed face to be met by arched black eyebrows, a blazing gaze of imperious outrage and the shrill warning, 'Come one step nearer, villain, and it will be the last thing you do!'

That voice! I blinked and peered at her in disbelief. The eyes, the fine brow, the small nose, the ruby lips, the abundant black hair, the defiant toss of the head . . .

But my eager bending closer to drink in anew these adorable features was utterly misinterpreted by their proud possessor, and my stupor was so complete at suddenly finding myself before my erstwhile mistress – who, I had discovered only afterwards, had been working for Kivami Bey all along – that I was quite unable to defend myself when she made her attack.

I dimly perceived her murmuring, 'I warned you,' and all at once she was hurling herself across the table at me. The wine glass went flying and smashed against the pillar in a shower of stars. I believe I saw the blade flash momentarily in a bright shaft of sunlight slanting through the green vine leaves overhead. She aimed straight and low and, as God is my witness, if the table had been half a span narrower, she would have made a eunuch of me. But the blow was slightly deflected when she overreached herself and lost her balance, and the steel missed my groin, plunging instead into the top of my left thigh.

The knife was thin and grooved down the centre, so that it penetrated deep. Blood spurted out of the wound, showering thick crimson drops on Sofia's white blouse and bared throat and neck. I grabbed her by the shoulders and tried to push her away from me with an incoherent shout.

Then I staggered backwards, baring my teeth in pain. And since she was still hanging like grim death onto the knife's ivory handle, the blade slid from my flesh, and I was left gripping my thigh in agony, watching the blood well out from between my fingers. Then I glanced up and to my horror saw that she was edging round the table, staring at me intently with an unwavering regard, the blood-stained knife still in her hand. She began to lift it in the air as though to strike again.

At last I found the voice that amazement had robbed me of until then, and backing off in terror, my right forearm raised to shield my body from the second blow, I managed to gabble out, 'For God's sake, Sofia, you stupid bitch, it's me, Barak!'

I had, to be sure, found easier ways in the past to win admittance to a beautiful woman's bed. But the ways of Fate are devious and strange. And in any case, what man would not have endured a hundred wounds to enjoy the artful ministrations of the black-eyed enchantress who was now devoting herself body and soul to nursing me back to health?

Nor could the not inconsiderable discomfort I was suffering as a result of Sofia's spirited attempt to unman me long delay the consummation of our miraculous reunion.

Lying in semi-darkness against a bank of downy pillows, on crisp starched sheets smelling as fresh and fragrant as a spring meadow, my leg dressed and bound up in a voluminous white bandage, the servants dismissed for the afternoon (so that I might rest!), I watched, dizzy with desire, as my beloved, ignoring my pleas to come to me at once that I might show her that I had forgiven her for her vicious and unprovoked attack on my innocent person, sat herself calmly before her mirror, removed her necklace, rings and earrings, then divested herself of her blouse, and dipping a sponge into a bowl of clear water, started to cool herself by applying it with alluring grace to her neck, her armpits, her breasts.

Once or twice she glanced up and, seeing in the reflection of the glass that I was following the progress of her toilette with rapt attention, she lowered her eyes as though abashed, yet stretching out one arm, then the other, she continued to pass the sponge over her skin in so leisurely and languorous a manner that I feared I might not be able to contain myself an instant longer.

After a while, she unfastened her hair and, shaking her head, allowed the luxurious black curls to tumble over her white shoulders and the lovely curvature of her back.

Then she stood up, wriggled free of her skirt, untied the knot that held up her petticoats and let them fall in a soft heap at her feet, revealing to my burning gaze a pair of voluptuously plump buttocks. Bending prettily to pick up skirt and undergarments, she cast them casually aside onto a chair, and proceeded to run the sponge over her trim calves and full, well-rounded thighs.

She gave me a sideways look over her shoulder, observed with apparent satisfaction and amusement the havoc this display of her nakedness was playing on that part of my being in which, in former times, she took so much delight, and began to dry herself with a towel. Then she took an alabaster vessel from her table, and applied to her neck, beneath her arms, and between her legs a heady perfume of musk, gazed at herself for a few moments in the mirror, then turned towards me with a little smile.

She came over to the bed, making no attempt to hide from me even those most private parts which, I observed, she still kept perfectly smooth and free from hair in the Turkish fashion, although she now dressed herself outwardly as a woman of the West.

I tried to raise myself on my elbow, but my nymph laid her delicate hands on my chest and prevented me from rising any further. She lay down beside me, pressing her breasts against me. I started to caress her between the thighs and found moist proof that Nature had already more than adequately prepared the way for me to enter her with ease.

But as I moved to pull her beneath me so that I might at last possess her, she slid deftly from my grasp and positioned herself instead astride my hips with her legs apart. Then, guiding me with nimble fingers into her belly's pink

322

honeyed cleft, she sank slowly on her haunches, impaling herself, with a low moan, inch by inch on the rigid staff of my tumescent manhood.

For a few moments she paused, panting, and gasped in a halting voice that I was never before so inhumanly large, and that she could feel already that I was doing her some fearful and irrevocable injury.

But then, surrendering her will to the unyielding grip of my strong hands about her slender waist, she closed her eyes and began to lift her hips and let them fall, her heavy breasts swaying with the even motion, and – though whimpering breathlessly all the while that I was killing her – to spread her thighs wider and wider so that I might penetrate her ever more deeply.

At length a series of shudders began to rack her whole body, signalling the imminence of her moment of gratification. Then, all at once, she threw back her head and gave a violent downward thrust that made her cry out with pleasure and pain. And seconds later, as I gave up the unequal struggle to hold myself back any longer, we dissolved in mutual ecstasy, as with rapid and irresistible spasms her hungry womb milked to the last drop the life-bestowing fluid from my convulsing loins.

It was shortly before dusk when we awoke.

'I still cannot understand', I said, 'why you did not recognize me sooner.'

'*I* recognize *you*!' said Sofia, full of indignation. 'If you had not been so preoccupied trying to look up my skirt, you would have seen that it was me. And after all, you had the advantage over me: *I* did not have a beard when you last saw me.'

She sat up and cast an appraising eye over my clean-shaven face, cocking her head a little to one side and frowning. Then she added, 'I cannot decide which way I like you best.'

She lay back again and I put my arm around her cool shoulders and began to stroke her silken, musk-scented hair.

'But surely', I said, 'Kivami Bey must have warned you that somebody would be coming here from Istanbul?'

'Kivami Bey', she said, 'told me nothing about sending anybody to see me. But anyway, you deserved to get yourself stabbed.'

'How can you say that, dearest?' I said. 'What fault was it of mine that you weren't expecting me?'

'Because you didn't reply to my letters,' she said with simple dignity.

'But I never received any. I promise you, before God!'

'I sent dozens,' she said. 'I can't remember how many. I suppose that monster Kivami Bey had them all intercepted somehow. But you could at least have tried to get word to me.'

'I did,' I said, 'but I could not discover where you had gone. The people in your neighbourhood in Fener said they knew nothing. Kivami Bey forbade me ever to mention your name again, or to try to find out what had become of you. I began – God forgive me – to think that something awful had happened to you, even that you were dead.'

'He's not a man, he's a fiend,' she said.

'And yet you made love to me on his orders, and tried to trap me into betraying secrets to you.'

Her hand tightened and her sharp nails dug into my arm.

'I no longer had a husband to look after me. What could I do? I was terrified of what Kivami Bey would do to me if I refused. But I loved you, you know I did.'

'You told him about us and all the things we did together,' I said bitterly.

'Not everything, my love, not everything . . .'

'And the Venetians,' I said, 'what were you doing for *them*?'

'Ah, so Kivami Bey told you about that, did he?'

'Only that they believed you were working for them.'

'I see. Well, what happened was this: I knew some women in Galata. One of them was the mistress of their most important agent in the city. He spoke to me one day and asked me if I would like to make some money by finding out about certain Greeks close to the Sultan. I went to Kivami Bey and told him I had been approached by this Venetian and he told me to play along with him, and that he would supply me with information to pass on to the Frank.'

'Why did you leave Istanbul in that case?'

'That was Kivami Bey's idea too. Eventually, he had me tell the agent in Galata that I thought I was suspected and my life was in danger. So with the Frank's help I fled to Venice.'

'And there you got married and became the Contessa Contarini!' I said, my heart filling with anger at the thought of some unclean Infidel having the impudence to enjoy my beloved.

She sighed. 'After I got there I did some small things for Kivami Bey, but it was very dangerous because I was being watched. When he discovered this, he seemed to abandon me. After all, he must have many other agents in the Republic, and in much more important positions than I was.'

'Why didn't you return to Turkey?'

'He wouldn't let me. He said he might need me in the future where I was.'

'How did you live?'

'I had a pension from the Venetians. A reward, they said, for supplying the State with intelligence. But it wasn't much. I was alone and I was unhappy. The Count was an old man, but he was kind and I thought he would protect me. Once or twice I even came close to telling him about Kivami Bey, but I was too frightened to in the end.'

'You were right to keep quiet,' I said, my heart suddenly beating faster. 'If you had talked, the Old Man would have got to hear about it sooner or later, and he'd have sent someone after you.'

'I know,' she said quietly.

'Did Kivami Bey tell you to come to Rome?'

'No,' she said, 'the Venetians did.'

'What for?'

325

'After I'd been married to the Count for a couple of years, he caught a fever in the winter and died. I thought he was wealthy when I met him, but afterwards I discovered that he was extravagant and had spent all of what he had, and more, long before. All I inherited were debts and a court case about some land that was far too expensive to pursue. Well, in Venice they have a secret council called the Council of Ten – they have people watched, pay informers, send agents to spy in other countries and commit assassinations.'

'Kivami Bey has spoken to me of this Council,' I said.

'Yes, I suppose he would have done. Anyway, the Ten knew of my circumstances. It was they who were my paymasters when I was in Istanbul, though I did not know it in those days. Eventually they summoned me and said: We will pay for you to plead your case in the Papal Court and make sure you live comfortably now and in the future. But you will have to go to Rome in person. And once you are there, all we require of you is that you report to us on certain men and women there – some Venetians, some not. You should have no difficulty in making their acquaintance – you are young, attractive, you have charm . . .'

'And you accepted their proposition?'

'One does not refuse a request from the Ten – unless you have grown tired of living.'

'And Kivami Bey?' I said.

'I sent word to him that I was coming here. Since then I have heard nothing. Until you came, that is . . .'

'So,' I said, 'now that it suits his purpose Kivami Bey brings us together again.'

'That's what makes me so afraid,' she said, laying her head on my chest. 'If only it had happened in some other way. I do not feel safe, even when there is a wide sea between that man and me!'

The servants could be heard now moving about on the floor below, and the footsteps of someone padding along the corridor outside the room in which we lay.

There was a light knock on the door of the room next to

326

ours. Sofia rose, put on a black velvet robe to cover her nakedness, and went through the double doors leading into the second room, closing them very quietly behind her. I heard her open the door to the passageway and speak in a low voice to her maid.

After a little while she returned.

'You will have to go soon,' she said. 'Anna I can trust, but the others are not my people and some of them, no doubt, are paid by the Ten to spy on me. If they see you here too often they may be tempted to find out more about you.'

'But, my darling,' I said, 'what are we to do?'

'You must take a house, somewhere discreet so that I can come and see you there. This Josef you have spoken of will be able to help you. I cannot come to see you in a tavern . . . after all, I have my reputation to consider.'

As she spoke, I began to kiss her throat and, opening her velvet robe, to nuzzle my chin against her breasts. Meanwhile, my hand found again that fragrant vale of delight between her thighs and the robe slipped from her shoulders and slid onto the floor. I pulled her onto the bed, where we exchanged burning kisses and intimate caresses.

Then, rolling her over onto her stomach and kneeling behind her, raising her haunches so that her elbows and forehead were resting on the bed and her rump was entirely at my mercy, I prised her thighs apart and, forcing my way into her gaping belly, I took her as a stallion takes a mare. Thoroughly inflamed by her moans of pleasure, I thrust myself into her with ever-increasing vigour until, finally, imploring the aid of the Blessed Virgin, she entered the last throes of her excitement and I copiously spilled my seed deep inside her once more.

Then all was quiet and still again, and as darkness gathered, we remained there for a while without saying anything, my exhausted dark-eyed Contessa lying trembling and weeping softly in my arms.

Within the week Josef had found a house at the edge of the Jewish Quarter, not far distant from the Sistine Bridge.

An old place in a quiet neighbourhood that had clearly

seen better days, it was solidly built in stone and surrounded by high walls, and though not large it had a squat
old-fashioned square tower surmounted by a tiled roof,
from which one could take in with a single sweeping
glance the wide loop the river makes as it passes through
the middle of the city, the greater part of the more densely
populated districts of the Town and, a little further off to
the north, the Vatican Hill and below it, on the bank of the
Tiber, the immense glowering bulk of the Castle of St
Angelo.

The house was entered from the street by a pair of doors
made of strong oak that could be bolted from the inside by
lifting into a place a heavy wooden beam. Once inside, one
found oneself in a cobbled courtyard bounded by stables
and storerooms. A small arch at the far end of the courtyard led into a second walled enclosure, where there was a
weed-choked trough fed by a spring pouring incessantly
forth from the mouth of a carved stone gorgon with
tangled locks and staring basilisk eyes, a handful of dusty
peach, orange and lemon trees, a patch of grass and some
overgrown and neglected vegetable beds. Beyond the end
wall of this modest garden was the river, which could be
reached by unlocking a narrow postern gate that gave
onto an old half-ruined quay with uneven steps leading
down to the turbulent, swiftly flowing water.

From the main courtyard there rose a stone stairway of
some twenty steps that led to a long open gallery covered
by a sloping roof. At the far end of the gallery was the door
to the half-dozen rooms overlooking the courtyard that
comprised the living quarters of the house. In one of the
rooms there was a fireplace and an enormous bed, for
which I bought a fine new mattress, pillows, blankets and
linen.

I sent word to Sofia.

She came the following morning with her young maid
Anna. I noticed for the first time that Anna was very
pretty, and reflected with pride that Sofia's choice of her as
a companion revealed her confidence in her own beauty.

I showed the Contessa my few rooms and took her up

into the tower to admire the prospect over the city. We descended and went into the garden beyond the court-yard, leaving Anna sitting on a little stool by the front door working on a piece of embroidery she had brought with her.

Sofia and I reclined on some cushions I had laid out on the grass beneath the spreading shade of a lemon tree. And at my urging, she began to relate to me the story of Jem's arrival in the city that spring.

For many months before he came, she said, it was rumoured that the Prince would soon pay a visit to Rome to consult with His Holiness about the great expedition he was planning to return to Ottoman lands and drive his brother Bayezid from the throne. And never, she said, even in the long memory of the most aged and venerable citizens, had the place been in the grip of such excitement.

For there was a prophecy, indubitably very ancient and known throughout Christendom, that in or about the year of the Lord Jesus 1484 a Turkish prince would come to the Eternal City and take as his place of residence the Apostolic Palace on the Vatican; and this event, according to the same prophecy, would herald the death of certain kings and princes, the decay of old Empires and the rise of new ones, and all manner of other awe-inspiring upheavals that would usher in a change in the entire order of the World.

Thus, when it seemed that what had been written by soothsayers and oracles of yore was going to be accomplished at long last by Jem's timely arrival in the city, the fervour and enthusiasm of the whole populace was almost indescribable. Indeed, hardly had Jem set foot on the coast of Italy at Civita Vecchia – having sailed from France in the Knights' Great Treasure Ship – than the news reached the expectant Romans and they jubilantly took to the streets to celebrate.

A few days later the Prince finally arrived in person, escorted by Guy de Blanchefort, Grand Prior of the Auvergne, a detachment of the Knights of Rhodes, and a magnificent suite of Turkish officers exotically attired,

329

like their Master, in turbans and eastern garb. They were met at one of the city's southern gates by Innocent's son Francesco Cibo, the Pope's equerries, his heralds, his interpreters, his Master of Ceremonies, a dozen Cardinals and their households, the Governor of Rome, his sergeants and men-at-arms and a glittering squadron of the Papal Cavalry.

After an exchange of salutations, the two parties rode into Rome in a single cavalcade and, passing through the Jewish Quarter and the Campo dei Fiori, they crossed the river by the Bridge of St Angelo and came at last to the Pope's Palace.

Needless to say, the whole city turned out to see the Prince and, lining the route of the procession, everyone – young and old, rich and poor – cheered wildly as he went by and crowded after him even as far as the Vatican itself, where they filled the square before St Peter's for hours after he had disappeared within the walls of the Palace.

As the vast crowd continued to ebb and flow outside, still applauding, still raising ragged cheers and hoarsely calling out his name, Jem was conducted by his hosts to the sumptuous apartments on an upper floor of the Palace set aside for the entertainment of visiting emperors and kings. There they left the Prince and his companions to wash and change their clothes and rest.

Presently, the Master of Ceremonies and various other Infidel dignitaries came to Jem to inform him of the manner in which they proposed that he should greet the Pope when the two men met.

'It is the custom', they said, 'for sovereigns and royal princes of every state when they come here to kiss the Pope's foot. Only the German Emperor kisses his knee, and that because it was his ancestors who granted Rome to the Papacy. Therefore, you should kiss His Holiness's foot – or at least, if this is unacceptable to you, his knee.'

But Jem replied, 'Why should this be? When other sovereigns and princes meet in these parts, the inferior is not expected to kiss the superior's foot. Besides, there are rulers whose power and magnificence greatly exceed the Pope's — how can they be expected to kiss his foot?'

'They hope', said the Master of Ceremonies, 'that by so doing they will earn remission for their sins.'

'If that is the reason,' said Jem, 'it would be of no benefit to me. For I seek forgiveness only from the One God, the Almighty, the Blessed, He who has no associate! So you see, I have no need of the Pope in this matter. And know this: I would rather die than perform an act that would bring indignity and dishonour to the True Faith.'

There followed a long discussion, in which the Infidels introduced all kinds of argument, but the Prince remained adamant, and nothing they said would make him consent to what they asked. So they went to Innocent and told him everything that had taken place.

But Innocent merely replied, 'Do not vex him like this. Whatever he wants to do, allow him to do it. Let him greet me in whatever way he wishes!'

The following day, a solemn audience was held in the Great Hall of the Palace. All the worthies and high officials of the Vatican and the City of Rome were there, as were the emissaries of the Kings of France, Spain, Portugal, England, Germany, Bohemia, Hungary, Poland and Muscovy, the envoys of the Dukes of Milan and Ferrara, the ambassadors of the Republics of Venice, Florence and Genoa, and a host of other representatives of smaller states, principalities and fiefdoms.

When all these ambassadors and plenipotentiaries had gathered and taken their respective places, the Pope himself entered, dressed in robes of gold adorned with priceless jewels. On his fingers were numerous rings set with fabulous gems, and on his head he wore his triple tiara, a tall crown studded with diamonds, rubies, sapphires, emeralds and other rare precious stones. And as all knelt before him, Innocent ascended his throne and his Cardinals seated themselves on their chairs to his right and left, while the Roman and foreign nobles rose to their feet and remained standing in deference to the Supreme Pontiff and the Sacred College.

Then the doors at the back of the hall were thrown open and Jem strode in, flanked three paces behind by the Grand Prior of the Auvergne and the Pope's son Francesco Cibo, and followed by his entourage of Ottomans. As Jem neared the throne, Innocent hastily got up, stumbling a little, seemingly astonished by the Prince's proud and regal bearing.

Without more ado Jem briskly and nimbly mounted the steps, took the Pope firmly by the shoulders and embraced him warmly, kissing him on either side of the neck.

Collecting himself and adjusting his cumbersome robes, the Pontiff said in a clear voice, 'Welcome! Welcome! And may you bring good fortune with you!'

To this Jem replied very courteously through an interpreter, saying he was very pleased to be in Rome, was obliged to the Pope for his kindness, and was confident that, if it pleased God, everything would be for the best. He added that there were weighty and important matters concerning which he hoped to confer with Innocent, and sought a meeting with him so that they might discuss them in private.

Graciously Innocent replied that he would grant the Prince an audience as soon as possible. At which Jem stepped down and began to embrace the Cardinals, who had risen in a body when the Pope stood up and were now gathered in a semi-circle around him. While Jem was engaged in greeting the Cardinals, his officers approached Innocent one by one, each in turn kneeling down to touch the floor with his right hand before raising it to his lips, and coming forward to kiss the hem of the Pope's robe.

Then, having reached the end of the line of Cardinals, Jem looked up once more at the Pope, inclined his head almost imperceptibly, and swept out of the hall, his retainers marching in step behind him, leaving the whole assembly standing in a stunned and amazed silence.

'And that', said Sofia, 'was the last time that Jem was seen in public.'

'Tell me,' I said, after pondering a while on what she had said, 'does the Prince receive visitors in private?'

'At present, very few. He never leaves the Vatican and everywhere he goes, whether in the Palace or in the gardens, he is closely guarded by the Knights.'

'The Knights?' I said. 'I thought they had relinquished him at last.'

'Some of them remained behind to act as his bodyguard. It was a condition the Order laid down when Jem was handed over to the Pope, though Blanchefort himself left the city some time ago – they say to go to Rhodes to consult with the Grand Master.'

'That is as well for me,' I said.

She asked me why and I told her of my adventures in Genoa, and of how Monsieur Guy and his comrades – God curse them! – had made it their business to attempt to terminate my existence. She listened wide-eyed, and seemed suitably impressed when I recounted my escape and my leap across the yawning chasm between the Banco and the building opposite, and laughed heartily when I described my collision with the pigeon on the other side. She begged me to tell her more but, promising to do so another time, I pressed her to return to her account of Jem's life in the Vatican.

Innocent, she told me, was terrified that Bayezid would send assassins to kill Jem before the Christians' plans for a Crusade could be realized. The Prince was, therefore, being kept almost as a prisoner, though in surroundings considerably more luxurious than those he had endured in France.

The only visitors he had received thus far were the Pope himself and close members of his household and family, and certain trusted Roman nobles and their wives, who were invited to the Palace to be presented to the Prince, to dine with him and alleviate the tedium of his confinement. And on other occasions, Sofia added darkly, Innocent had got his son to bring to the Turks' quarters certain notorious courtesans and boy harlots from the Town, who offered grosser forms of entertainment and were willing to satisfy the carnal needs of the incarcerated Ottomans . . .

Otherwise, she said, no foreigners, however noble

or distinguished, had yet been admitted to the Prince's presence – except the ambassador of the Sultan of Egypt – though it was now well known that Jem greatly desired to be allowed to lead a less circumscribed existence and constantly complained to Innocent about the excessive restraints placed on his person and those of his officers.

'So,' I said, 'you have not yet had the opportunity to speak to him yourself?'

'No. I've only seen him from a distance, walking in the gardens, when I have visited the Vatican. But I have been ordered by the Ten to try to meet him and make his acquaintance at all costs.'

'With what object in mind?' I said.

'For a long time,' she said, 'the Venetians have realized that if they could gain custody of Jem themselves the present peace between the Republic and the Porte could be guaranteed. In fact, you may be sure that if they could lay their hands on him, they would not hesitate even to hand him over to Bayezid – so long, of course, as the Sultan were prepared to offer a large enough reward in exchange.'

I gave a bitter smile.

'Then I see', I said, 'that far from working against each other in this case, the Convent and the Ten are now pursuing a common purpose.'

'What do you mean?' said Sofia. 'Surely the Sultan must desire only one thing.'

'Strange as it may seem,' I said, 'my orders are not to try to kill Jem, but, by posing as an agent of his partisans in Turkey, to persuade him to escape with me. Or, failing that, somehow to abduct him by force. But above all to try to get him back alive.'

Sofia had now sat up and was tightly embracing her knees with her arms and staring intently at the ground.

'Kivami Bey is mad,' she said at last, without looking up.

'He is acting upon the Felicitous Sultan's command. From the very beginning Bayezid has sought to avoid killing his brother.'

'Then the Sultan is mad too,' she said simply.

'Mad or not,' I said, 'you, my dear Sofia, are the one who

334

will have to act as a go-between. After what you have said, I can see that I myself have little hope of getting to talk to the Prince as things stand at the moment. But tell me honestly – what are your chances of obtaining an introduction to him?'

'I know certain Cardinals and also others in the Vatican. I have been pressing them for an invitation for quite some time now, and they cannot keep me waiting for ever.'

'Is there not a danger', I said, 'that they will become suspicious if you appear too eager to gain access to the Prince?'

Sofia burst out laughing, raising her hand to cover her red lips and her even pearl-white teeth.

'But, my dear,' she said, her eyes sparkling with hilarity, 'there isn't a woman in Rome who would not like to be able to say to her friends that she had dined with "the Barbarian", or even that she had shared some more intimate moment with him. In fact, the Prince is already acquiring something of a reputation with the ladies . . .'

I gazed at her gloomily. Still laughing, she gave a girlish pout and began to stroke my cheek.

'Don't look so depressed,' she said. 'I have a barbarian all of my own – why should I go in search of another?'

After a time we got up and strolled back to the house together. Anna was still at her embroidery on the stool outside the door. Sofia told her how lovely and cool and fresh it was in the garden, and suggested she take her needlework there to sit in the shade for a while.

Blushing, Anna curtsied to her mistress, gave me a sideways glance and a quick nervous smile, and then gathering up her skirts, she hurried away along the gallery and down the steps into the courtyard.

I guided Sofia into the house. She went before me with a lazy provocative swing of her hips, her full dress and starched petticoats rustling stiffly as she walked. When she reached the room I had set aside for my sleeping quarters, she sat down on the bed and, as I pushed the door shut, she took off her shoes and began to unlace the bodice of her dress.

Kivami Bey used to maintain that espionage was mostly pen-pushing and paperwork – and during that winter in Rome I began to see the truth in what he said.

It was impossible for me to get to Jem, so I could do nothing but report what I heard for myself in the city and, at second hand, what went on behind the closed doors of the Vatican. For this latter task I had at least the compensation of the unwitting assistance of the finest secret service in the West.

Sofia dined often at the house of Domenico Trevisano, the Venetian ambassador, who kept her briefed on the affairs of the Papal Curia, both from the official visits he made there and from the reports of Venice's agents and informers within the Palace. Trevisano also passed on to her instructions from the Ten, and conveyed her verbal and written observations back to them. Indeed, Sofia was now such a frequent visitor to the ambassador's residence that there might have been a scandal, had it not been known that whenever the beautiful Contessa and Messer Trevisano retired to a private room together – on the pretext of discussing the progress of the immensely complex and interminable case she was pursuing in the ecclesiastical courts – they were always accompanied by the ambassador's chaplain (a young priest from Vicenza who, unbeknown to the world, conveniently combined the roles of confessor and cipher clerk).

So, although Sofia had still not succeeded in securing a meeting with the Prince, I found myself privy to a substantial part of the secret intelligence gleaned by the Most Serene Republic's agents in Rome, and even gained occasional glimpses of the Ten's deliberations regarding Jem. And what I discovered must have made unedifying reading for my masters back in Istanbul.

For Innocent's plans for an unholy crusade against the True Believers were now gathering apace. And despite stories of the Pope's frailty and ill health, he appeared to work on the forthcoming expedition with all the persistency and determination of a camel. That winter he sent out legates to every capital and court in Europe, requiring every king, prince and state to send representatives to a great Congress to be held in Rome, at which a common strategy could be debated and the details of deployment could be agreed upon before war was declared on the Empire.

And every king, prince and state in Christendom duly responded by dispatching ambassadors – save Venice, whose Senate excused the Republic on the grounds that their attendance might be construed by the Porte as a hostile action and put in jeopardy their treaty of peace with the Sultan. Would that a single other Infidel state had declined to take part in Innocent's wild and dangerous schemes!

On the day of the Annunciation, ambassadors, envoys, ministers and plenipotentiaries from every corner of the Christian lands assembled together with the Pope and his Cardinals in a church within the walls of the Palace called the Sistine Chapel. After Mass had been said, at Innocent's instigation Pietro Mansi, the young Bishop of Cesena, mounted the pulpit and began to harangue the congregation about the 'Most Holy War' that the Pope was about to wage against the Muslims.

He told them that Prince Jem was an instrument sent by God, by means of which the power of the Turks could be overthrown; that it was the duty of every Christian to aid in the Crusade, or he would be a Christian in nothing but name, and that any man who tried to evade his duty would henceforth be obnoxious in the sight of the Almighty and, forfeiting Eternal Bliss, he would burn for ever in Hellfire.

The Ottomans, said Mansi, had long been thought to be invincible, and for decades had carried all before them. But now the tide of events was turning. Muslim even fought Muslim – had not the brave Sultan of Egypt recently inflicted terrible defeats upon the Turks in Karaman and Syria?

337

But, more than anything, circumstances were changed by Jem's providential coming to the West. For the Prince was the Conqueror's true and designated heir and was loved by all the Turkish people; whereas Bayezid, the usurper, was loathed by his subjects and went in constant expectation that the entire populace was about to rise against him. But, above all, Bayezid was terrified of his brother's return, which he feared worse than a visitation of the plague. And accordingly, since Jem had taken refuge in Christendom, the barbarian tyrant had not once dared to make war upon the West.

The Christians, however, must now use the Prince not just as a shield but also as a sword. Owing to the Holy Father's tireless and unceasing efforts as a mediator, there was peace in Italy and Europe – so at last all might join together to fight the common foe. And, said Mansi, they must seize this opportunity with both hands, before the Muslims had time to settle their own differences.

Amidst a rising swell of approbation, Mansi brought his speech to a close by urging his auditors not to delay a moment longer, but to march on Constantinople, liberate the former Christian cities of the East, retake Jerusalem and the Holy Sepulchre of the Saviour, convert the barbarians to the Catholic faith and leave to posterity such deeds as would be worthy of all praise and emulation on this earth and win heavenly plaudits from the angelic host in the Eternal Kingdom!

And barely had the Pope concluded the occasion by giving his benediction to the assembled foreign delegates than they poured forth from the Chapel and excitedly began to discuss – even in the very corridors of the Vatican, as they made their way to their own apartments and residences – their plans for gathering immense armies and mighty fleets to invade, overrun and lay waste the Guarded Domains of the Ottoman Empire.

It was scarcely ten days from the afternoon when Sofia related to me the unwelcome contents of Bishop Pietro Mansi's belligerent address that she came again without

338

warning, at the dead of night, with even more sombre tidings.

I had given her a key to the outside gate and the door of the house itself, so I did not hear her until, waking from a fitful sleep, I recognized her footsteps in the room next to mine and she called out softly to alert me of her coming. I got up, we embraced and at her insistence I put on some clothes and lit a couple of lamps. We sat down together at a table. Her face looked anxious and pale in the lamplight. The bell in the tower of the church at the far end of my street gave its hollow cracked chime for four o'clock.

'You should not have come here alone like this. This is not Istanbul. The streets are dangerous and these Infidel cut-throats and robbers are no respecters of the sex of their victims.'

'I would have come earlier,' she said. 'But I thought I was followed when I left Trevisano's house, and after I went home I had to wait until I was sure that everyone was asleep.'

She pulled up her skirts, reached down and withdrew from her stocking a piece of paper folded over several times. She unfolded it and smoothed it out on the table. Peering at it in the dim light, I saw that it seemed to be covered with tiny handwriting in Greek.

'What have you got?' I said.

'Innocent and the envoys came to an agreement yesterday. Trevisano received information about it earlier this evening while I was there. I put down everything I could remember as soon as I got home.'

'Wait,' I said. 'I'll need something to write with.'

I took pen and paper from the shelf by my bed, uncorked a new flask of ink I had bought a couple of days before and poured some into the pewter well I had found in the house, then sat down again.

'I'm ready,' I said.

'There are to be three armies,' Sofia said. 'The first to be raised by Innocent himself and the other Italian states; the second by the Germans, Hungarians, Bohemians and Poles; the third by the French, Spanish, English and Scots.

There will also be a fleet – provided mostly by the Italians and the French.'

'Strength of the armies?'

'At least one hundred and fifty thousand, probably more.'

'And the fleet?'

'Not less than a hundred sail.'

'Who is to lead the expedition?'

'Each army is to elect its own commander,' she said. 'But the Germans wish for their Emperor Frederick or his son Maximilian to be the Captain-General.'

'And the Pope?'

'He wishes to go with the Italian part of the expedition, and will do so if his health allows it. All but a few of the ambassadors maintain that his presence is essential in case disagreements should arise among the different Nations taking part. All of them know full well what calamities occurred in the past when the Franks began to fight each other in the East . . .'

'And where do they propose to strike first?' I said.

'The particular targets will be settled later between the Pope and the other Christian princes. But in principle the Germans and their allies will invade by Bosnia and Wallachia; the Holy See and the Italians will land by sea in Albania and the Morea; and the fleet will also attack the coasts of Greece, Anatolia and the Islands and land the army led by the French.'

'Which army will the Prince himself go with?'

'Jem is to go back to Karaman. The Egyptian ambassador has already given Kayitbay's pledge to gather an army in Syria in support of him, which will cross the border as soon as the Franks attack in the West.'

'Where will the fleet sail from?'

'Ancona, Brindisi, perhaps Messina in Sicily as well.'

'When?'

'This coming spring. All the attacks will be launched on the same day – this has not yet been named – including the Sultan of Egypt's in the East,' said Sofia, slowly folding her piece of paper again.

340

'Is that all?'

'For now, yes,' she said.

She held the paper towards the flame of one of the lamps, raising her eyebrows in a questioning look. I nodded and she set fire to it, taking the flaming paper and dropping it among the ashes in the hearth.

'Is it known what Jem has to say to all this?' I said.

'I gather he is behaving rather strangely. He is upset, they say, by the death of the Duke of Savoy.'

'Then Charles has died?' I said. 'I knew only that he was suffering from some illness. But he was young and people said he would recover.'

'It is almost certain that he was poisoned,' said Sofia.

'By whom?'

'The Duke of Milan, Charles's enemies in the Piedmont, the Knights of Rhodes – who knows? Jem was most distressed when he heard the news and has been getting drunk every day and refuses to see anyone. I cannot understand it. Apparently Jem and the Duke spent only a few days together. Yet the Prince is behaving, they say, as though he had lost a brother.'

'Ah,' I said, 'I can understand the reason well enough . . . But now I must get all this into cipher so that I can take it to Josef in the morning. Why don't you stay, my dearest, and send for Anna in the morning?'

'No,' said Sofia, shaking her head sadly. 'I had better go back. I don't want them to know that I've been out, if I can avoid it.'

'Then I will ride back with you,' I said, 'to see you safely home.'

How vividly I could picture to myself Jem's grief at the death of Charles of Savoy – the one true friend the unhappy Prince had ever encountered in the West, the sole Misbeliever who shared his lofty ideas of honour and chivalry, the only Frank of noble estate who had sought to aid the fugitive without considering what he himself might gain by doing so. And it seemed to me that the Prince – his judgement clouded by bitterness and disappointment at

341

the young Duke's demise – could now be more tempted than ever to acquiesce in Innocent's evil schemes, in the vain belief that in them lay his last hope of vanquishing his brother Bayezid.

After some time, it was said that Jem had recovered his spirits somewhat and had even started to complain to the Pope once again of the lack of civilized society. And thus, at last, Sofia's request was granted and she was informed by one the Cardinals that her name had been included on a list of guests to be invited to a banquet, which the Prince was to attend, to celebrate the accord reached by the Infidel Nations regarding the Crusade.

But the banquet never took place.

For there was at that time languishing in one of the filthiest and most noisome dungeons of the Castle of St Angelo one Cristoforo Castracano. This gentleman had once been the Lord of Castel Leone in the district of Fano, a place to the north of Ancona. But the Papal forces had driven him from his lands and given the fiefdom to another. Thereafter, Cristoforo had wandered, a penniless exile, even as far as Candia, Cairo and Istanbul. And some months before, he had turned up in Europe again, in Venice.

There he had presented himself at the house of the Pope's legate in the city; and having asked to speak with him alone, the dispossessed lord fell on his knees and began to pour forth the most extraordinary tale.

Whilst in Istanbul, he told the legate, he had been approached by an agent of the Porte who, to his amazement, knew who he was and all about the misfortunes he had suffered and the injustices of which he had been the victim. The Turk then assured him that if he was prepared to do as he was told, he would before long have the opportunity to avenge himself – and also to make himself a rich man once more.

Presently the agent took him to the house of a Pasha. There the Pasha enquired of him if he knew a certain fountain in Rome, just outside the Porta Viridaria, next to the Papal Palace. Cristoforo answered that he knew it well. Was he aware that the Pope and the other chief occupants of the Vatican had the water for their tables drawn from this very fountain? He was. And that Prince Jem too received his water from the same source? Cristoforo did not doubt that this was the case, as the water was held to be the purest and sweetest in Rome.

The Pasha then gave the Frank two small silver ampoules that had pierced in them a number of tiny holes sealed with beeswax. He told him that he was to go by night to the fountain and, pricking the holes beforehand with a pin, place the ampoules at the bottom of the small stone chamber within the fountain through which the water ran, where they would lie invisible to the eye while they did their fell work. The poison, said the Pasha, would seep out slowly, and those who drank the water would show no ill-effects for at least five days. By which time Cristoforo would be miles away, even in another country, and in not the slightest danger of ever being connected with the sudden deaths of Innocent and the Sultan's fractious younger brother.

Shortly after this meeting, when all had been agreed, Cristoforo said that he was even taken to the Palace and presented to Sultan Bayezid himself, who gave him two robes of gold brocade, a large amount of money and a diamond worth four hundred ducats and promised him gifts infinitely more lavish if he should succeed in the enterprise with which he had been entrusted. The following day Cristoforo left Istanbul to journey westwards to carry out the deed.

But no sooner had he left Turkish territory and set foot on the Christian soil of Corfu than he was all at once overwhelmed by the enormity of the crime he had undertaken to commit. In panic he threw the ampoules into the sea and took ship immediately for Venice, with the intention of revealing the conspiracy to the Holy Father's representative there.

And when he disembarked he went directly to the house of the Papal legate to confess everything and to crave through his intercession forgiveness from Innocent him-

343

self, without which, he now realized, he would never be able to save his poor benighted soul from everlasting torment and Damnation.

That night the legate had Cristoforo confined in his own house, and hastily sent word to the Ten that there was a dangerous criminal in the city with whom, as a mere man of religion, he felt wholly incompetent to deal. Acting swiftly on the denunciation, the Ten gathered at dawn and Cristoforo was brought before them.

However, having heard the story from his own lips and cross-questioned him about it, Their Excellencies came to the conclusion that Cristoforo was nothing more than a liar and a fantasist, and that he had made up the whole tale in the hope that, by revealing it, he would win some reward from the Pope – perhaps even the return of the lands taken from him by Innocent. The Ten agreed none the less that His Holiness should be informed of the incident.

Innocent took an altogether less phlegmatic view of the affair and insistently pressed the Ten to hand the offender over to him so that he could be questioned further. The Ten had little to lose by complying with Innocent's demands – they even hoped, by doing the Pope this favour, to placate his anger towards the Republic for its refusal to become involved in the Holy Father's expedition against the Turks.

Cristoforo duly arrived in Rome in chains, and Innocent wasted no time in having him put to torture. This seems to have had the effect of making the prisoner's feverish imagination run wild: he conjured up a host of additional conspirators, accomplices in the Vatican, Ottoman plans to land tens of thousands of Janissaries in Ancona, and a host of other extravagant follies, all of which Innocent seemed more than eager to believe. And when finally Cristoforo seemed to have nothing left to confess, the Pope had him thrust into a tiny cell, infested with tarantulas and worms, in the Castle of St Angelo.

Then an urgent dispatch arrived from the Ten informing the Venetian ambassador that they believed they had now uncovered a real plot, of which the Pope should be informed at once.

For the Ten had received intelligence from their agents in Istanbul that a desperado named Gianbattista Gentile had been in the city offering to undertake the assassination of the Sultan's brother. And though the Porte seemed to scorn his advances, he had suddenly disappeared from the city, and it was feared that Gentile had received a commission after all, and might even now be on his way to Rome. Every Venetian galley and sailing vessel had been ordered not to give the man passage, and all the Republic's captains and governors told to arrest him on sight. Yet he seemed, said the Ten, to have vanished into thin air.

But this time the Ten had gone too far in their attempt to win the Pope's approval with insincere shows of solicitude for his security and health. When the ambassador conveyed the warning to Innocent in a private audience, His Holiness visibly went white with terror. Already assailed on all sides by plots and conspiracies, real and imaginary, his mind seemed quite unable to accommodate yet another intrigue. He ordered the guard on the Vatican to be redoubled, Jem's banquet to be cancelled and all other visits to the Prince to be suspended forthwith.

The following morning the erstwhile Lord of Castel Leone was hauled from his cell at the Castle of St Angelo, stripped stark naked and dragged blinking into the courtyard of the fortress. There Cristoforo was put upon a cart and manacled, standing, to a stout stake that had been set up in the back of it. Already waiting to ride with him in the cart was a masked figure equipped with instruments of torture and a smouldering brazier. Before he began his business this sinister individual handed to his victim a little wooden image of the Lord Jesus upon the Cross, which the terrified Cristoforo clutched pathetically to his naked breast.

Then the gates were flung open and the cart started on its journey, leaving the fortress and rumbling over the Bridge of St Angelo into the city. In the mean time, the masked figure set about tormenting the condemned

345

man – searing his skin with glowing irons and tearing at his exposed flesh with red-hot tongs and sharp pincers. As they passed through the streets of the town, Cristoforo screamed and cried out in agony and begged for mercy and – prompted and goaded by the masked man – shouted out over and over again: 'Holy Father, forgive me for I have sinned!'

Having traversed the breadth of the city, the cart ascended the Capitol, the torturer still unhurriedly continuing with his work, and came to the square before the Governor's Palace that stands on top of the hill. There the cart stopped.

The masked figure was then seen to take a great wooden hammer, raise it high above him and bring it suddenly crashing down on Cristoforo's head, spattering his brains against the stake to which he was chained. Next, the executioner took a long dagger and plunged it repeatedly into his chest and heart. Then he unfastened the Lord of Castel Leone's broken body, which was by now a bloodied mess, covered from head to foot with gashes, cuts and burns, letting it crumple onto the floor of the cart.

On the Pope's orders the corpse was quartered where it fell: one section – part of the head, the chest and one arm – was sent to be hung up over the St Angelo Gate; another section dispatched to the Gate of San Paulo; another to that of San Giovanni; and the final quarter taken away to be suspended over the Porta del Populo. Thus, by the public exhibition of these ghastly talismans, did Innocent seek to ward off any of those who might have designs on his life or that of Prince Jem.

But the Romans, who like their ancestors are addicted to every kind of spectacle and usually attend executions in vast crowds, on this occasion turned away in disgust from this whole display, sullenly taking to their houses and cursing the Pope for his cruelty.

That afternoon a tremendous storm broke over the city. The air became thick and dark and turbulent, the wind roared and howled through the deserted streets, and a downpour began, the like of which had never before been

346

known, that lasted continuously for days on end.

And the people said that Christ was angry with Innocent. Because Cristoforo had freely confessed and should have been forgiven, not put to death in such a horrible fashion, and that by acting contrary to the example of the Saviour the Pope had invited not the approval of the Almighty but His contempt and wrath.

Thus, it was with grim satisfaction that the Romans learned in due course that Innocent had fallen seriously ill. For some days it was even rumoured that he was dead. During this time the fields and vineyards around the town were utterly abandoned, the shops and markets remained closed, and Romans and foreigners alike took to arms and barricaded themselves into their homes and lodgings, hourly expecting the city to erupt into tumult. But then it was learned that the Pope was recovering, and slowly life began to return to normal.

And before long the mob seemed to have forgotten all about Cristoforo Castracano. For its fickle attentions were now distracted by the tidings of a new event: the imminent arrival in the city of an ambassador sent by Sultan Bayezid.

I could conceive of no explanation for this unexpected embassy from the Porte – other than that the Emperor was playing for time. For now that Innocent's plans to make war on the Ottomans were so far advanced, all the Sultan could hope for was to try to delay the evil hour while he did what he was able to strengthen the Empire's defences to the East and West in preparation for the onslaught.

Bayezid had chosen for his emissary that Mustafa Bey who had been Head of the Convent during the Old Man's exile in Thrace, and who was now serving the Sultan as one of his advisers at the Palace. Not that I saw him except from a distance when he was in Rome, for I received orders from Kivami Bey just before his arrival on no account to attempt to contact Mustafa, since Bayezid had not considered it prudent to make him privy to my mission.

Mustafa Bey arrived at the Porta del Popolo on the morning of St Andrew's Day. I joined the crowds to watch him come in. He rode through the gate accompanied by a magnificent suite of his own and an escort of Knights led by Guy de Blanchefort, who had met the Turks in Rhodes, whence the embassy and the Knights had sailed together, in one of the Order's galleys, to Ancona.

I happened to be standing close to the gate itself and Blanchefort turned and glanced in my direction as he passed, which gave me an unpleasant feeling in my stomach – yet what chance had he of picking out my face in such a vast sea of others?

Mustafa Bey was formally greeted in the piazza before Santa Maria del Popolo, the church that stands just within the Gate, by Innocent's household, a dozen Cardinals, every Infidel ambassador then in Rome and what seemed like almost the entire population of the city. And when the Ottoman ambassador acknowledged with dignity the cheers of the mob, they rewarded him with a mighty roar of acclaim, while Blanchefort and his Rhodians looked on, stony-faced, and the Papal party, the Cardinals and the other ambassadors milled about in confusion, trying to get the procession into some kind of order that it might move off towards the Vatican.

The following day the envoy was granted his first audience with the Pope himself. But of course this and their subsequent meetings took place in private, so I had to rely on Sofia and the Most Serene Republic's agents in the Curia Romana to follow the progress of the negotiations.

The ambassador, said Sofia, came laden with lavish gifts: yards of cloth of silver and gold, exquisite tapestries and carpets, precious stones and rare furs of sable, ermine and vair. When these had been presented to the Pontiff, Mustafa added that he brought also the gold for Jem's maintenance but – in view of the fact that Jem had not been observed in public for some time – was not empowered to hand it over until he had seen with his own eyes that the Prince was still alive.

At this point the Pope, trying without success to conceal his astonishment, asked Mustafa how much gold the Sultan had seen fit to send to the Holy See.

'One hundred and twenty thousand ducats,' replied Mustafa. 'That is sufficient for the Prince's pension for three years, is it not, my lord?'

'This is the first', said Innocent, 'that I have heard of the Prince receiving a pension from his brother. Let alone one of such extraordinary magnitude. Since when has this arrangement been in force?'

'Why,' said Mustafa, 'the Felicitous Sultan has been paying Grand Master Aubusson forty thousand ducats a year – on condition, naturally, that the Prince is kept in custody and not permitted to disrupt the peace of the Empire – ever since Jem fled to Europe. And I am now bringing the pension to Rome instead of Rhodes because His Majesty assumed that, since the Prince has become Your Lordship's guest, this consideration should be paid henceforth to you.'

'Tell me,' said Innocent, 'is this all that has been given to Aubusson by your master during this time?'

'By no means,' said Mustafa Bey. 'And I can scarcely believe that the Grand Master has been so reticent with Your Holiness in this matter. Because there have been quite a number of additional payments – all of them involving substantial sums.'

The instant the audience was at an end, and Mustafa had withdrawn from his presence, Innocent called Guy de Blanchefort before him and began to question him about these enormous extortions from the Sultan. But Blanchefort was thoroughly evasive in his replies, and the Pope became so enraged by the recalcitrant Knight that his attendants feared he was about to have an apoplectic fit. At last, Innocent angrily demanded of the Grand Prior that he send to his uncle in Rhodes for a copy of the agreement between the Grand Master and Bayezid relating to the payment of Jem's so-called pension – but Blanchefort, brazen and insolent as ever, blandly denied that any such document existed, maintaining that verbal understandings between the Order and the Porte had always been deemed quite sufficient.

Innocent said: 'I refuse utterly to believe that an agree-

349

ment of this importance involving such vast amounts would ever be made as you say . . .'

But Blanchefort would concede nothing and soon he found himself peremptorily dismissed by the exasperated Pontiff. And from that day forth, Innocent was filled with the most profound loathing for Aubusson, his nephew Blanchefort and the entire Order of the Knights – God confound the whole pack of them!

Yet Innocent now found himself faced with a dilemma. For, as Sofia had revealed to me some time before, he was then in desperate need of money. His household was large, his numerous children and nephews, whom he had striven all his life to promote and enrich, were constantly increasing their demands on his wholly inadequate financial resources. And, as though this were not enough, his wastrel and profligate son Franceschetto had taken to losing thousands of ducats at the gambling tables and running up countless other debts, all of which his father had to pay off or suffer public humiliation.

Thus, the Emperor's offer must have seemed to Innocent almost too good to be true. Because to keep Jem and his suite, even in luxury, was, I knew from Sofia, costing the Pope no more than three hundred ducats a month. And as Bayezid no doubt carefully calculated, though there was little likelihood that Innocent could be persuaded by a bribe of whatever proportions to abandon the Crusade altogether, he might at least be encouraged to find excuses to postpone it while he replenished his empty coffers from the Sultan's rich treasury.

So, during the days that followed, Mustafa dangled this fat bait before the covetous Pontiff's eyes, cunningly maintaining all the while the fiction that it was merely a contribution to the upkeep of the Prince and his Turkish officers.

Finally Innocent could resist no longer. And at last, against the most vehement opposition of Blanchefort and the Knights, the Pope agreed to let Mustafa visit Prince Jem in his closely guarded apartments – the sole explicit condition laid down by Bayezid in return for the hundred and twenty thousand ducats brought by the ambassador from Istanbul.

On the day appointed, Mustafa was brought alone to a room decked out with silks and satins and cloth of gold, at the far end of which Jem sat awaiting him, cross-legged on a throne, surrounded by his loyal Turkish officers. And it soon became clear that the Prince expected his brother to go to any lengths to have him killed.

For the instant Mustafa entered the chamber, one of Jem's companions came up to him, searched him very thoroughly for arms, dusted his clothes all over with a piece of linen and then invited Mustafa Bey to lick the cloth to show that his garments were not impregnated with some deadly poison.

Thereafter, Mustafa approached Jem very humbly, three times prostrating himself on the floor as he went, finally kneeling, his head bowed low, before the throne. The ambassador was instructed to speak only if spoken to by Sinan Bey, one of the Prince's chamberlains. Jem asked the emissary if he brought any written message from his brother the Sultan. Mustafa showed the Prince a sealed missive he already held in readiness in his hand. But before the ambassador was permitted to go further, he was required by Jem's officers to lick the letter on the outside and, having opened it, to lick it within, before delivering it into Sinan Bey's hands.

Sinan studied the letter, then read its contents quietly into Jem's inclined ear. The Prince made no comment on what he heard, nor did he utter a word when Mustafa silently indicated a chest of costly gifts sent by Bayezid – certain rich cloths, jewels and fine books – that had been set down on the floor before the throne.

Then, at a sign from Jem, Mustafa was dismissed. Walking backwards and bowing, the ambassador withdrew, followed by those Infidels who had witnessed the meeting from the other end of the room, the doors were closed upon them by Jem's own attendants and the Prince's armed bodyguard of papal officers once again took up their positions outside his apartments.

That, more or less, marked the end of Mustafa Bey's embassy to Rome.

A few days later Mustafa left for the Porte without, needless to say, having secured any formal agreement with the Holy See on the Prince's future, but with the satisfaction at least of having got Innocent to take the Emperor's gold and having, into the bargain, sown dissension between the Pope and the Knights of St John. Mustafa and the Pope parted at last with a polite exchange of veiled threats, Innocent warning Bayezid that Jem would be used without hesitation to counter any hostile action on the part of the Ottomans, and Mustafa making it clear to the Supreme Pontiff that if the West should take the initiative in employing the Prince to the detriment of the security of the Guarded Domains, the Sultan would not hesitate to exact a terrible retribution upon those he considered responsible.

But it did not please God to allow Innocent to enjoy for long the gold bestowed upon him by the Sublime Porte.

Celestial Signs

And never was so short a time filled with so many ominous portents and signs.

These began some weeks after Mustafa had departed, when there appeared in Rome – whence, not a soul seemed to have the least idea – an old man, barefoot and clothed in rags, but calm and lucid of speech, who wandered the streets night and day, holding aloft a wooden cross and preaching sermons heralding imminent disaster and doom. 'Truly,' he said, 'the world will soon be overwhelmed with woe and lamentation. No Race nor Nation will escape this Divine punishment. Listen to me, for I speak the truth! Do you say now that I am mad, that these are merely the ravings of a lunatic? O, how bitterly you will regret the day that you said such foolish things . . .'

To begin with, the Romans shunned this curious prophet, some even laughing in his face or hurling insults at his back as he went by, and all but a few openly scorned his words. But presently reports started to come from every corner of the city of weird and supernatural manifestations that seemed to lend credence to the old man's admonitions and predictions that the world was about to enter on some new and fearsome phase.

Several churches and basilicas were said to have been suffused with a peculiar and unusual light; in some, pillars and walls were found to sweat and run with icy water; in others, warm blood trickled from the wounds of statues of saints and holy pictures, and in others still, the candles lit by the worshippers were suddenly snuffed out as though extinguished by an invisible hand, leaving the air heavy with foul and asphyxiating fumes.

Meanwhile, inexplicable irregularities were observed nightly in the Heavens. Fixed stars started to wander in the firmament; those that customarily alter their positions gradually with the seasons strayed from their wonted courses and certain planets appeared to remain stationary, glowing with an eerie incandescence or belching forth dense smoke. And as the weather grew hotter, great showers of shooting stars – said to be the fiery darts hurled by the angels to ward off Satan's spies from eavesdropping on the conversations in the Celestial Court – illuminated the skies from nightfall until dawn.

Then, day by day, news came from the rest of Italy of countless bizarre occurrences, subterranean rumblings, tremors of the earth, high winds, hailstorms and floods. In Arezzo, a she-wolf came night after night and stood howling before the town's gates, and in Florence a proud lion and lioness, displayed in a cage for the public's pleasure, turned without warning upon one another and fought in savage frenzy until both of them expired in a welter of their own gore.

Also, it happened in Florence that while a numerous throng of Infidels crowded into the city's principal basilica to attend a solemn Mass, all at once a woman began to cry out distractedly: 'Alas, alas, my fellow citizens! Do you not see the enraged bull descending with blazing horns to tear down this noble temple?' And at that moment the stone lantern in the high dome, the loftiest in all Christendom, was struck by a thunderbolt and massive pieces of masonry were dislodged and hurled to the ground.

Before long, certain merchants returned from Istanbul and the East, relating how an even more astounding occurrence had taken place in the God-guarded city. They told how on a clear and tranquil day a thick black cloud had been seen to gather and hang low over the Imperial Palace and the Mosque of Aya Sofia. And how suddenly it shot forth fire and set ablaze the gigantic gilded-bronze statue of the Emperor Constantine mounted on his war

354

steed, which monument had stood inviolable until then on its tall column for more than a thousand years. And this prodigy, it was said, was supposed by the people of the city, both Muslim and Infidel, to herald the imminent fall of Sultan Bayezid, and even, so the Adorers of the Cross dared to aver, the overthrow of Ottoman power itself.

Nor were there merely these signs sent from on high presaging future upheavals and catastrophes, but at the same time actual events revealed that the True Believers, before whom the Christians had become accustomed to bow in abject terror, were no longer immune to reversals and defeats at the hands of the Infidels.

Because that same ill-fortuned spring the Spanish dog King Ferdinand and his hell-cat of a consort Isabella launched the entire might of Aragon and Castile against Granada, determined now to extirpate with fire and sword every last Muslim man, woman and child in that most ancient and noble kingdom. At first Ferdinand had tried to seize this fair country by a stratagem, calling on the Muslims to lay down their arms and make terms with him – but they were only too aware of what would happen to them if they succumbed to the Infidels' trickery, and replied instead that if the King wanted their arms, he must come and get them for himself!

Therefore, in April, Ferdinand unleashed his hordes upon the Vega – that fertile plain that lies below Granada's walls – while its fields were green with waving corn, its orchards in full bloom, its vineyards sprouting forth their tender shoots. And for thirty days the Misbelievers ravaged the whole land, hacking, uprooting, burning and slaughtering every living thing they came upon. Then, when Ferdinand and Isabella – God curse them! – had reduced this abode of loveliness to nothing more than blackened earth and charred ruins, they threw up a siege-castle on an eminence opposite Granada, which they called 'Santa Fe', and from this unclean refuge they began to attack the city.

And though the Muslims defended their last redoubt bravely, and sallied forth again and again, wreaking havoc among the astonished besiegers and decimating the Spanish King and Queen's knights, the True Believers came to see that they could resist only for so long, unless relieved by supplies, arms and men from their allies. Thus, they appealed to Sultan Bayezid, the Defender of Islam, to send them succour quickly, before it was too late.

But now the twin spectres of the Crusade from the West and the Egyptian invasion from the East were looming larger and larger with every day that passed, the great-hearted Emperor could do little more than urge them to fight on alone until such time as the Ottomans were at liberty to assist them, and until then to put their trust in the Almighty and pray to Him for the deliverance of their city and the Faith.

At dawn on the first day of February, in the year from Jesus 1492, I was roused by a furious banging of bells in the church at the top of the street in which I lived. As I emerged from a deep slumber I realized that bells in the other churches and belfries nearby were also ringing, and the volume of this vile sound seemed to grow moment by moment. I turned to Sofia – for my beloved had passed the previous night in my bed – and, thinking the noise occasioned by some Infidel festival or holy day of which I was ignorant, I shook her shoulder, saying, 'What the devil is all this in aid of?'

She turned over, pushing aside the luxuriant mass of black locks that veiled her face, half opened her eyes, looked at me blearily, and mumbled some sleepy and indistinct syllables, not one of which I could comprehend. Then, giving me a sweet and contented smile, she lowered her eyelids and rolled over with a sigh, pulling her pillow over her head to muffle her ears against the din outside.

I swung my legs over the side of the bed, rubbed my unshaven chin, combed my hair with my fingers and rose shivering to my feet. I wrapped myself in my old fur-trimmed cloak, put on an icy pair of shoes and quietly left the room. Stiffly I ascended the winding stone stair to the small tower at the corner of the house.

I gazed out disconsolately over a city swathed in mist and drizzle in the dull grey morning light. The tumultuous clanging of bells had now reached such a height that the very hills around resounded to their noise and threw back their echo. Meanwhile, I could see the people of the neighbourhood taking to the streets, some still dressed in loose robes and gowns and night-clothes, raising their arms aloft, embracing and speaking to one another with wild gesticulations. But from where I was I could hear nothing above the turbulent and relentless clamour of the bells.

I descended and returned to the bedroom, where I observed that Sofia had added my pillow to the one already pulled down around her ears. I got into some clothes, unlocked the outside door, walked along the gallery, descended into the dank and chilly courtyard and unbolted the gate. Up the street I saw a crowd of people standing by the church door, so I started towards them. But before I reached them a crowd of a dozen or so boys came charging down the road, shouting at the top of their voice, 'Victory! Victory!'

As they stampeded past me, I seized one by the arm and said, 'What's going on?'

'Why, sir,' he said, 'haven't you heard? Granada has fallen to the King of Spain!'

And with that he rushed away to catch up with his friends.

On that day and the one after, the streets were washed and decorated by order of the Pope, and on Saturday the great bell in the tower upon Capitol Hill tolled out incessantly in celebration of these dismal tidings. And as darkness fell, bonfires were lit in all the principal squares of the Town, and the Vatican, the Castle of St Angelo, the palaces of the Cardinals and foreign ambassadors, and countless other villas, houses and other private dwellings were brightly lit up with tens of thousands of candles and lamps.

The morning following, I went down to the Piazza Navona, where the two Spanish bishops who served as their nation's ambassadors had caused to be erected two large and lofty castles constructed of wooden planks, one of which they called 'Santa Fe', the other 'Granada'. It was their plan that day to entertain the mob by re-enacting the assault and capture of Granada – while they and their guests looked on from 'Santa Fe' – offering prizes to the first to scale the wooden walls and reach the top of 'Granada's' tall tower. But the rain was so heavy and persistent that at length the spectacle was postponed until the next week, in the hope of more clement weather.

Yet the populace was not altogether disappointed that day, since not far away from the piazza, on the street that runs from the Campo dei Fiori to the Bridge of St Angelo, the Spanish Cardinal and Papal Vice-Chancellor Rodrigo Borgia, a man whose love of carnal pleasures and lavish entertainment had made his private life the scandal of the age, had fenced off with heavy beams part of the public thoroughfare outside his magnificent palace, in order to hold a display of men fighting bulls – a barbarous pastime of which the Spaniards are inordinately fond.

The Cardinal provided five animals for the purpose, but the bulls' prowess turned out greatly to exceed that of the swaggering young bloods who elected to do battle with them, and – to the intense delight of the onlookers – two or three of these bravoes were gored and trampled to death, and a dozen or more severely injured, before the bulls were with difficulty dispatched.

The festivities went on all week and did not end until the following Sunday, when vast quantities of food and wine donated by one of the Spanish bishops were distributed all day in the Piazza Navona, the representation of the storming of Granada took place, and more bullfights were held – but this time without loss of life, a horse being the only casualty. That day I saw my Contessa in the square, smiling and laughing with the Most Serene Republic's ambassador and a party of Venetian and Roman lords and ladies who had come to witness the various displays and place wagers on the races – customary in Rome on such occasions of public rejoicing – of old men, Jews, donkeys, courtesans, buffaloes and boys.

The day ended with a preposterous procession announced by criers as 'The Triumph of Ferdinand and Isabella'. First there came a squadron of cavalry followed by a cart drawn by four white horses. Sitting on mock thrones upon the vehicle were a boy and a girl, with crowns on their heads and gold palms in their hands, dressed as the King and Queen of Spain. Their feet rested on the prone body of a man, very ugly, his grotesque grimacing face blackened with paint, attired in a turban and silken garb and bound with chains, who was supposed to play the part of Abu-Abdullah, 'King of the Moors'. Behind the cart, all manacled and roped together and likewise blackened with paint, came a throng of men and women pretending to be Muslims, all blaspheming the Almighty by groaning and calling out His name. And behind them came a multitude of citizens on foot and on horseback, dressed as knights, pages, men-at-arms, foot-soldiers, bowmen, Roman caesars, senators, legionnaires, shepherds, nymphs, wild beasts, demons and pagan gods.

From a distance I saw Sofia and her companions turn to go, and ride through the multitude out of the piazza. Briefly she glanced over her shoulder, but she did not see me. Then I too turned for home, my heart full of melancholy and despair, in order to try to compose a dispatch relating what I had seen in Rome since the sad news of Granada's fall had arrived in the city.

May God Most High aid the Faithful to repair this grievous breach in the ramparts of Islam!

I saw Sofia hardly at all during the weeks that followed. She had become convinced shortly after her last visit that she was being watched more closely by her own people and, though we had taken so many precautions, that she had fallen under suspicion in some way, and that her every move was now being observed and noted. Nor was her disquiet in any way allayed by the arrival of a new ambassador from Venice, one Count Andrea Capello, who Sofia maintained was notorious for his ruthlessness, and whose appointment to the Most Serene Republic's embassy to the

Holy See she interpreted as being fraught with significance. Indeed, she believed it possible that Capello had been chosen by the Council of Ten with the express purpose of investigating their intelligence organization in Rome, that he might root out those agents no longer thought to be entirely reliable, or who had simply outlived their usefulness.

Needless to say, it was out of the question for her to come to my house. We still contrived, however, during this time, to meet briefly four or five times – once amidst the ruins of the Coliseum, on the other occasions in dark and ill-frequented churches, always taking elaborate measures against being followed, and approaching and leaving our rendezvous by different streets and alleys. In these dark places we would pass a few precious minutes together in furtive conversation before, with a touch of hands, going our separate ways. Each time she seemed more pale, more ill at ease. And to see her thus filled me with tenderness for her, and with every day that went by I became increasingly tormented by fears for her safety.

From these fleeting encounters I learned from my mistress that Venice's agents in the East were reporting that Sultan Bayezid was mustering a land army at Edirne and a sizeable maritime force at Gallipoli, and that this information had been conveyed to Pope Innocent by Andrea Capello – although the Venetian ambassador had to admit that, whether these warlike manifestations were intended to defend the Empire against the threat of Jem's return or were preparatory to some kind of pre-emptive strike against the West, the Serenissima's spies were at a loss to say.

Yet Bayezid – may God humble his enemies! – presently indicated that, though war now appeared inevitable, he had not altogether abandoned hope of gaining time by trying to suborn Innocent.

For the first days of spring brought word that a second Turkish emissary was on his way from the Sublime Porte to the Vatican, this time bearing a strange and unexpected gift from the Felicitous Sultan's treasury – the iron tip of the Lance with which, so the Infidels believe, the Roman soldier Longinus pierced the side of Jesus as he hung upon the cross. But even as the dispatch of the Holy Lance became public knowledge in the city, it was learned that Innocent had again fallen seriously ill, with a severe fever, and it was soon being said openly that it would be a miracle if the Pope survived long enough to witness the arrival of this venerated relic in Rome.

Nevertheless, Innocent clung tenaciously to life and in due course the envoy, a certain Kasim Bey, disembarked at Ancona with the Lance, which news seemed to cause a wondrous improvement in the ailing Pontiff's health. And despite his still weak and febrile condition, Innocent at once threw himself into making arrangements to have the Lance brought to the Vatican.

But when the Cardinals came together in the Pope's absence to discuss the matter, immediately questions were raised as to the manner in which the relic should be received, or even whether the Sultan's present should be accepted at all. Some Cardinals objected that there already existed two such relics – one in a town called Nuremberg, the second in the French King's chapel in Paris. Others replied that though this was undoubtedly true, this lance from Turkey was the real one. For had not the Venetians only a few years ago proposed to pay Sultan Mehmed seventy thousand ducats to gain possession of it? And had not their offer been rejected by the Conqueror as quite insufficient for the purchase of something so valuable? But others still argued that even if this was the real Lance the gift should on no account be accepted, since it came from the most violent and implacable enemies of Christendom, who wished by this gesture merely to mock and deride the Church and the followers of Christ.

Yet when afterwards Innocent got to hear of all this, he did not hesitate to declare the relic genuine, overruling all those whose opinions differed from his own, and hastily sent off to Ancona two of his bishops, a horse magnificently caparisoned, a special box usually employed to transport the holy bread and wine when the Pope goes out of the Vatican, a costly crystal vessel to contain the Sultan's gift, and a large golden lantern, so that day and night a light might be carried before the Holy Lance as it was borne with all solemnity through the lands of the Holy See on its way to the Pope's capital.

In no time, extraordinary stories began to reach Rome of the miracles performed by the Lance on its progress towards the city. Here a mute began to speak, here a blind person was restored to sight, and here a cripple bedridden for twenty years rose up and began to walk . . .

Then on Ascension Day, now looking extremely weak and sickly, Innocent reverently received the relic at the church of Santa Maria by the Porta del Popolo, amidst scenes of indescribable confusion – women weeping and fainting, overburdened branches of trees giving way under the weight of spectators, and guildsmen, monks and clergy battling with one another as they fought for precedence in the procession that was to bear the Lance to St Peter's. After an interminable delay the Pope and his Cardinals set off on the return journey to the Vatican.

When Innocent came to the steps of the Basilica, he gave his blessing by making the sign of the cross over the people, whilst his Vice-Chancellor Cardinal Rodrigo Borgia held aloft the crystal reliquary containing the iron lance-head. Then as the clergy were dismissed and the crowd urged to disperse, Kasim Bey, the Turkish envoy, respectfully approached the Pope to present him with the letters he had brought from the Sultan. But just as Innocent was about to have them opened, he was informed in a whisper by his interpreter that the documents contained references to a further forty thousand ducats sent with Kasim Bey, in payment of Jem's so-called pension. The Pope managed to croak out, apparently with extreme difficulty, the command: 'Later!' After which, visibly collapsing on his feet, the Pontiff was half-led, half-carried back through the gates of the Papal Palace.

From that time onwards, Innocent's life began rapidly to ebb away. Within a few days, archers and infantrymen were patrolling the streets and occupying the gates and bridges, and artillery was being deployed at vantage points around the city. And, as I learned some weeks later, for fear that during the riot and disorder that commonly erupt upon the death of a pope some attempt might be made to abduct or assassinate Jem, the Prince was moved one night to more secure apartments over the Sistine Chapel, and a hundred additional men drafted in and made to take an oath to guard him against danger.

Eventually, Innocent became so enfeebled that he could swallow nothing but a little woman's milk. And seemingly haunted in his delirium by memories of the Castracano conspiracy, and convinced once again that his enemies were trying to poison him, the old man even insisted on taking this sustenance directly from his unfortunate nurse's breast. It was also rumoured, though whether this be true or not I cannot say, that one of his physicians obtained the services of three boys, by giving them a ducat each, in order to attempt a transfusion of fresh blood into the Pontiff's desiccated veins; but the experiment failed utterly and all three boys lost their lives, without the Pope himself deriving the least benefit from this desperate enterprise.

At last the Cardinals had the recently acquired relic brought from the sacristy of St Peter's and placed by Innocent's bedside. But not even the Holy Lance could save the Pope's life. On the twenty-fifth day of July, he lost consciousness and the death rattle began. The following morning he gave up the ghost.

Thus, the meddlesome Infidel's lifeless corpse was carried forth from his rich and airy apartments in the Papal Palace, and the Recorder of the Court of Everlasting Decrees inscribed in his dread book as Innocent's new place of abode the dark and abysmal pit of Hell.

For ten days an eerie calm lay over Rome. Then when the Cardinals had completed their obsequies and bidden farewell to their late Lord, leaving the Papal forces, the foreign ambassadors, the Roman barons and their armed men in command of the government and security of the city, they held a secret assembly, which they call a 'Conclave', to decide which of their number should succeed Innocent.

For this purpose the Cardinals set aside a chapel in the Palace, and had built within it small wooden cells. Then they drew lots to see who was to occupy which cell and each Cardinal had his servants furnish the one allotted to him, so that he might live in tolerable comfort so long as the Conclave lasted. Meanwhile, all the doors and windows of the chapel were bricked and boarded up, only some openings high above the ground being left to admit light and air, and at the principal door a kind of hatch was constructed, through which food and drink could be passed to sustain those inside during their deliberations. Then, when all these preparations had been completed, the Cardinals entered, taking two attendants each to wait upon them. And after the chapel and the wooden cells (and even the privies, which were in a small chamber off the chapel) had been thoroughly scrutinized, to make certain that no one without the right to be in that place had been concealed anywhere, the doors were closed on the Cardinals and their servants, they bolting them from within, and the Captain of the Palace Guard in his turn locking them from without. And so were these venerable gentlemen confined in complete seclusion until they had elected a new Pope.

On this occasion twenty-three Cardinals entered the Conclave, and from that hour forth the entire city was gripped by a fever of speculation as to who would be named the next Pope of Rome. There were many who said Oliviero Caraffa, Cardinal of Naples, would inevitably carry off the prize, others that one Giorgio, Cardinal of Lisbon, was bound to triumph, while others loudly contested these assertions, enthusiastically pointing to the vastly superior cunning, wealth, brilliance in politicking and power of patronage of the various candidates they believed would win. And as wagers, some of them so large as to be scarcely credible, were placed on the outcome by men of every degree, from prince to pauper, the odds and favourites seemed to fluctuate and alter almost by the hour.

On the sixth day, the watchers who had gathered outside, on the rumour that a successful election had been achieved during the night, observed the bricks being removed from one of the windows of the chapel in which the Cardinals were incarcerated. Presently, a cross was thrust through the gap – the sign that one of the Cardinals had indeed managed, by outmanoeuvring his enemies, bribing his friends, and Heaven only knows what other skulduggery and intrigue, to obtain sufficient votes to secure ultimate victory.

Then one of the Cardinals appeared at the window and addressed in loud and clear tones the hushed and expectant mass of the people gathered in the court-yard below, saying: '*Nuntio vobis gaudium magnum. Habemus Pontificem . . . revertissimum dominum vice-cancellarium . . . qui nomen imposuit Alexander!*' Which means: 'I bring you tidings of great joy. We have a Pope . . . the most reverend Lord, the Vice-Chancellor . . . who has taken the name of Alexander!'

For a few moments these words were greeted by so complete and stunned a silence that one would have thought that Beelzebub himself had just been proclaimed Innocent's successor. But then the bells of the Papal Palace started suddenly to ring out, followed hastily by those in the campanile of St Peter's, the Vatican troops raised their weapons in the air with the cry 'Alexander! Alexander!' and all at once the crowd found its voice and the populace began to add its cheers to the now rapidly swelling tide of acclaim. And in this manner the world first learned that Rodrigo Borgia was to be Supreme Pontiff of Christendom.

It must have been about six weeks after the new Pope's coronation that I received Sofia's note telling me to come the following day to a villa some miles outside the city. I say 'villa', yet in reality it turned out to be little more than a half-ruined farmhouse. But the position was superb.

One reached the place by passing through a wide tract of marshland and low hills, so desolate that one hardly expected in such wilderness to come upon a single human habitation. But then the road climbed steeply to the crest of a ridge and suddenly, below, there lay a lush valley wooded with ilex, wild olive and oak. And there, standing alone in a green glade, looking out over the Campagna as it rolled away westwards to the Tyrrhenian Sea, was the old house Sofia had described in her letter.

I rode down the winding track through the woods and onto the grassy meadow before the villa, where I dismounted and, following the instructions I had been given, tethered my animal to a broken pillar beside a stone trough. Then I walked down through the clearing towards a little grove of trees, the sweet sound of running water growing louder and louder as I approached.

I found her sitting in sun-dappled shade, on a blanket spread out on the grass by the side of a shimmering pool, where the stream's flow had been arrested by an old moss-encrusted dam. She wore a white blouse and a blue cotton dress, and was barefoot, just as she had been when I came upon her that morning in the garden of the Villa Margherita. At the sound of my footfall on the path, she turned expectantly. The moment she saw me, her face broke into a radiant smile and she started to rise to greet me. Before she had the chance to get to her feet, I was there kneeling beside her, taking her in my arms and pressing my parched lips roughly against hers.

At length, I released her shoulders and she sank back on the blanket, closing her eyes, stretching her limbs invitingly and giving a long, almost purring, sigh. Hurriedly, with trembling fingers, I unlaced my breeches with one hand, whilst I pushed up her skirts with the other. When, with her help, I had completely uncovered her to the waist, I took her knees and forced them upwards and outwards, spreading wide her thighs and laying open to my impassioned and intense regard the soft roseate lips of her exquisitely smooth and naked belly. Seeing me gaze with such undisguised frankness at her most intimate parts, blushing, she covered her face with her hands and even tried to close her legs and wriggle free.

But resolutely holding her knees apart, I lunged on top

of her, as she laughed and tried to push me away. Then, abruptly abandoning all resistance, she reached out and took my swollen and importunate member in both hands. She clenched her teeth and gave a low moan and I felt her muscles tighten and relax in a series of sharp contractions as I entered her.

When I had entirely buried myself in my beloved's yielding womb, I began to cover her pale outstretched neck with kisses and – urged on by her breathless exhortations – I proceeded to make more violent and energetic love to her until at last I felt her nails dig into my back as she reached a sudden climax, and rapturously I discharged, mingling my virile seed with her abundantly overflowing nectar.

After a little while, I got up and went down to wash myself in the stream below the pool, drying myself with my shirt as best I could. Sofia did likewise, then disappeared barefoot into the trees. I heard a horse stirring in the undergrowth and realized she must have left her animal there so that it would be near at hand. Almost at once she returned carrying a basket and, kneeling on the blanket, she began to take out bread, cheese and fruit – all wrapped in little napkins – and finally a flask of wine.

'What is this place?' I said, jerking my head in the direction of the house.

'It belongs to somebody I know in Rome. But he has been sent on an errand to Naples by the Pope – and he seldom comes here in any case. So you see, my love, I knew that we would have it to ourselves.'

'And there is nobody here to look after the place, no servants?' I said.

'There was a man and his son, but the man died a few months ago and the boy ran away to Rome, and hasn't been heard of since.'

'Just the same,' I said, 'is it wise for us to meet like this, even here?'

Sofia smiled and said, 'Things are different now . . .'

'How so?'

'Well . . . There actually was somebody betraying the

367

Republic's secrets to the Vatican, somebody who knew a lot, here in Rome. Naturally enough, the Ten believed that I might be responsible. But it proved to be a secretary in the embassy – some stolen papers were found in his room and, when questioned, he confessed everything.'

'How did you get to hear of this?'

'Count Capello told me himself a few days ago.'

'And the secretary,' I said, 'what happened to him?'

'One does not enquire about such things,' said Sofia, lowering her eyes. 'But I am told that he had an accident, that he fell from a window . . .'

'So – God be praised! – they were not on to us after all?' I said.

'It seems not.'

'Though we cannot be sure . . .'

'No . . .,' she said. 'Yet I have the feeling that I am trusted once more. And so I should be, I have done some valuable work for them of late!'

'What kind of work?' I said.

She shook her head and, avoiding my eyes, said, 'Nothing that concerns Jem. Here, have something to eat.'

I took the bread and cheese she offered me and began moodily to chew it. I was about to ask her something to which, in truth, I did not want to learn the answer, then I thought better of it and remained silent.

She opened the flask of wine, drank and handed it to me. I shrugged and drank a little, then took a long deep draught. It didn't make me feel any better.

'What of this Borgia?' I said eventually. 'There are people who still seem scarcely able to believe that he succeeded in getting himself elected.'

'Then they knew very little,' said Sofia scornfully. 'He was the richest of all the Cardinals and was prepared this time to buy the whole Conclave if necessary. And in the end that's more or less what he had to do. To Cardinal Sforza alone he gave not only his Palace in the Town and the assurance of the vice-chancellorship but also a pile of gold and silver besides. And the other Cardinals, even the less important ones – houses, villas, the promise of lucrative office in the Curia, church estates and dioceses. Not one of those prepared to accept the Spaniard's largess found himself wanting. In fact, from what I gather, Borgia divested himself of almost everything he owned. But he'll make the Papacy pay and end up richer than ever, you'll see.'

'And Innocent's Crusade,' I said, 'what will happen to that now?'

'Borgia was the Cardinal Protector of the Knights of Rhodes,' said Sofia, 'so of course they're delighted that one of their patrons has got hold of the papal chair. They're convinced that he'll go through with the Crusade – they're even calling him "the New Alexander", and urging him to outdo his namesake's conquests in the East . . .'

'Ah,' I said, 'are they, indeed? But now that Borgia is Pope, will he listen to them? If, as you say, he is so determined to feather his own nest, perhaps he will find his ardour for war has somewhat abated. After all, that the Sultan was sending gold to Innocent seems to have become common knowledge. Would a man like Borgia refuse the same opportunity to enrich himself?'

'Perhaps,' she said, 'perhaps not. But Borgia is not without ambition to leave his mark. He has long believed that the Papacy should rule with a stronger hand in Italy – and if a Crusade against the Turks seems to be the means of realizing his aim, then he will do what is necessary to promote it. As a matter of fact, it appears that he has already begun.'

'How?' I said.

'There's talk of a new league between the Pontiff, the Duke of Milan and the Doge of Venice. And if Borgia brings it off, the Venetians will have to forget their Peace Treaty with the Porte and add their fleet to the Crusade . . .'

This was bad news: the last war with Venice went on for many years and, though we achieved victory in the end, what a price we had to pay for it!

'How the devil did Borgia get the Venetians even to talk about joining this damnable expedition? Innocent, for all his threats and promises, got nowhere in his attempts to involve the Republic . . .'

According to Sofia's sources, the Venetians reckoned it was only a matter of time before the Turks made war on them again. The Venetians had long believed that if they could acquire custody of Jem, the Sultan would think twice before putting into operation any plan of attack.

'So in exchange for their support, they've got Borgia to agree to give them Jem.'

'How soon?' I said.

'Who knows? But probably not before next spring.'

'In that case,' I said, realizing the hopelessness of my mission, 'something will have to be done before then.'

'I'm afraid', said Sofia, 'that's going to prove rather difficult . . .'

It seemed that, of late, Jem had become so sick of the delays that he had made up his mind to flee the Vatican, go back to Egypt and throw in his lot with Kayitbay again. He'd even managed to make contact, through a go-between, with a Venetian captain – a rogue with a reputation for undertaking risky commissions – who was to bring his vessel up the Tiber on the night of his planned escape, to take him downriver and into the open sea, where an Egyptian galley would be waiting to take him to Alexandria.

'Great and good God!' I said. 'What an opportunity for us to get hold of him!'

'And so it would have been,' said Sofia with a sigh. 'But the Captain got cold feet. In fact, the whole idea scared him so much that he went to the Ten and warned them what was going on.'

'And then?'

'The Ten instructed Andrea Capello to inform the Pope of what was afoot – after all, the last thing they wanted was to have the Prince absconding from the Vatican just when Borgia was about to hand Jem over to the Republic.'

'So what has the Pope done about it?' I said.

'He's had Jem moved from the Palace and locked him up in the Castle of St Angelo.'

'God damn and blast him!' I said, a great surge of anger and exasperation rising in my breast. 'At this rate, it'll take the entire Imperial Army to wrest Jem from the clutches of these accursed Infidels!'

That afternoon, like benighted savages who think nothing of yesterday or the morrow and neither know nor dream of any other life, nor care anything but for the fleeting pleasure of each bewitching moment, we made love and swam in the cold clear water of the pool, and lay naked on the grass and stared up at the blue sky, the passing clouds, and the autumn swallows swooping and diving high in the air.

The shadows were already growing long by the time this bright illusion of forgetfulness began to fade, and wearily we dressed and prepared to leave the valley. As I led Sofia's animal slowly up through the meadow, she walked beside me, one arm clasped about my waist, whilst with the other she held up her skirts to prevent them catching in the long grass.

I glanced at her and saw that her expression was troubled.

'What is it?' I said.

'I did not want to tell you before . . . but very soon I shall have to return to Venice.'

I felt sick to the pit of my stomach and my voice sounded strange and faint when I spoke: 'What for?'

'The Ten wish to speak to me in person,' she said. 'But don't worry, my love, it is not unusual for them to summon people in this way.'

'It may be a trap,' I said anxiously. 'Perhaps they mean to do you some harm.'

'No,' she said. 'I do not think so. Besides, what choice have I but to obey?'

'I would take you back to Istanbul at once – but I have orders to remain in Rome . . .'

'I know,' she said, and she turned to me and tried to smile, but I saw that tears were now trickling down her cheeks. I stopped and embraced her and she buried her face in my chest.

'You must not go,' I said.

'It will only be for a while,' she said, 'and then I am to

371

return to Rome. Count Capello has told me so himself.'

'God grant that what he says is true,' I said. 'For if they do not send you back soon . . . by Heaven, I will come to Venice and fetch you back myself!'

But Sofia was too overcome with misery to make any reply, and leaning back in my arms she simply gazed at me, her eyes overflowing with tears, biting her lower lip and slowly shaking her head, almost as if it were I, not her, who was the one to be pitied.

And, alas, as the weather grew colder and the rains set in, my beloved duly received the expected summons to return to Venice.

The day she left I remained the whole afternoon in the tower of my house, brooding and looking out over the rooftops at the fortress of St Angelo, where Jem now languished under the grey wintry sky, awaiting still his hour of glory when he would, so he fervently believed, return in triumph to the land of his birth. At sunset I descended to my bedroom. Sitting at my table I took pen and paper and started to draft a letter to Kivami Bey, informing him that I had now become convinced that a successful seizure of the Prince alive was utterly beyond the realms of feasibility and that, in view of the likelihood that Venice was now prepared to throw her maritime might behind the Infidels' Crusade, if the Felicitous Sultan wished to remove once and for all the insupportable threat that his brother's continued existence represented to the security and stability of the Empire, he should send three or four suitable men to assist me in an attempt to penetrate the castle and carry out the Prince's assassination.

I delivered the letter to Josef later that night, and a courier left with it the next day. For a long time the Old Man did not send any reply whatsoever, so long in fact that Josef could not conceal his surprise when time after time I passed by his shop and there was nothing for me. But finally a message came. It was written in cipher – yet I recognized Kivami Bey's clumsy and awkward hand at once. It was a single line that read: '*Your request forbidden. Continue to carry out your original orders.*'

Soon afterwards I received a signal from Sofia – sent via Josef, and disguised as an order for one of his concoctions – indicating that she was safe and sound and would presently be returning to the Villa Margherita. And return she did, just as she had promised. Though, God knows, I wish now that I had never set eyes on her again.

The Overwhelming Event

So I continued my existence in Rome, condemned by my masters to watching and biding my time, a mere observer, fruitlessly (I was convinced) awaiting some alteration in Jem's circumstances that might enable me to attempt the Prince's abduction.

Meanwhile, Pope Alexander brought to a triumphant conclusion his schemes for an Italian alliance. And on the Feast of St Mark the air resounded to the peal of bells and the earth trembled to the crash of the Castle of St Angelo's cannons as the Holy League was proclaimed: a confederacy, it was revealed, that included not only Rome, Venice and Milan but also the Republic of Siena and the rich duchies of Mantua and Ferrara. In this manner, hardly nine months after his accession to the throne, Alexander gave notice of his resolve to bring fame and renown to his papacy, and win glory for the House of Borgia.

And even before the first year of his reign was out, news started to come from France that the new monarch of that land, who had inherited with his crown the title of 'Most Christian King', was marshalling an immense army and a powerful battlefleet, with the purpose of bringing them to Italy to join the long-awaited expedition against the Ottomans.

This Infidel's name was Charles, and though he had succeeded his father during the early days of Jem's captivity in France, being a minor he had ruled at first under the tutelage of a regent and had only recently come of age. It was said that he had spent much of his youth

374

reading romances and studying the martial exploits of
his barbarous Frankish forebears; this was not difficult
to believe since it presently became evident that, far
from being content with the fair and fertile kingdom
bequeathed to him by his father, Louis, Charles har-
boured in his young breast the most violent and insatiable
longing to conquer the lands of others.

At first the Pope praised the enthusiasm of the Most
Christian King, seeing only too well what harm this belli-
cose prince could inflict upon the Muslims. Yet Borgia
began to have second thoughts about the desirability of
the King's army entering the Peninsula on its way to the
East when he discovered that Charles also seemed set
upon reviving France's claim to the crown of Naples, an
ancient despotism that brought with it the appellation
'King of Jerusalem', which city – may God defend it –
Charles had pledged himself one day to possess.

Nor was this the only title that this vainglorious youth
had set his heart on. For soon the Vatican learned that
Charles, in anticipation of his successful siege and capture
of the God-guarded City, was in the process of trying to
have himself declared Emperor of Constantinople, by
purchasing the name from one Andreas Paleologos, a
pathetic Greek exile then resident in Rome, who sup-
plemented his wife's earnings (he had married a Roman
whore called Katerina) by disposing of, for a fee, such
honours as he fancied himself still to retain.

I wrote of all this and more to Istanbul, and the contin-
ual demands for further intelligence – 'at the Felicitous
Emperor's express command' – left me in no doubt that
Bayezid was filled with consternation by this latest
untoward turn in events, and that for all King Charles's
posturing, the Sultan (whose golden judgement had been
proved right so often before) did not in the least underestimate the dangers represented by this aggressive and
ambitious Frenchman.

Then Fate seemed to take a malicious delight in bringing
matters to a head. For on the twenty-seventh of January,
from Jesus 1494, it was learned that, having ruled for

375

well-nigh forty years, King Ferrante of Naples had suddenly died. Within weeks, ambassadors from Charles were in Rome demanding that Pope Alexander delay the investiture of Ferrante's son, Alfonso, so that the French King could come to Italy to press his claim, and warning the Pontiff that since the use of the ports of Naples, Brindisi and Otranto would be essential to the French to launch their attack upon the Turks, if the Most Christian King's legitimate claim to the Neapolitan kingdom should by any chance be denied, Charles would not hesitate to use armed force to secure it.

Alexander equivocated, appealing to the French King to be patient until after the Crusade. Then, in the fond hope that Charles would refrain from carrying out his threat, the Pope gave his blessing for Alfonso's coronation to proceed. But this time Borgia, so smooth, so capable, so expert in the art of compromise that he seemed quite to have forgotten that other men existed in this world whose impetuous spirits would brook no concessions, finally overreached himself. Before the summer was out, Charles had completed his preparations to lead his troops into the field. By the end of August his fleet was putting to sea and he himself was leading his army southwards towards Italy.

And then . . . but who alive does not know of the awe-inspiring story of what happened in the weeks that followed? How the Gallic hordes crossed the Alps and how town after town, city after city, state after state opened wide their gates to the invaders until it seemed that, without a shot being fired, Charles would soon make himself master of the entire Peninsula?

And yet, how many are still living who know of the dark and murderous dealings that went on in secret during those dreadful times, during which no prince, king or emperor seemed so strong that he could not, in the twinkling of an eye, be overthrown?

By mid-November Florence had fallen to the French King, and Charles remained there for some days while he strengthened his hold over the city and the surrounding territory, before completing his march over the Apennines to Rome.

On the last day of that same month I returned to my house around noon to find the apothecary's son Ishak waiting concealed in a doorway opposite my gate. Catching sight of him, I did not go into the house but continued walking and turned into a narrow deserted lane running down to the Tiber's edge. A minute later the boy caught up with me.

'What is it?' I said.

'There's somebody at the shop to see you – a woman.'

'Who?'

'The Contessa Contarini.'

When I got there Josef was standing in the dimness behind the counter. As always he had an air of immense dignity and calm, but as I came closer I could see the disquiet in his eyes. Without a word, he lifted the curtain covering the entrance to the corridor that led to the back room, and with a glance over my shoulder I dived through the opening.

Sofia was sitting at the table under the window, her hands clasped together, almost as in prayer. She looked up with a start as I came in.

'Thank God you're here,' she said. 'I was about to leave.'

'You shouldn't have come here in the first place,' I said, avoiding her anxious gaze.

'I had no choice,' she said.

I sat down at the other end of the table from her.

'Well?'

'An agent came to the Villa Margherita a couple of hours ago,' she said, pausing to reach down into a small basket full of crimson apples on the floor by her side, and pulling out of it a flat leather case that lay hidden beneath the fruit. 'He didn't want to be seen going to the Venetian embassy himself, so he gave what he had brought to me so that I could deliver it.'

She opened the case, pulled out several pieces of stiff paper folded in four and pushed them in my direction.

'What are they?' I said, unfolding the wad.

'They're copies of official – and not so official – letters from Sultan Bayezid to the Pope. Kasim Bey was on his way to Rome again from Istanbul, in the company of the papal nuncio Giorgio Bocciardi, who was sent by Alexander to the Porte earlier this year. Just outside Ancona, despite their diplomatic immunity, the two of them were set upon by Giuliano della Rovere and a band of his men. The Turkish envoy – he's an excellent horseman, apparently – fought his way out and got away. But Bocciardi and all their baggage was captured. And hidden among the Turk's things they found not only forty thousand gold ducats bound for Borgia but also these letters . . .'

'How did the copies come to be made?' I said, as I shuffled through them.

'When Giuliano realized what they were, he had them sent at once to Florence – his brother, Cardinal della Rovere, is there with the French King. As you know, the Roveres are no friends of the Borgias and would dearly love to see Charles expel Rodrigo from the Vatican . . .'

'Then the letters are probably forgeries,' I said.

She shook her head, saying, 'The agent examined the originals very carefully before he paid Cardinal della Rovere to have the copies made. If they were fakes, the agent would soon have sniffed them out – he's expert in such matters. No, he believes they're genuine, and so do I.'

'So what's happened to the originals?' I said.

'The Cardinal has given them to Charles.'

I began to study the first sheet. It was a letter thanking Alexander for sending his nuncio Bocciardi to the Sublime Porte and assuring him that his ambassador had carried out his duties most satisfactorily – all in very elegant and high-flown language, of course, but amounting to no more than that. Then I perused the second, and found it full of polite formalities and well-turned locutions but signifying, as far as I could see, virtually nothing of any import. I moved on to the third.

But then Sofia said, 'Don't bother with those now. I'll

tell you what's in them another time. Look at the last one.'

I pulled the final sheet from underneath and held it out to her with a questioning look. She leant forward and glanced at it and nodded.

It did not take me long to realize that this one was something else altogether. In fact, it was nothing less than a personal letter from Emperor to Pope, written in such familiar terms that you would have thought the two men had been friends and allies all their lives. And it did not take much longer to see that this missive was intended to be read by Borgia, and Borgia alone. For in it the Sultan most warmly thanked the Pontiff for the warning, sent via his nuncio, that the French King was determined not only to seize the Kingdom of Naples (of which he made no secret) but also forcibly to deprive the Pope of the custody of Jem, in order to take the Ottoman Prince along with him on his expedition against the Turks – an act which, Bayezid agreed, could have incalculable consequences for both himself and Alexander. Accordingly, Bayezid proposed, since his brother Jem was, like all men, mortal and must die sooner or later, the time had come to make certain that this now occurred as soon as possible. Therefore, he beseeched His Holiness to see to it that the said Jem be released from the narrow confines of this world, so that his soul might seek refuge in some higher place where it could enjoy a more perfect repose than ever it could find here in this world. For this act of charity, Bayezid pledged himself to pay Borgia 300,000 ducats (on receipt of the Prince's corpse), swearing by the True God, Creator of Heaven and Earth, that he would keep his side of the bargain, so long as Borgia kept his . . .

I finished reading and quietly laid down the letter, my mind growing numb with the realization that things had now come to such a pass that this noble heir of Mehmed Khan, the world-conquering *Gazi*, whose very name had brought terror and despair to his enemies, was reduced to seeking such an infamous favour from a scoundrelly Infidel like Borgia. How I yearned to be told that this letter was nothing more than a cunning plot . . . yet I knew in my heart that every accursed word of it had indeed been written by the Sultan.

I looked up and saw that Sofia was already on her feet.

'I must go now,' she said.

Almost in a trance, I folded the letters, put them in the leather case and handed them back to her.

'I wanted you to see for yourself,' she said.

'I would scarcely have believed it otherwise,' I said.

Before I could utter anything more, Sofia had slipped the case into the basket and vanished down the corridor.

As night was falling on the eve of the new year, Charles and his host came within sight of the gates of Rome. A deathly hush lay over the whole city. The bells of St Peter's were silent, the Papal Palace was darkened and desolate against the low overcast sky, and only a few uncertain lights glimmered faintly in the gathering dusk on the high tower of the Castle of St Angelo, where Borgia and his household had hastily taken refuge.

The Porta del Popolo stood opened wide, its strong wooden doors flung back by the fearful citizens who, convinced of the futility of resistance, hoped by this gesture to save Rome from pillage and massacre at the hands of the French King's troops.

I stationed myself in the shadows of a church porch on the Via Lata, a couple of hundred yards from the gate itself, and watched Charles's men come in by torchlight to the slow and monotonous beat of their drums.

First there came company after company of Swiss pikemen and halberdiers, ten thousand at least by my reckoning, all dressed in slashed and parti-coloured clothes; then, almost the same number of French and Breton archers and infantry and, after them, several thousand Gascon crossbowmen, small, swarthy, agile men with pinched features, who eyed with hostile and suspicious glances those few Romans that had dared to venture out of doors to watch the army's entry; and then, with a deafening clatter of hoofs against the cobblestones, came four or five thousand French knights, in heavy armour, bearing lances and maces and riding on immense chargers, each knight followed by three or four pages and armed attendants, also on horseback.

Behind these came the King himself, attired in black velvet and a cloak of gold brocade, his lance held resting against his hip to signify his coming as a conqueror, and surrounded on all sides by his mounted bodyguard of Scots bowmen, bestial, broad-shouldered, thick-armed colossi, with red hair and beards, their weapons strung and at the ready to defend their master. And after these came a great crowd of nobles, courtiers, gentlemen and retainers, among whom I espied several Cardinals and priests, including the renegade Giovanni della Rovere. Then, after several thousand more Infidel footsoldiers and archers had gone by, I watched in wonder the procession of the French artillery. I counted thirty-six stupendous bronze cannons, each one mounted on an enormous wheeled carriage; and after these prodigious and fearful monsters, so many smaller cannons and field pieces that my head reeled to the counting of them.

The gate remained open all night, and all night the army poured into the city like an incessant flood. By the early hours of the morning when I turned for home, every square, public garden and open piece of ground was filled with men, huddling around fires lit against the wet and cold, or simply lying stretched out asleep on the ground where they had lain down, exhausted after the days of forced marches through wind and rain.

When I re-emerged from my house an hour or so before midday, I discovered that the French King had taken up residence in one of the Cardinals' palaces, the Palazzo San Marco, below the Capitol Hill. I wandered over there and joined the curious crowd of onlookers that had gathered to watch the King's men pulling down the houses around the palace – a measure designed to give their guns a clear line of fire, the better to protect the building should it come under attack (though quite from what quarter was difficult to imagine, since the Pope had days before withdrawn his greatly inferior forces to the Vatican and the Castle, abandoning the town altogether).

I did not see the King that first day, but my patient vigil was rewarded the day after, when in the early afternoon Charles came out of the palace for a few minutes to make an inspection of the artillery that was now in place.

Charles was then in his twenty-fourth year, and though Sofia had spoken to me before of what she had heard of the oddity of his appearance, I gazed with incredulity at the figure I now observed. Even on horseback I had noted his awkward posture and smallness of stature, but on foot he seemed a veritable hunchback and a dwarf. His head, moreover, was much too large for his body, his enormous nose took on in the daylight a ludicrous beak-like aspect, and his pendulous lips – permanently wet and half-open – gave him a positively cretinous air. He shambled rather than walked, made jerky and inelegant gestures when he spoke, and to make matters worse, he wore peculiar round-toed shoes that served only to emphasize his deformity. In fact, he had more the appearance of a court buffoon than a monarch, and but for the mighty army at his back he would have excited laughter rather than fear. And yet this man held the Fate of half Christendom in the palm of his hand, and was now poised to unleash chaos and civil war upon the Guarded Domains.

Strange and ineffable indeed are the instruments of Destiny!

Here, then, in the Palazzo San Marco was the King, and there, on the other side of the Tiber in the Castle of St Angelo, were the Pope and Jem. But though all concurred that Borgia would sooner or later have to surrender the Prince to the French, the Pontiff seemed prepared to go to almost any lengths to put off the evil hour. Indeed, after several days had gone by in tortuous negotiations, the Most Christian King became so exasperated with Borgia's refusal to agree a day and hour for the transfer that Charles was restrained by his ministers only with the greatest difficulty from ordering his artillery to commence the bombardment of the Castle and the Papal Palace.

Meanwhile, as the delegations daily went back and forth between the Royal and Papal courts – struggling to find some solution to the impasse – the luckless inhabitants of Rome began to pay the price for their master's evasions and vacillations. For apart from anything else, the army was far from adequately provisioned and the influx of tens of thousands of additional souls into the city had emptied the markets and shops of food overnight. Thus, the troops, their meagre marching rations at an end, were soon going from house to house demanding to be fed, and terrorizing anyone who showed the least reluctance to cater to their needs.

Moreover, although at first the French officers made a half-hearted attempt to billet their men in an orderly fashion in suitable buildings in the Town, as the weather grew colder the troops themselves wasted no time in seeking out their own quarters and installing themselves wherever they thought fit. And within a few days, well-ordered homes had been transformed into squalid and vermin-infested slums, churches and chapels into filthy latrines, and rich palaces into human pigsties.

Then at the end of the first week of the occupation the Swiss went in force into the Jewish quarter, looting and killing wherever they went, and setting fire to the principal synagogue. Josef – praise God! – escaped this massacre, having shut his shop and retired with his people, for safety, to some upper rooms. Even so, he was fortunate not to be burned alive when the tenement next door was put to the torch by a gang of these Infidel mercenaries.

Nor were the Town's Christian inhabitants altogether spared. Numerous houses were broken into and their occupants molested. The two young sons of a Roman noble were hacked to pieces while defending their father's house from an invasion of intruders. And even the house of Vanozza – the Pope's onetime mistress and mother of several of his children – was beset by a huge mob of soldiers and ransacked, while their French officers looked on impassively.

At last Charles issued an edict ordering that the

lawlessness cease. And it is true, some malefactors were executed in the Campo dei Fiori as an example, and others hanged from the eaves and windows of the houses in which they had been caught red-handed committing crimes. But in spite of the King's appointment of squadrons of cavalry to patrol the city, still hardly a night went past without some new outrage being visited upon the cowed and defenceless citizenry. And all this from an army that, according to the French King's proclamations, came as pilgrims to the Eternal City!

How my house escaped the attentions of this murderous rabble of Misbelievers I shall never know. No doubt the poor and neglected aspect of that obscure quarter down by the river made it less inviting than other districts that held out the promise of much richer crops of booty. But still, early one morning, I came out to find some poor devil lying in the street in a pool of his own blood – he had been set upon by a band of soldiers and robbed (so a sobbing old woman told me) of nothing more than a few silver coins.

That day I resolved to go once more to see how things were faring at the Villa Margherita. I had already passed by there twice since the arrival of the French and had been relieved to find the gates manned by a company of the Venetian ambassador's men (who had draped a banner of the winged lion of St Mark from a balcony to show that the residence was under the Republic's protection).

Yet when I went back that morning, I discovered that the men were gone and the gates were gaping wide. I strode into the courtyard and, finding the main doors of the house also open, I went inside.

My nostrils were instantly assaulted by the smell of stale wine, urine and vomit. A soldier was lying on the floor of the hall, gently snoring, a blanket thrown over him. I wandered from room to room, in every one coming upon more troops asleep in chairs, or stretched out on the flagstones amidst the scattered debris of shattered glasses, bits of food, broken furniture and crumpled hangings and tapestries that had been torn down from the walls to serve

384

as bedding. Reaching the back of the house, I encountered a group of men slumped around a table in the kitchen, three or four of them still awake but very drunk and arguing in loud voices.

I said in French, 'Where's your Captain?'

'Us-stairs,' said one of the men in slurred, wine-sodden tones, before rejoining the incoherent dispute.

I discovered, after some searching, that the Captain had installed himself in Sofia's room. The door was not shut, so I walked right in. There was a sickening smell of unwashed flesh and sweat. I pushed open the shutters. On the bare mattress there sprawled a fat heavy-jowled Frenchman, still in his boots and covered in a heavy mud-stained cloak. Roused by the light, he slowly pulled himself up on one elbow and peered at me with blurred and bloodshot eyes.

'And who might you be, monsieur?' he said, his voice still thick with sleep.

'A friend of the family,' I said. 'What's happened to them?'

The Captain sank back on the bed, covering his eyes with his hand to keep out the light.

'They all left yesterday . . .,' he said.

I glanced around the room and saw that Sofia's wooden chest and her mirror had gone. I went over and looked inside her cupboard. All her dresses were gone, nor could I see anything else of hers left lying about the room. That at least suggested a reasonably ordered departure.

'Where did they go?' I said.

'How should I know?' said the Frenchman. 'They could have stayed, but the lady didn't seem to appreciate company . . .'

'Really?' I said. 'You surprise me.' But he just looked back at me with a stupid uncomprehending gaze. I reckoned I had probably asked too many questions as it was, and decided it was time to leave. So I turned to go outside to get myself some fresh air.

She came to me on Thursday, towards the end of the second hour of the night. For two whole days before, the French army had been mustering in different parts of the city, as though its departure from Rome was suddenly imminent and the invasion of the Kingdom of Naples was about to begin.

The night was cold and very dark and sleet had been falling since dusk. I sat on my threadbare carpet hunched in front of the fire, staring into the flames and listening to the steady dripping of the water running off the eaves outside.

Then there was a light tapping at the door and I heard Sofia calling out softly, 'Barak . . .'

I hastened to the door, unbolted it and let her in. She was shivering and very white, a bluish tinge about her lips and below her eyes, and damp snow flakes were clinging to her fur-trimmed cloak and the black shawl covering her hair. I put my arm around her and led her to the fire, took her wet things and spread them out to one side of the hearth to dry. She sat down on the carpet, her teeth chattering and held out her hands to warm them. Meanwhile, I fetched a blanket and draped it around her shoulders, and poured some red wine into a pot and hung it over the flames to take the chill off it.

I helped her off with her sodden shoes and stockings, and began to dry her feet with a cloth. Then I took her hands in mine and rubbed them to get some heat back into them.

'Where have you been?' I said.

'At the ambassador's house – the swine billeted soldiers at the Villa.'

'I know,' I said, 'I went there a few days ago.'

'I would have sent word to you about what had happened, but I was constantly surrounded with people and I thought it too risky.'

'What about tonight?' I said. 'Are you sure you weren't followed?'

'I'm sure,' she said. 'I came all the way on foot, and I was very careful. And anyway, I'm certain nobody saw me leave. I have been a little unwell these past days, so I said I would retire early. Then, when the others were at dinner, I slipped out. Nobody is expecting to see me now until tomorrow morning . . .'

'But what if somebody calls for you?'

386

'Anna and I are sharing a room – she'll say I'm asleep and not to be disturbed.'

'What news, then?' I said.

'Jem has been handed over to Charles. He went in disguise with an escort to the Palazzo San Marco a couple of hours ago. His Turkish officers are to follow later tonight.'

'From all the activity,' I said, 'I guessed as much. Will Charles and Jem be leaving Rome at the same time?'

'No. The Prince is to start early tomorrow morning, while Charles takes his leave of the Pope. The King will join Jem later on in the day at Marino. Then they'll set off for Naples together. And there they will meet up with the fleet and the additional troops and supplies coming from France by sea.'

'So,' I said with a bitter smile, 'Jem is on his way home at last . . .'

I got up and poured some wine into a cup and passed it to Sofia. Then I poured some for myself and swallowed a mouthful.

'I'm surprised,' I said, 'after all these delays, that the Pope gave up Jem at all in the end. Alive, that is. I gather he knows now all about the Sultan's letter and how much Bayezid was ready to pay to get his brother put out of the way . . . Strange, isn't it, that Borgia didn't take the Emperor up on his offer?'

'That', she said, shrugging, 'might have been going too far, even for him. Besides, the French King told the Pope that if there were any more delays, he would have his artillery bombard the Papal Palace and the Castle – and given the power of the French guns, I don't suppose that Borgia much relished the idea of being buried alive in the ruins of his own fortress.'

'Ah,' I said, 'but would Charles really have carried out such a threat?'

'He'd have done it all right,' said Sofia, 'and Borgia knew it. The Venetians think that Charles is actually insane – and they're not the only ones . . .'

And so we went on talking for an hour or more, as we

lingered by the fire, speculating on what would happen now that the die had been cast and the expedition against the Ottomans, so long promised by the Infidels, was finally about to take place. Then we grew tired of such great affairs and retired together to bed.

When we had finished, we lay in silence for some time, watching the reflections of the flames dying in the hearth flickering spectrally on the ceiling.

After some while, Sofia said quietly, 'What will you do now?'

'What can I do?' I said. 'I shall follow the Prince when he leaves Rome tomorrow. And when – God willing – I find the opportunity, I will do my utmost to kill him.'

'In the midst of a whole army?' she said. 'Are you mad, my love?'

'If you have courage,' I said, 'you can achieve many things that the fearful would deem impossible.'

'Yes,' said Sofia, 'that is true. But this time it is different. The Prince will be guarded night and day, not only by his own companions but also by the King's archers. They will be expecting attempts on Jem's life – of that you may be sure.'

'No doubt,' I said coldly, 'but it is my duty to try.'

'Have you orders from Kivami Bey to do so?'

'No,' I said. 'But communications have been abominable since the coming of the French. Not that it makes any difference. The Sultan's wishes are quite clear, you know that as well as I do.'

'The Sultan', replied Sofia haughtily, 'asked Borgia, not you, to do his dirty work. If he had wanted you to do it, he would have sent orders long ago.'

'Circumstances have changed. I have no choice in the matter . . .'

'No,' she said tearfully. 'You have done enough. Nobody will gain anything. You will die, that's all – and for nothing.'

She turned her face away from me and shook my hand from her shoulder when I reached out to her. I sat up and bowed my head, my heart heavy with gloom.

388

Then, without looking up, I said, 'I am the Sultan's servant. To run away now would be a betrayal not only of my master but also of that Faith which we Muslims hold more dear than our own lives. How could I go on living afterwards? And how could I stand in the presence of God on the Last Day without covering my face for shame?'

'Neither Emperor nor God', said Sofia angrily, 'requires a faithful servant to throw his life away recklessly and to no purpose. You have done everything you could. If this quarrel between Bayezid and Jem cannot be settled except by another war – so be it! Nothing you can do will prevent the inevitable from happening.'

'You do not understand,' I said.

Sofia sat up, clutching the blankets around her. I gazed at her tear-stained face, and she looked back at me with an unwavering glance.

'It is you', she said, 'who do not understand, not I. I am a mere woman. Why cannot you, a man – so much stronger and surer in mind, in body, in everything – understand that if it is God's will that Jem should overthrow his brother and become Sultan in his stead, no man on earth will be able to stand in his way?'

I awoke to find Sofia was no longer by my side. I felt a sudden pang of anguish – but then I saw in the dim light that her dress was still draped over the chair, where she had left it the night before. I got up and put some clothes on, and crouched by the hearth blowing on the embers, adding dry wood to revive the flames. As the fire started to come to life again, Sofia returned to the room.

She looked still more pale and wan than on the previous evening. As she sat down on the carpet in front of the fire, she wiped a little perspiration from her forehead with the sleeve of her shift.

'What is wrong?' I said, watching her intently.

'Nothing,' she said. 'I am sick in the morning sometimes, that's all.'

'Then you are ill,' I said.

'No, not ill, my love,' she said, ruefully gazing at me

389

with her clear brown eyes. 'It is just that . . . well, my blood has not come as it should . . .'

'Since when?' I said, thunderstruck.

'Since the last time we . . .,' she said, lowering her glance.

'But I thought you could not.'

'So did I,' she said.

'God is most bountiful,' I murmured.

'Yes . . .,' she said with a sigh.

I took her hands in mine and passionately, reverently kissed her palms and pressed them against my face.

'Why didn't you tell me before?'

'I was not sure myself,' she said without conviction.

'Was it because you did not believe me when I said I would take you back to Turkey with me when this business was over?'

'No, no . . .,' she said.

'You could have told me last night,' I said, suddenly feeling very foolish for not having guessed what was the matter with her.

'What would have been the point?' she said sadly. 'Perhaps it would have been better if you had never known.'

'Come, my darling, I am not quite as impetuous as you seem to think. And I have every intention of staying alive, God willing, for some years yet.'

'Oh, how I wish I could believe what you say!' she said.

'It will not be long now,' I said. 'I'll be back, in a few days, you'll see. And I swear to you that if I cannot do what needs to be done alone, I will not attempt anything stupid.'

'God willing,' she said quietly, 'God willing.'

I persuaded her to go and lie down on the bed while I gathered a few things together to take with me on my journey. Before we departed I gave her a hundred ducats and a piece of paper, leaving her my property and goods in Turkey. And I told her, if I should not return within ten days, to start without me for Istanbul, and I would follow as soon as I could.

As I spoke she seemed to listen attentively, nodding her

head from time to time, but she did not say anything.

I helped her on with her cloak and slung mine over my shoulders as she covered her hair with her shawl.

'I will see you as far as the church near the Venetian embassy,' I said, 'and return here afterwards for my things.'

We went into the hall. I unlocked the door and pulled back the bolt. Sofia seemed a little unsteady on her feet, so I put my arm around her and ushered her ahead of me through the door and onto the gallery above the courtyard.

I did not see the man until too late, far too late. He must, I suppose, have been pressed very close against the wall by the door. So the first I knew, he was suddenly there before us, his right arm already raised high above his head. Then the arm fell at tremendous speed and Sofia let out a sharp scream and fell against the doorframe.

The man's arm shot up again and my eye caught the glint of a fine steel blade. But by this time I had got past Sofia and clear of the doorway.

For a split second the bright knife seemed to hang motionless in his hand against the leaden sky. Then it started to descend. But before it could reach its target a second time, the mace-like ball of my clenched fist hit him full in the face and the knife flew from his hand. Crumpling under the force of my blow, the man crashed against the gallery rail, which instantly gave way beneath his weight with an ear-splitting crack – and he went over backwards, disappearing from sight, his hands clawing blindly at the empty air. A moment later, his cry of terror was abruptly cut short as his body slammed heavily onto the cobbles down below.

I swung round to find Sofia bent almost double, clutching at her chest and moaning through clenched teeth. I grabbed her round the waist, dragged her back into the house and kicked the door shut with my foot. Still holding her up, I reached out and shot the bolt back into place. As I did so, she began to slide to the floor and I sank down with her to prevent her from striking her head against the tiles. Then I managed to get a firmer grasp of her, cradling her body in my arms.

Very gently I moved her hands a little from where she was still pressing them against her chest. She scarcely resisted at all. And for a moment my heart leapt with joy. There was only a small slash in her dress, hardly bigger than her own slender thumbnail, nor did there seem to be the slightest trace of bleeding.

Slowly, so as not to move her too much, I reached with my free hand for the knife I kept concealed in my boot, cut through the laces of her bodice and pulled the material aside. Then I ripped open her shift, exposing her left breast. There was a great purple bruise but otherwise . . . Then my stomach jumped into my mouth. At the centre of the bruise a trickle of thick blood was slowly beginning to ooze from a deep dark-crimson cavity. I knew then that the blade must have gone through her ribs after all, and penetrated her heart.

I felt her small hands clutching like a child's at my forearm. Panting breathlessly, she was trying to speak.

I inclined my ear and she gasped, 'Oh God, my darling, forgive me! This is the Ten's doing . . . and now I've led them to you. Leave me, please, and save yourself . . .'

'Don't talk,' I said, 'you'll exhaust yourself. I'll get you to the bed and then I'll go for a surgeon.'

But she started to struggle to free herself from my grip, saying urgently, 'No, no, it's no good . . . go away, now, before it's too late . . .'

I tried to raise her slightly, very slowly at first, but I'd hardly lifted her at all before she cried out in agony, her face contorted by the pain. So I let her gently down again on the floor, resting her head against my knee and trying to soothe her.

I took her hand and surreptitiously searched her wrist for her pulse. It was very weak by now and fluttering wildly. Meanwhile, her breath seemed to grow shallower and shallower by the second. I met her gaze, too overcome to speak, and an unbearable expression of tenderness filled her eyes. When she somehow managed to give me a shy little smile, a horrible sob rent my chest – a ghastly, desolate, inhuman sound.

She tried to smile again, but it seemed to hurt her too much this time. Then she whispered, almost dreamily, 'Kiss me . . .'

As I bent over her, I could see her eyelids beginning to close, as though she were too drowsy to keep them open any longer. When my mouth touched hers, her lips parted a little, and she even pressed them softly against mine. Then, as I drew back, I felt a tiny, almost imperceptible exhalation of her breath against my cheek and her lips ceased to move altogether.

What happened afterwards, I cannot recall in detail. All I know is that by the time I started to come to my senses it was already dusk. Sofia was lying on the bed, looking so serene, so beautiful – you would have said she was asleep. I was sitting beside her, still holding her hand. And one of the first things I remember thinking was: The fire has gone out, that is why her hand is so cold.

The bells of the church at the top of the street began to ring, as they always did at sunset, for what the Infidels call 'the angelus'. Perhaps it was this sound that roused me at last from my stupor. I straightened up, withdrew my hand from Sofia's and got to my feet.

I went into the hall. The door was unbolted. I could not understand why. Then it began to come back to me.

I had gone out at some point to see about the man. I had found him lying where he had fallen, his neck twisted round at an impossible angle, the back of his skull a sticky mess of blood, bone and matted hair. His eyes were open and I didn't bother to try to close them before I dragged his body into one of the storerooms under the house and threw a piece of canvas over him. Then I had gone back to the house to be with Sofia.

When night had properly fallen, I lit a storm lantern. I thanked God that neither the yard nor the garden was overlooked by the houses around. When I went out, I found that the sleet had turned to rain, but the air was still very sharp and I could see my breath in the lamplight.

I descended to the storeroom and hung the lantern from a beam. I searched the man's body but could find nothing to show who he was – but then I didn't really expect one of the Ten's assassins to have a letter of commission in his pocket. Roughly, I stripped off his clothes and tied them in a bundle around a heavy stone I had come across lying on the floor. When I pulled off the man's drawers, I observed with a start that he was circumcised. So the bastard must have been a Jew, or even some abominable renegade from our side . . .

I hoisted the man's corpse over my shoulder and walked with it out into the courtyard and through to the garden. With a bit of kicking and cursing – the wood seemed to have swollen in the wet – I got the postern gate open that led onto the ruined quay. I squeezed with my burden through the narrow doorway and glanced both ways to check if there was anyone about. But the night was pitch black and I could hardly see five yards in either direction. I went on to the quay and down the slippery and uneven steps towards the rushing and hissing water's edge. I nearly fell a couple of times.

When I reached the bottom, I heaved the body into the river and the dog's carcass – may it rot for ever in Hell! – hit the dark water with a noisy splash and was immediately carried away on the Tiber's swirling muddied flood. Then I went back for his clothes and tossed them in after him.

Afterwards, I returned to the storeroom to get the lantern and a spade. Below a tree in one corner of the garden, just by the wall, there was a large slab of marble laid out flat on the ground. I levered it up with the handle of the spade, dragged it to one side and started to dig. The ground here was sandy and loose, and I had soon excavated a sizeable hole. Then I fetched some short lengths of old board I had noticed in the storeroom and leant them against the wall.

I went back to the house. The candles I had lit and placed by the bed cast their warm light on Sofia's lustrous

394

hair and waxen features. Her hands rested folded on her stomach, where I had placed them. Tenderly, I wrapped her in the sheet on which we had spent our last night together, and tearing the other sheet into long strips, I bound her tightly up in this poor shroud, leaving only her sweet face exposed. Then I lifted my beloved in my arms and carried her out along the gallery, down the steps and across the courtyard into the garden. By the light of the lantern, I laid her in the grave. Then I put the boards in place, one by one, below the surface of the ground but leaving a good space beneath so the earth would not press down directly on her body.

At last only her head remained visible. I went down on my hands and knees and kissed her lips, her eyes, her white forehead. I took a final look at her and, having covered her face with her shawl, put the last piece of wood into place.

The lantern started to flicker and the wind to bluster and moan in the bare trees, making their branches dip and sway and creak, as I filled the grave. It began to rain again, the cold drops striking my face and neck and bare arms. Finally, when I had finished, I smoothed out the surface of the ground with the spade and then my hands, and scattered the remaining earth about the garden. Then I dragged the marble slab back into position, aligning it with great care, in the hope that nobody other than myself would be able to tell that she lay there. And having done this, I sank to my knees and wept, and though the downpour was now falling harder than ever, nothing, not even the rain, seemed able to wash away my tears.

At first light I rode out of that accursed city and set off after Jem, my heart filled with murderous determination to avenge myself on that person who now seemed to me the prime author of my misery and grief.

But the roads and the weather were appalling, and by the time I made it as far as Marino, I learned that the Prince had already left with the King and the royal suite to accompany the French march southwards into the Kingdom of Naples. And so for the next few days I followed in the wake of the victorious Infidel army, tracking my prey from town to town, camp to camp, halting place to halting place, until fifty miles before Naples itself, in a town called San Germano, I caught up with the Prince at last.

By then I had realized that, with the fifty or more Scots archers said to be guarding Jem whenever he travelled or ventured outdoors, I could forget even thinking of trying to kill him in the open, since anybody who came anywhere near him would certainly be shot down in a hail of arrows long before they laid a finger on him. So I decided to gamble everything on one chance: I would attempt to talk my way into Jem's presence the next time they stopped for the night and then, if the trick paid off, when I was brought to him, I might – by God's grace – just have time to retrieve my hidden weapon from my riding boot, take a lunge at the Prince and deal him a fatal wound in the throat or stomach, before his officers and guards woke up to what was happening. Of course, I knew I would be searched before I was allowed to see him, but the knife I had chosen for this desperate undertaking fitted so exactly in the narrow cavity I had fashioned between the stiff outer leather and the inner lining of the boot that I was almost certain that it would evade detection, unless I was extremely unlucky. So, you see, I had thought of everything – everything, that is, except the possibility that Jem might be already expecting me.

The Prince was lodged that night not with the King and his suite – as he had been on some occasions on this journey – but in a large house of his own, just off the town square. As I left the square and walked towards the house, I felt strangely calm – considering that I expected to be dead within the hour.

When I reached the gates, I found my way blocked by a dozen or so Scotsmen armed with bows and axes. And when I bid them good evening in French, one of them came forward and demanded peremptorily in that same language to know what my business was there.

'I am', I said, 'a Turkish officer. And I have vital information to communicate to His Highness – please inform his officer Sinan Bey that I am here, at once!'

The captain of the guard eyed me suspiciously and said, 'What is your name, monsieur?'

'That I may reveal only to the Prince himself,' I said. 'But you may tell his officers that I am sent by Sadi Bey.'

At first the captain said nothing and continued to look me up and down. But then he turned away and knocked imperiously on the door, and spoke loudly in some tongue that I did not understand. Presently, there came sounds of the gates being unlocked from the inside.

As he disappeared into the house, the captain said, 'Wait here . . .'

I remained standing in the street for quite some time, until eventually the doors opened a little, a command was barked out from within and the guards who had barred my way smartly stood aside. Then another voice from inside said pleasantly in Turkish, 'Dear friend, welcome! We have been expecting you for some time.'

It was too easy. I should have realized that something was badly wrong.

Urged politely to come in without delay, I crossed the threshold and found myself in a dim passageway, in which I could discern a flight of gently sloping steps leading up into a large twilit courtyard. The warm yellow glow of lamps suffused the upper windows on the other side of the yard, but not strongly enough to cast anything but the faintest light into the passageway. The door creaked shut behind me and I heard a key being turned.

The man who had spoken before in Turkish said, 'This way . . .'

I turned slightly in the direction from where the voice seemed to be coming, and perceived now in the shadows the outline of someone wearing a long cloak and turban. I took a step forward.

The man said, 'That's right . . .'

Then the only thing I can remember is feeling a blinding pain, as if my skull was being cleft in two; and darkness came flooding in, like a black tide, from all around.

I do not know for how many hours I was dead to the

world, or even whether it was day or night when I emerged from that profound and dreamless state of oblivion, because when I woke I discovered myself to have been thrown into some kind of cellar where no ray of sunlight could penetrate.

When I first came round, I thought I was alone. I was lying on an earth floor, and when I opened my eyes I could see nothing but the black ground itself and a dimly lit section of wall, the stones mottled with moss and glistening in places with moisture. I tried to move but my limbs felt peculiar and constricted, and my head and neck throbbed with nauseating and dizzying pain.

Eventually, though, I managed to get a grip on myself and, gritting my teeth, I rolled over to see what was behind me. It was then I realized that my boots and most of my clothing had been removed, leaving me wearing nothing but my breeches and shirt, and that my wrists and ankles had been manacled with irons, which in turn were attached to a long chain fixed to a ring in the wall. I started to rattle these shackles, trying in vain to pull them apart, and as I writhed about on the floor, I glimpsed at the other end of the vault the legs of a table and chair, and a man's feet.

Almost at once the feet came to life and moved rapidly towards me, and a bright lamp was held up over me, shining in my face and dazzling my eyes so brightly that I could see nothing of the features of the person holding the light aloft. Then the lamp swung abruptly away and I heard heavy footsteps receding and a door being opened, then slammed shut and bolted.

A few minutes later, I heard the door open again, the light came back, and I found myself being hauled up into a sitting position and propped against the wall. Blinking, I stared into the lamp, and as I fought back the piercing pain radiating from the back of my head, my vision very slowly began to adjust. I now saw above me two bearded gentlemen in Ottoman dress, who gazed down at me, frowning with a grave preoccupied air.

For a little while the men just stood there. Then without

a word they turned and left the room, taking the lantern and closing the door behind them, and leaving me on my own. After which, I heard nothing for a time, until the dull clatter of what sounded like horses' hoofs passed somewhere above my head, and silence descended once again.

So I sat there in the blackness of that dismal place, contemplating with as much equanimity as I could the abject hopelessness of my position and wondering if they would soon send a suitable hireling to finish the job with cord or dagger, or if they had, as I now suspected, decided instead to let Nature take its course, and starve and freeze me to death by just leaving me there without food and water.

Yet neither was to be my Fate. For, as I learned presently, Destiny had one final task still for me to perform that this grim drama might at long last be brought to an end.

The two Italian Infidels came for me shortly before midnight. By that time, as I managed to work out afterwards, I had been in that wretched dank vault for about five days – my only sustenance some water that trickled down the wall and gathered over a period of hours in a shallow depression in the floor just within my reach.

The men first struck off the iron fetters round my wrists and ankles. Then, whilst one of them covered me with his sword – as though I was in a state to attempt anything heroic! – the other gave me a little food and drink, which I devoured greedily with trembling hands. After that, they gave me water to wash myself with, and helped me into some warm clothes they had brought with them.

As they half-pushed, half-carried me up the stairs, I said, 'Where are we going?'

They said, 'To Naples.'

'Who sent you?' I said.

'The Turks,' one replied. 'The Prince wishes to see you . . .'

The courtyard was dark and deserted under a clear and starry sky and the air was cold and fresh and good to

399

breathe. One of the men disappeared for a few minutes and returned with three horses. As I mounted, the dull cracked bell in the town square began to strike for twelve o'clock. At that moment I thought I had never heard a more lovely sound.

We travelled by night, resting and sleeping during the day. On the journey my guides told me that when they set out the French had been on the point of entering the capital of the Kingdom and that, since the Neapolitan King had fled in terror to Sicily, Charles would certainly by now have taken the city.

Towards sunrise on the third night, we crossed a broad fertile plain and Naples came into view, lying on a wide sweeping bay beneath the slopes of a high, cloud-shrouded peak they call Vesuvius. And even from a distance I could see the countless vessels of the great Christian fleet riding at anchor in the bay. We entered the city by one of the principal gates and repaired to a tavern for some time, while one of the men went to make enquiries. Afterwards we passed by a large fortified house, and one of these Misbelievers said:

'Prince Jem and his officers are lodged here.'

But we did not go directly to this place. Instead they took me to another house nearby, where they locked me in a room, saying they would return later.

For most of that day I heard cannon fire coming intermittently from the direction of the waterfront. I learned, when the Infidels returned, that this was because, although the Neapolitan King had indeed fled over the sea to Sicily, leaving Charles in possession of the town, two castles on the shore had still refused to surrender to the French and were consequently under siege.

After nightfall my two escorts led me through the empty streets to the house where Jem and his people were lodged. At the back of the house there were some stables and inside one of them I found waiting for me two of Jem's officers, who said their names were Sinan Bey and Ayas Bey. Having given the Infidels money, they dismissed them and set about searching me very meticulously. They even took

400

my boots away from me – by which I knew that they must have found my concealed weapon after they had rendered me unconscious in San Germano (although they said nothing about this openly). Finally, Ayas Bey tied my hands tightly in front of me with a length of strong rope.

Once inside the house, Sinan and Ayas took me up a steep winding stair and through a low door into a narrow corridor. On the left was a solid stone wall, but on the right there was wooden panelling. When we had gone a few yards Ayas Bey stopped and tapped very lightly against the wood. Seconds later the section swung soundlessly open – for it proved to be a hidden door. Sinan took me by the upper arm and pushed me ahead of him into the spacious high-ceilinged apartment on the other side.

Inside, standing around the room in the lamplight, were half a dozen other Turkish officers of Jem's suite, all armed with swords, who watched me closely, their hands resting on the hilts of their weapons, as Sinan guided me across the chamber towards a large canopied bed.

In the bed lay the recumbent figure of a big man, with a broad chest and stout stomach, his head and shoulders resting against a bank of piled-up pillows, his arms stretched out, inert, on the white sheets before him. That the man was Jem I did not doubt, yet so utterly was he transformed in appearance that, in truth, I barely recognized him. For his entire face and neck were grotesquely bloated and distended, his eyelids purple and swollen, and his once alabaster-white skin the colour of old ivory. Great beads of sweat stood out on his furrowed brow and prominent aquiline nose, and his lips, formerly so rounded and red and sensual, were now emaciated and slack and of a ghastly greyish-black hue.

When we reached the bedside, Jem turned his head very slowly towards us, partly closing one of his eyes, as though straining to see. I felt the pressure of Sinan's hand on my arm and I responded at once by going down on my knees. To my surprise, the Prince offered his hand to me, sluggishly and painfully moving it across the sheet. When I kissed the tips of his fingers I could feel with my

401

lips – even on this brief contact – the intense heat of the fever burning fiercely in his veins. Then he slowly withdrew his hand and, breathing in short wheezing gasps, motioned with his bloodshot eyes towards a low carved chest by the head of the bed. With bowed head, I obeyed and sat on the chest. Sinan sat beside me, his hand still firmly gripping my upper arm.

'It is over . . . ,' the Prince said at last in a hoarse whisper. 'What you sought to do has been done by another. I have been poisoned . . . I beg you to go now to Istanbul as quickly as possible to inform my brother of what has befallen me . . .'

'So that is the reason my life has been spared!'

'Yes,' said Jem, 'for I fear that these Infidels will keep my death secret in order to prolong civil strife in the Empire, while they launch their expedition against my brother . . . My officers will be imprisoned – Charles may even have them executed – to ensure their silence . . .'

'God forbid!' I said. 'But would the King not be equally certain to have me put out of the way?'

'The French believe you to be dead,' said Jem, 'and buried in the cellar of the house in San Germano.'

'What of the Infidels who brought me to Naples?'

'They are Neapolitan nobles who hate Charles and will do nothing to assist the French invaders . . .'

'In that case,' I said, 'I stand some chance of getting out of the Kingdom alive.'

'You will do as I ask, Captain?' said Jem.

'For the sake of all of us, I will try.'

'God be praised!' said Jem with a deep sigh, closing his eyes. 'Now that my prayers have been answered, I am at peace . . .'

So saying, Jem seemed to fall into a kind of faint, his head lolling to one side, at which his officers rushed to his bedside, clearly afraid that the Prince had breathed his last.

But he somehow clung to life for several hours more, his officers taking it in turn to sit by him and gently wash the feverish perspiration from his brow.

Then, just as dawn was about to break, Jem suddenly opened his eyes and uttered the confession of the Faith, saying in a clear and strong voice, 'There is no god but God, and Muhammad is the Prophet of God!' And thereupon his spirit departed his body.

Thus did the unhappy Prince drain the last bitter dregs of the cup of his misfortunes on this earth and go to seek in the Gardens of Perpetual Abode the sweet wine of Paradise.

On the sixth day I made it to Ancona and secured a passage in a Ragusan vessel bound for Dubrovnik; from there I made my way in an Albanian caique to Avlona, where I found in residence in the governor's house Bayezid's former envoy to Rome and Head of the Convent, Mustafa Bey.

Mustafa had, he told me, been sent to Avlona some months before, in order to keep the Sublime Porte informed of the Infidels' belligerent preparation across the straits in Italy and, as he freely confessed to me, he was now expecting daily to see the sails of the Misbelievers' fleet appearing on the western horizon. Indeed, so gloomy had Mustafa's prognostications become by the time I arrived on the scene that, at first, he greeted my momentous tidings with utter incredulity. And it was only when I described in detail Jem's demise in Naples that his doubts were finally overcome, and he dispatched Tatar couriers to acquaint the Emperor himself with the fact and circumstances of his errant brother's death.

So, my vital message safely delivered, it should have been as much over for me as for the Prince himself . . .

Yet there is something about a sea voyage that clears and concentrates a man's thoughts, and brings home to him things that elude his understanding on dry land. And, alas, by the time I reached Avlona and stepped ashore, onto that very quay from which I had set sail an eternity before in search of Jem, everything had become horribly transparent.

I set off for Istanbul slowly and with a doom-laden

heart, wrestling within myself mile after mile as I rode through mountain, forest and plain, trying to conceive of some way of extricating myself from the impasse into which my unwelcome new-found knowledge had led me. But what could I do? I had to act as I did – or else betray Sofia.

They say that Bayezid wept like a child when he learned of the death of Jem; and when he heard the account of it from my own lips, certainly the tears seemed never far from his eyes. When I had said my piece, he questioned me closely as to which of the Infidels could possibly be responsible for poisoning his brother. I replied that his officers believed it to have been the work of Rodrigo Borgia, who sought thus to avenge himself on the French King for forcing him to relinquish this most prized hostage. But even that, I had to say, was mere speculation, and I expressed my view that the identity of the culprit might for ever remain a mystery.

Afterwards the Felicitous Sultan asked me if I had some request that he might grant me as a reward. I told His Majesty what I desired more than anything else in the world, and he appeared pleased and said that the favour I asked was the very thing already in his mind, and graciously acceded. Then I kissed his beneficent hand and our interview came to an end.

Since my orders had been to present myself at once at the Palace on my arrival in the God-guarded city, it was not until I had seen and spoken to the Emperor that I had the opportunity to go to the Convent to settle what was now my one outstanding account.

The morning was sharp and bright and breezy, the sky clear and almost cloudless, the buildings, mosques, minarets, gardens, streets and squares all wet and sparkling after a heavy shower. The kind of morning, in fact, that ought to make you feel glad to be alive. But I had other things on my mind.

Kivami Bey was alone in his room, his table, the floor and the old couch piled high as ever with reports, docu-

404

ments and files. He looked uglier, more obese, more unhealthy, more pockmarked, more malformed than even I could remember. He greeted me with his customary lack of ceremony.

'You have just come from the Palace . . .,' he said brusquely.

'I have,' I said.

'Did they tell you the news?' he said.

'Davud Pasha told me that Jem's death is now known throughout Italy, Charles's Crusade against us had to be abandoned and the Sultan of Egypt is sending ambassadors to the Porte to sue for peace . . .'

'H'm!' Kivami Bey said grudgingly. 'I suppose that's about the top and bottom of it.'

'So the schemes of the Infidels have been confounded at last!' I said.

'Indeed,' he said, nodding slowly. But then added, with a bitter edge to his voice, 'Yet this business has left the Empire in a bad way . . . it will be many years before it becomes as strong again as it was in Mehmed Khan's day.'

'Yes, that is true,' I said. 'Which is the reason I shall shortly be returning to sea to command one of His Majesty's ships.'

Kivami Bey frowned and fixed me with his cold steely grey eyes.

'That is impossible,' he said flatly. 'I cannot spare you.'

'The Sultan has just now granted my petition,' I said.

'Has he taken leave of his senses?' said Kivami Bey. 'I forbid it. I will speak to Bayezid myself. I will oppose your transfer.'

'You wish to have me near you so that you can keep an eye on me?' I said.

'What are you talking about?' he growled angrily.

'Cannot you guess?' I said. 'Anyway, what does it matter? The decision has been taken out of your hands.'

'I will not release you.'

'I think you will,' I said. 'Because if you do not, I shall be obliged to tell the Emperor that ever since he came to the throne you have been secretly and consistently working for the return of Jem alive, so that his younger brother might supplant him . . .'

'You are raving mad,' said Kivami Bey. But at that same moment a strange look, which in another man I might even have called fear, began to creep into his eyes. I saw a taut nerve twitch in his cheek and, involuntarily, he raised a stunted misshapen hand to still it.

'If only I were . . .,' I said.

'Consider carefully before you say anything more,' he said, glaring at me with burning intensity.

'It is too late for that now . . .,' I said.

'And also be warned', he said, 'that whatever insane ideas you may have dreamed up – you will not be able to prove any of them.'

'Ah, but I can,' I said. 'So, now will you listen to me?'

'Say what you will,' he said, with an exasperated, dismissive wave of the hand. 'It won't do you any good.'

'At first,' I said, 'your devious plans were easy to disguise. Because the Sultan himself still wanted, if possible, to have his brother brought back alive. But after Jem went to Rome, and the Infidels started talking of a Crusade, His Majesty must have known that more drastic action would have to be taken.'

'Go on,' said Kivami Bey, watching me steadily, as though he expected me at any moment suddenly to draw a knife and lunge at him.

'And yet when I asked permission to mount an operation to assassinate the Prince, it was refused. By you, Kivami Bey – without the Sultan's ever knowing of my request.'

'What I did,' said the Old Man, 'I did for the best . . .'

'Did that include trying to have me killed?' I said with barely suppressed rage. 'Only killing Sofia by mistake instead . . .'

He gave a start, as if I had slapped him hard across the face.

'The woman was killed by the Ten. You said so yourself in the report you sent from Avlona.'

'That is what she thought – may God's mercy be upon

406

her!' I said. 'And so, at first, did I. I only began to wonder when I saw the naked body of her murderer – but still I could not work it out . . .'

'Why should I have wished to have you killed?' said Kivami Bey coolly.

'Because', I said, 'you were afraid that I was about to make an attempt on the Prince's life. But it was Sofia, not I, who was the first to walk through that door . . .'

For a while Kivami Bey did not reply, but stared fixedly at the table in front of him avoiding my unwavering and hostile gaze. Then, without looking up, he said in a hollow mechanical voice:

'I wished you no harm as a man. I had no choice . . .'

'How so?' I said.

'You are a dangerous and determined fellow, Barak. And I knew by then that you would be aware, through the Venetians, of Bayezid's letter to Borgia. And I knew also that, once you had made up your mind that Jem would have to be stopped, you would almost certainly succeed in killing him, even if you lost your own life in the process.'

'I suppose', I said caustically, 'that I should be flattered you still had such a high opinion of my dedication . . .'

Kivami Bey raised his eyes slowly and gave me a bleak look.

'You are also a clever fellow, in your way,' he said. 'When was it you became convinced of all this?'

'Why,' I said, 'when I fell into Jem's hands. His officers had been forewarned, they were expecting me! And when I spoke to Jem just before he died, he even addressed me as "Captain". I knew then that someone had betrayed me.'

'It need not have been me,' said the Old Man with a shrug.

'Only two people here in Istanbul knew that I was in Rome. Yourself and the Sultan. What reason would Bayezid have to warn his brother I was on my way to try to kill him?'

As I spoke these words Kivami Bey threw up his hands in a gesture of hopelessness and despair, sinking back on

407

his divan, his head bowed between hunched shoulders. For a long time he remained silent, but at length he sighed and said:

'What I did, I did for the future of the Empire. Jem was Mehmed's true heir and would have been as great and glorious a Ruler, perhaps even greater . . . if Fate had not turned against him. Bayezid is an ascetic, not a *Gazi*. Why. the people call him "*Sofu*" – the Mystic! But Jem – God forgive him! – was a true Ottoman, a fearless warrior, a leader of men, like his father . . .'

'Jem should not', I said, 'have thrown in his lot with the Infidels. That is what led to his downfall. And you should have had more wisdom than to go on supporting him when he was consorting with our enemies.'

I got to my feet and, seeing me rise, Kivami Bey seemed seized with a kind of panic. Clumsily he reached for his silver-handled canes, and shuffling sideways along the couch, he struggled awkwardly to get up.

'What are you going to do?' he said.

'Nothing.'

'What in God's name do you mean?' he said, spluttering and wild-eyed.

'If you retire, I will say nothing to a living soul. For what you did to Sofia, God will punish you . . .'

I turned to go and Kivami Bey came after me, staggering on his sticks and nearly falling as he pursued me to the door. As I reached the threshold, he hissed:

'I could have you killed.'

'I would not advise you to try again,' I said without looking back.

I walked through the antechamber and out into the open air. I heard the Old Man's sticks clattering against the flagstones and his feet dragging painfully along behind him, and the familiar wheezing pant of his breath. When I was about halfway across the courtyard, he cried out:

'Come back! You don't understand . . .'

But I kept on walking. When I passed through the gate and into the street, the call to the midday prayer was just coming from the mosque nearby. I noticed that the sky had clouded over again and the first few drops of rain were beginning to fall.

Atik found him early the next morning. The doors of his inner sanctum were barred from the inside, and when the Old Man failed to reply to his faithful servant's usual knock, Atik became anxious and fetched a couple of the Convent mutes to help him break the doors open.

Kivami Bey lay on his back, the divan soaked in his blood, the carpet sticky with gore. The windows, with their view over the blue spring waters of the Golden Horn, the Bosphorus and the green Asian hills beyond, stood wide open. As the doors gave way to the powerful shoulders of the mutes, a swirling gust of breeze blew through the room, scattering the few cold grey ashes in the hearth – all that remained of the half-dozen or so pages extracted from the Jem file that lay open on the table before the couch, spattered here and there with small dark congealed spots of crimson.

At first they thought that Kivami Bey had been murdered by some intruder; but then they saw the sharp slender paper-knife tightly clenched in the Old Man's right hand and the deep gash in his throat where he had cut through his own jugular.

Sometimes I ask myself why he did it. Did he think that sooner or later I would expose him, despite what I had said? Yes, perhaps that was it. For, as he never tired of saying, Kivami Bey had never trusted another man or woman in his whole life. In that he was different from me . . . from Jem . . . from Sofia.

They buried him with honour in the garden of the Conqueror's Mosque, close by Mehmed's own mausoleum. The headstone was simple and unobtrusive, according to the Old Man's wishes, as befitted the last resting-place of this secret warrior for the Faith. Atik told me afterwards that the Felicitous Sultan believed that Kivami Bey had killed himself for grief at failing to bring Jem back alive from the lands of the Infidels. Which of course, in a way, was true.

Here end the Memoirs of Captain Barak

Epilogue

Jem's body, embalmed after his death and put into a sealed lead coffin on the orders of King Charles, was not returned to Turkey until the spring of 1499, when he was at last placed in the tomb awaiting him at the Muradiye Cemetery in Bursa, where he lies until this day. As for his companions, all of them were generously received back into the Ottoman fold by the Sultan and given pensions and positions at court in recognition of the steadfast devotion they had shown to their Prince through the trials and vicissitudes of his ill-fortuned existence. Also returned were Jem's books, jewels, clothes, his drinking cup, chess-playing ape and even his parrot, its white plumage now dyed deepest black by Jem's officers, and saying no longer 'God give victory to Prince Jem!' but instead 'God have mercy on Prince Jem!' – hearing which, it is said, the whole court was moved to tears, and bethought themselves of the transitory nature of life upon this earth.

On 12 August of that same year, the Ottoman and Venetian battle-fleets met off Prodano, a small island on the coast of Messinia in the far south-west of Greece. Finding the channel between the island and the mainland blocked by the Republic's ships, Captain Barak resolutely steered his vessel into their midst in an attempt to force a passage. At once he was assailed by a dozen or more Venetian galleys and brigantines but, unable to withstand the unexpected ferocity of his fire, several were set ablaze or sunk, and the remainder put to flight. But then two large cogs bore down on Barak's vessel and succeeded in grappling him to port and starboard.

411

A protracted and bloody hand-to-hand fight ensued, during which Barak tried to extricate his vessel. But, finally, seeing that it was in danger of being overwhelmed by the Infidels, he ordered naphtha and fire bombs to be hurled into their ships. Fanned by a strong breeze, the fire soon took hold of the Venetians' sails, and rapidly spread to Barak's own ship.

Those who witnessed the engagement avow that Barak could have saved himself by jumping into the sea with the rest of his crew. But it seems that his gaze was already set upon a martyr's reward in Paradise and, sword in hand, he fought on until at last his own ship and the two Venetian vessels – whose desperate efforts to free themselves proved to no avail – sank together beneath the waves, a roaring inferno of billowing smoke and leaping flame.

Meanwhile, the Christian fleet – thrown into confusion by this unexpected turn in events – was breaking up in disorder and running for the open sea, leaving the Turks free to pass unimpeded through the strait between Prodano and the Messinian coast and continue their progress northwards. A few days later the Ottoman fleet sailed into the Gulf of Corinth and took the Venetian stronghold of Lepanto.

In remembrance of Captain Barak's glorious death, Prodano was renamed by Turkish seafarers *Barak Adasi* – that is, Barak's Island.

There is also a curious footnote to this whole affair; fourteen years after Barak's death, Guy de Blanchefort, Grand Prior of the Auvergne, entered these same waters on his way from France to Rhodes, the Knights having elected him Grand Master of the Order. But on the voyage out Blanchefort fell ill. He died on board ship – while the vessel lay at anchor off Barak's Island.

Messinia, Greece
June 1987

POSTSCRIPT

This story is based on real characters and events that actually took place. It was inspired by the recent discovery of fifteenth-century secret service documents in the Ottoman Imperial Archives of the Topkapi Palace, Istanbul. The author has endeavoured to respect historical accuracy. To avoid confusion, he has slightly altered the name of Mehmed the Conqueror's Grand Vizir.